STORM IN THE MOUNTAIN

THE ELEUN CHRONICLES

A. E. ARMITAGE

DEDICATION

To the younger me, who dared to dream.

CHAPTER
ONE

The kidnappings were all over the news.

The authorities had assured that measures were being taken to target and bring down the assailants, but victims were still going missing, causing a nationwide investigation.

"Stick together," the police had announced over the last month. "In pairs if you can, but groups are better. The larger the group, the more likely you'll be safe."

Mum had taken the warning to heart, demanding my siblings and I follow the instructions given.

And yet, despite her constant nagging, I was alone this afternoon, power walking along the path as the overcast sky grumbled, every news report and reminder from Mum running through my head as I looked over my shoulder, sure someone was following me.

I hadn't seen anyone to confirm my theory. But the sense had been nudging at me all day during school.

I'd been in a rush to leave, wanting to get home where I knew I would feel safe, and only realised my mistake when I got halfway home. There was no turning back now.

I sped through the housing estate, jumping at the slightest noises that I thought unnatural at this time of day. The storm over head grew in intensity faster than I could walk, the sky darkening with each step. After threatening to worsen all day, Mother Nature had finally decided to act, as if in solidarity with my feelings of uncertainty.

Lightning flashed across the sky, brightening clouds that churned overhead as another rumble filled the air. Rain fell in large drops, pelting my skin and soaking into my uniform.

I picked up the pace.

As I rounded the next bend, the sky lit up once more, illuminating a figure across the road. I jumped back with a scream. From this distance, I shouldn't have been able to see the figures eyes, but they glowed green as they locked onto me. Backing up, I blinked, and the figure was gone, a tree standing in its place.

Heart pounding, I took deep breaths.

Stop being silly. You need to get home.

I took off, wiping water from my eyes.

Thunder vibrated through me as another boom erupted, as if to say, *you can't run from this.*

More lightning, and I shrieked, my mind creating scenarios of being caught by this ever-growing storm, or maybe the kidnappers. I didn't want either. Home was close, a few blocks away. I would be safe there. I just needed to keep moving.

Of all days, I had to choose this one to leave early when I could have holed up in the school library to finish off my homework. Then I could have caught a ride with Nicole, ensuring I got home safely.

The wind picked up, blowing through the trees. I darted my head back and forth at anything that moved, the sense of someone close overwhelming. Perhaps they were using the storm to hide their movements, waiting for the opportune moment to strike.

Lightning forked its way down, striking a tree two houses away. I stopped breathing as branches snapped. Sparks flew as a branch split, one half falling across the road.

Breath short and sharp, I stared in surprise.

Did that just happen? It was so close.

My stomach turned and I looked over my shoulder, everything on high alert.

Nothing.

I sprinted off.

Distance. I needed to widen the gap and get out of sight of my unknown pursuer.

I will not be taken next.

Hair stuck to my face, water streaming down my cheeks as I raced under the overpass. Thunder boomed louder, the lightning weaving through the sky as a heavy downpour assaulted me when I emerged from beneath the overpass. The eye of the storm was on top of me. I didn't need to look up to confirm it.

All I wanted was to be home, warm, safe, and snuggled under my blankets.

My front lawn came into view. I whimpered in relief.

But even as I pushed onwards, I knew it was too late.

I won't make it. They've found me. I don't know how. I don't know who, but I can feel it deep within me.

My fingers buzzed, like electricity charging through me, or maybe charging me… I was drawn to it, almost hypnotically. There was a zap in the air, and I pulled my hands in toward my body as if I'd touched a live wire.

The sky lit up in quick succession all around me. I stopped running, awed and shaken all at once at the tentacles scaling the sky. Strikes arched toward me.

I threw my hands over my head as lightning cracked the air apart. The bolts crashed into the ground nearby.

I screamed.

Shaking, I hesitantly looked up. Three black and cracked spots appeared nearby in the grass along the path. Smoke rose from where the lightning had struck.

That was too close.

My heart pounded against my chest, and fear coursed through my bones.

Straightening, I took a step back. A bright light caught my eye.

It took me a minute to realise what I was seeing.

One of the lightning strikes had stopped mid-strike directly above where I'd been standing, frozen as if time had halted its progress.

I stood wide-eyed in disbelief. I'd never seen anything like it before. I'd never heard of anything like this.

I wondered if I could touch it. Reaching up my arm, I hovered just on the edge, caution warning me against it.

The tips of my fingers tingled, and I pulled them back, logic telling me it was a stupid idea.

It could still electrocute me.

As I lowered my hand, the lightning came back to life, striking the ground with a loud crack.

I jumped, squealing.

The lightning vanished, leaving the cement at my feet black and dented.

Glancing around, I hoped someone had witnessed the scene. I found my surrounds bare.

No one would believe me if I told them what had just happened.

My unease had vanished. The fear of being watched and chased had disappeared. Like the panic of almost dying by lightning had driven it from me.

Unsure whether I was losing my mind, I ran home, trying not to think about the strike.

My house came into view as I rounded the corner. The front slope of the lawn was already muddy from the downfall with small trails running down it toward the drains. I sloshed through them on my way to the front door, not caring that my shoes were now mini pools.

I ran past the actual pool and onto the veranda.

Pulling open the door, I bee-lined straight for my room, not even stopping to greet Mum, who was seated at her computer typing madly as strands of her dark brown hair fell into her face.

Slamming the door behind me, I moved to close the window, pulling the blinds over the top. I didn't want to hear, see, or even think about the rain.

How could a bolt of lightning stop *mid-strike,* as if someone had pushed pause? It just wasn't possible.

I sat on the floor with my arms wrapped around my knees, rocking back and forward, trying to calm myself. Breathing deeply, I tried to think about something else, anything. But the lightning strike kept playing over and over.

What had just happened?

CHAPTER TWO

"**P**aige, wake up."

Startling awake, I pushed away the hand on my shoulder.

I blinked, trying to see clearly, but the images and feelings from my dream wouldn't dissipate.

A man with green eyes had chased me as I ran along an unknown road, knowing that if I stopped, my life would never be the same again. Lightning forked across each scene as it changed, bringing with it the memory from earlier in the week. The lightning that could have killed me, but by some miracle, hadn't.

My breathing heavy, I pressed the palms of my hands over my eyes willing myself to come out of my sleep haze.

The lights in the rec hall circled and beamed in time with the beat of the music as half-time started. The cheering from the crowds along the bleachers grew, the MC trying to rev up the horde around the basketball court.

Reality crashed back into me.

"Are you all right?" Nicole asked.

I took in my best friend: loose brown hair, brown eyes, untucked uniform, the school day long over.

"Yeah, I'm fine," I said, but she didn't look like she believed me.

"Are you sure, because this has been happening a lot?" she said over the noise, eyeing me carefully.

"What has?"

"You," she said. "Falling asleep in random places. It's like the fourth time this week. Twice today if you count Math, and I know that's boring, but it's not like you."

Biting the inside of my lip, I shrugged.

"I haven't been sleeping well. It's nothing," I said, facing the court again.

I didn't need to look to see her roll her eyes. She knew something was up.

It had been four days since the incident with the storm, and the longer I thought about what had happened, the more baffled I'd become. Lightning doesn't stop in mid-air; I'd looked it up.

A few times, I'd thought about telling Mum or Dad about what had happened, but I couldn't help but think they would consider my mental health. I knew I wasn't crazy and had no plans to see anyone about it.

So, I'd kept the memories of the afternoon to myself, hoping the whole event would fade from my mind with time.

"Whatever. A bunch of us are heading out to set up for the after party. You want a ride?" Nicole said, thumbing over her shoulder.

Ready to answer that I was more than willing to leave, I never wanted to be here in the first place, I followed her thumb to see two girls and a boy chatting by the exit. One of the girls, tall and slender, sleek blonde hair and a petite nose, eyed me disdainfully, before whispering something I knew wouldn't be complimentary to the brunette beside her.

Instead, I said, "Is Sophie coming?"

Nicole grimaced, noting my line of sight. "Yes, but only because everyone will come if she's there. Otherwise, it won't be a party."

I slumped, ready to decline her offer,

"You'll hardly see her, I promise," Nicole added in a rush. "You never come to parties. Please come."

I lifted an eyebrow at her. She sighed, knowing it was a lost battle.

"Okay, fine, at least let me drop you home," she said, and swinging her arm around my shoulders, she pulled me next to her. I grabbed my bag and we headed toward the door. "Your mum will freak if you walk home alone, again, then she'll call me to see if my cars still working, and I really don't want to have that conversation again."

I laughed at her worry.

Mum had not been happy about me arriving home by myself on Monday, a fact she'd cornered me about the next day as I was leaving for school. Nicole was none too happy when she'd received the phone call from Mum asking if she could keep me accountable.

The topic wasn't funny, not in the slightest. Everyone was worried. How could they not be? No one knew when the kidnappers would strike again, or where.

At Nicole's car, I sunk into the front seat, the lively chatter in the back from Sophie, Isabella, and Matt, about a fancy silver vehicle they'd seen on the side of the road, a stark contrast to the dreary feel the weather was giving off at present. The sky had been overcast for days.

Just the thought of stepping out in this weather made me grumpy. The weather was the only reason I'd agreed to watch the basketball game in the first place: so I wouldn't have to think about what was happening outside.

After Monday, I'd been more than happy to follow the rules Mum had laid out. But being cooped up was taking its toll, and I was eager to get outside with some sunshine.

I sat upright, eyeing the local oval. As if by some miracle, a ray of sunshine broke through the clouds, lighting it up in seeming invitation.

I hadn't been running in at least two weeks. I had been forced to schedule my training days around when Mum and Dad were available, or during the lunch hour at school. And given the current weather, I hadn't been motivated to get out there.

I considered my options.

It hadn't rained since Monday and if that ray of sun was anything to go by, perhaps my luck was turning around.

Mum was also out with Dad at a company dinner tonight, so they wouldn't be home till late, and she thought I was at the basketball game until Nicole dropped me home after the party.

Liam and Eva, my siblings, would be the only problem. They'd rat me out the moment they had the chance.

But I itched to move. To feel my lungs burning under the pressure of a good run. The week had been long, and I needed to release all the frustration that had built up.

Turning to Nicole, I said, "Pull over. I'll walk home from here."

Nicole's eyes bulged as she registered what I was saying, then filled with understanding as she took in the oval, shifting to unease.

"I know, I shouldn't be alone," I said, beating her to it. "My mum will have a mental break down, then you'll be to blame. But I promise I'll only be half an hour, and I'll even run home. Age champion three years running, remember? No one will catch me."

I gave her a pleading smile, all that had happened earlier in the week fading away to a distant memory at the prospect of doing what I loved.

I could see she wanted to argue. She was only looking out for me. But when she pulled over, I leant across and hugged her.

"Call me when you get home, yeah?" she said as I slid out, the three in the back barely pausing their conversation to acknowledge my exit.

"Aye, aye captain," I said, saluting her, and she laughed, shaking her head.

Waving, I closed the door and she pulled away from the kerb.

The sky lightened further as I dropped my bag and began loosening my muscles, the clouds thinning as I eyed the track.

Three turns of the oval later, I was warm and my breathing laboured, but feeling good.

This was better than a party, where the music was always too loud and the rooms far too crowded. I should have come here instead of the basketball game, then I could have stayed longer. With the sun going down my time was limited. I picked up the pace, readying for some sprints.

Fifteen minutes later I slowed my speed, staggering to a stop by my bag. I dropped my hands to my knees to catch my breath, smiling at the time I'd just run.

Looking skyward, sad the sun had begun to sink behind the treetops, I placed my hands behind my head and strode back to the start line for one more sprint. That's when I saw them.

A group of figures settled on the hill by the road, watching me. They were all male.

I eyed them as I slowed, my concerns easing slightly as one of them drew the attention of the others. The men looked at something on his phone, laughter following.

There were four in total. All well-built and older than me by at least ten years.

I swallowed, Mum and Nicole's warnings ringing through my head.

Making a split decision, I began stretching instead of preparing for the next sprint, while walking back toward my bag.

Keeping my head down, I powered through my stretches. Why were they here? I tried to ignore the gut feeling inside me that said it wasn't good.

"Is that it? Surely you can do more?" one of the guys called out, his red hair striking in the dull light. His tone was encouraging, and yet there was something else in there I didn't like. "You were only getting started."

One of them had shifted closer, standing directly where I'd walk to go home. I glanced in the direction of my only other route out. Toward the school.

I swung my bag over my shoulder and power-walked toward in the direction of the school. A blast of wind almost knocked me over, blowing my tied hair all over the place.

"Hey, wait!" the red headed man said. "Do I know you from some-where?"

I didn't turn around. I'd seen enough of them to know I didn't recognise *any* of them.

Quickening my pace, I reached the far end of the field, and continued across the road. The school wasn't the most ideal place to go, but considering what might lay behind me, it seemed like a haven.

"Oh, come on!" the same voice called.

Shocked to hear him so close, I swiveled my head back. They were only ten metres behind.

"Can't we just have a chat?"

Fear tingled down my back as my breath hitched.

Picking up the pace, I was almost running up the hill toward the school gates.

Once inside there were sure to be teachers still milling around before they headed home. If I could just get to them, I would be safe.

The footsteps behind me quickened. I took off at a run.

The gates loomed ahead. I smashed into them, tightening my hands around the green metal. I shook the gates, but they didn't budge.

They were locked and I was trapped.

CHAPTER
THREE

The school gates were never locked, at least not whenever I'd been around… which admittedly hadn't been at this time of day. Surely with the game still going the school would have left them open.

Then I remembered the rear gates and cursed as I realised that would be where most of the spectators would go afterwards, since it led straight to the car park.

A panicked groan escaped my mouth, my breathing speeding up.

"There you are!" a voice said from behind me.

I spun around to find the four men corner had cornered against the bars, cutting off any exit routes.

My heart felt like it was going to jump right out of my chest.

"I was beginning to think you were avoiding us," the man second from the right said.

That's because I was, I thought, desperately looking around for anyone who might come to my aid.

But the place was deserted. It seemed that once school was out, there wasn't a single person who wanted to stick around. Even the houses across the road were quiet and bare, too early for those who worked to be home yet.

The guy who spoke was tall and looked like someone in a fashion magazine, with chiselled features, his muscled chest showing through his fitted black shirt. He had jet-black hair spiked away from his head and a matching goatee in the shape of an upside-down triangle.

He stood casually, as if everything was going to be fine. As if he hadn't just surrounded a seventeen-year-old girl, frightening her half to death.

His eyes were a deep piercing green.

I almost stopped breathing. I recognised them from my dreams over the last few days.

Averting my gaze, I took in his companions. In case, by some miracle I managed to escape, then I could inform the police about what they looked like.

To the right of him stood the ideal body builder, the one who'd spoken first at the oval, with broad shoulders, massive chest, and slim waist. His skin was fair which made his red hair and, if I wasn't mistaken, red eyes as well stand out all that much more. On his face was plastered an excited grin, which told me that he thought the fun was only just starting.

Directly opposite him to my left stood the shortest of the group by at least a head, with light brown hair, and brilliant yellow eyes. Although smaller in size he in no way was lacking in the built department.

The remaining man, standing next to him, appeared the least pleased to be here. In fact, he looked like he would rather be anywhere but standing in the circle they'd formed around me.

He didn't even fit the mould, compared to the others, with hardly any muscle at all, shocking blond hair, and, purple eyes.

"Looks like you've put her off chatting." The red-head laughed. "Pity, I enjoy hearing their threats."

Well, if that wasn't something to put me on edge then I didn't know what was. Clearly, they were not here to chat or talk about how they 'knew' me.

I considered making a break for it, but a force of wind passed me, catching me off balance and almost knocking Red Eyes over. The trees around us shook violently.

All eyes turned to the brown-haired man.

"What, it caught me by surprise as well!" he said, but I didn't understand what he was trying to prove, as he looked skyward.

I followed his gaze, and my eyes widened.

Fantastic, just to make my situation even worse, it was going to rain!

The clouds darkened, the winds intensified, Mother Nature finally deciding to unleash her power upon us.

How had this come on so quickly?

Rain began to fall, hitting my clothes and soaking into the fabric. Visibility dropped until I could barely see the men in front of me.

"Let's get this over with," the red-head said, his voice a low growl.

The green-eyed man turned to his left, motioning for Purple eyes to move forward.

"You know what to do," he said with a smile.

The man who seemed so out of place locked eyes with me. He sucked in a deep breath and…

Did he just shudder?

He took a step forward, reaching toward me.

The rain fell heavier, large droplets drenching the lot of us. It smashed against the fence behind me, making a ringing sound that was almost deafening. Water ran through my hair, plastering loose stands over my face. The rain ran down my neck, squeezing between my back and bag, not leaving anything untouched, or allowing much to be seen beyond the semi-circle the men had created around me.

Purple Eyes had paused in his approach, his eyes narrowed as if trying to understand something. Then he turned back to Green Eyes.

"I think we're too late," he yelled over the sound of the storm, then pointed to the sky. "This isn't a normal storm."

Green Eyes seemed to be the one in charge by the way the rest of them looked to him for instructions. He strode toward me, and I pressed harder against the bars, gripping them behind me.

A boom of thunder erupted through the sky, startling all five of us.

"See!" Purple Eyes screamed, as if that explained everything "She's too advanced. The process won't work on her!"

What did that even mean?

Green Eyes took hold of the front of Purple Eyes shirt, and leaned his head in close.

"Just do your job, Turi, or things will turn out very badly for those you love!" he said.

Was he being blackmailed? Guess that explained the fear.

Green Eyes turned to me, Turi, stiff and shaking, following suit. Something wove around my waist pulling tight, the metal poles behind me pressing into my back.

I sucked in a deep breath, feeling light-headed as the bond squeezed around my middle, and I tried to pry away something firm and barky.

Turi turned back to Green Eyes. "Was that really necessary, Dominic?"

Dominic smiled. "Now she's not going anywhere." His voice turned deadly. "Move it!"

Dominic shoved Turi toward me, and he took another hesitant step closer.

My eyes widened at his approach. My legs gave way and I found myself on the ground, knees bent in front of me, whatever was binding me to the fence preventing me from correcting the fall.

A bolt of lightning struck less than two feet from my toes, my breath hitching as I scrambled to claw at my restraints. Dominic and Turi jumped back, clearly taken by surprise, their gaze falling to the now cracked bit of concrete at my feet.

Not again. Images from a few days ago came back to haunt me.

"What the hell was that?" Red Eyes yelled, his body angled away from me, ready to bolt, my final stalker right behind him.

Another bolt landed beside the first. Turi took two, then three steps back, chest rising and falling rapidly. When the third strike came, he turned tail and ran back the way he'd come.

I doubled my efforts to free myself, panic setting in.

Dominic barred his teeth as he growled in my direction. Even as the fourth strike came down, he pushed forward not ready to leave me behind, no matter how dangerous.

Tears joined the rain drops on my cheeks as a whimper escaped through my lips.

"I don't care if you can sink the ground," he said, "you're worth far more to me than anyone's life!"

His words washed over me, not making any sense.

"Leave me alone!" I sobbed. Another bolt hit directly in front of him as if in warning.

Then ice began to fall, hard and fast. The remaining two in the circle raised their hands above their heads and flinched every time a large piece came close to hitting them.

"Hell, Dominic," Red Eyes yelled, "I didn't sign up for this crap!"

He turned and ran, followed closely by the final member.

Dominic took two steps toward me.

The hailstorm intensified with larger balls of ice falling from the sky. He got close enough for his fingers to graze my elbow.

I cried out in terror. *This was it; he had me. If the storm didn't get me first.*

Another blast of wind, more powerful than before, blew him off balance. Thunder crackled loudly through the sky. Two more bolts of lightning blocked his path toward me.

I screamed at the turbulence. I wanted everything to stop and go back to normal.

I should have just gone home. I should never have gone behind Mum's back.

The storm was out of control, wind billowing ferociously around me. Hail crashed into the fences across the street. Cars parked along the side became dented in seconds. Water pounded against the ground, thunder boomed, the ground felt like it was shifting underneath me. I blinked as the bright light flashed through the sky.

Anyone stupid enough to be out in this storm had disappeared by now, leaving me the only one remaining. Well, me and the tall figure of Dominic as he shifted from side to side avoiding strikes of lightning, his footing looking shaky each time he placed it down.

His eyes were murderous, the frustration of not achieving his goal eating him up. But when his stance stumbled, a forked flash of light coming just a little too close, he grunted in disapproval and said,

"This is not over."

Then he ran, lightning bolts chasing him back down the road.

But I was too worked up to be relieved, because I was stuck here, the mysterious bindings around my waist, that felt oddly of bark, holding me secure. It was only a matter of time before another bolt came again, and despite what people said about lightning never hitting the same place twice, I knew it was coming for me, to finish me off once and for all, like it should have days ago.

Closing my eyes, I prayed for the end to be fast, hoping I wouldn't feel too much of it.

"Hey, are you all right?"

My eyes snapped open to see a man crouched in front of me, his face full of concern.

"What are you doing out here? This storm is crazy," the man said, sounding breathless. "I need to get you out of here."

While the storm raged around us, he hooked a hand under my elbow to get me to stand. But even if I could, my bindings were tight.

Blinking a few times, I willed the man to leave and save himself, but my vision swayed, and I was in need of air. I couldn't find enough of it.

The man's expression turned anxious, but it seemed like there were two of him and everything began to blur.

"Oh crap," he said, taking in the wildness of the storm. "This is you, isn't it? Right, well then, you *have* to calm down. Calm yourself and this will go away."

He motioned to the looming storm, but none of his words were making any sense.

Storms didn't just disappear when people remained calm.

My breathing sped up as I anticipated my imminent doom, sad that this kind stranger would probably go down with me.

"You're hyperventilating," he said, and I marvelled at how he was managing to stay so calm. "That's not good. Try taking deep breaths, in through your nose, out through your mouth."

I tried his suggestion, but after two attempts gave up as more lightning bolts hit the ground along the road.

"Right, not helping," he said. Focusing on my waist, he removed whatever was holding me there.

Pressure released from around me, I gave a pathetic hiccup noise before my attempts to suck in air continued.

The guy bit his lip, eyes roaming around looking for another solution.

"Um, close your eyes and think of something happy?"

He didn't sound too sure of himself.

Unable to focus on anything, I did close my eyes, tears slipping down my cheeks as I hiccupped and gasped.

Something soft and warm pressed against my lips.

My eyes shot open, to find the man's face directly in front of me, his lips against mine.

My first instinct was to shove him away, but seeing as I was still in shock, I couldn't register movement for any parts of my body.

I realised then that I'd stopped breathing altogether, the sudden contact catching me off-guard and bringing me back to reality.

He let out a slow breath and pulled away to a respectable distance, his eyes wary of what had just transpired between us.

That was when I finally took him in.

He looked a few years older than me, probably nineteen or twenty. From his crouched position I guessed he was half a head taller than me, though that was hard to tell for sure since we were both still on the ground. He had fair hair with slight tinges of brown flaked throughout the strands. In this light his eyes were the colour of grey stones, which made his appearance seem strange and otherworldly. His clothes, a grey shirt and pair of jeans, were fitted and drenched, showing off his well-defined body.

As I took him in, he seemed to be doing the same to me.

"See, I told you the storm would pass," he said, grinning.

Blinking, I looked around. The ferocity of the storm had vanished, as if it had never happened.

I didn't understand.

My hands were still shaking by my side, so I balled them into fists, digging my nails into the flesh. I realised the shaking wasn't because of the storm, but from what this man had done.

He'd kissed me!

And not just any kiss; it had been my first kiss, something that was now claimed by a stranger. An outrageously good-looking stranger, I'd admit, but someone I didn't know all the same.

I shook my head. What was wrong with me?

My vision blurred as dizziness overwhelmed me, and I leant back against the gate.

"Whoa, you don't look so great" he said, genuinely worried, "We should get you some place safe."

Couldn't argue there.

"Can you stand?" he asked.

I grimaced, my legs stiff and arms sore, which made no sense since I'd barely done anything.

Slowly, and with the support of the bars behind me, I pulled myself up. But as I let go, I stumbled, the ground racing toward me, black spots appearing in my vision.

An arm caught me from behind, breaking my fall and I looked up into his grey eyes.

"Okay, baby steps," he said, soothingly. "Don't want you hitting your head so soon after that display. Wow, you feel like ice. How are you not shivering?"

Weird, I didn't feel cold.

He narrowed his eyes as he contemplated something.

"Who are you?" I asked.

He pursed his lips together.

"Someone who wants to help," he said.

Before I could press him further, he brought his other arm under my knees and swung me off the ground and into his arms, cradling me against his chest.

"How about we get you safe, then you can ask questions?" He smiled down at me.

I wanted to protest; demand he tell me exactly who he was. After all, he could have been some psycho-kidnapper and I was falling right into his hands…

But mostly I just wanted to curl up and go to sleep.

It was very comfortable in his arms, and he had said we were going somewhere safe. I didn't have time to pause and think what that meant, because exhaustion took over and I blacked out completely.

CHAPTER
FOUR

The room was quiet.

I rolled my head side to side, and my eyes fluttered open.

Blinking, I carefully sat up, taking in the room. A wave of dizziness caused my head to spin.

Then I remembered the events that led here.

Dominic, the storm, and the stranger who'd helped me.

The room was an array of pastel colours, from the blue walls to the corked aqua flooring, right down to the white bed sheets. It screamed hospital.

What was I doing here? Did the man think I was that beaten up?

Taking a breath, I calmed myself. I *had* passed out. He'd probably thought I had a concussion. I should have thanked him, not that he appeared to have stuck around. I registered the empty room.

On the bright side, it didn't seem like he was out to hurt me.

The door to my left opened and a nurse entered, dressed in simple grey pants, a button-down shirt all covered with a white coat open at the front and hanging to her knees.

"Good afternoon, Paige. How are you feeling?" she asked.

Her brown hair was pulled tightly at the top of her head into a bun, and she looked in her mid-forties.

Her eyes were downcast as she entered, but once she plucked a clipboard from its hook by the door, she turned and smiled warmly at me.

I reeled, catching sight of her eyes.

They were purple.

The colour matched with the man outside the school.

I reconsidered if the stranger had been kind at all. Had he been working for my pursuers all along, only pretending to help when the four of them had disappeared?

Her smile dropped as she took in my defensive position, legs bent up against my chest, eyes wide and cautious.

"There's no need to be afraid," she said, lowering the clipboard, "I'm not here to hurt you, just to check your vitals."

I didn't move, not sure what to believe.

Being in the hospital should have been comforting. Surely if someone attacked, I could call for help. But her presence set me on edge. I didn't know why she was here.

"Who are you?" I said carefully, my voice shaky. "And why are your eyes a different colour?"

She let out a relaxed laugh.

"My name is Karen," she said, placing a hand to her chest, "and my eyes, well, that's a bit of a story. I'm sorry if they scared you. I know they can be a little strange at first."

I didn't relax, although I was beginning to feel that I'd overreacted.

"I promise you," she said, then leaned forward and lowered her voice. "I'm not here to hurt you, just to make sure you're feeling better."

Slowly I nodded, letting my legs stretch out.

I wasn't in my clothes, but a pastel green hospital gown.

Fingering the material, I pulled it back down over my knees.

"Where are my clothes?" I asked, turning back to Karen.

She had begun writing on the clipboard and didn't look up to answer.

"You were completely saturated when you arrived. I had them taken to be washed and dried. You'll get them back soon," she said.

I bit my lip.

"Have you called my parents?" I asked.

After everything, I should have wanted them to know straight away, but I cringed, knowing the lecture that would follow when they learnt what had happened. I didn't want them to worry. I was already doing enough of that on my own.

Karen looked up, her expression guarded, which surprised me.

The first thing the hospital should have done when I arrived would be to find out who I was and upon learning I was underage, call my parents.

She'd already used my name when she walked in, so I figured Mum and Dad weren't too far behind.

"Not yet…" Karen answered slowly. "I wanted to make sure your… condition was stable."

My breathing quickened as my mind began to reel.

Condition? I'd blacked out. How bad could it have been?

"Which hospital am I in?" I asked, my earlier concern re-appearing. "Where's my phone? I want to talk to my parents now."

I leaped off the bed, ready to storm out the door in search of the exit.

Karen stood in my way, her hands raised, palms out to stop me.

"It's okay," she said, looking anxious. "You will be able to go home, but not just yet."

My gaze flittered around the room, searching for a way out. The door behind her was the only exit.

"You still haven't answered my questions," I said, looking for a way around her.

"I…" she started, before stopping, her voice uncertain. "I don't think I'm the right person to tell you."

The door burst open, revealing the strange man who'd found me outside the school.

So, he hadn't left after all.

He also had a knack for turning up when tensions were high.

"Hey," he said, still holding the door, "what's going on?"

There were others standing outside, two figures both dressed in black. They didn't enter.

Karen gave him a pointed stare. "She's just a little confused. Maybe you should have had that talk you were supposed to have *before* bringing her here."

He relaxed, sighing.

"She wouldn't have heard it," he said. "If you remember, she was unconscious."

"Well, if you'd followed orders, *Jayden,* we'd have been there to stop her losing control when it happened!" Karen said.

"Not a lot I can do when I get a flat," Jayden said easily. "It takes time to change a tyre."

I looked between the two as each spoke, not understanding what was going on.

"I'm right here, you know," I said, bringing their attention back to me. "Whatever you want to tell me…"

I lifted my arms to indicate they could fire away.

Karen lifted an eyebrow expectantly toward Jayden.

He rolled his eyes and finished with a grin.

Happy about something, Karen gave me a brisk nod and placing the clipboard back on its hook, disappeared out the door.

Jayden turned to the two figures in black outside the door.

"You guys can go. She won't be any trouble," he said.

The two shot wary glances at me, before leaving their post.

Jayden grabbed hold of the door and began to close it, but I stepped forward, hand raised.

"Can you leave it open?" I asked not wanting to be left alone in a room with a strange guy. Stranger danger and all.

Shrugging, he obliged, and motioned for me to take a seat, while he took the chair at the end of the bed.

I remained standing in case I needed to run.

"So, you're probably out of your mind right now, huh?" he said, noting my fight-or-flight stance.

I lifted an eyebrow as if to say, 'no kidding', and the corner of his lips curled upward.

My eyes stayed on his lips, recalling the kiss we'd shared, how soft and warm they were, how it had caught me off guard but had been the thing to calm me down.

I shook my head. What was wrong with me?

"What's with the guards?" I said, gesturing to the now empty hallway. "Last time I checked, I wasn't a wanted fugitive."

His smile lingered as he took me in.

"Maybe I am?" he said, his lips curving ever so slightly.

"So, what, I can't trust you?" I pushed.

He shrugged. "I'm pretty trust-worthy, so I'm told. You on the other hand, are a very lethal weapon."

What the hell did that mean?

Sighing impatiently, I glanced around the room. "Look, I don't know what game you're playing, but I can assure you I'm not *that* dangerous. Now can you please explain to me what's going on?"

"You're really not good with pleasantries, are you?" he said, a smirk plastered on his face.

"Again, with the unanswered questions." I dropped my hand to my side. "What don't you want me knowing?"

"Nothing," he said. "I just don't think you're ready."

"Ready for what!" I shouted.

"For the truth." He shrugged.

I stared at him, willing whatever information he had stored away in that big head of his to miraculously appear before me.

I gritted my teeth. "Try me!"

His grin widened. "You might want to sit."

"I'm fine standing, thanks."

"Okay, but don't say I didn't offer. What would you like to know?" he asked.

"How long was I unconscious for?"

"Couple of hours," he said dismissively. "And no, I did not undress you."

He nodded at my attire, and I blushed, remembering what I was wearing.

Why would I have thought he'd undressed me, since we were in a hospital?

Although, something now told me that wasn't true.

"Where am I?" I asked.

He pursed his lips.

"In the hospital," he answered, but I could tell there was more and gave him a pointed stare.

"Which one?" I pressed.

He didn't answer.

"What's with all the secrecy? Clearly you don't want me leaving."

"True," he said softly.

"What truth don't you want me to know?" I asked, trying to find the right question, because I knew he was avoiding something.

His lips formed a hard line, almost turning white, his eyes crinkling disapprovingly.

I scoffed. This was getting ridiculous.

"Fine, don't tell me, but I'm out of here!" I turned for the door.

He grabbed my wrist. I yanked against his grip but he pulled me to his chest, holding me tight against his body.

"If you go out there, you may not like what you see," he said, mouth close to my ear.

I shivered. Now I really wanted to see what was out there.

"Isn't that for me to decide?" I said, trying to sound brave.

He didn't respond right away, just held on.

My heart beat fast. I'd never been this close to a guy before, and it was making my body respond in ways I wasn't used to.

"I suppose so," he finally said, "but you've been warned."

He released his hold on me.

I stepped away from him experimentally and when he didn't move to grab me again, I bolted out the door hospital gown and all.

Running down the hall I passed doors leading to other rooms with beds, some occupied, most empty. I didn't know where the exit was, but up ahead the light was different, and I took my chances there.

Charging through the archway, I burst into a large room.

It was as wide as two basketball courts side-by-side, the floor a light brown colour. The roof towered like a cathedral, although not structured like one, more domed. The far wall was utterly plain with nothing but the white paint it sported. A doorway to the right opened to a small room, where three black clad people stood talking.

Doorways lined the side I'd appeared from, with corridors running down different angles, leading to unknown areas.

There was a second level with a long curved wooden staircase connecting the two together. I assumed there were more corridors extending from the balcony that lined the edge but didn't venture further to clarify.

Scattered around the space were groups of people, eyebrows rising as they took in my attire, some even giggling. Three adults stood chatting nearby. A bunch of kids sat by the far wall laughing, while another played a game of handball closer to the staircase.

I took a step back. Just as Karen's eyes had been otherworldly, so too were many of the eyes that stared at me.

But they weren't just purple. Some were yellow and a deep red, making even the smallest of the kids look dangerous and scary. At least the blue and green eyes seemed more normal, but even they gave me a sense of unease as they took me in.

I took a step back, my chest rising and falling rapidly, scenes from outside the school re-surfacing. Why did everyone have strangely coloured eyes? Why were there so many kids? Was it a children's hospital? And why were there guards?

This was not any hospital I was used to.

"I did say you might not like it," a voice said from behind.

Spinning around, I found Jayden leaning against the archway I'd run through.

"Where am I?" I asked, voice shaky. "And don't say a hospital, because…"

I gestured to the scene behind me, where those who'd stopped to see the running spectacle, had started moving on, no longer interested, and very much healthy and unharmed, at least from the outside.

"This is Havasek, or Home," he said. "You're at one of the headquarters for the organisation and safety of Elementals."

He pushed off the frame, walking toward me.

The way he spoke made me feel like this was the most important place I would ever go visit.

I blinked. "The what?"

"How about we head back to your room? As much as you look…comfy, I don't think you're really in the appropriate dress for a tour."

I took in my minimal clothing.

Agreed.

As he ushered me back down the hall, I paused, having the sudden urge to glance over my shoulder into the large room.

Doing so, I found myself looking at a set of double doors almost opposite me.

It was strange, but I felt a pull, a beckoning to enter the doors and see what lay behind them.

"You coming?" Jayden asked, breaking the urge.

I turned to follow him as he led me back to my hospital room, and I took a seat on the bed as he closed the door, before resuming his own seat.

"What is this place?" I asked, dumbfounded.

"It's a safe haven," he said, "somewhere we can go so that certain, uh, people won't find us."

I narrowed my eyes. "Who are you hiding from?"

He didn't answer right away, and I began to get impatient.

"People who aren't like us," he said finally.

Like us? What did that make *us*? Why were we different?

"I don't understand," I said. "Why are we hiding?"

"We're hiding because we aren't human, and if people found out about us, we would be the news of the century," he said, his gaze hard, telling me that this was the truth.

I couldn't stop the laugh escaping and slapped a hand over my mouth.

"Sorry," I said through my hand, "but I think I heard you wrong. You said we aren't human?"

He nodded, expression not faltering.

"That's a little hard for me to believe since, you know, I look like a human, talk like one, and pretty much all out am a human."

I jumped off the bed, searching for a new way out. I couldn't leave this *haven*, since I had no idea where the exit was, so my only option was to remain here until my clothes were done and I was shown the way out.

"I know it's hard to believe," he said softly, "but it's the truth, and if you'll listen, I'll explain how it's possible."

I turned on him, my mind racing, plausible possibilities for what I was hearing coming to the fore.

"Is this some sick joke?" I shot at him. "You find a girl in distress, kiss her, then take her to some cult? It's not funny!"

His eyes found mine. Sympathy shone back, as if he was sorry this had happened to me.

Without a word, he rose from his seat, and left, the door slamming behind him.

I scowled.

Well, if that wasn't the most human thing I'd seen.

I scrunched up my fists, sending a dirty look at the door, pent-up frustration over what I'd been through over the past few hours exploding out of me.

How dare he accuse me of not being human! Bring me here and expect me to believe every word out of his mouth.

Well, he was just going to have to suffer in his jocks, because this *human* was not going to be swayed!

The door burst open, revealing Jayden again, a pile of clothes in his hands.

"Get dressed," he said, throwing them on the bed, before walking back out. "We're going on an excursion."

Glad to be out of the airy gown, I opened the door to find Jayden in the corridor, leaning against the opposite wall, head down, staring at the ground.

When I appeared, he straightened.

"This way." He nodded back down the hall.

I followed, wondering where we were going.

Instead of venturing out into the large room, we took a sharp left turn and stopped at a set of double doors.

Lift doors.

Jayden hit the down button.

"Where are we going?" I asked.

He didn't look at me. "To *show* you the truth."

The door dinged, opening, and we entered. We travelled in silence, until the doors re-opened, and I followed Jayden out.

Turning to our right, we entered an even larger space than the one upstairs, although the roof wasn't nearly as high.

The room wasn't as bright and welcoming as the foyer above. In fact, everything down here was either black or brown, with the occasional white lines.

The wall with the lift ran along one side, closed doors set further down to our left.

As we moved across the hall, Jayden opened a door to another room that wasn't empty. The low ceiling ended, opening to a football-field-sized room, revealing a glass roof, light from the end of the day shining through.

Wow, that's high.

I took in the people, all dressed in workout gear. Some were partnered up and practicing hand-to-hand combat, while others remained alone, performing a routine of movements in slow motion like a dance.

I didn't see how this was supposed to convince me of un-human-like behaviour, but I continued to follow him.

Coming to a stop by another door, opposite again from the one we'd already passed through, Jayden punched numbers into a keypad beside it and then pulled it open.

Without waiting for me, he strode through, and I followed.

We were outside. The air was clear and fresh, and a little brisk from the wintery night ahead. Before us stretched a large open field, about the size of a football stadium. Surrounding the field lay a stream of water, looking unnatural as it shaped the grassy land between it.

Four people occupied the field, and between them lay a single ball.

They could have been playing soccer, had there been goals at each end. Instead, five coloured rings were positioned, scattered in random places. The rings stood as if in mid-air, some lower to the ground and others impossibly high for anyone to reach.

What held them up?

As we watched, the ball passed from person to person as if by invisible hands, rolling along the ground without so much as a single foot or hand touching it.

Scrunching up my face, I turned to ask Jayden how that was possible, but he merely pointed to the scene in front of me and said, "Keep watching."

I did, albeit reluctantly. I blinked back my surprise as a woman with blonde hair kicked off the ground, shooting into the air impossibly high before diving for the ground as she scooped up the ball. She shot it through a ring that hovered only a few metres from the ground.

Before I could take that in, a larger woman with a buzz cut fisted her hands and red-hot fire shot out of them, directed at the ball as it landed on the grass once more. Fire nudged the ball to the right where she raced for it, the remaining two opponents hot on her heels.

The lead woman charged ahead of her pursuers, the blonde one still in the air diving after her, or rather the ball. Fire shot from the buzz cut woman's palm. The blonde zig-zagged so as not to get scorched. Then, reaching down, the woman with fire tossed the ball into the air, followed by a blast of fire to push it further upwards and toward the highest ring.

A stream of water shot from the side, knocking the ball off course, and toward another ring lower down. The ball sailed straight through.

I couldn't take my eyes off the people as each one did incredible, but impossible... well I wasn't sure what I was seeing.

How were they able to do that?

I forced myself to look at Jayden, ready to demand he explain what was going on.

He was already watching me, smiling as if everything before us should have been explanation enough.

I did not agree.

Rocks or mounds of dirt – I wasn't sure which – popped up amidst the grass, nudging and guiding the now-ground-borne ball toward a ring almost touching the tips of the green stems at the far end of the field.

Fire shot from the buzz cut woman as she tried and failed to shift the ball, but the ground sprouted larger mounds and rocks as a blonde-haired male ran a few metres behind.

Then a lasso of water rose out of the stream, flooding the path of the ball, taking it along in its current back the way it had come, dodging the still rising, and now forgotten mounds of rock, as it hurried for our end of the field.

I stumbled back, not sure if what I was seeing was real, the sight before me turning blurry.

Closing my eyes, I backed all the way up until my back hit the wall of the building behind me, a strange feeling erupting through me.

Sinking to my knees I gripped my hair between my fingers, feeling the strain from my pressure.

What had I just walked in to? How was any of this possible?

My breathing became laboured, something inside of me unleashing.

"Paige?" Jayden said, concerned "You, okay?"

I couldn't answer, didn't know *how* to answer, or whether I would ever be *okay* again.

He knelt in front of me, his hands against my cheeks.

"Breathe, Paige," he said. "Don't let it take you again. You're stronger than it is."

What was he talking about?

I opened my mouth to ask him.

Then the sky exploded, and it started to rain.

CHAPTER
FIVE

"**L**ook at me!" Jayden said.

His grey eyes locked on mine, as he tried desperately to convey something across the link.

"Focus!" Jayden said, squeezing the sides of my shoulders. "Take. Back. Control!"

What did he mean?

A crack echoed through the sky, followed by a bright flash.

What was it with the thunder and lightning lately?

"Jayden, what are you doing?" a voice yelled over the heavy down-pour. "It's raining buckets out here. Get inside!"

He didn't look away. "You go. I have to stay!"

His words sent a wave of gratitude through me and immediately I felt a rush of air flow into my airways.

"That's it," he encouraged reassuringly. "Slow, deep breaths."

I managed to keep my breathing even for two long inhales, before another crack sounded and the sky lit up again, bringing with it the scene of the four people performing impossible things from moments before, though they'd long disappeared from the field when the rain hit.

A whimper escaped, and I began to panic again.

"No," Jayden said. "Come on, stay with me. You're stronger than this!"

I focused on his face, those eyes holding my gaze.

"Don't make me kiss you again!" he said.

A strange noise half-way between a laugh and snort escaped me.

The corner of his mouth twitched.

"Only if you promise I won't collapse again," I said between heaves.

He smiled. "That was all you, if I recall."

I smiled, my body jerking awkwardly as I finally took back control of myself.

Continuing with that incredible smile, he slid his hands from my shoulders down my arms and took hold of my hands where he secured them in my lap, squeezing them.

I concentrated on breathing until I wasn't shaking anymore.

Jayden helped me to my feet, his hands still clasped around mine.

"How are you feeling?" he asked, the look in his eyes telling me I'd done something right.

Not trusting my voice, I nodded.

"Good. Let's go inside." He motioned toward the door of the building.

We started back along the outer wall. The sky caught my eye and I stopped.

"What happened to the storm? It was just here…"

The sky had cleared from dark grey, with a few clouds still drifting, but the thunder and lightning had stopped along with the rain that had been bucketing down like crazy a moment before.

It was just like what had happened outside the school.

A troubled look crossed Jayden's face. He was hiding something.

"Jayden, what's going on?" I asked a little more forcefully.

"Do you remember what you saw before?" He waved a hand across the field, and I nodded.

"Well, the storm disappeared," he said slowly, cautiously, "when you calmed down…"

I narrowed my eyes.

Did he think that *I* was the cause of the storm?

He grimaced, and I took that as an affirmative.

"I…" I started to speak but I couldn't form the words.

As wild as his explanation was, it would explain a lot of things. The lightning strike that had come close to taking my life but stopped midway. The storm outside the school and then here.

My heartbeat skipped a beat.

How was it possible? People couldn't control the weather.

My breath sped up, terror stepping in.

Jayden squeezed my hands. I took a deep breath, closing my eyes, not wanting to lose it again.

If all this was true, and by the looks of things it seemed to be, I was in way over my head.

"Can we go inside now?" I said, my voice still shaky. "This time, I want the full truth. Don't leave anything out!"

Jayden nodded, leading the way back inside.

"We're called Elementals, or in the old language, Eleun," Jayden said, as I settled in the corner of the meditation room tucked away past the gym facilities.

It was a large, square space with mirrors down one side and blank walls along the other three, with noise-canceling material from floor to ceiling. The lights were set on low and moody, presenting a relaxed environment.

According to Jayden, it was a regularly used space, currently empty aside from the two of us, which made the room seem bigger. Towels were stacked inside a shelving unit, an incense table next to it with unlit candles spread out along the back. Messily rolled-up yoga mats lined the rest of the wall.

Ell-ay-oon. I sounded the word out in my head as I shook water drops from my arms.

"And strictly speaking, we aren't human," he said, giving me a pointed look, arms folded across his chest. "Not fully anyway. Our ancestry hails not from Earth, but a planet called Marcious, where everyone could manipulate and control the elements – Earth, wind, water, fire, and mind."

He counted each off on his fingers.

Having seen at least four of the elements being manipulated out on the field, I nodded, though the news about us coming from another planet put me on edge.

"When the planet fell under siege, the people were forced to leave or forfeit their lives along with the planet. So, they travelled through space and came here, the only livable planet they'd come across since leaving their home."

Jayden looked at me, making sure I was keeping up. I paused from scrunching up my shirt – and letting water drip to the floor to nod, deciding that I would hear him out before asking questions.

Eyeing my attempts to dry off, he strode over toward the towels. Picking one at random he returned, handing the towel to me.

I took it gratefully, wrapping it around my shoulders, willing the water to be soaked up so I wasn't wet anymore.

I noticed he was dry from the waist up, his leather jacket clearly having protected him.

"The Elementals kept their abilities hidden as best they could, but sometimes it isn't easy, especially when an Elemental first discovers their gifts, causing phenomenal displays of power to ensue. That's why they built safe houses, places we could go to shape our abilities, become familiar with them and control them. A place to call home – Havasek."

I realised the word was probably from the language of these people.

"Acclimatising wasn't easy, but after proper training and guidance, it became a way of life and the people settled into it quickly."

Holding the towel together with both hands, I let out a controlled breath. Not willing to lose control again, I asked, my voice steady, "So, I'm a descendant of these Elementals?"

"As am I, along with everyone in this building."

Jayden turned for a panel on the wall, punching some buttons that lit the screen up, and air began to flow from the ceiling.

I slowly took this information in, still not sure if I was ready to accept it.

"And these Elementals, Eleun, our…" I paused, the thought sounding so strange to speak out loud. "Our ancestors? How long were they in space? How far away is this planet, Mar-si-ous, right?"

"From all the logs I've researched, it's hard to say for sure how long they were in space, but they estimated about a year in Earth cycles. Their technology was far more advanced than on Earth, but a lot of their navigating equipment was damaged when they left so it was hard to track the time."

How strange to be talking about aliens and space travel as if it were an everyday occurrence, considering it took years of study and training if you wanted to travel in space as an astronaut.

"How do I know you're not just pulling my leg?" I asked, looking for a way out.

He grimaced.

"You don't, but after what you saw," he said waving in the direction of the field, "is it so hard to believe?"

With a dismal sigh, I shook my head.

He was right. What more evidence did I need that this planet and its people existed? And if what he'd hinted at before was true, then I was just like them.

"The storm?" I said, wanting to move away from strange planets and ancestors. "Why does it pop up when I panic?"

"It appears because you lose control of your emotions and the element inside you, which is connected to your emotions, takes over."

"What, so I can never get angry or scared again?" I asked, frustrated. *That was going to be hard with siblings like mine.*

He chuckled, backing up to the table next to the towels and lighting the incense. "Well, right now, while you're untrained, it's best you stay calm, but once you've been taught properly, then it shouldn't be a problem."

That was the first good news I'd heard all day.

"Will I be able to do what those four on the field were doing?" I asked, picturing myself in their place. Surprisingly, I liked the idea.

"I don't know," he said, striking a match to light the candles. "Everyone has different abilities here. That was one thing that changed when the Elementals started breeding with humans. The gene that provided the element changed slightly with every new Eleun born. It was studied extensively, and in the end, it was discovered that human DNA was not the same as the Elementals' which mutated the Eleun."

"So, how will I know what I can do?" I asked.

The situation was becoming more confusing by the second.

He turned, giving me a mischievous smile.

"With practice," he said, his hand hovering over a wick. "But I don't think you'll have a problem adjusting. From what I've seen, you're pretty powerful, even more than first Eleun that landed here."

I screwed up my face.

"The first Eleun?" I said. "You make it sound like you've met them."

His story had sounded like it was hundreds of years old.

He lifted an eyebrow as he crossed the room to another table of candles, this one in front of the mirror wall.

"I've met a few of them. There aren't a lot around these days, but they come and go as they please."

"When exactly did you say they first landed here?" I asked.

"Eighteen ninety," he answered, flames sprouting as he bobbed his hand across the table.

My jaw dropped.

If any of them were still alive after fifteen decades, plus however long they'd lived on their own planet, they would be well over one hundred years by now.

Jayden's smile gradually grew until he was laughing. He shook the matchstick flame out.

I glared at him. "Are you pulling my leg?"

"No, it's just that your face right now is priceless!"

I narrowed my eyes, my teeth gritted together.

"Okay, okay," he said, and I relaxed the stare as he slowly came back to me. "A longer life span is also something we inherit from the Eleun, along with a little tougher skin so we can take a hit and speed up healing."

"How much longer are we talking?" I pushed.

It was probably the only aspect of the three I wasn't over the moon about. I'd read books about people who lived forever and had to watch all their loved ones grow up and die, while they stayed the same. While they were fictional, it didn't exactly sound like a good time.

Jayden shrugged. "A couple of extra lifetimes, nothing that would have us walking around till the end of time."

"Because you know when the end is coming and all?" I threw at him.

He pointed at me "Touché."

"This rapid healing…" I backtracked, wanting to know more. "If I stuck a knife through my chest, would I see it heal before my eyes?"

"If you could keep yourself alive without bleeding to death first, sure, but no, our healing might be sped up, but only by cutting the time in half, nothing like you're thinking."

So not as great as I hoped, but still cool.

"What about the tough skin?" I asked.

"You can still be beaten pretty badly, but it takes a bit to get you bleeding," he said with a shrug. "Pretty handy in a fight if you ask me."

When he put it that way, I didn't like the sound of it. What would cause someone to *want* to beat me black and blue?

I paused before asking my next question, having an idea but not certain.

"You said you thought I was powerful. What element will I be able to control?"

He scrunched up his face.

"It's difficult to tell. Usually, the telltale signs are in your eyes." He motioned toward mine. "With yours being blue, I would have automatically thought you'd control Aquenel, or water, but from what I've seen you can create storms, which also involves wind."

"Could I have both?" I asked.

He shook his head. "It's impossible to wield two elements, always has been. It could be that your power has been mutated and therefore your eyes don't tell the full story, like mine."

"What do you mean?"

"Well, I control the Terralin Eleun, the Earth element, and usually that would mean I'd have green eyes, but…" He hovered his hand under his eye. "They're grey, which makes sense when you know exactly what I can manipulate."

He didn't elaborate on what he could do, and I didn't push.

"We won't know until you've been trained, but I'm certain that's what it is," he concluded.

"So, when do I have to undergo this training?" I asked.

My gaze fell on the clock by the door.

Nine-thirty.

I shot to my feet. "I need to get home!"

Mum was going to kill me when she learnt I'd been out all night. She and Dad were at a work dinner and wouldn't be home till much later, but with Liam and Eva in the house there was no telling what they would spill.

Jayden stood, his expression unsure. "I don't think that's a good idea."

I rounded on him. "Why not! This is my family we're talking about. They'll get worried!"

He nodded, but still he looked hesitant. "Yes, but you're not stable. You've already lost control twice today and the more your element is left untamed, the easier it is for you to wreak havoc."

I scoffed. "So, I'm just to stay here until I've got a handle on things and let my family worry what happened to me?"

"It's safer for you and your family if you stay here," he said, trying and failing to comfort me. "At least we can talk you through any outbursts and minimise the damage here. But if you're at home, there's no saying what will happen, or who will see."

His words made sense, even if he seemed more worried about witnesses than my family's worry.

"Okay, so teach me. Let's get this done," I said.

Jayden didn't move, and I knew there was something he'd left out.

"It's not something you can learn in one night," he said slowly.

A lump formed in my throat.

"What are you saying?" I said, a gut feeling growing inside me. One I didn't like.

He cleared his throat. "I'm saying you can't go home tonight, not until we're sure you have full control, and that could take days, weeks, sometimes even months, or…

"Don't say years." I held up a finger in warning. The walls crept in.

I had no idea where the exit was, but I wasn't going to let this guy tell me where I could and couldn't go.

"I'm going home," I said. "Tell me how to get out of here."

"I can't do that. You must stay here," Jayden said.

My hands shook as I eyed the door behind him.

"You have no right to keep me here," I said.

He didn't stop me as I brushed past him, back through the gym and out to the dark floor.

I took a right, hoping one of the doors there would lead outside.

It might have. I didn't find out. Because my vision blurred, then blackened, and I fell to the ground.

CHAPTER
SIX

Bolting upright, I gasped, my heart thudding in my chest, as I wildly searched for trouble.

Instead, I stared back at myself in a mirror. Dark hair dishevelled, clothes crumpled, and my eyes deep navy, with a crazed look about them. I recoiled.

I looked like I'd run out of the woods after an animal had chased me.

Peering down at myself, I gripped the front of my shirt. I was still in my running gear, the material dry and rumpled.

In the room, two matching beds rested, a set of bedside tables between them. On the opposite side, filling the entire wall, was a closet, one of the sliding mirror doors pushed to the side where a pile of clothes, and a towel, along with a jug of water and a cup sat.

Where was I?

I didn't recall going to bed last night. In fact, I didn't remember doing anything. After Jayden had told me I couldn't go home, I'd just blacked out.

Had Jayden knocked me out? I wasn't sore anywhere.

Where did my parents think I was?

Throwing back the covers, I swung my legs over the bed, my feet landing on my runners, still a little damp. I searched the room for any more of my belongings. Nothing. They'd taken my bag and my phone, no doubt so I couldn't call home.

Pulling on my shoes, I opened the door to the room, surprised when it did.

They hadn't locked it. That had to be a good sign.

Should I leave the room?

I caught myself. I'd been kept here against my will. I needed to get home.

A long hallway extended to my left, other doors set into the walls on either side. Voices echoed from the end of the hallway, and I shrank back, not sure if I was supposed to be wandering around.

Water splashed behind me. The jug of water was on its side, its contents soaking into the towel and clothes, and running down the shelves to the carpet.

I must have bumped into it in my haste, though I didn't recall hitting anything. Ignoring it, I stepped out of the door, closing it behind me, grateful when no one appeared. I found the exit of the hallway, entering the atrium I'd seen the night before, only this time I was on the second-floor balcony staring down at the cathedral-sized space.

The atrium wasn't as busy this morning. I assumed it was morning given how well rested I felt. Guards lingered near a small box shaped room, chatting and laughing together, mugs in their hands. A few casually dressed people strode across the floor from underneath where I stood, toward the corridor that led to the hospital wing. An echo of others nearby floated up, but I didn't know from where.

I kept away from the railing, skirting along the walls as I made my way to the staircase. When a group of boys appeared farther down, I turned around to look at some paintings on the wall, hoping they wouldn't notice me.

A groaning noise sounded nearby, like the pipes in the walls were struggling to push through water. I took a step back and the noise stopped,

Plumbing issues?

The boys didn't look my way, and I made to follow. Before I did, I really took in one of the paintings. Strange symbols were etched into the corner of the painting.

The picture seemed to be moving. Not like on a television, but as if a slow-motion breeze had blown through the trees, the branches swaying with it.

I blinked, but found the same result, my mouth dropping open at the sight.

More voices sounded, and I put my head back into escape mode. I hurried to the top of the staircase. Leaning over the railing, I watched the boys descend the last step and vanish into a room.

Slowly, I began my own descent.

Almost directly in front of the bottom step, a set of double doors opened wide, revealing long wooden tables filled with people talking and eating.

This was where the voices were coming from.

Grateful no one was paying attention to me, I raced around to the other side and hid behind the railing, trying to figure out where the exit to this place was. There were so many doors along the wall that wrapped the inside of the building, I decided to try them all until I found a viable route.

I hurried for the double set of doors I'd noticed the night before. As I drew closer, I felt the same pull that enticed me forward. It was as if I needed to find out what lay behind it.

Maybe it was telling me I'd found the exit.

I listened.

As I turned the handle, a loud squeal echoed through the atrium from the eating area. Heart thundering in my chest, afraid I'd been caught, I wrenched the door open. Throwing myself into the room, I collided with someone.

Hands pressed against my shoulders, keeping me upright, as I tried to skirt around them, not looking at the person.

"Slow down. No one wants to study that badly on a Saturday morning," a boy said.

I stopped, taking in the rows of shelves, study nooks and computers along the walls. It was a library.

Annoyed my instincts hadn't been correct, I backed out of the room. "Hey, wait," the boy said, following me out the door.

Ignoring him, I ran for the two doors on the opposite side of the room set inside a nook, near the hospital wing. My feet echoed in the near empty area, drawing the attention of the guards by the blank wall as they drank from their mugs. They didn't pursue me.

"I wouldn't go in there if I were you," the boy said, his voice right behind me as I reached for the handle of the left door. "You'll end up on toilet cleaning for the next month."

I paused, not having a clue what he was referring to, but deciding against opening the door, I moved to the door on the right two steps away.

"Best to avoid that one too," the boy said, standing by the first door. "I can help, if you tell me what you're trying to find."

I finally looked at him. He was tall, a head over me, with shaved blond hair and bright yellow eyes that reminded me of pineapples.

He was wearing a loose singlet, running shorts, and a pair of flashy basketball shoes.

"Hi," he said, then stuck out his hand. "I'm Bree. What's your name?"

The fact that he knew I wasn't local told me I had been caught.

Looking from his hand, then back over the atrium, I decided to try and make this work. If all Jayden had said last night was true, then everyone here had abilities of some kind. I didn't know what Bree could do, and I didn't want to find out.

"Paige," I said, not accepting his hand. "I'm looking for the way out. I need some air. Is it over here?"

I pointed to the lift, remembering the numerous doors down on the lower level. Without waiting for a response Arnse, I strode toward it. Bree followed.

"The Pina told us about you, well, sort of," Bree said, a step behind me. "They said a new Eleun had arrived, and we were to make you feel welcome. I thought one of the girls might bring you down, but I guess you woke up before the breakfast bell rang. That's okay. I can show you around if you like."

"I think I can manage," I said, punching the down button. The fact that Bree hadn't called for a guard made me hope I might just escape without trouble.

Bree leaned against the wall, watching me curiously.

"How old are you?" he asked.

Starting to get annoyed by his lingering, I said, "Seventeen. Why?"

He shrugged.

"Just trying to get to know you. What are you into?" He took in my day-old workout gear. "You look kind of sporty. That's good. It means you won't have to start from scratch. Heaps of us did, and trust me when I say, it wasn't fun."

"Yeah, I like sports," I said, punching the button again. Nothing happened, and I reined in my groan.

"Nice. You should come watch our game of Elemucka," he said, reaching into his pocket. He pulled out a bag of gummy worms and threw two in his mouth. When I didn't reply, he added, "Powerball?"

"Like… the lottery?" I asked, holding back a laugh. "Didn't think gambling was allowed for underage kids."

He burst out laughing, holding a hand to his stomach.

"No, not the lottery, but I can see why you'd think that. Elemucka is a Marcian sports game, but only people with powers can play it. Well, you don't have to have powers, but it makes it wicked fun."

Still not following, I stared at him.

The idea of a sport for another species piqued my interest, for about five seconds, before I remembered that I needed to get out of here.

I punched the button again, maybe a little too hard.

"What is taking so long?" I said, scanning the rim of the lift for any indication of where it was. The place couldn't be that big.

"It's probably not working," Bree said, shoving another gummy worm in his mouth. "The Jalin like to shut it off sometimes to conserve power.

Just quietly, I think they like to torture us by making us use the stairs. Something about exercise and it building character."

"You're telling me this now," I said, glaring at him. "Where are the stairs?"

A low chiming sounded through the building, and I tensed. They were after me.

I searched for a new escape route.

Bree's eyes lit up.

"Finally, breakfast time. You coming?" he asked, passing me for the double doors leading into the dining room I'd seen earlier. I'd almost done a full three-sixty of the floor.

I relaxed. Shaking my head, I said, "I really need some air. Where's the door to get out of here?"

He snorted. "Good luck with that. At this hour you'd have a better chance walking through that wall than finding a door."

He pointed at the large blank wall, opposite where we stood. I shrank back as I realised he wasn't going to help me. Did they have specific opening hours? Perhaps being a secret alien race, you had to have strict rules.

"Hey, I get that you're nervous and everything is new. But I promise it's not that bad," he said. "Come and eat something. We get an hour for breakfast before we're due on the field."

Bree took half a step toward the dining room, his expression hopeful.

The field. The words sparked an idea. That was outside, and once I was out, I was sure to find a way home from there. Wishing I could just book it downstairs right now, I decided to play along. Bree would lead me right to the exit. Plus, I hadn't eaten since lunch time yesterday. The thought of food made my stomach growl.

"Okay," I said.

We fell into step with each other.

Inside the dining room, those who had been eating before, were now packing away trays and dishes into trolleys along the right far wall, before exiting the room.

Bree and I joined the line forming along the left wall.

"There are two meal sessions a day. Jalin get the first session, and we get the second," Bree said, motioning to the line of kids and teenagers behind us, a few adults littering the line as well.

I nodded, deciding to play along.

"What are Jalin and Pina?" I asked, having heard both words.

Bree pointed to a duo in the black uniform leaving the room as we shuffled down the line. "Jalin is Marcian for guard and Pina are educators. I know the lingo is a bit confusing to begin with. It gets easier if you use the terminology for everything."

"Why not use the English word for everything? Seems like that would be easier for everyone," I said.

Bree smiled. "True, but Havasek like to bring the Marcian culture into everything we do, so we don't forget our ancestry."

Reaching a trolley that held empty trays, plates, and cutlery, we collected a set of each and moved closer to the glass screens along the back wall. My stomach growled in anticipation as the aroma of food wafted under my nose.

I filled my plate with a bit of everything: toast, eggs, bacon, hashbrowns, sausages, then joined Bree and his friends in the centre of one of the long tables.

Bree introduced me to those who sat around us, but I forgot their names immediately, my focus set on eating. Missing a meal had done no favours to my appetite.

When everyone had finished, I followed the other kids down to the field. My stomach now filled, I was once again determined to get home.

The stairs, as it turned out, were directly to the right of the lift, behind a closed door, which was never locked, according to Bree.

I sent a glare in his direction when I learnt this, wondering if he'd intentionally kept that piece of information from me.

Crossing the large open space with the glass roof of the lower floor, I eyed the door leading outside to the field only steps away. I was almost home free.

As Bree's friends opened it, a voice sounded from behind us.

"Paige, would you mind coming with me?"

Without turning, I contemplated making a break for the door but thought better of it. Apart from knocking me out last night, these people had been nice so far. I wondered how long that nicety would last if I openly displayed my disapproval by running away.

I found an older woman who looked to be in her fifties standing behind me. Her amethyst eyes locked with mine, and I felt like she was looking into my soul.

We were the same height, and she had light brown hair cut to a bob. She stood tall with excellent posture as she smiled warmly at me.

Bree gave me the thumbs up before continuing with the others out the door, mouthing the words, "Good luck." For what, I had no idea, but I hoped whatever she wanted wouldn't take long.

"You're younger than I thought you'd be," she said, her gaze travelling over me.

"What do you mean?" I asked. "Did Jayden tell you I was older?"

The woman shook her head, and said, "I just hope you're up for the task ahead. My name is Katalya. I'm here to guide you in your first lesson of control."

She stuck out her hand.

Jayden had told me that I couldn't leave until I could control my abilities. I should have been grateful they hadn't forgotten about me and were trying to help me, but who knew how long these control lessons would take. I needed to leave now.

"Hi," I said, timidly taking her hand.

The door to the outside banged shut. I swung around as it locked in place. I felt a tug in my stomach. Water burst from small holes in the walls, streaming from all angles, pooling on the floor and soaking our clothes.

I let out a squeal as I became drenched. The water died down as if a hose had been turned off.

The corner of Katalya's mouth lifted.

"I guess I came at the right time," she said. "Best we start this training now so that doesn't happen again."

She waved a hand at the mess on the floor.

Had I made the water appear? Why were there holes in the wall?

I eyed the security keypad next to the door, remembering that Jayden had entered a code to exit last night. Bree and his friends must have known it, but I didn't.

I should have paid more attention.

Still holding my hand, Katalya said, *"That isn't the only way out you know. Just one that isn't guarded all the time."*

Tensing, I cringed. Had she known I was trying to leave?

"The lock, and the Jalin, are not here to keep you in, but to keep others out."

It took me a second to realise that her mouth hadn't moved. I'd heard her voice in my head.

I pulled my hand out of hers, taking a step back. Was she inside my head? What had she seen? Would she lock me up again for trying to leave?

Panic set in and I kept moving back.

Jayden had said there were five elements. Katalya must have an ability that involves the mind. Could she make me do things I didn't want to?

Katalya chuckled.

"I'm sorry I frightened you, Paige. That was not my intention," she said, this time with her mouth, the sound echoing off the walls of the empty room. She remained rooted to the spot, watching as the distance between us grew, until my back hit the wall.

"I'm not here to harm you in any way," she said, her demeanour peaceful. "I've been assigned to help you understand your gifts, if you'll let me."

It was then her words about the lock and the Jalin keeping others out registered.

"If the guards aren't here to stop me leaving, then why can't I go home?" I asked.

Everything about this place confused me.

Katalya sighed. "I believe Jayden already explained that to you last night. Those rules are for your benefit and those you love. I promise that your family will be none the wiser to your disappearance. When you do return, it will be as if you never left."

I narrowed my eyes, not following.

Katalya strolled toward me.

"It's a simple trick we perform to keep suspicion away from Eleun, and homes intact as much as possible," she said, though a sad look crossed her features. "Not everyone is as lucky as you were when you first displayed your powers. Often, once loved ones find out about an Eleun's gifts, it is hard to keep it a secret from them for long once their memories have been modified. Though we try to avoid altering humans' minds, it's sometimes unavoidable."

Altering their mind? I didn't know how I felt about that. Was it safe? I didn't want my parents' minds being scrambled because someone didn't know what they were doing.

"I promise, it's perfectly safe," she answered my unspoken question, fuelling my suspicion that she was reading my thoughts. "Once you return home, the modification will lift and it will be like you were always at home, their minds filling in the blanks with a plausible reason."

"My brother and sister, Did you change their minds as well? What about my school? Won't they question my absence?" I said, looking for a way past this silly rule of not being allowed home.

"The process will take care of itself. The modification isn't a complete changing of minds from anything your parents would normally do," she said. "We simply put a suggestion in your mother and fathers' heads, that while you're away there is a good explanation for it. Their minds will find something that makes sense to them as to why you're not around, and they will set the ball rolling themselves, your parents being the ones that will notice your absence the most."

"They'll call the school themselves?" I said, hoping I was following along.

Katalya nodded. "And find an excuse that your siblings will believe."

I guessed after a hundred years of practice, Havasek would be adapt at keeping things quiet. After everything I'd seen about these people, there no doubt had been outbreaks. The only way any of this had remained a secret was because these mind Eleun made it so.

The idea that I was one of these Eleun, an alien race, was still new and completely foreign. I was descended from a race of supernatural people.

I supposed to them it was just biology, and nothing supernatural at all.

I wondered which one of my parents had the gene and if they knew about it. Had either of them manifested abilities and kept it a secret all this time? Or did it skip a generation and they were none the wiser? What about my siblings, grandparents?

There was still so much I didn't know, and yet, I didn't want to ask for fear of my life changing more than it already had.

Swallowing, I nodded at her explanation.

"What do we do now?" I said, hoping to seem compliant. Now that I knew about this mind changing business, I didn't want to get on anyone's bad side. But I still hadn't given up on trying to leave this place.

"We are going to make your Eleun fall in line," Katalya said simply. "To do that you will have to find its source, something we call the Myun, and then complete a true merge which is known as the Myundun, a sacred bond you make with your Eleun."

This sounded complicated…and weird, like a ritual…

"How am I supposed to know what or where it is?"

She smiled reassuringly. "It is inside you, and I will talk you through the process to help guide you, but ultimately you will have to do the seeking."

Not really understanding, I nodded. I'd always been a-learn-as-you-go type of person. It was probably better to just get on with it.

"Come," she said, motioning for me to follow her. "Let's continue in the meditation room."

Begrudgingly, my clothes wet and shoes once again squelching as I moved, I trailed after her, covertly glancing back at the door that had almost been my exit.

The meditation room was lit up as it had been the night before, the lavender incense strong under my nose as we entered.

"Please take a seat, Paige," Katalya said, two yoga mats already laid out on the floor. Choosing one at random, I did as she asked.

"Close your eyes," she said, sitting on the other mat. "And clear your mind of everything."

I closed my eyes, but clearing my mind wasn't so easy, fuelled as it was with my will to escape. Images from yesterday and the feelings I'd felt experienced before my eyes, and I shook my head a few times before I finally managed to push it all away and focus on the task at hand.

As if knowing exactly when I was ready, Katalya, gave me the next instruction.

"Relax your body, feel each limb loosen, and release your tension."

Exhaling, I let my body go slack, moving up from my feet all the way to my shoulders and neck. It was kind of nice.

"Now just breathe…in…and out… imagine the Eleun you hold and how you think it will work."

Sceptical of the ease in her voice, I recalled Jayden saying he thought my element was water and given the display I'd put on just before, I focused on that.

"Sometimes, visualising can help. Think about what it does when it moves or is touched," she said.

I thought of how water fell from the sky, not difficult since the last day had been filled with rain. Drop by drop, it could form puddles that rippled and sloshed underfoot. I remembered the feel of the raindrops on my skin, how they ran down the length of my body, connecting with other drops before dripping to the ground. The pitter patter sound as they hit surfaces, creating a loud symphony of noise. The smell of clear fresh H2O cleansing the world around us to start anew.

I inhaled sharply as something stirred in the pit of my stomach, coming alive. It beckoned me forward.

I felt a pull and wanted nothing more than to take that leap and let it consume me.

"Don't be tempted," Katalya said. "Go to it on your terms. The Myun needs to be disciplined. That is the only way it will not lash out again."

Sweat formed along my brow as I fought to stay back.

"But I want to go to it. It's…calling me." I breathed heavily, all doubt evaporating.

"That is its allure, complete power. It wants to be free and wild, but you must not let it," she said, voice stern. "I'm going to place my hand on you to guide you forward and help you complete the Myundun."

I didn't know what she was talking about.

She rested her hand on my knee, and I felt something enter my mind, like someone opening a door to access a room, only this was more personal.

"What?" I cried out.

"Relax. It is just my presence you feel. I will not harm you, trust me."

Swallowing hard, I tried to calm my beating heart, feeling self-conscious about her presence… whatever that meant.

"Now, go toward the feeling," she said calmly. "The power of the Eleun will not take you. I have a firm hold of your conscious mind."

Somehow, through the process, my mind's eye had taken over and I could see a vast colourful expanse that called to me, urging me to keep going.

"Are you ready?" Katalya asked, excitement in her voice.

I nodded, even though she probably couldn't see me.

"Let the feeling consume you."

Feeling myself fall into this overwhelmingly powerful entity was like being hit over the head with a bucket full of iced water. The sensation was euphoric, intense waves of happiness and excitement rolling through me, my breath coming out in deep gulps.

My heart sped up as I felt as if every inch of my body being filled with this overstimulating power. My hands began to shake. I tried to gulp in air, the feeling overwhelming me.

Was I going into shock?

CHAPTER
SEVEN

I rocked back, hands catching on the ground behind me before I could fall over. Air filled my lungs as my body acclimated to the surge of feeling rushing through me.

Katalya laughed as she lifted her hand off my knee, "Exciting, isn't it?"

Not trusting my voice, I nodded.

"You've successfully completed the Myundun," she said, the corners of her mouth lifting with pride. "You and your Eleun of Aquenel are now one, linked forever."

She was right. I could feel it. No, I could feel everything that was connected to the substance of water. It was as if everything had been hidden from my sight until this moment. The pipes running under my feet and above my head were filled with water, running inside the metal tubes. The water that surrounded the field outside registered in my mind. Currently the water was being lifted and splashed around as the kids on the field manipulated it in their game.

Moisture droplets in the air brushed against one another; although minimal, I knew the water was there. Sprinklers spinning into action hundreds of metres away sprayed out over the ground. Puddles from the storm yesterday trickled in various directions.

"This…this is amazing!" I said. "Who would have thought something like this was possible?"

"Familiarise yourself with the feeling," Katalya said. "Be aware of everything and it will be easier for you to find tomorrow."

I didn't think I would forget this feeling for a long time, even if I never felt it again.

After I further explored and got to know this new part of me, Katalya assisted to pull me away.

I couldn't help but feel a sense of loss wanting to experience the euphoric feeling again, and soon.

Blinking back a wave of tiredness that appeared when I opened my eyes, I focused on the room again, thankful the lights were dim.

"Eventually, you won't need to release its hold, but can stay in the Myun all the time," Katalya said. "With practice, it will be as easy as blinking an eye."

I was stunned by how respectfully she spoke about the process. Every time she mentioned Myun, or Eleun or Myundun, I felt as though angels might fly down from the skies and start singing praises.

Did she expect me to talk this way as well?

"Does this mean I can go home now?" I asked.

I felt bad for asking it so bluntly, but I had to know.

Her calm, respectful expression remained as she said, "I'm sorry, Paige, but no. Completing the Myundun is not enough to deem you in control. While you've tamed the beast, so to speak, any erratic emotion could set you off again, and who knows, it could be your siblings that you cause the lightning to strike next time. How would you feel then?"

I pressed my lips together, remembering the strike that had frozen in mid-air. I still hadn't told anyone about that. Until yesterday, I had almost made myself believe that I'd imagined it. I knew better now. Though why it had stopped, defying all logical and scientific explanation, still had me reeling.

Was it just a manifestation of the gift I could control? Jayden had said that the gifts born to those on Earth varied. Perhaps this was something

I had to figure out on my own? Not that I had any plans to stand under a lightning strike again.

I opened my mouth to question Katalya about it, but a yawn escaped. A wave of fatigue swept over me, and I swayed.

"There it is," Katalya said. "I think it's best you head back up to your assigned room. While your Eleun is powerful, you will need a lot more rest until you're accustomed to merging with it. I will find you when its time to continue your training."

Wanting to fight her on the notion, I was assaulted with another yawn.

Katalya smiled knowingly, helping me to my feet.

I let her lead me through the halls back to the room I'd woken up in. Then I sank onto the mattress, my eyes closing as she murmured something about me showering the next time I woke up.

I dreamed about five strange symbols. They formed a circle spinning until they vanished altogether. Then slowly, they reappeared one at a time, the top one lighting up like a beacon followed by the second, third, fourth, and finally fifth.

Zooming in, I converged on them, and they all clumped together before they were so close, I felt they were about to knock me over.

Then I was sitting upright in bed, my breathing heavy, sweat sliding down my cheeks.

What a strange dream. It felt as if the symbols were trying to tell me something.

And yet, it was a dream. How could that be?

Running a hand through my hair, I slid out of bed, my mind needing a few seconds to remind me I wasn't at home. The light was off, but the glow from under the door was enough to guide my way as I padded over to the cupboard. There I sculled two full glasses of water from the jug that had been refilled as I slept.

What was my life turning into? First the revelation of the Elementals, and now this strange dream?

Yawning, my eyes still full of sleep, I made my way back to bed, eager to fall back into oblivion.

When I woke again, it was almost dinner time. Katalya had left a note by my bed with instructions on where to find the girls', or the Lamonas', as it was said in Marcian, bathroom. She'd also laid out fresh clothes for me and sheets too, as I'd fallen asleep wet after my lesson.

I followed two girls Bree had introduced me to this morning to the dining room for dinner, finding a seat in the corner farthest from where the line extended as kids trickled in.

I scarfed down the shepherd's pie I'd chosen. I was contemplating re-joining the line for a second helping, when Jayden strolled through the door.

Conflicting emotions filled my insides as I took in his tall frame and wide shoulders, the black shirt and pants he wore reminding me of the military uniform.

My quick assessment of him from yesterday was unchanged. He was good looking and wearing black only intensified that. But he'd also kept me from leaving, somehow knocking me out, which I was still mystified about.

Even after my lesson today, which had given me a better understanding of what I was, I was still angry at him.

I lowered my head, hoping he wouldn't notice me. Too late. Our eyes met and he strode over to me.

"How did you find your first day?" Jayden said, stopping on the other side of the table. His tone was polite, as a host would be at a dinner party.

Sliding my knife and fork together on my plate, I held them in place as I stood, preparing to leave.

"Fine," I said, my pointed stare saying otherwise. "As fine as it can be when you wake up in a strange room with a building full of foreign people who won't let you go home, or even talk to your family."

Jayden followed as I rounded the table to place my dishes on the trolley. "You like to hold a grudge," he said, a smile playing on his lips. "Good to know."

I continued toward the door, thinking he had come in here for food and wouldn't follow me.

"Katalya told me how your Myundun went," he said, trailing me out the door. "Even after all that, you still want to leave?"

I turned left, no plan in mind except to be away from Jayden, my gut leading me where I felt I needed to be. I'd only seen parts of the building and had no idea where I could go to unwind.

"What I want is to not be kept a prisoner even though everyone keeps saying they aren't keeping me here against my will," I said, through my teeth. "I mean, how does a girl get a little fresh air around this place, or some exercise?"

Though I was secretly hoping he would show me the exit, my body did feel agitated. I needed to move. I wanted to run.

"You might be sorry you said that," Jayden said, chuckling. "Once you reach a certain level of control, a lot of your lessons will depend on your physicality."

"Yes, Bree told me about that game you have them play on the field outside, Ele…moock or something, and yet, apparently I'm not allowed out there," I said, throwing my hands up in defeat.

Stopping at a set of doors, I pulled one open and froze.

The library… again?

"It's called Elemucka. That's one way of training, yes, and you'll get to see it for yourself soon enough," Jayden said. "For now, it's best you focus on the Myundun. You'll have to complete it a few more times before your Eleun isn't affected so easily by your emotions. Aren't you going in?"

I was staring into the room, confused. I felt as though I was supposed to be here, but I had no idea why. Eva, my ten-year-old sister, was the reader in our family, finding pleasure in spending hours of her time in any library she entered. I had no such inclination. So why was I suddenly feeling like I needed to explore every inch of the one here?

"Paige," Jayden said, waving a hand in front of my face. "Are you going in?"

Blinking, I hadn't realised I'd zoned him out.

"No," I said, releasing the handle and allowing the door to close.

The tugging feeling in my gut was still there, urging me to walk through the door.

This place was weird.

Turning back the way we'd come, I acted on my need to move and ran across the atrium floor for the stairs that led to the lower level. The lift was up and running, but it would take too long.

Jayden followed easily.

"Where are you going?" he said.

"If you're not going to let me leave, then stop bothering me," I said, and a few passersby stared at me.

I hurried down the stairwell.

"I was only trying to help you," he said from behind me, his tone asking me to see reason. "I thought you might have questions. I know I did when I first got here."

"I've only got the one question, and everyone is determined to avoid answering it," I said, the hollowed space echoing my words. "Apparently the only special treatment I'll be getting is when you kissed me, and what a shame I was too worked up to enjoy it. At least I know how this place works now. You give something, you get something."

A group of teenagers entered the stairwell from below, taking in every word.

I knew he'd only kissed me to help me focus again. It hadn't meant anything else. But I was frustrated. I wanted to go home, control over my powers or not.

The group of teenagers snickered. Two girls at the back whispered to one another as they sent Jayden and I curious looks.

Jayden, to his credit, didn't seem affected. Not missing a step, he reached my side. Wrapping his hand around my wrist, he pulled me with him as we raced down the last few steps to the door.

Out on the bottom floor he continued dragging me into the room with the glass ceiling and over to the door with the security panel.

Keying in the code, too fast for my eyes to see, he pulled the door open, and we strode out into the night-filled sky. Ground lights lit up, rimming the field and stream that surrounded it. Spotlights from the edge of the building flashed on like a soccer field.

"You want to have fresh air, then have at it," Jayden said, practically throwing me ahead of him. I stumbled, catching myself before I fell over.

He stood with his arms folded as if waiting for me to enjoy this brief freedom, or to thank him, I couldn't tell which.

I took in the tree line that bordered the field. I couldn't make out what lay beyond it. If there was anything. We could be in the middle of a forest for all I knew, with nothing for miles.

Walking toward the opposite end of the field, I cautioned a glance back at Jayden. His eyes followed me, but he didn't move.

At closer range, I still couldn't make out anything beyond the tree line. I knelt by the stream's edge and scooped up some water. The sound of the water trickling over the stones at the bottom was soothing.

When I'd connected with my Eleun, I'd felt the water out here. I wondered what it would feel like to manipulate. When would Katalya let me try it?

Standing, I faced Jayden, who leaned against the building, still watching me. The wall was made from grass, like the field, then domed upward toward the sky, imitating the inside we'd just walked through, flattening out at the top.

I walked the perimetre, looking for any sign of human life past the trees. Nothing.

"Where are we?" I asked Jayden when I was close enough for him to hear.

"Havasek."

I sent him a no-kidding look. I knew he wasn't going to elaborate. I didn't bother asking my follow-up questions.

Instead, I walked right past him to inspect the last side of the field.

There was a low ridge of dirt, or rock, I couldn't be sure, with trees growing on top and behind it. Perhaps this was the way out, the mound there to shield whatever lay beyond from seeing in.

Jayden had lost interest in my wandering and was looking at the ground, rather intently, a small smile playing at the corner of his lips.

Why was he so happy? Did it matter? This was my chance.

I hurried toward the stream and leapt to cross it.

I scrambled up the mound.

Heart pounding in my head and without looking back I took off down the other side, using the tree trunks to stop me from falling. I bounded through the trees, hoping I was moving in a straight line.

My mind raced as I wondered if I'd gotten a good enough head start. Had Jayden come after me? I'd heard no shout, or foot falls to suggest he was pursuing.

I had to assume I had outsmarted him. I ran on.

The ground beneath me began to shake. Wobbling, I hugged a tree.

Was this an Earthquake?

The trees swayed, some sleeping birds taking flight at the disturbance. The ground settled, my heavy breathing the loudest noise in the darkness.

I'd never experienced an Earthquake before, but I hoped that was the end of it. Standing upright, I picked a direction and began moving again. The lights from the field faded as the trees grew thicker.

The ground began to shake again. I lost my footing and fell into the undergrowth with a squeal. Seated as I was, hands on the ground behind me, I gave another yelp as something moved under my fingertips and butt. Pulling my arms in, I tried to find what had touched me, but I couldn't make it out. The rumbling continuing.

The ground itself wasn't moving; there was something under the dirt. Was it an animal? I thought of badgers and moles and wondered if we even had those in this country.

Completely freaked out and wanting to put some distance between whatever it was, and me, I pushed up to my feet and took off. The rumbling seemed to follow me. Every now and then my feet would roll or slide off something smooth, and I would change direction. The rumbling became so intense that I skidded to a stop, hoping to ride it out. As soon as the rumbling eased up, I put on a burst of speed through the trees as lights appeared.

I sighed in relief. I was out. I would track down a phone, call my parents and finally go home.

At the edge of the tree line, I came to a stop as I squinted at the lights glinting off a stream of water. My heart deflated.

I was staring at the field next to Havasek. Jayden, positioned in the centre of the field, was looking directly at me, his feet planted apart, arms outstretched.

No. How could I be back here? Had I run in a circle?

"Enjoy your bush walk?"

The ground at my feet shook. I gasped as my feet rolled off something smooth and I slipped, falling into the stream, landing on my butt, hard.

Wet from the waist up, I watched as eight rocks under the water rolled out of the stream bed and onto the field. They circled Jayden once before returning to the water where they lay motionless.

I glared at Jayden. It hadn't been animals or Earthquakes, but Jayden's element at work, herding me back toward Havasek. He'd let me run off, knowing he could reel me back in when he wanted to.

I clenched my fists, ready to give him an ear full.

"You did say you wanted some exercise," he said, a smug knowing smile spreading across his face. "I made it happen. I would hate for you to think I've not accommodated your needs while staying here against your will."

He cocked an eyebrow, goading me.

I had nothing to say. Or at least, nothing that would give me the upper hand in this situation. Embarrassment and rage boiled inside me as our eyes locked in a staring competition. I wanted nothing more than to hurl something at him.

I felt a tug in my stomach and then two columns of water rose from either side of Jayden, dousing him from head to toe.

It happened so fast he wasn't prepared for the assault, his fingers stiffening as the water gushed over his head, drenching him completely.

Stunned, I watched as the water slid over his body and onto the ground, my eyes placing every drop, until the bulk of it sank into the ground at his feet.

I waited for him to yell at me. Or say anything. But he stood there, processing what I'd done. And I just stared at him, dumbfounded that I'd manipulated the water.

He cleared his throat and shook out his arms, droplets flying off him.

"I think that's enough fun for one night," he said, avoiding eye contact. Oh, he was mad. "If you wouldn't mind leading the way back inside, I'd like to call it a night."

He stood back, waiting for me. He might be mad, but he would make sure I complied with this stupid rule of staying here.

All my fight had left me. My run through the bush had tired me out, and my display of Elemental usage had drained me further. All I wanted to do was have a hot shower and curl up in bed for the night.

I did as he asked.

Trudging through the glass room, I felt his irritation at being doused. Mum's voice in the back of my head told me I should apologise, but my anger at him chasing me through the bush kept me from saying anything.

At the thought of Mum, I longed for home, wishing it was her here telling me off, not some stranger I barely knew.

At the lift, he pushed the button for the first floor and stood back as if he wasn't coming up.

"Katalya will want to know what happened out there," he said, dutifully.

I nodded. The lift dinged. Jayden waved me on, holding a hand over the door to prevent it from closing.

"I wouldn't be so quick to judge this place," he said. "Yes, its foreign, and yes, you can't go home, but it's not forever. Everyone here went through a similar experience when they discovered their heritage, some far worse than yours. But they all stayed and are free to leave at any time. What you're experiencing is but a short time of your existence. This is where you get to discover yourself, your true self, without judgement from anyone knowing your history. Don't let it go to waste."

He met my eyes, the grey almost silver in the low light driving his words home. I felt the intensity as he willed me to not let my desire to leave overpower what I had discovered.

I believed him. I wanted to find out who I was with this knew knowledge, these new gifts. I wanted to become someone more than I had been, more than I ever thought I was capable of.

Despite myself, I nodded once.

"Katalya is the best Myundun Pina you could ask for. She knows more about Eleun than anyone I know," Jayden said, almost as an afterthought. "But then you'd expect that from someone who lived and grew up on Marcious. Don't be afraid to ask questions. That's the only way we learn, after all."

Letting his hand drop from the lift frame, he walked out of sight, my mind reeling over the knowledge that Katalya wasn't part human like Jayden and me.

She was a full-blooded Marcian. An alien from another planet.

CHAPTER
EIGHT

My Myundun, or control, lessons the next day were like the day before.

Mostly I breathed, became utterly aware of my body and then finally, after some achingly painful moments of waiting on the brink of my Eleun Myun, I was able to enter, the euphoric feeling lacing every inch of my body once again.

"Why does it feel like this?" I asked, trying to see how far I could sense water from a distance. I estimated I was sensing water for at least a few kilometres.

"Your Eleun is raw power and energy," Katalya said. "When we tap into it, the Eleun gives over reserves for us to manipulate. The Eleun is part of you, always has been and always will be, but only after you complete the Myundun can you fully use it in a safe manner."

"What happens if I die? Does it live on?"

"No, it will pass on just as you do."

At least it wouldn't leave my body and form a mind of its own. I'd seen all too well what it was capable of unchecked.

Katalya smiled as if she'd heard me.

Narrowing my eyes, I asked, "You're a mind Elemental, right?"

She nodded. "Entina Eleun, that's correct."

"What does that involve exactly?"

I'd seen the other four elements in action. I didn't quite understand the mind enough to know how she might manipulate it.

"It's a mind enhanced ability," she said slowly. "On Marcious it was seen as the peaceful Eleun, the one that brought everyone together and prevented contention."

She scowled, as if remembering something.

"On Earth, however, it's not as easy to explain our role. I, for instance can enter a person's mind, like I do with you," she said, indicating her hand that lay across my knee, "but only when I touch you. With the connection, I can read your mind, thoughts, feelings, even change them or convince you to do things you wouldn't normally."

My eyes widened and I was eager for her to release me right away.

She smiled warmly. "Don't worry, I won't make you do anything you don't want to. That's another aspect of being an Entina Eleun. We have stricter rules regarding our abilities, well, everyone has rules, but for us, we must always have permission to enter a mind, unless of course the person poses a threat. Then we act as necessary."

Her words weren't making me relax, but I continued to listen.

"With the combination of human DNA and Eleun, there are a lot of different abilities out there and not everyone can do what the original Eleun could."

It was the first time she'd mentioned her home planet. Now that I knew she was an original Eleun, my interest was sparked. I hadn't been game to ask her about it when I'd first arrived this morning, since they had been forced to leave it, but now that she'd brought it up, I couldn't resist.

"What was it like there, on Marcious?"

She fell silent, her gaze wandering off beyond me as if seeing something I couldn't, a small, sad smile appearing on her face.

"Absolutely beautiful," she said simply. Blinking out of her reverie she said, "Let's move on, shall we?"

With that, the conversation ended.

Katalya helped me in and out of my power a few more times, giving me an array of confused looks, as if she couldn't quite add something up. But when I asked her, she just shook her head and said it was nothing.

Any hope of sending ropes of water through the air like a whip or forming shapes, was shattered when Katalya explained that I wasn't ready and wouldn't be for a while.

My eyes were heavy as I stood to leave, and I knew if I didn't reach my assigned room soon, I would end up sleeping on the meditation room floor.

All this element work was exhausting, which didn't make sense since all I'd done was sit in the same spot.

"Why am I so tired?' I asked, rubbing my eyes.

"Connecting with your Myun, or using your Eleun in any way, is just like training your muscles, only more extreme," Katalya said, pushing the door open for me to lead the way out. "Your body is unused to accepting the power that resides in you. Every time your Eleun floods your system, your body must work harder to support it."

"All I'm hearing is that it will take a long time before I get to go home," I said, fighting back a yawn as we navigated our way through the gym equipment. Stumbling, I almost fell onto a rack of dumbbells had Katalya not caught me in her surprisingly strong grip.

She laughed. "With training and practice you will get stronger, your ability to sustain it lengthening in time, allowing you to manipulate the water around you as you wish. But you'll be able to go home before that point."

Gripping my elbow, she steered me out of the gym heading for the lift.

"Our main goal is to stop the outbursts when your emotions flare up," she said.

"Can I at least have my phone back?" I asked, hoping she might take pity on me in my current state. "It would be nice to hear my parents' voices to know they're not worried. I only have your word that they aren't organising search parties for me."

Katalya didn't answer right away as we rounded the corner. She pressed the call button for the lift. I watched her mull over my question.

"Normally, there is no contact with the outside until you're able to complete the Myundun by yourself," she said finally. Her tone told me she didn't completely agree with the rule. "But I will try to get it returned to you. I can see how worried you are. Your feelings and intentions are pure."

It took me a second to understand what she was saying, before I remembered she was touching me, and must be hearing my unspoken thoughts.

The idea still weirded me out. But then this whole place felt like a foreign country. Aliens from a destroyed planet, rocks chasing me through the bush, emotions causing teenager tantrums times fifty, right down to the fact that no one could stop them but yourself.

Even though I was part alien, I didn't feel any different, aside from the slight warmth inside me that was the source of my new power.

The lift doors opened.

"Is there something you needed to tell me?" she asked, eyeing me calmly.

I stared back, not following. "No, why?"

She pressed her lips in a thin line, her gaze stern like she already knew what I'd done wrong.

"Something about being chased by rocks and tantrums?" she said.

Embarrassment flooded me and I dropped my head, recalling Jayden's order to tell Katalya about my exercise the night before.

I opened my mouth to re-tell the events, but she cut me off.

"I've just seen it through your eyes," she said, lifting a hand to silence me. "You should have told me before we started lessons today. In the future I need to know of any outburst. Small mishaps are fine, but if they get any larger than last night, then it could cause a flow-on effect which could lead to bigger and more disastrous events we may not be able to talk you through. We have our methods to stop you, but I'd rather it never got that far."

I didn't like the way her voice dropped as if these *methods* weren't favourable.

I nodded, hoping it wouldn't come to that.

"Paige, what about you?" Amelia asked me. She had berry blue eyes and wild curly brown hair. She stared at me expectantly.

Ten other sets of eyes also found mine, each one a different shade of red, green, blue, purple, or yellow. I swallowed, taking them all in.

We were sitting in the common room, a large space on the top-level set between the boys' and girls' living areas amongst the schooling rooms. The common room was filled with couches and tables, board games, TVs and other electronic equipment. My fourteen-year-old brother, Liam, would be in technology heaven if he was left here without parental supervision.

Even I had to admit, the room was perfect.

After watching me wander around Havasek Wednesday afternoon searching for a way out, Bree had invited me to join them. Having exhausted all the doors I could find in the place, I'd agreed to come along, thinking that if I appeared to be settling in someone might slip up and tell me how to get out of here. So far, no one had been helpful enough to point a way out to me, but they'd also not tried to stop me. Either the Jalin were confident that I wouldn't find a viable exit, or they were enjoying watching my attempts.

Tonight's activity comprised of performing Elemental party tricks without adult supervision. According to Bree, you had to reach a certain level of control before you were allowed to use your ability without a chaperone. That didn't seem to deter these kids though.

"Surely, you've tried something by now," Amelia said. "On my second day, I was trying to lift water out of jugs."

A few boys laughed.

One said, "Yeah, and managed to set off the fire hoses instead."

"It was an accident, and the Pina never found out it was me," she said, giving the boy a shove.

"Yet," the boy said, almost under his breath.

I smiled, enjoying the comaraderie.

I'd already watched in awe as most of them performed some kind of trick. Amelia had already displayed her water wielding skills, shaping the water into farm animals, and sending them galloping around the room. I'd been a little worried the fire alarm would go off when a red-eyed girl had made fire girls dance the macarena along her arms. But my favourite had been when Josh, a mauve-eyed boy with shoulder-length sandy hair, had pulled an image from a girl's mind, then with a single look the image had appeared onto a blank piece of paper as if he'd painted it himself.

"I can't do anything, sorry to disappoint," I said, eager for them to move on from me.

"Oh, come on, it's all in good fun."

"No one will say anything."

"The number of times we've played this and the Pina have no idea."

I tried to shake them off. After having witnessed some amazing feats, my heart wasn't in it. But I agreed to try.

Closing my eyes, I made the merge with my Eleun.

Katalya had encouraged me to perform the Myundun by myself Tuesday morning, and after staring at me like I was some sort of phenomenon, that was how we began all our sessions from then on. It had felt natural to merge with my Eleun unassisted, easy, and I wondered why she'd insisted on helping me as long as she had.

"Often, Eleun can become overwhelmed with the power they hold in the early days of training," Katalya had said. "If the Myundun isn't completed properly, the Eleun can take control, wreaking havoc in the elements around them. That's why new Eleun are always assisted to begin with."

I'd already seen what my Eleun liked to do on its own. I didn't have a desire to repeat the experience.

Now, I focused on the water jug that had been placed on the centre table. I didn't know if I could make the water move, but I would try.

Staring at it now, all I wanted was for the water to lift and drop back down, just to appease the crowd in front of me, to show them I could do something.

In my mind, I told the water to move. Nothing. I tried again, staring so intently I wondered how long it had been since I blinked.

The water rippled. Two girls pointed out the movement, clapping.

I kept staring. I could do this. The longer I stared at the water, the more I understood it, like the knowledge on how to make the water move the way I wanted was at the edge of my mind but kept evading me. If only I could…

A single drop rose from the surface, lifting a metre over the rim of the jug. Concentrating on the drop, I willed more to follow, my breathing speeding up under the strain of focus. Three more drops floated to join the first, the four merging to create a larger drop. I could hear cheering as those around me applauded, but I wasn't paying attention, determined to do better.

I lifted my hand as if it would help move the water ball, even though I knew my mind had control of it. The ball circled the rim of the jug, progressively widening its arc until the floating ball almost touched the knees of those in the circle.

Knowing I could do more, I told the ball of water to continue the movement, drawing my eyes back to the jug, determined to get the rest of the water out as well. It came slowly, thinning as it edged itself out of the jug then clumping over the top in a dome.

Sweat beaded along my brow, starting to slide down the sides of my face. I ignored it. I could do more. I could do so much more.

Flattening the dome of water, I made it into a thin disc, the top appearing like the surface of a lake rippling in the wind. Holding the disc aloft, I diverted the small ball of water that continued to circle the room, sending it up through the centre of the disc and back down like a dolphin entertaining an audience.

My hands began to shake, but I held the display steady.

"Paige, you can stop now," Bree said beside me. "You'll over work yourself."

I shook my head.

"I can do more. I know I can," I said through gritted teeth. "This is nothing."

I made the disc twist and wobble, like a piece of paper floating on a breeze, all the while the ball dipping and diving along the edges and middle.

Black spots appeared in my vision. I blinked them away.

"Paige, really, you can stop," Bree said, sounding worried.

Clumping the water together I rolled all of it up into a triangular prism, spinning it tip down. The movement was hypnotic, and I lost myself in the feel of the connection, a sense of peace and contentment filling me as everything around me drowned out even as I strained to hold the water firm in my grasp.

Drops of water flew everywhere. Some protested at the unwanted shower, calling for me to stop as the kids stood, backing away. But I couldn't. I had more to show.

"Paige, stop. That's enough," Bree said, his voice sounding far away. "Amelia, can you take over? She's not ready for this."

"I already tried. She's holding it too tightly. I can't get a grip."

"Paige, stop, please."

I was lost in the rhythm, the feel of my connection to this element. It was me, and I was it.

Yells and protests grew louder.

"What's going on here?"

"Jayden, she won't stop. It was only a bit of fun."

The pyramid was spinning out of control, and water seemed to be coming from everywhere, too much for the amount I'd pulled from the jug. I knew I should stop, but something told me to keep going, that I only needed to get past this stage before controlling my element became easier.

The water clumped together, forming long lines flowing in an organised symphony, breaking apart as people moved for the door.

Someone shook my shoulders. "Snap out of it. You have to stop."

The water collapsed, splashing all over the furniture, technology, and anyone left in the room.

Trance broken, I blinked, feeling lightheaded. My knees buckled. Someone caught me and I looked up into a pair of silver-grey eyes filled with fury and worry.

Knowing I'd gone too far, I severed the connection to my Eleun before fainting.

CHAPTER
NINE

I startled awake, jerking upright in bed. I scrambled backwards pulling the blanket to my chin.

Jayden sat on the other bed, watching me as if I might start attacking people.

Releasing my grip on the blanket, I let out a relieved breath.

"Why are you in my room?" I asked, then groaned when my head throbbed like I'd been hit by a rock.

"Keeping an eye on you," he said, voice tight as if he wanted to say a lot more but was holding back.

"Why? I didn't lose control and haven't all week. I don't need a babysitter."

Swinging my legs over the side of the bed, I walked to the cupboard. Filling the glass cup with water, I gulped it in one, then refilled the cup. The water was refreshing and eased my headache.

Jayden, unmoving, watched me.

"What you did in the common room shouldn't have been possible at your stage," he said, in a low voice. "The others shouldn't have encouraged you either. That's on them. But that kind of manipulation is usually months away from when you first discover your Eleun."

I shrugged.

"That still doesn't answer my question," I said, though it was good to know.

He sighed. "Someone needed to keep an eye on you and Katalya was busy."

I rounded on him. "But I wasn't out of control, so there wasn't any harm in it going further. I even made sure I disconnected with my Eleun before passing out."

His narrowed his eyes. "There was water flying everywhere, Paige. It certainly looked like you had lost control."

"Well, I didn't," I said, then sipped from the cup. "If you were so worried, why didn't you have someone take control of the water, so it didn't cause damage?"

"Katalya didn't tell you?" he asked, as if I should already know the answer to this question.

"Tell me what?"

"Two Eleun cannot control the same section of element simultaneously. One must release it, before the other can take over."

I was once again, baffled by how things worked around here.

Jayden stood up and crossed the room to me. He eased the cup from my grip as I stepped back, uncomfortable with him in my space.

"I wasn't done with that," I said.

He held up a finger for me to listen.

"I was only able to take it because you let go in the first place," he said, then pushed the cup toward me again. "Now take it back."

Playing along, I wrapped my hand around the top of the glass. Jayden held it tightly, the two of us fighting to take the cup from the other. Water splashed over the rim and my hand slipped, Jayden claiming the glass again.

"When two Eleun try to manipulate the same section of element, a battle ensues and the one with the strongest grip wins," he said. "Sometimes it's a long battle of the mind. Others times, there's no fight at all depending on the strength of the wielder. It all comes down to training."

"Are you saying no one interfered because they knew it was pointless?

Because I've only been at this for less than a week. Surely anyone else would have been stronger than me," I said, extending my hand for him to return the cup so I could finish my drink.

"Amelia tried to take over, but she couldn't even get a grip. She said your hold was like steel. And even a two-year Reku-lee, like Amelia, should have been able to sway someone so new to our ways."

Whatever that meant. Jayden handed the cup over and I swallowed the rest of the water.

"Does this mean I'm progressing? That's good, right?" I said, deciding not to voice my eagerness to go home. "If Amelia couldn't get a grip on the water, shouldn't that have told you I was in control? You staying in my room all night seems pointless, unless you're some creepy stalker."

He squinted at me as if trying to see something he hadn't before. I didn't like that look and regretted the stalker comment.

"It was just a precaution," he said. "Sometimes, an Eleun can seem in control, only for them to lose it completely soon after, and you being so new… I couldn't risk it. You put a lot of lives in danger for some silly dare."

A knock sounded at my door.

"Finally," Jayden said, opening the door. "You made it. How did it go?"

"Not good, I'm afraid." Katalya's voice sounded from the other side.

I shifted to take her in. She was dressed in the black Jalin uniform, her hair out of place, dirt smudges along her front.

"We were too late. The damage was severe –" Katalya caught sight of me and cut off whatever secondary conversation they were having. "How is everything here?"

Jayden told her about my water manipulation dare, rehashing everything I'd just told him. I was surprised when she turned to me with the same look of intrigue that Jayden had, like they could see something I couldn't.

"And she's had no outbursts since?" Katalya said, still looking at me but directing the question to Jayden.

I was okay with this, having half expected her to lay one on me.

"Not a single drop of water out of place," he said. "Plus, she wasn't out for nearly as long as I would have thought. It's only been an hour."

I snapped my gaze to him. Only an hour? Even with my head hurting, it felt like I'd slept half the night.

"Interesting," Katalya said, finally addressing me. "Can you do it again?"

I shrugged, not sure what answer she wanted me to give. I gave the honest one.

"Maybe. Probably not now. I still feel tired."

"Then I want to see it first thing tomorrow. For now, get some sleep," she said, her voice authoritative.

I nodded.

Turning back to Jayden, Katalya said, "We should talk more about what happened tonight. It might help."

Jayden gave me a brief nod before following Katalya out into the hallway. I moved to shut the door, glad to see them gone, but their words made me freeze before it could click closed.

"How bad was the place?" Jayden said, their voices trailing toward me.

"Ruined," Katalya said, clearly dismayed. "There was a tree growing through the centre of the house, the branches spreading out into every room like they were searching for them. They didn't hold back and there was no trace of their departure."

What were they talking about?

"Were there any witnesses?" Jayden asked.

"A few of the neighbours, but we took care of them after we got their accounts," Katalya said, sounding tired now.

"Did the neighbours give you anything we can use?"

"Most of them only heard noises," she said. "By the time they ventured out to investigate, they were too caught up watching the tree spread through the house to notice anyone's faces. But we got enough to identify the family taken."

They were talking about kidnapped victims.

Was Havasek investigating the kidnappings? Had the kidnappers progressed to taking whole families now? From Katalya's words it sounded like this one had involved Elemental usage. Were Eleun the cause of the disappearances? After my experience outside the school and now this account, it wasn't a big stretch to assume as much. The questions kept on coming, but I pushed them aside to continue listening.

"We'll add them to the watch list," Jayden said, resigned. "Not that it's helped in our search."

"Everything helps," Katalya said, reassuringly. "We can only do the best we can."

"We need *her*," Jayden said, pointedly.

Who was this girl and why was she sought after?

"Without her, we are severely disadvantaged," he added, his voice becoming more worked up. "This is the second time we've been late. We'll never arrive in time by following police scanners. And unless we've got an Eleun in every few suburbs, we'll never feel any Elemental disturbances. We're spread too thin as it is. Humans will start to notice something if we don't find a better way."

"She's not ready," Katalya said, trying to calm him. "We need to hold out a bit longer. It's the only way to be sure she's prepared for the role."

"We're talking months, Katalya," Jayden said, his voice a hushed shout. "That's how long it normally takes, and that's for the ones that pick it up quickly. We could be waiting a whole year before she's proficient enough to go out. That's too long. We need her now."

Wait, were they talking about me? It was a guess, since no names had been mentioned, but the way Jayden's voice kept lowering as if he was conscious that someone close might overhear had me thinking it was me.

"The Welka have made it clear that she can't accept the role until she's in control, and Harmsworth is standing by them," Katalya said. "There's nothing we can do but wait... though there is something about her that tells me we won't be waiting as long as a year."

Jayden drew his sigh out. "I know. But there're a lot of people getting hurt because we aren't at full strength, not to mention the correspondence I'm getting from other Havasek about the situation. The Likonan aren't happy. It's only a matter of time before we slip up and miss someone who saw something."

"Everything will work out, Jayden," Katalya said. "She was chosen for a reason. We must have faith that it will all turn out."

Jayden didn't sound convinced as he blew out a breath.

"Come, I need to eat and clean up," Katalya said, "Plus Harmsworth will want my update. I walked straight past her on my way up."

"Lucky you're the only one who can do that. Anyone else and she'd have our heads," Jayden said, laughter in his tone.

Their footsteps disappeared down the hall. I waited until their voices trailed off before slowly closing the door. Pins and needles prickled through my hand as I let go of the handle. I'd been holding it rather tight.

My back hit the mirrored door of the cupboard as I ran over what the two had been talking about.

There was a lot I couldn't follow. But what I had picked up on was that both Katalya and Jayden were worried. Something was going on outside these walls and it wasn't going to plan.

Pushing off the door, I shook my head. Why should I worry about it? I was currently stuck in this place with no way to venture out. Clearly, Katalya and Jayden were handling the situation, and no doubt others as well. I should be focusing on getting out of here.

Trying to shove the worry I'd heard in their voices aside, I slipped into bed, determined to get some rest. But my dreams had other ideas.

A tree trunk spread through a house, the branches extending out of the windows and high into the sky as people ran from the doors screaming in fright.

The green eyes of the man who chased me flash, a wild mechanical laugh ringing through my head.

"This isn't over," he said, over and over.

Then the strange symbols were back, brightening with each turn of the circle they formed until they were one giant ball of light that blinded me.

I fell out of bed, the blankets slipping off with me. My heart thudded in my ears, my breathing heavy.

The symbols had looked similar to many I'd seen around Havasek. Was it just my subconscious filling my sleep with things I'd seen here?

I pushed myself off the floor.

What was my life turning into? First the revelation of Eleun, and now this strange dream.

Yawning, I noted the light under the doorway. It was brighter than when curfew was enforced, telling me the new day had started.

Opening the door, I peered out. All was quiet. There was no way I was going back to sleep. I was too riled up. I felt stronger today, more than I had since I'd arrived here. That had to be a good sign.

Dressing into my workout clothes, the only ones that belonged to me, I made my way down to the gym. While I couldn't leave Havasek to go running, there were plenty of treadmills that would serve my purpose.

After breakfast Katalya tracked me down, insisting I re-enact last night's performance.

It took just as much focus to make the water lift and spin, then clump and dive, but I did everything the same, right down to dropping the water as the room filled with liquid lines, a splash sounding through the meditation room.

If Katalya was mad about the carpet being wet, she kept it to herself. I hoped another water Eleun would be able to pull it back out of the carpet. I was spent.

"Very good," she said smiling. "I'm impressed with your progress, and it seems your control is well and truly in check."

As with every session we'd had, Katalya had connected with my mind by resting a hand on my knee, to observe my progress from the inside.

Slowly, I pulled my inner self out of my power.

"Does this mean I can learn more advanced things?" I asked.

Throughout the week, I'd seen some of the Eleun in the Rekulanna manipulating their elements. I'd been enthralled by what they could do.

Katalya chuckled. "Don't be in such a hurry, dear. A lot of those Eleun have been training for years, and it takes just as long to be disciplined. Your time will come."

Looking at her hand on my knee, I realised she must have seen some of what I pictured in my mind and looked away, embarrassed by my eagerness to be so bold.

She pulled her hand back. "But it does mean you can go home."

I snapped my gaze back to hers.

"Really?" I said, hoping I hadn't heard her wrong.

She smiled. "If you can do all this again tomorrow morning, we can have you home after lunch."

I felt as if I couldn't smile wide enough. I was going home. I could see Mum and Dad again. I could sleep in my own bed. Then a thought pierced through.

"Why now? You said it would take months before I was ready?" I asked, wondering if I'd gotten excited too soon.

"That is true, yes, and in most cases, it does take months to reach a level of safety before we let an Eleun venture outside alone," she said, her amethyst eyes conveying something deeper. "But that's only a precaution. Everyone progresses in their own time, though I will admit you've done so far sooner than anyone in history."

That was interesting. Why was I so different? Not that I was complaining. But I could see that the notion had Katalya baffled.

"Your liberation will come with rules," she said.

"Rules?" I said, sounding a little whiny.

"You will be required to return here every day to train," she said, chuckling. "Only with daily use of your Eleun will you become proficient in using it safely, and ultimately becoming fully aware and in control with it so you don't put yourself and others at risk."

It wasn't ideal. But after seeing the damage I could do, and hearing about Eleun manipulation gone wrong from some of the other kids, it wasn't a hard promise to agree to.

I met Jayden in the Rekulanna the next day after an encore performance for Katalya, proving to her that I was ready to venture outside.

I could barely hold in my relief to be going home, as Jayden wrapped up his conversation and waved for me to follow him.

I hadn't been thrilled that it was him taking me home, but since I had no other option, who was I to argue?

Jayden pushed open one of the doors I'd tried earlier in the week with ease. It led to a large garage, cars filling the spaces, a good portion of them being black vans or beat up cars you'd find at the dump. Except for one.

My jaw dropped when I saw the car Jayden led me to. Its slick silver body ran smoothly from back to front, the frame sitting low, appearing ready to take off at any moment. Just looking at the thing, I felt as if I was going a million miles an hour.

"This is yours?" I took in my second round of the vehicle.

Jayden smiled. "Just get in."

He ducked into the front seat and revved the engine. The vehicle roared to life, and I found myself laughing. Any hint of discomfort over him being my driver vanished.

The passenger's door lifted open, and he leaned across the seat.

"Or do you prefer to walk?" He gave me a cheeky grin.

His comment made me pause. Perhaps I should be cautious about getting into the car with a man I barely knew. One who could manipulate rocks at that. I still hadn't forgiven him for the stunt he'd pulled a few days ago.

He'd brought me here almost a week ago, on top of telling me a lot of wildly outrageous new facts about the world I lived in to help me survive. Aside from not letting me leave, no one had physically hurt me during my stay here. Surely, I could trust him to take me home, no matter how much

I was still unsure about him.

Besides, I really didn't have a choice. It was either go with him or stay at this place.

I entered the car, aware of the leather seats and beautiful interior, as I placed my bag on the floor. Katalya had returned my phone and belongings the night before, when I'd made a phone call to my parents to let them know I was coming home the next day.

Jayden took off through the garage and zoomed out the roller doors and onto the road.

I was eager to get a look at the building that housed the super-secret alien race. Turning in my seat, I found myself looking not at a building but a dry hill. A big one, but it was not what I expected to see.

The crest of the hill ran quite a way to the left, tapering off at a slow angle until it appeared to flatten out if the surrounding trees didn't obscure it from view. That must have been where the field lay hidden. The other end looked to be a large stone wall.

A small children's playground that had seen better days lay metres away from the road.

We'd not exited from the hill, that I assumed was Havasek, but one of the surrounding house garages that backed onto the bushy landscape. Some of the houses were old and run down, others nicer.

I turned back to Jayden to ask him about the facility.

"It's under the hill?" I said, staring at him dumbfounded.

"Havasek was built inside the hill, to keep its extravagance from attracting attention, especially surrounded by all this." He waved at the houses we passed. "If people saw a great big building sticking out that had people coming and going from it all the time, questions would be asked. Questions we don't want them asking."

"What about the houses?" I asked. "Surely someone would notice a lot of activity around a plain old hill."

Jayden shook his head. "They're either empty, or Eleun live in them.

Havasek owns the entire estate and uses it as a cover to stop people from entering the area."

"Empty? Why not utilise them?" I asked. "Seems a waste to let all this space go unused."

"It would draw too much attention to us. People would notice cars coming and going from the one house that leads to the basement of Havasek. It's better this way. Besides, we do use them. There are plenty of Eleun who struggle to find places to live and work, not to mention those who live at Havasek full time, so when it's needed, we do up a place and they move in."

Something still didn't make sense.

"Wait, so you have this super-secret hide out right smack in the middle of suburbia. What happens if a helicopter flies over and sees something strange? Wouldn't that raise suspicion? I mean, it seems to me that you'd be better off having this place somewhere less busy, like the countryside?"

He chuckled. "First, we aren't amateurs. We have connections and talents of our own. So this place has a no-fly-over zone plastered on it, though the government doesn't know it wasn't them who made that decision. Second, we do have other Havasek in the country, and by the ocean, and desert, and any other location you might think of, but with the main population being in the city, it seemed silly not to have one close by. Anyone could develop abilities at any time and a quick reaction time in finding them is usually the best and safest solution."

Huh, that did make sense. Guess they had it all sorted.

He pulled out of the abandoned suburb and sped up along the main road.

I was silent after that, processing what he'd told me, then when the silence became too much, I said, "If you wake up tomorrow and your car's missing, I didn't take it."

Jayden chuckled, shaking his head. "If you make it past security, then you deserve to have it!"

Lifting an eyebrow I shot a look at him, suddenly interested in his story "Security?"

He pressed his lips together so they formed a white line. I got the message loud and clear. He wasn't going to elaborate.

Instead, I started directing him toward home.

"Take the next left, and then..."

"I know where you live, Paige." He smiled apologetically, turning back to the road again. "I was assigned to keep an eye on you, with instructions to bring you in if things got bad, but not before."

"How did you know about me?" I asked, not following "And where I live?"

"It might surprise you to know that we can operate technology," he said, smirking. I rolled my eyes at his jab. "Plus, we have our own way of knowing when someone is…changing."

I wasn't sure if that was comforting or not, reminded about his conversation with Katalya a few nights back.

"So how long had you been watching me for?"

I remembered his comment about fast reactions being a good thing when getting to Elementals.

He didn't answer for a bit then said, "A week."

So much for being fast.

If that were the case, he would have missed my first lightning encounter.

I nodded. "Why did you have to wait?"

He was silent as he focused on the road, deciding what to tell me.

He sighed. "You were sort of… bait."

"For whom?" I said, my voice rising, although I had a strange feeling I already knew.

"Some people we've been trying to track down."

"What do they want?" I pressed.

Was my life expendable enough to be put on the line like that?

"People like us," he said simply.

Anger filled me, my mind racing with how events could have ended if my element hadn't kicked in and thrown a storm at Dominic and his gang.

"Paige, are you all right?" Jayden asked.

I rounded on him. "No, I'm not alright! What if they'd taken me? You never would've found me. What then?"

He cringed. "I'm sorry. Look, I thought I had everything under control. I hadn't let you out of my sight all week."

I recalled Matt, Sophie and Catherine ogling a silver car the day I was chased and realised that must have been Jayden.

"But when you left the school and I went to follow, my tyre was flat, so I had to go out on foot. It took time to find you."

The rational part of me told me to forgive him and move past it, but I was too wired up for rationality.

"Well, you're damn lucky they didn't," I shot at him, "because they came awfully close to abducting me and if it was –"

"Wait, what?" Anxiety laced through his features. "They were there? How many? What did they look like?"

I threw my hands up in annoyance. "Yes, there were four of them and they had me cornered, which was why I lost it and the storm appeared."

I could see him putting everything together, his gaze not entirely on the road ahead.

Then he slammed a hand across the steering wheel. "I'm such an idiot! It all makes sense now. The tyre was slashed. Of course, it wasn't a coincidence. They knew I'd be there, but how?"

I wasn't sure if I should say anything.

He turned back to me, fierce determination in his eyes. "Paige, I am so sorry for putting you in danger like that. I only wanted to stop them, or at least get a good look at them, but I guess they're more organised than we thought."

"Stop them from what?" I said.

His eyes glazed over before he shook his head.

"Never mind, that's a story for another day." He motioned a-head and I realised we were a street away from my house.

Wow, that had been quick.

I was still curious about his untold story, but my need to be surrounded by familiar people and inside my home overpowered the curiosity. I pushed the door open.

"I can pick you up tomorrow afternoon for your lesson if you want?" Jayden said, his features guarded after our conversation. "Four o'clock?"

I nodded, though I would have been fine not to return to Havasek, all the strangeness still overwhelming me.

What choice did I have?

Un-clipping my seatbelt, I turned to Jayden. Although I was still mad at him for using me as bait, I needed to know the answer to my question, so I put my anger aside.

"You said on my first day, that we were descendants from the original Eleun that landed here. Does that mean one of my parents has a gift as well?"

He leant against the door. "Not necessarily. We've found it can often skip a generation or two, showing up out of nowhere further down the line. When we learned of your change, we did some research and couldn't find any link between you and anyone we have on record, but it was only a brief search, so the link might show up eventually."

"It should go without saying that you can't tell anyone about your abilities or Havasek," Jayden said. "We've only lasted this long without discovery because it's been kept a secret, and it's one of Havasek's rules for using it as a safe haven."

My shoulders dropped at this news. Though I hadn't decided how I was going to tell my parents that I was different, I had wanted to do it. His words buried that thought instantly.

Part of me could understand why, but the other half wanted to rebel.

Wanting to see my family, I decided to push the issue another day. Maybe after I'd had more time to think about it and come up with a better argument.

I stepped out onto the front lawn of a neighbouring house.

"Thanks for the ride," I said simply, not sure what else to say to him.

He smiled and I closed the door so he could pull away from the kerb. I watched as he drove off down the street and around the corner.

As I crossed the road, I took in the view. My insides filled with warmth that I was finally home.

The house was set on the corner of two streets, the front lawn a grassy slope as the house commanded the flattened top half. A brick fence hid most of the front windows, curving with the footpath that attached to the driveway, where the pool stood.

The house wasn't anything fancy. A modest four-bedroom, two-bathroom, with a small granny flat we used for guests. Mum's flower garden lined the front of the granny flat, looking like she hadn't given it any love in a while.

I smiled with happiness. I could already see the shoes stacked against the wall as I opened the front door, no doubt a trail of school bags and uniforms leading to various rooms as I moved through the living room and into the kitchen. We weren't the tidiest bunch, a fact Mum was always yelling at us to correct, but the thought made me pick up the pace so I could hear her voice again, in whatever mood she was in.

Stepping onto the front lawn, I was about to run the final distance when a car pulled into the driveway. It was black and small compared to the two cars already parked ahead of it.

Wait, two cars?

The first belonged to Mum, a red four-wheel drive, old and dusty, a dent or two in the back from the various road trips we'd taken over the years. Dad hadn't seen the point in getting them buffed out as the car worked fine.

The second car was bigger than ours, its white frame far newer. The car had been washed recently. I didn't recognise it.

The black car pulled to a stop and the door opened. A boy stepped out of the driver's seat, a plastic bag in one hand.

The boy was my age, wearing dark jeans and a bright orange T-shirt fitted nicely with his athletic build of a body. His hair was dark brown with a hint of curls, but what caught my attention were his eyes; they were a piercing dark green, much like another pair I'd seen recently, only these were far more dazzling.

My breath caught in my throat. I took a step backwards, not from fear, but because I felt as if I recognised him.

Our eyes locked. I became entranced by his gaze.

Who was this boy? And why did I have the sudden urge to feel his arms wrapped around me?

CHAPTER
TEN

"Paige?" the boy said, the words breaking my trance. How did he know my name? And yet, I enjoyed the way it rolled off his tongue.

Mentally slapping myself for being ridiculous, I nodded hesitantly, not trusting my voice.

He gave a heart-breaking smile and leant back slightly. "Wow, you look so much like Angela. She said you'd be coming home today. How was your trip?"

Who was this guy?

I cleared my throat. "Do we know each other?"

Shock spread across his face.

"Oh, my fault. Of course, you probably think I'm some weirdo."

A hot weirdo! I mentally slapped myself again for thinking that.

"It's been a good seven years, so I guess you wouldn't recognise me. No doubt you've progressed from playing mudpies in our back yard, so maybe that's why you don't…"

Everything clicked together.

"Ryan?" I said stunned.

He flashed me a grin. "In the flesh."

Before I could stop myself, I ran toward him, flinging my arms around his neck. My abrupt assault almost had him falling backwards but he righted himself and pulled me in for a hug.

Ryan was the son of Mum's oldest friend, Sharon. The two had grown up together, living next door their entire lives, attending the same schools, even working at the same places for a time. We had been close with the Drake kids.

But seven years ago, they'd moved down south when Sharon's husband Colin started up his company, a good twelve-hour drive away, and we hadn't seen them much since. Mum and Sharon had made the trip a few times, but they'd never taken us along.

"Whoa, let's not knock out the zombie," Ryan laughed. "I've been driving non-stop for six hours."

His words triggered the reason why he was outside my house, and I pulled back making eye contact again.

"I'm sorry about your dad," I said. "I wish I could have been there for you, and everyone."

His smile dropped.

Way to bring up a hard memory!

"Thanks," he said kindly. "I know you would have if you could."

Last year, his father had been killed in a work accident. A lab experiment gone wrong was the official report.

A few months after the funeral, when Mum had been visiting the Drake's, Sharon had expressed her need to start a new. Fast forward nine months and here I stood with Ryan in my driveway.

I'd known the Drakes were moving up here, but through all that had happened in the last week, that fact had completely slipped my mind.

Looking into Ryan's sad eyes, words failed me.

I'd never lost anyone before. How did you comfort someone who was in mourning?

Then his smile began to lift again. It wasn't as broad as before, but there was hope in his expression.

I mirrored his smile, before I realised his arms were still around my waist. They were surprisingly warm and comfortable.

Looking over his shoulder, I noticed the empty seats of the car.

"Where are the rest of your family?" I asked, taking a deliberate step back, even as my body told me to stay put.

The plastic bag he was holding rustled as he dropped his arms.

"They're inside. I just ducked out to get a few things for Mum," he said lifting up the bag.

"When did you get here?" I asked, looking at the house, but I couldn't see past the tree blocking the windows.

"About two hours ago," he answered.

Now I understood his zombie reference. Sharon and Ryan must have driven both cars up here.

"Should we go inside?" I asked.

"Yeah, Mum is eager to see you," he said, as I led the way to the front door. "She was sad when we arrived, and everyone was still out. We forgot about the time difference."

When I stepped inside the house, I was almost knocked back by a booming voice.

"Oh, Angela! You did not do any justice to your daughter!"

Sharon pulled me into a tight embrace, squishing every bit of air out of me. Then she pushed me back, running her gaze up and down me.

My cheeks heated.

"Hi Sharon," I managed, still trying to gather myself.

"You are gorgeous! Oh, I love your hair, so long, and those eyes, very striking," she narrowed her hazel eye, shaking her head. "I still can't see any resemblance to your parents. If I didn't know better, I'd say you were adopted, I've said that from day one."

Sharon was a little taller than me, her body curvy around the middle but not overweight. She had dark brown hair, close to Ryan's, with blonde streaks falling from the centre.

Sharons comment about me being adopted wasn't a new one to me.

Over the years, many people had said the same thing, joking that mum needed to confess something she'd been holding back. Mum had always laughed it off assuring them that I was her biological mother. I'd grown used to ignoring the comments.

But now that I'd learnt I was Eleun… did that explain the difference?

Sharon turned to Mum, who sat on the couch a few steps away. "I'll be taking the role of descriptions from now on, Angela dear. I don't trust yours anymore. Wouldn't you agree, Ryan? Angela dramatically understated her kids."

Mum, her dark brown hair pulled back into a loose knot at the nape of her neck, shook her head, chuckling. Eva, who sat beside her, ducked her head, her sun-kissed blond hair falling over her face, as she hid a smile, pretending to read her book.

Muffled laughter trailed out of the kitchen next door. Liam was getting a kick out of me being singled out. No doubt he'd been under Sharon's gaze already and was glad I wasn't being let off the hook.

Ryan chuckled. "Sure, Mum."

That wasn't enough for Sharon, who stood me directly in front of him.

"Come now, tell me Paige isn't a beautiful young lady?"

Liam howled with laughter from the kitchen again.

Ryan tipped his head.

"She is very beautiful," he said with a smile.

I tingled inside as heat spread across my face.

Catching on to my uncomfortable positioning, Mum piped up. "Let's leave the kids to it. What can I help you with to get ready for the move?"

I excused myself, eager to change my clothes and needing to get some distance. My element fed of emotions, and I didn't want to lose control again, especially since I seemed to be feeling a plethora of new ones at present.

When I rejoined everyone, I curled up on one of the front room couches, listening to Sharon and Mum chat idly. It was so good to be home, made even better with the presence with close friends.

Early the next morning, Mum had everyone out the door by nine o'clock for a trip into the city.

Sharon seemed eager to do some sightseeing and Ryan and his siblings showed the same enthusiasm.

We all loaded onto a ferry the size of a small house that would take us along the harbour.

As soon as we boarded, Ryan's six-year-old sister Lucy's hazel eyes lit up and she begged her mother to let her go off and explore the boat, her bobbing brown ringlets swinging over her eyes. Sharon agreed so long as someone went with her, so she and Eva took off toward the front.

Peter, Ryan's fourteen-year-old brother, headed down the back with Liam. The former was tall and lanky, his strides doubling those of Liam's. Mum, Dad and Sharon found seats inside, leaving Ryan and me alone.

"Come down the front with me?" Ryan asked with a nod in the direction Lucy and Eva had disappeared.

I followed him along the outside walkway as the engine revved and we pulled away from the dock.

Leaning against the railing, I stared out over the water as it swirled past the side of the boat. For some strange reason, the motion reminded me of running, of having the wind brush past me. I sighed as the memory sent a calming effect through my body.

"What are you seeing that I'm not? You look so entranced." Ryan's voice interrupted the silence.

He watched me curiously.

Smiling, I returned my gaze back out over the water. "Nothing, just thinking."

"I think I'd pay a little to find out what's going on in your mind," he said with a chuckle.

Feeling a heat rise to my cheeks, I lowered my head.

"My thoughts aren't that interesting, trust me," I replied, thinking of the craziness of the last week.

How would he react if he knew who or what I really was?

Ryan's smile was lopsided as he studied me. "I don't know, I think they'd surprise me."

You're not wrong there.

"Rye?" Sharon's voice called from the door and we both turned to face her. "Can you watch Luc? Eva's just come in and said she isn't feeling well."

He sighed, giving me an apologetic look, before heading inside to follow his sister out the back.

Turning back to the water, I watched as it swirled and tumbled against the boat and amongst itself.

My mind raced with thoughts of how I would control this element, how it would move and the types of things I would make it do. The possibilities seemed endless, enthralling and scary all at the same time.

My senses took over, and I was one with the water below, feeling it rock and sway as objects moved along its surface, causing the coils of water to spin and swirl into small whirlpools. I moved with the water, the churning intensifying as the boat picked up speed and broadened its range.

Shouts sounded around me when the boat gave a sharp rock.

Why the loud screams? It wasn't anything to be afraid of, just a bit of turbulence.

My back slammed into the ground. My senses came back to reality as the boat rocked heavily from side to side.

I blinked, my vision clearing. A man stood over me.

"You okay?" he asked, grasping my shoulder. "You took quite a fall."

I gasped as I felt the familiar sensation of the after-effects of connecting with my element. I pulled myself up and leaned over the railing.

The water still swirled and tossed. Dread filled me, my heart pounding heavily against my chest. I'd lost control.

CHAPTER

ELEVEN

I watched the water begin to settle and fall back into a gentle roll along the surface.

My heart beat rapidly at the prospect of what had almost happened.

I'd almost created a whirlpool. One that could have taken out everyone on board.

I'd just put my family and friends in danger.

"Hey, you doing alright? You don't look so good," the man who'd first appeared said. "Maybe you should head inside?"

Slowly, I nodded, and he helped me through the door.

"Paige!" Mum's worried voice sounded in my ear. "You're pale. What happened?"

She grasped my other arm and led me to a seat.

"She took a fall outside," the dark-skinned man told my mother.

"Thank you for bringing her inside," Dad replied, shaking the man's hand.

"Are you all right?" Mum continued to fuss over me, feeling my forehead and offering me water.

I nodded and leant back against the seat, trying to ignore the rocking of the boat.

Sharon leaned over and placed a hand on my knee.

"It's all right, dear. Sea sickness is my weakness too. That's why I stay indoors," she said, then lowered her voice and added, "and drug up for trips like this."

Her smile was reassuring, but I wasn't feeling it. The thought of harm coming to those I loved, by my hand, was enough to scare me into the reality of my situation.

"Hello, Earth to Paige?"

I blinked, focusing on the voice beside me.

Ryan.

I hesitated. "Sorry, what did you say?"

We were walking along the pier where the ferry had dropped us off at the harbour. Sticking to my seasick façade, I had hung back behind the cluster of my family, trying to keep my focus away from the water. Ryan had fallen into step next to me.

"I just asked how you were feeling," he said.

Shrugging, I replied, "Better, I guess, now that we're off the boat."

It was a lie I didn't want to keep up.

Ryan gave me a comforting smile. "So, what do you like to do Paige Munro?"

His question caught me off guard, not because it was unusual, but by the way he used my name.

"Nothing interesting," I said, brushing him off, my mind unable to come up with anything but my Eleun life. It was still fresh in my mind.

"I don't believe that for a second," he said. "A great girl like you has to have plenty up her sleeve."

My cheeks heated, and I ducked my head to hide my embarrassment.

I watched the seagulls land along the pathway, scavenging for food, then fly off when anyone got too close.

"Well, I like to run, and I'm okay at most sports." I shrugged, trying not to make a big deal of it. "Other than that, I'm your average teenage girl."

"Average girl? What does that even mean?" He brushed the air in front of him. "The way I see it, there's no average anything."

"I guess," I replied. "But honestly, there's nothing special about me, no deep secrets or hidden talents."

My heartbeat skipped as I desperately tried to think about something, anything, to talk about.

To cover, I uncapped the water bottle Mum had given me on the boat and took a drink.

"Are you on the school track team?" Ryan asked.

Thankful he'd reverted to something I could answer, I said, "Not since last year. School got too hectic, so I pulled out and just run for fun now."

"Mind if I come along sometime?" he asked.

I snapped my gaze to his, surprised by his question.

He wanted to spend time with me.

Covering my hesitation, I took another drink. Unfortunately, my mind went to answer his question at the same time and water came spilling out of my mouth, splashing all over my shirt and pants.

Springing backwards, I held the bottle away from me.

People stopped to stare at me.

I wanted to disappear.

Well, that was one way to get Ryan's attention. Now he would remember me as the water girl his mum forced him to talk to.

Trying to ignore everyone's eyes, I attempted to swipe the water off my clothes. Ryan pulled off his sweatshirt, extending it out to me.

"It's okay, it's just water," I said, waving him away.

"I insist," he said. "Here, give me the bottle."

When he reached for the plastic, his fingers brushed against mine. My hand relaxed at his touch, the bottle falling to the ground, spraying us both with water.

I groaned dismally.

Ryan chuckled as he bent to retrieve the now empty bottle. Muffled laughter surrounded us. Mum and Sharon had stopped to check on us and were stifling grins.

I glared at them. They had the good sense to turn around.

"I'm so sorry," I said to Ryan as he righted himself. "I'm such a klutz."

He smiled. "It's okay, seriously, I needed a shower anyway."

I chuckled, glad he wasn't making a big deal of my clumsiness.

I started forward, not wanting to be left behind.

Ryan caught my wrist. My heart stopped, heat flaring through me.

"You didn't answer my question," he said, and when I looked confused, he added, "About running?"

A scream issued from up ahead, and we both jumped. Ryan released my hand, as we turned toward the sound.

Eva, Lucy and the boys ran up the large stone steps to the Opera House at the top, screeching with joy.

I relaxed. All the strangeness lately had put me on edge.

Forgetting my fake façade, I smiled in Ryan's direction.

"How about now?" I grinned.

He didn't quite catch on until I took off.

The pounding of his feet wasn't far behind me, as I reached the bottom step, taking them three at a time, lunging and pulsing upwards.

We passed Lucy first, then Eva and Peter. Liam beat us to the top, shaggy brown hair flopping around his face. He might be short, but he was fast.

I sucked in a deep breath and let it out slowly, feeling my heartbeat rhythmically against my chest after the exertion of exercise. It felt so good to be moving again, to have the rush of adrenaline coursing through me, bringing me to life.

"What a view!" Ryan said, as we looked out over the shops that lined the water's edge. "Beautiful day for it too."

I couldn't agree more. The sky was bright and blue, clear of any clouds. Seagulls soared high above, singing their calls loudly for all to hear. Tourists were out in force as they walked along the boardwalk, enjoying a Saturday morning with friends and family, taking photos and feeding the birds.

Closing my eyes, I took another deep breath, letting the fresh air fill my lungs as I felt the watery depths around us, the smell of salt brushing my senses.

I pulled my mind away from the ocean. I couldn't afford to lose control again, not today.

The air had a tinge of a pungent odour. I wrinkled my nose.

That hadn't been there before, had it?

Another scent filled my senses, sausages cooking on a BBQ, onions sizzling away beside them.

It was more welcome than the last, but I didn't remember seeing anyone along the way who had been cooking.

Then the whiff of gas hit, followed closely by petrol fumes.

"Ugh," I said out loud, the stench overwhelming me.

The air could do with a good freshening up. I wished it would rain. The aftereffects of a good downpour would purge the air of most of the unwanted odours.

A strong wind blew past me, whipping my hair away from my face. I stood my ground as the force almost knocked me over.

The sun continued to beat against my skin, but the cooler breeze helped to lighten the force. Then a light patter of rain began to fall.

With no clouds about?

The rain became heavier, followed by a loud *boom* through the sky.

It was no longer a sunny day. The sky was now a dark mass of grey as the wind pulled and tugged at anything that wasn't secured down.

Uh-oh!

I rested my hands in my hair as I took in the scene before me, the strands soaking wet and slapping my face.

There was no more laughter or pleasant chatter of tourists enjoying their day. Instead, the tourists darted toward cover, calling out to loved ones or just from the sheer shock of the unexpected storm.

A storm that was entirely my fault.

Again.

"Paige!" a voice yelled over the next loud boom.

I turned to Ryan as he pointed toward the bottom of the stairs. His hair was plastered against his face, clothes drenched and clinging to his body.

Below, our families beckoned the younger members closer as they headed for shelter along the shop front.

Ryan and I took off down the stairs after them.

My mind raced with how I was supposed to handle this situation. Without Katalya or Jayden, I didn't know if I could calm myself.

I realised I wasn't hyperventilating like all the times before. In fact, I was completely calm, aside from the slight edge of the catastrophe on my hands.

But if I was calm, then why was there a massive storm raging, when only seconds ago everything was clear?

Continuing to run, I tried to come up with a solution as we reached the bottom of the steps and began across the open pavement.

Keeping my gaze down, I focused on not tripping.

Hands grasped me under the arms, and the ground suddenly dropped away as I was lifted into the air. The pavement grew further and further away.

I let out a scream.

Panic took hold and my head shot from one side to the other, trying to come up with an explanation for this madness.

I found it from above, in the form of a girl with blonde hair that blew around her face in the wind as we flew through the sky.

"Who the hell are you?" I shouted, wriggling in her grasp. "Put me down!"

"Stop moving, or the fall won't be pleasant for either of us!" she said.

Seeing the growing distance, I halted my struggle. I didn't feel like going splat today.

We moved through the sky, away from the main thoroughfare and toward the grassy landscape of a hill.

Flying had not been on my list of adventures for today, but it seemed the element that resided in this girl allowed her to do just that.

When we dropped altitude, the ground raced up to meet us. I braced myself for impact. We hit the ground hard and rolled halfway down the hill.

I sent a death stare at the girl. "Couldn't you have landed softly?"

"You try landing in a hurricane!" she shot back as we both got to our feet, her yellow eyes lighting up.

"This is hardly a hurricane," I said brushing off my clothes.

"Oh, really? I guess you haven't seen the best part." She nodded behind me.

Slowly, I turned to see what she meant.

Out over the water raged an enormous swirling waterspout.

I took a step back, almost falling over as I slipped on a wet rock.

Had I done this?

The circulating mass pulled at the surrounding water, rising into the sky, stray spurts flying through the air from the fierce wind. Boats struggled against its flow and fought to escape the danger zone, but it was futile. People daring enough to withstand the storm stood along the water's edge, phones out, filming the entire show.

I fell to the grass beneath me. "How do I..."

Words failed me and all I could do was stare.

Then a face appeared in front of me, his features hard and determined as he focused on me. I reeled back.

It was the man from the boat, the one who'd found me on the ground.

His skin was dark, making his purple eyes stand out. His hair was pulled into dreadlocks and he looked barely older than me.

"You," I said. "You were on the boat?"

"Yes," he yelled over the noise of the storm, "but right now you need to concentrate!"

His words didn't sink in.

"Are you from Havasek?" I asked, wanting answers.

"My name is Danny. Please listen to me or a lot of lives are going to be damaged," he said.

With another look at the waterspout, I nodded.

"Close your eyes and breathe," Danny said.

I did as he asked, remembering Katalya's instructions in our lessons.

The noise outside was deafening and I found it hard to stay focused, my attention continually being pulled back to the ocean.

"Paige, please," he said. "I can help you, but you have to start the process."

I took his meaning to say that he could talk me through this mess and pulled my mind back into the room Katalya and I would sit for our lessons each day.

It was quiet. There were no raging storms, no screaming people, and no gigantic waterspouts. Just the closed, soundproof room in the basement of Havasek.

Somehow, I felt the beat of my power inside me come into focus.

"Now merge so we can end this," Danny said, loudly but calmly as if he'd done this plenty of times.

"How? I've barely controlled my element before," I admitted.

His hand rested over mine, and his voice sounded through my head.

"My ability allows me to control other abilities once they are merged. You won't have to do a thing, just relax."

He could control my ability? I hadn't expected that.

Slowly, I moved toward the source of emanating power. As I came closer, I could feel it was out of control and wanted to do a whole lot more than merely start up a water spiral.

Entering wasn't like all the other times. There was still the elated feeling of euphoria, but it came slowly, almost as if the element was pre-occupied. Which of course it was. I knew when I had fully merged with it, because it was intoxicating.

I wanted to be just as reckless and carefree as the storm that raged. I wanted to explore every part of my element to see just what I could achieve.

The thrill of what was going on around us pulled at me, sweeping me away.

My eyes flashed open. Danny's hand was still over mine, but he was looking at the connection as if something was wrong.

He shut his eyes as he concentrated, but utter bewilderment set in his features.

I didn't care so much right now.

Standing up, I moved away from him and walked down the slope, my eyes glued to the water that spiraled and twirled before me.

I could see how it worked, how it was formed, how it pulled at the surface of the water and worked its way upwards to the sky.

It was like I'd been downloaded with the knowledge of everything water… just by looking at it.

I was aware of everything that went on through the storm that loomed and even though I'd barely had any training with controlling my element I knew exactly what to do to put it right again.

But part of me didn't want to. The carefree, unworried part fell under the spell of power, my eyes closing as my mind drifted away into the swirl of hypnotic supremacy.

My mind spun round and round, feeling the flow of water as it churned and tumbled. I smelled the fresh watery scent, heard the lapping and splashing, the rushing and crashing.

"Paige, what are you doing?"

Danny stood in front of me holding my shoulders tight.

"Why can't I control you? I can't get into your mind." He was frantic.

I blinked a few times, coming back to myself.

"I…I don't know," I said, "but I think I know what to do. It's strange but it all makes sense. It's… amazing!"

A shaky laugh escaped my lips, and I looked Danny in the eyes as if that would convey everything I felt.

He just stared back, confused.

"Can you stop it?" He nodded to what lay behind him.

I smiled. "Yes."

"Well, now would be a good time." His voice was shaky.

I stepped away from him, concentrating on the waterspout.

The lure for me to re-join its intoxicating adventure pulled, but I held my ground as I thought of my family and friends, of all those who would be in danger should I let it continue.

Funneling just enough of myself over to the force, I flowed with the movement, implanting myself in amongst it, steadily taking control and slowing it down until the water spurt came apart entirely, the water falling back into the ocean.

Breathing out, I turned my attention to the storm overhead and using the same techniques, gave part of myself to it. Just as before the storm slowed and calmed. The clouds drifted on, parting to show the clear blue sky once more, the sun taking force again.

Turning back to Danny, I smiled.

He nodded approvingly. Exhaustion swept through me, and I collapsed.

CHAPTER
TWELVE

Opening my eyes, I registered that I was lying on grass with two faces looking down at me.

"It's about time!" the blonde girl said.

Slowly, I sat up, taking in my surroundings.

We were back on the hill, hidden away behind a small jutting of rocks. There wasn't much to see from my position, but from what I could make out, life after the storm was back under way, with people moving about freely again.

"How long was I out?" I spoke.

"Not long, ten minutes, tops," Danny said.

I blinked a few times to clear my blurry vision.

Danny was kneeling by me, his expression guarded as he surveyed me. Water droplets slid down his jacket, remnants from my control issues.

The girl, whose name I still didn't know, was standing, her long blonde hair clumped and dripping around her shoulders. She wore faded black skinnies with boots and a bright yellow T-shirt that clung to her tiny waist. I realised then that I had seen her before. She had been on the field the day Jayden had brought me to Havasek.

At least I knew where they'd come from now.

"How do you feel?" Danny asked cautiously.

I'd been sure I was bound for the concrete when I'd fainted, but at the last second, Danny had caught me before I'd lost complete consciousness.

"I'm fine, thanks. Were you following me?"

The two shared a look.

"Yes," Danny said. "Libby and I have been with you since you got on the boat."

I glanced between the two, looking for more even though I wasn't sure what. "Why?"

Libby snorted. "Do you even need to ask?"

She was right. It was clear why they'd been on my tail.

"Did Jayden send you?" I asked Libby.

"Yes," Danny replied, "he just wanted to make sure you had help should you need it."

"Guess that turned out badly, didn't it?" I sighed.

"Yeah, about that…" Danny said. "Why couldn't I control your element? That's never happened to me before."

I shrugged. "You got me, but it was like you were never inside my head once I'd merged."

He nodded slowly then pulled himself together.

"Regardless, you're okay now and it seems, more capable than we thought. We can't have our Remana breaking down. You're too im –"

Libby coughed and shot him an accusing glare.

I tried to make sense of what he'd just said. What did they mean by 'our Remana'?

"You should get back to your family," Libby piped up. "They're probably going frantic."

"What were you talking about?" I asked Danny, standing. "Why did she just cut you off?"

He scratched his head.

"It's not important," he muttered, looking down. "She's right. You should go."

"No!" I pointed a finger at him. "I don't like secrets!"

Danny stood too, avoiding eye contact.

"You'll find out soon enough," he said. "Make sure you keep yourself in check. We'll be around, but hopefully you won't need us again."

The two of them headed around the side of the hill, but I wasn't going to let them leave without an explanation.

"Wait, you can't just leave me hanging like that. Tell me," I said, following them.

Without a glance back, they took off at a run. I was still exhausted from using my element and couldn't keep up. They disappeared out of view.

Damn it!

"Paige!"

I spun around, before I was engulfed by arms and a face full of hair.

"We were so worried. What happened?"

Catching my breath from the knockout, I pulled back to see Mum, the rest of our entourage following close behind.

"I'm fine," I said, taking in her worried expression.

"One second you were behind Ryan, the next you were gone. We thought the storm had swept you up!"

I almost laughed. She wasn't wrong there.

Giving her a reassuring smile, I tilted my head as I searched for a plausible explanation.

"I just… took a wrong turn, that's all."

She tucked a loose strand of hair behind my ear. "Well, I'm glad you're okay."

"I don't know about anyone else, but all this excitement has made me hungry. Who's up for lunch?" Dad said, patting his belly.

Liam and Peter cheered.

Mum gave my arm a quick rub before moving to Dad's side.

"That water spurt was freaking awesome!" Liam said. "Did you see how wide it was? And it reached the sky as tall as ten buildings!"

"Probably closer to fifteen," Peter said, just as excited. "No one will believe we had front row seats!"

Great, if two teenage boys found the waterspout exciting, there wasn't much hope that the news channels would overlook it later this afternoon.

As we walked back along the waterfront, I fell behind, going over everything that had happened.

Controlling the storm had been incredible.

I couldn't wait to do it again.

But what Danny hinted at had me concerned…

"So, I'm confused."

I jumped at the sound of Ryan's voice.

"What about?" I asked, trying to sound calm.

"What happened?" he asked. "I swear you were right on my heels."

I lowered my head and swallowed.

"Honestly, I don't know." I paused as if trying to make sense of it. "I *was* behind you and then you weren't there and I… I can't really explain it. I continued running until I came to the waterfront, so I just stayed there until the storm passed."

Ryan nodded and I hoped he believed my story.

"Well, I'm glad you're okay." He smiled. "It was pretty scary when I turned to see you weren't there."

I nudged him playfully. "Miss me much?"

"Perhaps." He laughed, dropping his gaze. "Next time, I'll have to make sure you *don't* wander off."

A thrill of excitement filled my insides, his words not lost on me.

We followed our families as they turned toward a street filled with people.

When our trip to the city finally ended, I was relieved. I wasn't worried I would lose control again. In fact, I was pretty sure I had a good handle on my powers now.

I just wanted to get home and into bed where I could curl up and sleep off my exhaustion. As it was, I fell asleep on the ferry ride, and almost in the car as well.

After explaining that I was spent and planned on skipping dinner, I excused myself to my room.

Opening the door, I didn't even bother turning on the light, just shut the door behind me and felt my way to the bed. A hand latched onto mine.

Jumping back, I hurled myself against the door and slammed on the light, my heart racing.

Gasping for air, I doubled over as I took in the person sitting there.

"Holy hell, Jayden, you scared the pants off me," I hissed at him.

He was dressed in faded jeans, a grey shirt, and jacket open in a way that showed off his muscled chest.

"We need to talk," he said, folding his arms.

"Yeah, well, you could have given me a heads up," I said. "The whole house probably knows you're here now."

His gaze shifted to the door.

As if on cue Dad's voice rang out. "Paige, you alright? Sounds like something fell?"

I lifted an eyebrow as if to prove my previous statement.

"No, Dad, all good, just bumped into my bedside table," I called back in my best calm voice. "Good night!"

"Okay, sleep well honey."

I let out a breath, relieved that he wasn't going to come in and check on me then leaned against my chest of drawers.

"So, why the urgent visit? It couldn't wait till I managed to get away?" I asked.

Jayden shook his head, his gaze serious.

"You missed your training session," he said, his brow furrowed. "I would have thought after your outburst today you'd have made sure to be here for it. I need to hear your side of events."

Danny and Libby must have explained the day's events to him and now he was here to reprimand me.

I didn't blame him. I had just caused a massive spectacle in front of plenty of spectators, and there would be some fallout that needed attention.

I wasn't dreading it, though. If Jayden wanted a recount, then that was my chance to find out what this Remana business was.

"From what I heard, there was a lot Danny didn't understand," he continued when I didn't start talking. "He seems to think you have a better hold over your element than you've been letting on."

I kept my lips pressed together as I thought about this. Did they think I was holding back on purpose?

Yeah, well, two could play at that game.

"Paige," Jayden said sternly, "this is important."

"What is a Remana and why did Danny seem to think I was important?" I asked instead.

Jayden was good. He didn't show any sign of recognition over the title, just continued to give me his expectant stare.

"I asked first," he said, holding my gaze.

"But you're not the only one I can ask about this," I said. Danny and Libby knew, and I could go to them if he didn't tell me.

"True. Unfortunately for you, almost everyone who knows won't talk if I tell them not to."

I rolled my eyes. "Fine, but only if I get my explanation."

He didn't reply for a long time, and I was afraid he wasn't going to agree, but then he finally stood.

"Okay, but not here," he said. "It's better if I show you."

CHAPTER
THIRTEEN

"What do you mean *show me*?" I asked. "You afraid someone will hear us?"

Jayden's face faulted as he smiled. Pulling out his phone, he pressed a few buttons before pocketing it.

"No," he said, "you just won't believe me if you don't see it for yourself."

"Oh."

After everything I'd already seen and learnt, what more could shock me?

"But I should warn you, once you understand, you won't be able to take it back," he said.

"Whatever." I was determined to not be left in the dark. "Let's just go."

I paused at my door.

"Wait…How exactly did you get into my house?" I asked, facing him again.

His smile turned mischievous as his stance relaxed.

"I have my ways," he answered simply.

I glared back at him, but he held his ground.

"Well, however you did it, I hope it doesn't involve getting seen on your way out, because it's going to have to be our exit route."

Sighing, he turned to the window. I hadn't noticed it was open.

He unhooked the latches along the sides and removed the fly screen, gently lifting it outside and onto the grass below.

I was going to have to remember that one.

He effortlessly jumped over the seal.

Clumsily, I followed, landing hard on the ground.

"Are you sure your parents won't check on you through the night?" he mocked, looking back into the room.

Truthfully, I wasn't, but he didn't need to know that.

Regardless, Jayden jumped back through the window, stuffed some clothes and pillows under the bed sheets and quilt so that it looked as if I were asleep, then switched off the light. He re-joined me back outside and re-attached the flyscreen.

"Can't be too careful," he said. "I'd hate for them to worry because you were missing."

His lip curled, and I scoffed as he was clearly patronising me, considering all my worries while I'd been away this last week.

"Ha-ha," I said, and followed him around the side of the house and across the street to where his car was parked.

Once we were on the road he said, "Okay. You first. What happened today?"

I recounted what had happened on the boat, then along the waterfront with Danny.

"Once I made the connection, everything became obvious. I just knew what to do to right everything," I concluded.

We'd almost reached Havasek.

His expression was confused.

"What's the matter?" I asked. "Isn't it normal, what I did today?"

"No, most people take weeks to get through the control lessons, then months more to get the hang of using their element. What you did today was beyond anything I've seen, or heard of. No one has picked it up so fast before."

I was beginning to get tired of hearing this. But I finally understood Danny's confusion over not being able to control my element. I was different, advanced possibly… or maybe it was just a side effect from originating from Earth?

"What does it mean?" I asked.

He sighed, shoulders slouching slightly. "I don't know, but the Likonan will want to hear about it."

I shot a look at him, remembering hearing the name a few days prior. "Likonan? Who's that?"

"It translates to captain. She… runs this Havasek," he said.

"Why haven't I heard of her?"

"It hasn't come up until now." He explained simply.

I focused on the road ahead as the car turned down a street and raced to where Havasek was hidden.

Stepping out of the car once it was parked, we made our way into the Rekulanna.

"It's your turn now," I said with perhaps a tad too much accusation in my tone. "What is a Remana?"

Jayden didn't stop, just kept walking as he headed to the lift.

"Keep up and… keep an open mind, okay?"

What did that mean?

He wouldn't give me anything else as we rode the lift to the atrium floor, crossed the open space, and stopped in front of the library doors.

Like every other time, I had a strong urge to enter and see what lay beyond the doors.

"This is as far as I go." Jayden motioned to the wooden frame. "Katalya will meet you inside and explain."

"Wait, what?" My gaze darted from the door to Jayden. "Why aren't you coming? You said you would explain!"

He dropped his head before sheepishly looking back up.

"I know I did, but it's not my right," he said, "and truthfully, I only know part of what you need to hear. Katalya can tell you the rest."

I swallowed nervously.

What had I got myself into?

He left me, disappearing into the dining room.

Facing the library doors again I gave into the urge and pushed them open.

Standing in front of me were six rows of shelves lined one behind the other, each filled with books.

Venturing farther into the room, I ran my hand along the end of the bookshelves. Something caught my eye and I stopped, my brow furrowing.

I pulled a book from its place and stared at the cover. It was completely green in colour except for a bunch of symbols along the top. The symbols matched the symbols I'd seen on the bottom of the paintings in the hallway upstairs. They also resembled the ones I'd seen in my dreams, but after a quick scan of the page I realized none replicated the one's that had been plaguing me night after night

Opening the book, I flipped through the pages and found the same symbols covering almost every page with various images on others.

"What sort of book is this?" I spoke out loud, even though no one was around

"A Marcian original," a voice spoke up, startling me so much I almost dropped the book.

"Katalya!" I breathed. "I didn't know you were here already."

She stood by the end of the last shelf, her gaze resting on me as I studied the book in my hands.

She smiled, reaching out for the book. I handed it to her.

"This one is about plant life," she said, flicking some pages and stopping at a drawing of a forest, though not quite like the forests I'd seen before. "Terralin Eleun would usually consult this type of book to understand the element they control."

My shock dissipating, I nodded. "Is the writing Marcian too?"

Katalya nodded. "And quite beautiful when spoken aloud, although it's not often done so these days."

She sounded sad about that. Carefully closing the book, she placed it back on the shelf.

"Do many people speak it?" I asked, curiosity getting the better of me.

Giving me a sorrowful expression, she replied, "Not as many as I would like, but it's hard when you live on a planet where it isn't even known as a dialect."

"Will you speak something for me?" I asked, eager to hear this beautiful language.

Katalya smiled. "Not today. We have important business to discuss."

She headed toward the back of the room.

Sighing, I followed.

"But if not many people speak it then why have books written in the language?" I asked, not willing to give the conversation up just yet.

"Preservation," she replied. "Not many things from our home planet survived. We must preserve whatever we can, so our past isn't forgotten."

Part of me wanted to see more of these foreign items, but I could sense Katalya was ready to let the topic drop.

She stopped beside a row of desks with computers perched atop them.

Turning to me, she said, "I heard about what happened today, and though I'm glad everything worked out, I'm amazed at what Danny told me. You've gone from barely being able to perform party tricks to manipulating an entire storm. I must say, even I'm shocked at your progress. And I've seen my far share of Eleun in-training. Care to fill me in on the details?"

Apparently, I was the topic of the day. But all I could say was what I'd told Jayden, unable to explain it in any other way.

Katalya mulled over my explanation.

"I guess we will see how your ability continues to grow over the next few weeks," she finally said, before changing the topic. "Why don't we get to the reason you're here."

I nodded, eager to learn of this Remana business.

"Now, I know you have a lot of questions," Katalya said. "Normally,

I wouldn't agree to this so soon, but after today and sensing that there is something different about you, I think now is the time."

My curiosity intensified at her change of mind.

Katalya turned to the wall to her left and pressed her hand to a panel I hadn't noticed.

A light appeared as it scanned her hand. The wall in front of us slid open, revealing a corridor.

Without hesitating, Katalya strode through the door and I followed.

We took the left-hand turn, coming to a stop outside a door.

"This door can only be opened by a handful of people," Katalya said. "What lies inside is our most valued possession."

"If it's so important, why show me?" I questioned. Surely my mere curiosity hadn't been enough for them to explain whatever lay inside.

She smiled softly. "Because you will be one of those people who can open the door."

"What?" I said, but Katalya pressed her hand to the door and closed her eyes as she concentrated.

There was a light click and the door slid open.

If I was expecting a room full of gold and riches to come tumbling out, I was wrong, very wrong. What did occupy the room was far from anything lavish or expensive. A mere wooden stand stood erect in the centre of the space, much like a stand in a lecture hall where a professor would place his books to teach a class. And that was exactly what was placed in the centre of the stand – a small midnight blue book.

My eyes narrowed.

Why was a book the most important thing in the building?

Katalya entered the room and walked around the stand, watching the book reverently.

I followed, with less reverence. The insistent pull seemed to come from the book.

I still didn't understand what was going on.

"We call it Salyunda," she explained.

Again with the weird names. Clearly a remnant of the Marcian language.

"Why is it in a room all by itself, when there is a library full of other books out there?" I asked, thumbing toward the room we'd just left.

"Because it is the one thing that is able to unite our people across the globe."

"How?" I asked staring down at the simple object.

The insistent pull intensified.

"Salyunda is the source we turn to, to find others, to teach them who they truly are."

My eyes locked with hers as I remembered Jayden telling me that Havasek had its own ways of finding people.

"So, this is how you found me?" I clarified. "Why didn't you just say so? Jayden made it sound as if it were the biggest secret on the planet."

"It's one of the biggest secrets we hold," Katalya said continuing her walk around the room.

"I don't understand. Then why tell me? I mean how do you know I can keep a secret?"

I peered down at the book again, that elusive pull still lingering.

"Because only one person can actually read Salyunda. That person is known as the Remana." She looked at me as she rounded the stand, her gaze trying to convey something more than I understood.

There was that title again. The same one Danny had used this afternoon when he had called…

"You mean me?" I gaped, putting everything together.

Did they think I was the one supposed to read this book? To find other Eleun? Surely, they had it wrong. I wasn't even that much of a people person.

Katalya nodded. "It would seem Salyunda has chosen you to be the next Remana."

"Wait just a minute, the *book* chose me?" I asked, not understanding how a book could choose anything. "And how can only one person read it? It's a book. Everyone reads books."

"I can see how this may be confusing," she said with a warm smile, "but trust me, Salyunda chose you because it saw certain qualities in you that a Remana needs to find others. You see, it's not just a cover, bindings, and pages. It's also made up of an ancient magic, one not created from any mortal."

I shot a doubtful look at her.

"Salyunda was made by Lalanthal," she said. "In your tongue it translates to the gods."

"Gods?"

This was beginning to get weird.

"Yes, the same Lalanthal that created Marcious, in fact."

Well, that was a bit of history that was left out.

"You mean like, the Creation, Adam and Eve, and all that?" I rambled. "I've never been a big religious girl. I don't believe the big bang theory, but gods, as in multiple…" I shook my head, this revelation too much.

"That is Earth's beginning, yes. Marcious's was… similar in the planet's forming, only there were five Lalanthal who worked together in creating the world I grew up in."

I needed to sit down. This was making my head spin.

Backing up, I hit the wall by the door and slid down until I sat with my knees bent in front of me, my arms resting atop them.

"So are you saying that gods really exist or is this just what was passed down from generation to generation?" I asked, hoping this would help me understand it all better.

Katalya looked at me solemnly. "I know that religion is a complicated thing here on Earth, and there are many different beliefs, but on Marcious, there was only one, and everyone believed the same thing, well… for the most part."

"But how do you know? Was there proof, or was it all just a blind belief that had everyone following stories?"

She smiled grimly. "I know this is hard to take in, but when you have the ability to manipulate the elements, is there really any more you need to know?"

I sighed. "I guess not."

It still wasn't enough, although she did have a point.

"Once our planet was destroyed, however," Katalya said, "and the day of Nelayunda happened, when we arrived on Earth, our makers did show themselves to us."

My head snapped up.

"You saw them?" I asked, louder than I anticipated.

Katalya nodded. "They offered us help, in starting a-new, guiding us through the struggles of blending in with this world and teaching us many things in order to survive."

I stared wide-eyed, not sure if she was pulling my leg or being serious.

"What happened after that?" I pressed.

"They are still here," she said softly, her gaze drifting to the ceiling, "watching over us. And they are also the creator of Salyunda."

She motioned to the small book on the stand.

"They made it from parts of themselves, giving over certain aspects so that it would notify its Remana when someone was ready to be told the truth."

"What, so these *Lalanthal*…feel people coming into their power and then transfer it to Salyunda?"

Katalya shook her head. "No, Salyunda has a mind of its own, from what the Lalanthal gave it. It is connected to them, yes, but it thinks and acts for itself. Salyunda finds our people, notifies the Remana, and then we do the rest."

My gaze drifted to the book, and I had an urge to pick it up. However, I resisted after hearing its origins.

Was I really worthy to be this Remana?

There was a long silence as I stared at the book, Katalya watching me.

"You don't have to be afraid," she said. "It has already chosen you. You are the Remana."

I swallowed. Hearing the words said bluntly like that made me feel even less worthy.

"How do you know it chose me?" I said, my voice shaky.

"The last Remana made contact from our Havasek in Peru, and told us about you after reading your name inside as a developing Eleun. We thought it was just a routine find, but while we spoke, he became frantic and said he couldn't find Salyunda anymore. It had disappeared. To lose something that important would send anyone a little crazy, but having seen it before I knew what had happened. All Remana do once their time comes to an end. It's hard to accept when it happens."

"Why, what happened?" I asked.

Katalya smiled and motioned to the book. "It came here. It had chosen a new Remana, releasing its previous one from responsibility."

I let out a shaky breath. "So because I was the last name read, I'm also the new Remana?"

She gave a single nod. "Yes."

"Why not tell me when Jayden first brought me in? Why keep it a secret?" I asked. "If I'm the only one who can read it, why wait?"

Their conversation from a few nights ago suddenly made sense. They had been talking about me.

Katalya sighed loudly. "You were not ready for the task. You were untrained and the information would have been too much. There are many who still think this."

I had been told a lot that first day.

"How hard can it be?" I shrugged, "Read the name, find the person, done. Sounds easy enough."

The pep talk was more to calm my overwhelming mind as it processed everything, but when Katalya spoke I felt a little worse.

"Once upon a time, that would have been the case," she said, eyes sorrowful. "But the responsibility of others is a heavy burden. It's more involved these days."

I got to my feet, my butt having gone to sleep. "What do you mean *involved*?"

"I'm not sure now is the right time for this conversation," she said. "You still have to accept your role and the Likonan will want to speak with you before you leave."

I remained silent, feeling slightly intimidated by meeting this leader.

"It is not hard. All you must do is pick it up and you will be bound," Katalya said, reading my silence wrong.

I turned to the book again. "What if I don't want to be this Remana?"

"Then you had better be sincere. Otherwise, Salyunda will not choose another person until you are."

This whole book-can-think-for-itself thing was starting to freak me out.

But I had to admit, all I wanted to do was pick up the book, fulfill the pull that drew me closer until I was standing directly in front of it, my hand hovering over the top.

Jayden's words replayed in my mind. *Once you understand, you won't be able to take it back.*

This seemed like it was a big task, one I shouldn't take lightly.

Now that I was so close, the pull was intense, and it took all I had to resist as I tried to think logically about the decision before me.

Perhaps I would give it a go. How hard could it be? If I didn't like it, I could always change my mind. Right?

Anticipating something magical to happen, given it was a book made by gods, I placed my hand around the spine of the book, and lifted it gently off the wooden stand.

There was no glow that surrounded me or bright angelic music that announced I had accepted the role, just a feeling of rightness and relief at having satisfied the pull that had tugged at me ever since I entered the room.

Katalya nodded approvingly and turned for the door. I followed, clutching the book to my chest.

Once outside in the hallway, Katalya said, "Protect Salyunda with your life. It's the key to our survival and continual peace within our people. Without it, many would drift away."

I didn't like the sound of that. In fact, it made me less enthralled to have this massive responsibility thrust upon me.

"If you ever need to hide it, place it on a bookshelf with other books, and only you will be able to locate it," she said as an afterthought. "Now, you will have to lock the door. Place your hand over the frame and merge with your Eleun."

I did as she instructed. There was a soft click before the door stayed firmly shut.

"To open it, you do the same, however you probably won't need to use the room again. Its best if you always keep Salyunda on you, so you will be ready to read the names that appear."

"What do I do when a name does appear?" I asked.

Katalya led the way back down the hall as she spoke. "Call Havasek straight away and then get here as soon as possible."

I nodded.

"You'll be required to go out with a team but I'm sure Likonan Harmsworth will go into more details about that," she said.

Great, how much more did this job require?

As I followed Katalya back through the library, across the atrium floor, and into the lift, I stared at the book in my hands.

It was so small, only a little bigger than one of my hands. When I looked closer at the cover, I found that it wasn't entirely blue at all. It had very fine silver lines weaving before my eyes. It was mesmerising.

When Katalya pulled me to a stop, I realised we were standing outside a door connected to the Rekulanna. An eye was etched into the wood, a large L across it.

It occurred to me now that the 'L' must stand for Likonan, and I swallowed in anticipation.

"Likonan Harmsworth is very straight forward. She doesn't like to beat around the bush, so when you speak, just get to the point," Katalya said in a stern tone. "She's a very busy woman and doesn't like nonsense. However, having said that, she's also one of the best Likonan we've ever had in this building."

Katalya pushed the door open.

The rectangular room wasn't large by any means, but it was bigger than my bedroom and the long edges of the room framed me left and right.

This half of the room was bare, the other half contained a bookshelf to my left and vanity cabinet to my right. Near the end stood a wooden polished desk, two chairs facing the one that resided on the opposite side.

In that single chair sat a woman, who I assumed to be Likonan Harmsworth.

Her head was bowed over a stack of paperwork and she moved a pen across it. When I entered, she looked up.

Her gaze fell upon me first and a look of annoyance crossed her face, but upon seeing Katalya, she smiled and stood.

"Katalya, good news, I hope?" Her voice boomed around the room.

Likonan Harmsworth was taller than me by at least two heads. She wore a white uniform that mimicked those of the Jalin, a large 'L' stitched over her left breast and various items hanging from the belt at her waist. Her black hair was pulled back into a tight ponytail and as we got closer, I saw that her eyes were a piercing green. She was a Terralin Eleun.

"Yes, Likonan." Katalya smiled warmly. "May I introduce Paige Munro, our Remana."

The green eyes found mine.

"So you're the young girl who's caused me so much trouble today." The Likonan surveyed me sternly. "You know, it's not an easy task trying to cover up a waterspout in the middle of the city with so many witnesses, plenty of whom took videos and are currently trying to sell them to the news channels."

I felt her reprimand keenly and my gaze dropped.

"I'm sorry. I didn't realise what I was doing until it was too late."

"Yes, well, next time be on your guard."

I felt as if Mum were standing over me giving me the riot act.

"I can't afford any more mistakes," the Likonan said. "It takes up too much time."

If this woman ran this place, she no doubt would be involved in whatever the Remana did. Which meant I'd have to work with her. From everything I knew about her, I got the sense she would only accept perfection.

I already didn't like her.

CHAPTER

FOURTEEN

Katalya cleared her throat. "Perhaps its best if you explain the responsibilities involved as Remana?"

The Likonan nodded curtly.

"Right as always, Katalya," she said, and I got the sense the Likonan looked up to her.

Probably because Katalya was much, much older than her.

"I assume you've informed her of the heritage of Salyunda?"

Katalya nodded and the Likonan pointed to the chairs in front of her desk. "Right, have a seat."

We all sat, the little book, Salyunda, lying across one of my knees.

"Being Remana is an important role for our community," Likonan Harmsworth said, her hands intertwining as she placed them on the desk, "not only because it prevents outbreaks that could cause major damage, but it brings our people together and ensures that we continue to grow and stay united. Without Salyunda, there wouldn't be a worldwide Havasek organisation."

Worldwide!

"That's right," she said, correctly reading my astonishment. "We cover the globe, with many different buildings used for safe havens. In each one, there is a trained team ready to mobilise the instant they get the news of a new Eleun."

133

She stopped, waiting for that to sink in.

My mind was still reeling with the knowledge that we existed all over the world and yet I hadn't met anyone like me until earlier this week.

The knowledge that I was half-alien was still rattling around in my head as if someone were about to jump out and scream, 'April Fools.' Given Eleun had been on Earth for over a hundred years, it shouldn't have been a stretch to believe that they lived everywhere.

"Now that you have been chosen, we will oversee notifying the areas when a name appears close to them," the Likonan said, "and you will be required to locate these people alongside those teams."

"Me!" I shot out before I could stop myself. "How would I even get to these places? Can't a team just find them once they know the name?"

"They could, yes," she said slowly, surveying me, "and for the interim that is how it will work since you're still undergoing your training. But once you have completed your training and are deemed in control, then you will be required to travel the distances to accomplish your mandate."

She made it sound as if it was a binding law.

I nodded, though I still didn't like the sound of it.

"We can go into more depth around that travel when the time comes," she added. "However, in order for you to be a part of the teams, you will have to undergo training, both physical and Elemental."

That didn't sound good.

The Likonan turned to Katalya. "Would you mind finding Jayden and bringing him here? I think he was headed to the field."

Katalya bowed her head slightly and disappeared out the door, leaving me alone with this woman.

Likonan Harmsworth turned back to me, her gaze hardening. "The training you will go through will not be easy. In fact, your instructors will be particularly hard on you because of the circumstances that linger on these missions."

"Why? Is it dangerous?" I asked, vaguely remembering something

Jayden had said yesterday afternoon.

"Very. We aren't the only ones looking anymore. Over the last year, we've had Eleun go missing before our teams could arrive. Its only in the last few months that we've learnt that another group has been taking our people and just recently that the other group aren't human."

My mind went straight to Dominic and my encounter outside the school.

As if reading my thoughts, the Likonan said, "Yes, it was the information you gave Jayden that told us they were like us. What we don't know, however, is why they want our knew Eleun and how they are able to locate them before we do. It has put a lot of Havasek on edge. Some have even limited contact to remain hidden and safe."

"Wait a second," I said, something occurring to me for the first time. "These disappearances don't have anything to do with the ones on TV lately, do they?"

She didn't answer, just kept eye contact, but that was answer enough.

"So, humans don't have to worry, then," I said, relieved that my family would be safe. "These people are looking for Eleun."

"It would seem so," the Likonan said. "However, there have been some humans taken as well…"

I swallowed hard. "So… these outings, will they be dangerous? I mean, the training is only a precaution, right? I won't have to use it?"

Even as I said the words I recalled Jayden and Katalya's conversation about a tree growing through a house and realised what she must have been doing the night I drenched the common room.

Likonan Harmsworth didn't respond, looking at me with an unimpressed frown.

Her gaze locked with mine. "Why did you pick up Salyunda?"

I felt like I was in an exam.

"Because my name was last to appear inside it," I said.

"No, your name appeared in Salyunda because it sensed qualities in you worthy to fulfill the role of Remana. Why did *you* choose to pick it up?"

The scrutiny in her voice was intimidating.

"Katalya told me it's an important role. I figured I couldn't say no," I said.

My mind was a blur, trying to give her what she was looking for.

Likonan Harmsworth sighed impatiently. "Being Remana is not for the faint of heart. It is both physically and mentally draining and will test your limits. If you can't answer the simple question of why you chose to pick up that book, then you better think about it long and hard to find the reason. Otherwise, you will fail, and the end result might not be favourable, to anyone."

Her gaze was hard, boring into mine.

"I allowed Katalya to acquaint you with Salyunda because it is our custom, and something this important cannot be left sitting in a room, unread. You've chosen to pick up Salyunda, so I will allow you to go ahead with the training, for now. But mark my words. If I find you are not up to this task, I will find a way to remove you from the role. Do I make myself clear?"

I was saved from responding when the door opened, revealing Jayden.

"We're all gathered," he said.

Likonan Harmsworth stood with a nod and motioned for me to follow her.

Glad to be out of her firing line, we entered back into the Rekulanna where a group of people waited.

They all turned.

"This will be your team," the Likonan announced. "They've been working together for some time now and do so quite well, so I expect you to become just as efficient."

So much expectation. She really wasn't going easy on me.

"Jayden, I'll leave you to do introductions. I've other things to take care of." She gave me a sideways glance, and I knew by the deepening of her brows that it had something to do with my display by the harbour.

She strode out of the room, the door swinging shut behind her.

Five pairs of eyes, all different colours, stared at me. I clutched the book more tightly to my chest.

"You sure she's the one?" A girl with long blonde hair that draped flawlessly around her shoulders asked. "Because she's really young, not to mention inexperienced."

I did a double take. It was Libby from this afternoon, the one who'd flown me up onto the hill.

A few of the others cracked smiles, all except Jayden.

"Yes, Libby, and I'm sure she's already worked up enough. Give her a break."

Libby rolled her eyes.

"Yes, Master," she said with a salute, sarcasm filling her tone.

Jayden turned to me.

"Usually, there are only five on a team," he said, motioning to the five that were gathered, "but since you aren't fully trained, we're going to have six for a while."

I nodded. I was fine with that news, seeing as there might be danger involved.

He waved to Libby first. "Libby. You met her today. Her element is Breezen or wind which allows her to fly, among – other things."

She'd changed since our encounter this morning, now sporting a pair of denim short shorts and a purple singlet. She threw me a nice-to-meet-you-but-not look.

"Nicolas is our Entina or mind Eleun," Jayden continued around the circle. "and he can move things with his mind."

Nicolas was tall and lanky, his black hair shaved close to his head. He, out of everyone, smiled warmly at me and extended a hand for me to shake.

"Nice to meet you," he said, his voice deep but welcoming. "I never thought we'd actually host Remana again, not in my lifetime anyway."

I smiled back, not sure how to respond.

Again? Had the Remana been found here once before?

"Bradley is our Aquenel or water Eleun; however, he has a military background which helps in tight situations."

He was tall with wide shoulders leading to a slim and cut waistline. His hair was chocolate brown and hung around his ears. His eyes, like mine, were a deep blue.

"And finally, this is Naomi, our Furno or fire Eleun, and also your Reku instructor," Jayden finished.

As I looked at her, I gulped. She was massive!

Not tall-massive, as the Likonan had been, but big boned and body builder-type massive. I'd never seen any woman her size before.

I had no idea what a Reku instructor was, but hearing that she was to be that person, I didn't like the thought of what she had in store.

I shuddered as I took in her eyes. They were red, just like one of Dominic's men outside the school. Now I understood why.

Naomi gave me a nod but didn't extend any niceties.

"And you already know me, so that's all of us. Thanks guys." Jayden nodded to the group, and they all strolled back toward the lift, except Naomi and Jayden.

"I hope you're ready to get sweaty kid, 'cause we start tomorrow afternoon," Naomi said, waving her hand to encompass the room. "And once I'm done with you, you'll wish you never became Remana."

I shuddered involuntarily, before she followed the other three out of sight.

Did I really want to be Remana after hearing everything that was involved?

"Is it too late to say no?" I said, my eyes glued to the corner they'd disappeared around.

Jayden burst out laughing. "I did warn you that you may not like it."

I gave him a horrified look as I wondered what I had gotten myself into.

"Don't worry about it – she's not that bad," he said. "In fact, you're lucky to have her. She's one of the best."

"What is Reku?" I asked.

"Reku roughly means fight training, or close to it… There is an ancient Marcian fighting style that goes by the same name, but since there are so many different styles on Earth, the name has been used for all disciplines, Muay Thai, Karate, Taekwondo, Jujitsu… you'll be doing a range of different things with her."

I was going to have to write these names down if I was to remember them all.

"Do I need to update my Will before tomorrow?" I said nervously.

He laughed.

That was enough to calm my nerves.

Before Jayden drove me home, we made a trip to the dining room. Hunger had nagged at me as the night wore on, and Jayden insisted I eat after hearing my stomach growl.

After a large helping of lasagna, fresh bread rolls, and a garden salad, we hit the road home.

We mostly talked about my new Remana role. It turned out that Jayden didn't know much about Salyunda's history, except that it found new Eleun.

I wasn't sure if I was supposed to mention anything Katalya had told me to him, and disregarding how he'd treated me these last few days, I had to talk to someone about it. He was right there, so I took the opportunity.

As we neared home, I asked, "The story Katalya told me about the Lalanthal, the gods, that isn't true, is it?"

Jayden seemed like someone who would give me a straight answer.

"I mean, if there were god's, they wouldn't show themselves to us mere mortals, would they?" I finished hesitantly.

Jayden shrugged, looking as if he really had no idea. "Maybe. Who can know for sure? I mean, if you think about our history here on Earth, there are plenty of recounts that tell of God appearing to humans. Who's to say that story isn't something similar for Eleun?"

"So, you don't believe it's true then?" I asked.

"Honestly, it seems to me like it's just a story, something to keep us younger generation in line and believing in some higher power. But whether I believe it or not, it doesn't change my stance about this place or what we do, because ultimately, we are doing a good thing and that's enough for me. Plus, I've met some incredible people in my time here, so I wouldn't give that up for anything."

I nodded absentmindedly.

When Katalya had talked about the Lalanthal, there had been a reverence in her voice that told me her experience had been more than just some story she rattled off to the kids.

I didn't fully understand it, but I didn't want to worry about it. I already had enough on my plate.

"How dangerous do these missions get?" I asked, changing the topic, not sure if I wanted to hear the answer.

Jayden exhaled loudly, his shoulders rolling back as if my question was a tough one. "Usually it isn't that bad, not to mention it's rare that we have many Eleun found in our area, but we've heard stories from other buildings that have put us on edge."

"The kidnappings." I said.

"Attacks as well," Jayden said, nodding. "Houses destroyed, teams coming home severely injured, but it's nothing we can't handle. Everyone has recovered and with each incident, we learn more about the group behind all of it."

"What about the victims?" I asked.

"There's nothing we can do for them." His expression dropped. "We have no idea where they've been taken or what these people want. We can only compile information and hope we find something that leads us to them."

"You make it sound like there isn't any hope," I said, my voice soft.

Jayden didn't reply straight away, and we drove almost the remainder of the way home before he said anything.

"There's always hope. We can't give up, those people depend on us."

Pulling to a stop two houses down, we both got out of the car and walked the rest of the way to my house.

Likonan Harmsworth's question floated through my mind again. I still didn't have an answer. Did I honestly want to put myself in danger like they all kept telling me?

Salyunda, at my chest, hummed as if knowing my thoughts. It gave off a reassuring warmth, as if to say: *It's okay, I picked you for a reason.*

I wasn't sure if that made me crazy, but I felt calmed by the feeling.

"You might want to consider coming up with a solid excuse for getting out of the house in future or your parents are going to get suspicious," Jayden said.

I sighed. He was right. With my new role as Remana and all the extra training I was going to have to endure, I needed something that Mum and Dad would believe and allow for me to leave the house regularly.

"Any ideas?" I asked hopefully.

"Ever think about getting a job?"

That wasn't a bad idea. I was old enough.

Jayden rattled off some ideas, ones that wouldn't involve too much parental involvement – fast food, retail – but I turned them down. They weren't bad ideas, but they were also jobs at which my family and friends could pop by and 'surprise' visit me any time.

Walking around the side of the house, we lowered our voices.

"I'll ask around and see if anyone can come up with something," Jayden said as we stopped outside my window. "Alternatively, you could move out of home and live a Havasek full time."

He grinned wickedly.

"No, thanks," I said, knowing he was joking, but needing to be clear that it wasn't happening. "I do like my life out here, even if it means commuting to and from Havasek regularly."

He silently unlatched my flyscreen and I climbed inside, then watched as he re-attached it once more.

I placed Salyunda on the bed-side table.

"Hey," I whispered loudly, placing a hand on the edge of the window.

"Yeah?" Jayden moved closer to the window.

"How do you manage it… living two separate lives?" I asked, not wanting to pry but needing to feel less alone in this craziness, especially after the day I'd had.

I'd noticed that Jayden usually only came in to Havasek in the evenings throughout the week. Which had got me wondering about what he did during the day.

He considered my question, then said, "When you're different like we are, it's more about survival, because you never know what will happen if people find out about us, but… if you find something to ground you, to push you through, then it's easy, or at least less of a battle."

I nodded, thinking that over.

"What is it for you?" I asked hesitantly.

He smiled. "Helping people. I know firsthand what it's like to be rejected and ridiculed for what I am, so I'm doing everything I can to make sure others don't go through the same thing."

I thought of him driving me to and from Havasek. Then I thought of the times he'd not been so nice. He had a roundabout way of showing his helpfulness. But he had been there for me, even when I didn't want him to be.

"Hey," he interrupted my thoughts, "it takes time as well, and help from others. Don't worry, you'll find your reason."

I smiled, even though he couldn't see my face through the flyscreen. "Thanks for being honest with me today. I really appreciate it."

"You're welcome, but next time, you don't have to cause a spectacle to get my attention."

I felt the heat of a blush, thankful he couldn't see me in the darkness of my room.

"Goodnight, Paige," he whispered and then his footsteps faded away.

"Night, Jayden," I said long after he'd gone.

I dreamt of a tall mountain surrounded by bushland as far as the eye could see.

My focus on the mountain intensified, and I found myself standing at the bottom looking up. It didn't have a peaked top but more of a rounded one. Along the slopes leading upwards there were various rock faces and caves with trees, grass, and shrubs.

Before I could take in too much more, the scene changed. I stared out over the inside of a domed building. The structure was hollow from the bottom up, but around the edges ran walkways with no stairs leading to the top of three separate levels.

In the centre of the massive room stood large boxes, shipping containers and crates, stacked high, with a walkway down one side that led to the back.

Noises issued at the other end, mechanical and human.

A scream echoed through the building. I shot up out of bed.

My breath came fast, and my hands shook on the blanket atop me. Squeezing them tight, I shut my eyes again and tried to calm down.

It was just a dream. That was all, nothing to be frightened of.

Eventually, I drifted back to sleep, trying in vain to block the images from my nightmare.

"Have you seen the tally today?" Dad asked over breakfast the next morning. His iPad was propped against his protruding belly and the edge of the table, showing the daily news. "It's almost doubled from last week. The police must be getting desperate with all these disappearances."

I paused midway between lifting my fork to my mouth.

Act normal. You don't know anything. How could you? You're a seventeen-year-old girl.

Slowly, I placed my fork into my mouth but the blissful flavors from two seconds ago had vanished. All I could think about was the doubled number of victims who'd been abducted.

After sleeping in late, I'd entered the kitchen to find Mum and Sharon had cooked up a massive breakfast with everyone's favorites on the menu: hash browns, pancakes, fried eggs, and bacon.

The adults and Ryan were all that remained at the table. They'd chatted quietly as I'd sat down, except for the latter, who was sliding his thumb across his phone screen.

I hadn't been paying attention to the topic of discussion while I'd made a plate for myself, until now.

"How awful is it all?" Mum replied. "They're saying that people are being taken from their houses now, whole families."

I dropped my fork, no longer hungry.

This situation really was getting out of hand.

"That is scary," Sharon said. "Are we even safe anymore?"

Mum rested a hand on her shoulder. "You'd want to hope so. It doesn't sound good."

I couldn't sit here and listen to this. It was too much.

"You guys all finished?" I asked, collecting the empty plates where the kids, long gone now, had been sitting.

"Yes, I think so," Sharon said with a smile, "but dear, you haven't finished your own food."

"I'm not hungry. Guess I took too much."

Lifting the pile, I carried them to the sink and began stacking them in the dishwasher.

Ryan came over with the second pile and scraped the leftovers into the bin.

"Thanks," I said, "but I got this. You go sit down."

"No way. In our house, you gotta earn your keep, and I already offered to help clean up."

I didn't fight him and together we managed to pack the dishwasher tight.

"So…" Ryan leant against the counter. "Got any plans for today?"

I looked at the clock. "Not until six. Figured I'd get some schoolwork done, unless you've got a better idea?"

He smiled. "Wanna go for a drive? You could show me where everything is."

I weighed up my options. On the one hand, I wanted to open the pages of Salyunda to see if I was able to read it. But I was still a little hesitant to confirm what Katalya had said about me being the only one capable of doing so.

However, spending some time with Ryan was definitely on my to do list and he'd just openly said he wanted to spend time with me, so what was another day?

"A drive sounds great!" I said.

After a hurried shower to get yesterday's stench off me, I sat in Ryan's car as he manoeuvred it out onto the main road.

The further we got from the house, the more uneasy I felt about something, I couldn't place it though, and I spent a good part of our drive trying to figure it out.

What was so bad about being in the car with Ryan?

"You okay? You've not said anything since we left." Ryan spoke up, breaking the silence.

"Yeah, sorry, I just have this odd feeling, like something's not right."

"Don't trust my driving, huh?" he joked. "We can turn back if you want?"

I shook my head, giving him a smile to ease his mind.

"No, your driving's fine. It's just a weird feeling, that's all."

I tried to brush it aside and changed the subject.

Our afternoon was spent driving around to the local landmarks: shopping centre, popular parks, and the school. Once we'd covered the basics, I directed Ryan to a few off-the-radar spots, showing him my favourite locations. I asked him about the life he'd left to move up here; the friends he'd had, places he'd visited. In return, he asked questions about me and what I did.

When the sun began to lower in the sky, I directed him onto the freeway, motioning for him to turn off. He obliged, and the car tilted slightly as we drove up a hill.

Reaching the top, Ryan parked the car and I got out.

"This place popular too?" he asked, following me to the railing that looked over the tree-tops and slow-moving traffic below us.

I smiled. "Not really. It's off most people's radar, but it's one of my favorite places."

His eyes widened as he took in the view.

Despite the noise of everything below, there was a sense of awe that ran through me as I stared at the distant city. Its tall buildings were merely Lego pieces from this distance. But what I loved most about the view was the sun, as it shimmered between the cracks and crevasses, continuing to light up the sky in magnificent gold, red, and orange making everything that lay in front seem like a dream. One that would only last for these few brief moments each day.

"Wow." Ryan leaned against the fence line. "That is something."

"It's not a sunset over the beach, but it seems unreal. It's why I like it so much."

"Well, then, we'll have to add a beach sunset to our list of things to do," he replied, and I couldn't help the laugh that escaped.

He had such high hopes for our friendship. It was nice.

If only the uneasy feeling in my gut, that had persisted throughout our whole trip, would go away. I pushed the feeling aside, willing it to not ruin my evening.

We moved to sit on the grass in front of the fence.

I picked up a rock, rolling it in my hands as Ryan continued to watch the last remains of the setting sun. I studied him, trying to figure out what exactly it was about this guy that made me so calm and relaxed, and if I wasn't lying to myself, drawn to him.

When the last of the light faded, he turned to face me. I was already staring at him.

"Is there something on my face?" he said with a laugh.

"No, I just…" I didn't know how to say it without coming on too strong. I'd only known – well, gotten to re-know – him, for two days and yet I knew I could trust him.

It was an odd feeling, but I felt it was true, nonetheless.

"I had a really great time with you today, and I'm not just saying that. I feel like we've known each other for decades, maybe lifetimes… There's just something about you that says I can trust you," I said, hoping my words didn't sound creepy.

The corner of his mouth lifted into a crooked smile, and I thought he was going to laugh, but instead he said, "I had fun too, and I'm glad you feel you can trust me. I'm here for you, whatever you need."

I felt my cheeks heat and was glad the darkening sky hid it from him.

"Now, didn't you say you had to be somewhere at six?" he asked.

With his words, whatever peace I'd managed to find this afternoon, vanished as the uneasy feeling returned.

Tossing the rock to him, he caught it as I pulled out my phone. It was quarter past five. Jayden would be arriving outside my place soon. I needed to get home.

"I almost forgot. We should get going."

I followed Ryan back to the car, annoyed this feeling was so overwhelming.

Why was I so anxious?

CHAPTER
FIFTEEN

Entering my room back home, I felt a pull from the direction of my desk. My gaze lingered on the pile of books. Trying to determine what was so urgent, I moved closer.

Sure, I did have homework to complete, but didn't think my drive was that dedicated.

Slowly, I picked up each book, re-stacking them into a new pile, until my hands fell upon Salyunda.

I felt calmer, as if having the book in my hands was the only comfort I needed.

"Strange," I muttered.

Was it Salyunda that had me so on edge? Was it trying to tell me that it needed me to find someone?

As I carefully turned through the pages, nothing stood out telling me to go on a search and rescue mission. The Marcian symbols were unreadable as ever.

So much for me being the only one who could read it. How was I supposed to do that when I didn't know the language?

Closing the book, I slipped it into my bag.

I would have to ask Katalya about it.

Adding two other books to the bag, in case Mum got suspicious, and a set of gym clothes, I zipped it up and exited the room.

There was no inspection check as I said my goodbyes, however, and I hurried out the door.

Jayden sat waiting in his car a street over.

"What did you tell your parents?" he asked with a sly sideways glance.

"That I'm studying with a friend," I replied, giving him a smug grin. "It happens often enough."

Satisfied, he nodded and didn't press the topic.

Something had changed between us. Jayden wasn't treating me like a two-year-old who needed rules and constant surveillance anymore. Was it because I'd mastered control? Or maybe that I'd taken on the important responsibility of Remana?

Either way, I liked this version of him far better.

The closer we got to Havasek, the more nervous I became.

"Relax. Naomi isn't going to kill you. You might feel like she has, but you'll be fine."

I fake-whimpered. When had *I* gotten so comfortable around him?

He laughed when I sent him a death stare, so I refused to look at him for the rest of the drive.

The car came to a stop, and we got out, Jayden leading the way into the Rekulanna.

He stopped halfway across the room.

"Naomi should be here soon," he said, giving me a once over. "You gonna work out in that? I can find something else if you want."

Lifting my bag, I turned and headed for the bathroom.

After changing, I gave myself a quick look over: dark brown hair pulled into a ponytail, blue eyes that stood out strongly, black singlet that clung to my frame, and long legs covered in black tights that moulded them. It would do.

Jayden was no longer alone when I exited.

Naomi had arrived.

The two were moving one against the other with quick sharp jabs and lashes, striking out in some sort of defensive routine I couldn't make out.

They were fast, and I had to catch myself a few times as Naomi went to take a hit at Jayden, but at the last second, he counteracted, only to be blocked as well.

Was this the kind of thing I would be learning?

My stomach dropped.

Yup, I wasn't leaving here alive.

I had to admit, the movement was beautiful to watch in its deadly way. The force and agility they showed was amazing.

I was mesmerised by it all and couldn't take my eyes away.

Finally, Jayden got the better of Naomi, and with a strength I'd never seen anyone possess, he swung her up and over his head. She landed heavily on the other side.

He straddled her, pinning her, until she voiced her surrender.

"Never said anything about powers," Naomi muttered, getting to her feet. "Show off."

Jayden laughed. "Wasn't about to let you beat me. That would have ruined my image."

He gave me a quick wink.

"Besides, I'm not the student today," Jayden said.

"Guess that was a good look at Reku," she said to me. "Something you can aspire to achieve. Of course, cheating isn't something I take lightly."

She glanced in Jayden's direction. "Despite Jayden's lack of following the rules, I won't tolerate the use of powers in my class. This is solely a physical training session. Save any element usage for Katalya."

Seeing the stern look she gave me, I nodded, although I didn't understand why Jayden had been reprimanded. I hadn't seen any elements being used, which had me wondering if there was more to his gift.

"Right." Naomi clapped her hands, pulling me away from my thoughts. "Before we begin, let's look at you. Stand up straight."

Not wanting to get on her bad side, I dropped my bag by the wall and came to stand before her.

She circled me, her gaze surveying me like she could read my soul.

Thankfully, I knew she couldn't since she was a fire Eleun.

"Not too bad." She nodded, though her eyebrows still knit together. "You look fit enough, though you'll need some muscle on those bones. Do you do any sports?"

"I'm on a soccer team and I used to do track as well," I answered proudly, hoping that would win some points.

"So you'll have some stamina and endurance. That will help, but your upper body will be weak." She came to a stop in front of me, peering down, still not entirely impressed. "At least we won't have to start from the beginning, though we still have a long way to go, but first, we warm-up. Follow me."

She began to demonstrate the first stretch, motioning for me to fall in line.

"This is where I leave you," Jayden announced, and he smiled backing up to the door. "Have fun, you two."

Naomi led me through a series of moves that ranged from what she said were yoga positions to the slow-moving Tai Chi movements. Along the way, she added in a bunch of successive fast jabs, ducks, and swerves, which I thought were made to catch me off balance and sent me tumbling to the ground looking like an idiot.

My body ached once she called a halt.

If *that* was the warm-up, I was not ready for the actual training session.

There wasn't a single layer of sweat on her, nor was she even the slightest bit out of breath.

I felt ridiculous.

"That was the easy part." She grinned.

Sighing, I walked to my bag where my drink bottle sat beakoning me.

After drinking deeply, I sat the bottle back down with a sigh of resentment.

Did I really want to subject myself to this every day until Naomi said I was ready?

I hadn't thought about Likonan Harmsworth's request since yesterday, but I'd told myself I would attend the first training and see where it led. So that's what I would do.

"Now, I'm not your soccer coach, so don't expect me to coddle you. You're here for a reason and that is to learn to defend yourself and attack if needed, however… seeing as they will both take time and consistent practice, if you do encounter trouble, your best bet is to run away as fast as you can," she said pointedly, reminding me once again that being Remana could be dangerous. "Hopefully, your track experience will help you out there."

I swallowed, trying to keep my nerves in check.

"Your training will focus on different styles and forms to build up your strength and knowledge," she said, choosing to ignore my wide eyes as I took in her words. "We'll start with the common strikes. Have you ever done any martial arts or boxing?"

I shook my head.

She pursed her lips. "Then pay attention."

My Reku lesson consisted of Naomi telling me how to stand in a way that prevented me from falling over but so I was always ready to move. How to punch, though I never actually hit anything, and that when I didn't do what she wanted, I received a very hard, very painful, slap to my cheek, as a reminder that I always needed to be prepared for an attack.

I lost count of the number of slaps I received.

Naomi constantly yelled for me to, "Stand up straight, round your shoulders, fists protecting your face, eyes on the target, from the hip, the hip!"

More than once I envisioned dunking her head in a bucket of water and wondered how angry she would get if I broke her rule of no Elemental usage.

I didn't understand how any of the boxing strikes were going to help me in a fight, seeing as I didn't hit a single target. Surely landing a punch, was an important step?

But considering how sore I was just from hitting open air, I wasn't about to bring that up.

By the time we were done, I was sweating profusely. My shoulders, back, and arms were on fire from holding my hands up over my face the entire time, and my butt and thighs were so sore I knew it would be hard to get out of bed in the morning.

"Kill me now!" I called to the roof.

Jayden laughed, as he walked up to us from the other side. "Not quite what you expected?"

"Worse!"

"I did warn you it wouldn't be easy."

"Yeah, but you also said she wouldn't kill me. I don't think I'll be able to move for a week."

He shook his head. "I'll be your live-in nanny if it's that bad, but right now, I think Katalya wants to see you."

Groaning again, I stood up.

Great, now for the mental work out.

Katalya stood by the door to the gym, her composure relaxed as if she could wait there all day.

As we approached, she opened the door and motioned for us to enter. Jayden headed for the mens, or Ganens bathroom, and I was left alone with Katalya.

Being so tired from my physical workout, I found it hard to concentrate on staying awake as I breathed in and out to focus on my element. However, after a short reprimand from Katalya about this being important and needing to practice every day, I did my best to stay on task.

Once I did, I realised how easy it was for me to find my Elemental source and merge without feeling as though it were seeking to take over. I remembered the storm in the city yesterday and the feeling of complete control that had come over me as I sent the water spurt packing.

Katalya instructed me to perform a few tasks all with containers of water spread around the room.

I made the water rise from all five buckets in long spiraling columns, reaching to just under the roof, not wanting to damage the room. I shifted them, then cut off the connection to the buckets to lay them vertical in long lines. Intertwining them, I made them look like an intricate braid, then from the far end shattered the link holding the water aloft so that the room was filled with tiny droplets all spaced evenly.

Katalya looked impressed.

"This is beyond what I thought capable from someone so new," she said from her cross-legged position near me. "It seems we will need to take your training to the next level, probably for the best now that you've accepted your role as Remana."

The praise from her seemed like the highest of all honours. I didn't know why, since I barely knew her, but maybe it had something to do with the knowledge that she was an original Eleun from Marcious.

After a few more water manipulation exercises, I replaced the liquid into the buckets and drew away from the merge with my element.

"Tomorrow, we'll have our lesson outside. I'd like to see your range on a larger scale," Katalya said, "then perhaps we can run through some defensive moves."

I swallowed, not liking the sound of having to defend myself.

Was it inevitable that I would be attacked on these missions?

All this talk of defending and escaping put me on edge.

Katalya dismissed me then and I started toward the door.

Then I paused turning back to face her "Katalya? I felt something strange today, with Salyunda."

She lifted an eyebrow, her curiosity sparked.

"Oh? It's not uncommon for the book to make a connection with its Remana," she said, smoothing out the invisible wrinkles in her skirt. "You are, after all, it's only outlet and without you, the people in that book would never be found."

I bit my bottom lip, needing more. "So it wasn't trying to tell me someone needed help? I thought maybe I'd missed something."

Katalya smiled warmly. "You'll know when that happens, trust me. The words will literally translate for you."

I hesitated again before waving and heading out the door.

Jayden stood by the garage entrance, waiting for my arrival.

"You look ready for round two," he said with a smirk.

"Just take me home, please," I said, shoulders slumped, barely able to lift my soles from the ground. "I need to dissolve into my bed before I collapse."

Chuckling, he followed me through the door.

"I wish you'd warned me Naomi was so heartless," I said. "Best teacher or not, I still can't feel my cheek from the slapping she gave it."

"Her methods might be different, but they're effective."

"Say that again and I might just drown you for trying to make light of my soreness," I muttered.

"What was that?" he said as we both slid into our seats.

Plastering on a smile, I said, "Nothing, just take me home."

Maybe it would be better if he didn't suspect it when I unleashed the waters of hell upon him.

He started the engine, the loud hum preventing us from saying anything else until the doors were closed.

"Oh, and I never said Naomi was the best teacher. That title is reserved only for me." He winked then revved the car unnecessarily before taking us out onto the road.

"So, you teach me then," I said once the car had joined steady traffic. "If this training is so important, I might as well have the best?"

"No can do, Likonan's orders. I might not always be around. I do have other responsibilities to attend to, you know."

"Like what?" I pressed, wondering what he had disappeared to do this evening.

He laughed. "Aren't you the persistent one? But that's classified, sorry."

"I thought we weren't keeping secrets anymore, now that I'm Remana and all."

He shrugged. "We aren't, but the Likonan doesn't want this getting out just yet, so I'm not going to be the weak link."

"Fine." I huffed, sitting back in my seat and folding my arms. "Keep your secrets. Maybe I'll take the bus tomorrow."

"Well, if you insist," Jayden said with a laugh as the car sped up.

I lay on the floor of the Rekulanna, breathing hard and sweating profusely after torture day number two with Naomi.

After a sleepless night of dreams plagued with strange symbols, it had gone as well as the first day. My constant yawning earning me a one-way trip to being flipped over by Naomi and landing hard on my shoulder, which was still roaring with pain.

Footsteps pulled me from my daze, and I lolled my head to see Jayden and Katalya approaching.

Looking up at the ceiling, I groaned. "Is it home time yet?"

Jayden chuckled, as he stared down at me.

"And miss the most important training of all?" Katalya said. "I think not."

Jayden pulled me to my feet.

Katalya was already at the door. We followed to catch up.

She led us out to the centre of the field.

"Jayden has kindly agreed to help in your training today," she said with a nod at him.

He smiled as if it had been his idea.

"But before we get to that, connect with your element and find the water sources around us," Katalya told me.

It wasn't hard to see the water channel that surrounded the field, but somehow, she made it sound as if there were others I couldn't see.

The connection was as easy as breathing, even in my exhausted state, I'd barely closed my eyes before the surge followed.

The channel was the first source I felt, but there were in fact others that littered the field. Water-filled pipes ran underground, leading to the surface for access.

I swirled the channel, creating a current that rushed through its bed. Every few metres, I made water spurt up, leaping into the air and landing back among its liquid companions before continuing the course. Deciding to have a little fun, I played with the water in the pipes, causing it to shoot upwards in organised synchronicity, with each hole erupting one after the other.

As the spurts made their way toward us, I misjudged where one sat, and doused myself in a spray of water. The display ended abruptly as I stood in shock, my clothes drenched.

As the droplets touched my skin, I felt them absorb on their own, and with every new drop, my energy returned. I felt more awake, the pain from the last two days of physical training becoming less, as if the water was healing me.

I stared at my hands, not sure what I was feeling. This must be another aspect of my power.

Reaching up, I touched my shoulder. The pain from my impact earlier had dissipated.

I did a once over of my body, ready to run a few laps around the field.

"Okay, either you've had an epiphany, or you've discovered something new," Jayden said.

"I think the water just gave me energy," I said. "It dissolved into my skin and now I feel amazing."

Katalya and Jayden's eyes widened as they looked at one another. Clearly this added feature of my ability wasn't normal.

Before I could ask them about it, Katalya started on her next instructions.

"Jayden, if you'd kindly take your position, we'll begin with some defensive moves."

I cringed. I hadn't expected to be attacked so soon.

As Jayden moved down the field, Katalya, smiled encouragingly at me.

"Your challenge today is to defend yourself," she said, motioning toward Jayden who'd turned to face us. "From anything he throws at you."

I eyed him, remembering the rock chasing stunt he'd pulled on me my second day here. Jayden was skilled at this. I didn't know if I was ready to face him.

This wasn't going to be fun.

CHAPTER
SIXTEEN

Jayden stomped his foot, sliding it in my direction. A small tremor shook the ground, and a rumble of rocks surfaced close to me, more continuing to upturn as the cluster approached.

I was so awed by his ability, I forgot what I was meant to be doing.

The rocks converged. I hopped and jumped from their path, narrowly avoiding rolling my ankle on them. Another line of upturned rocks was coming at me from beneath my feet. I stumbled and fell, the rocks enclosed my feet to the ground, pressing in tightly, as I tried to escape.

"Concentrate, Paige," Katalya called from the sidelines. "This is not for your amusement – Think!"

Biting my lower lip, I tried again to loosen my feet, but they remained stuck.

Katalya had praised me for progressing with my element so quickly when others had not. I was determined to do better at this type of training than I had with Reku.

Think, Paige! Think!

I didn't know if water was the stronger element in this scenario… or if there *was* a stronger element among any of the five.

Whichever took the highest rank, I knew one thing was for sure, I needed to get out of here.

On a whim, I pulled water from the pipes around me, covering the rocks, creating a clear dome of liquid that encased my feet, up to my calves.

Not sure what I was doing, I pressed the water down, filling every crack and crevice. With a final push, everything, water and rocks combined, exploded around me, freeing my legs.

Bits of rock flew everywhere, some rebounding against the ground and back at me. I shielded against them with my hands. A few pelted my arms and side.

Katalya tilted her head toward Jayden. I followed her gaze.

Jayden was stomping his feet against the ground. Every time he did, something shot from the surface until a line of floating objects hung in the air, ready to hit their target – me.

My mind raced as Jayden directed the first one at me. It was a rock.

Instinct kicked in and I sent a spurt of water from the ground at the small object, redirecting it off to the side. The next two came flying through the air.

Using the same manoeuvre, I discarded them and continued for the next few shots. Jayden increased the number of attacks, and I narrowly avoided being hit by a few of them.

His attacks sped up and I found myself ducking and swerving as I knocked obstacles away before they slammed into me.

We kept at it, the renewed energy I'd gained from my water dousing wearing thin, until I panted with exertion.

Finally, when I could take it no more, I fell to all fours, yelling for him to stop.

The already flying rocks halted mid-strike and fell uselessly to the ground. I rolled to my back and collapsed on the grass.

Jayden and Katalya approached me.

"I don't know… how you… keep that…up." I spoke between gasps.

Jayden laughed, but he was heaving deep breaths as well.

I hadn't seen *that* from the distance between us. It seemed he'd used up just as much energy as I had.

"That was a pretty good run for your first defence attempt," he said. "Most people give up after five minutes."

I smiled, happy to take the compliment, but mostly because the praise had come from him.

"How long has it been?" I asked, my breath coming back.

"Forty-five minutes," Katalya said, "and he's right. I didn't expect the session to last that long. You did exceptionally well, Paige."

It had felt longer than that as we'd exchanged blows but thinking about it now, I realised the sun had barely even lowered as we sparred.

"Well, I could do with another good dousing," I said, a wave of fatigue floating over me.

Jayden and Katalya shared a worried glance.

"What?" I asked, warily. "It helped earlier. Why not now?"

Katalya narrowed her eyes. "I just don't think you should rely solely on that form of energy boost."

"Why not?" I sat up to face her. "It's a part of my ability, so surely it's okay if I use it?"

She sighed. "Despite the fact that you are capable of these things, you still need to remember that you're part human as well. The best way to get your energy back up is through a proper meal and rest."

At the mention of food, my stomach growled. Not feeling up to arguing, I let it go with a sigh.

"Well, point me in the direction of food and I'll be a happy girl," I said.

Jayden offered me his hand, and I accepted it gratefully. He led the way to the dining area.

Smelling the incredible food, I forgot about my other option and piled my plate with spaghetti bolognaise. Afterwards, Jayden drove me home, sleep threatening to take hold of me now that I had a full belly.

When I arrived home, the house was still awake and buzzing. That was what happened when you had an extra family living with you.

Mum and Sharon sat in the front lounge looking through old photo albums, reminiscing about past adventures and times when they were younger and child-free.

Sharon tried to encourage me to join them, hinting that one such story involved a possum, a cow, and a guy she had a crush on in their first year of university.

I was tempted, but decided to decline, my bed beckoning.

The television blared from the rumpus room, and Liam and Peter yelled at each other as they fought it out on the screen.

Mum had left a plate of what looked to be Pad Thai for me on the kitchen bench. Grateful she'd thought of me, I pulled out a plastic container and scraped it inside to take for lunch the next day.

Food stored in the fridge, I headed for my bedroom.

"Hey, how was soccer practice?" Ryan asked, coming out of the rumpus room.

I only narrowly managed to cover my cringe as he rehashed the lie I'd told him for coming home late. Well, it wasn't a complete lie. Soccer practice had happened. I just hadn't attended.

When Jayden had messaged to say he would meet me after school, I'd told him about my extracurricular activities. He'd stressed the importance of my training, and I'd decided I could skip one practice.

"Tiring," I answered honestly. It was the truth nonetheless.

The corner of his mouth lifted in apparent amusement.

"You all set for tomorrow?" I asked, remembering he was starting school the next day. Sharon had taken Ryan and the others to acquire all their school supplies today in preparation.

"Yup, ready to go. Hey, are you up for a run tomorrow morning before school? Might be good to calm the first day jitters with some exercise," he asked. "No pressure if you're not up for it."

I hesitated. I was already tired from all the extra training I'd been put through.

On the other hand, this was Ryan and a part of me was screaming to accept.

"Sure," I said. I was going to regret it later, but I didn't care. "But don't get your hopes up at beating me. I don't go easy."

I goaded him with a cheeky smile.

"Is that so? I do like a challenge." He looked down at me, an eyebrow raised "I'll see you bright and early then. Sweet dreams, Paige."

With that, he turned on his heel, heading for the room he and Peter were sharing.

I couldn't help but notice his incredible physical shape and wondered if I'd bitten off more than I could chew.

The mountain range extended far beyond what the eye could see. Wind blew the leaves on the trees back and forth.

Then I was pulled forward, and I stood at the bottom of one of the smaller peaks. The top slanted slightly to the left, majestically displaying dark rock. The rest of the slope was covered in trees and green moss that hid the underlying rock.

The scene changed. I was in a large open cavern, the roof extending high above me, doming at the top. The walls were made of dirt and stone, roots and grass sticking out at odd angles.

The first half held walkways running inside the walls, three stories high. Black clad men and women walked along them while other white coated people headed toward the walls and disappeared.

The ground level of the cave was covered in large crates, containers, and boxes of all shapes and sizes, creating a maze toward the back of the cavern, obscuring my view of what lay beyond.

A scream sounded. I stood alert, looking across the sea of containers, trying to make out what was going on.

"Please, no, don't do this. I have a family – they need me," a male voice cried. "I'm begging you. I'll do whatever you want, just don't…"

His screams filled the room once more.

I bolted upright in bed, shaking. My alarm started to blare.

I hit the snooze button and rubbed my eyes.

What was that about?

Glancing at the clock, I groaned, the urgency of the dream dissipating. Why had I agreed to an early morning run? I was way too exhausted.

I changed into running shorts and singlet, then pulled my hair back into a ponytail as I entered the kitchen.

"You are some serious competition," Ryan huffed as he sat down beside me on the front lawn of my house two hours later. "I don't think I've pushed myself so hard before against a girl."

My legs burned from the exertion of our sprint at the end of our early morning run. Our laughter had carried behind us, not deterring me from giving the race my all.

I feigned offence. "Well, now that I know you're a boys-are-better-than-girls advocate, I think I might just un-friend you."

"After that run, I take anything back that makes me a part of that club."

"Hmm, I'll consider re-friending you later… once I've cooled down." I stared up at the sky. It looked like a clear sunny day ahead.

"Guess I'll just have to beat you next time."

He winked.

Delight swelled inside me that he wanted there to *be* a next time, and I found myself smiling stupidly.

"So, is there anything I should know before I hit the school gates today?" Ryan asked.

"What do you mean?"

"Oh, you know crazy people that might lead me into dark corners or direct me to class and it turns out to be the bathroom…"

I raised an eyebrow and he smiled.

"What you might want to avoid is the crazy horde of girls that will probably want to interrogate you."

He looked taken aback. "What's that supposed to mean?"

"Oh, you know, you're a hot guy. They'll try and get in your good books the minute you cross the threshold."

As soon as I said it, I wanted to smack myself.

Did I just admit to him being good looking… to his face?

He cleared his throat, dropping his head. I focused my gaze on the garden bed lining the house, searching for something else to talk about, my mind blank.

The flowers were far brighter than they had been a week ago. All this rain was doing some good.

"Hot guy, eh?" he mused. "Your words, or is this just what everyone says?"

It was a way out and I took it.

"Well, it depends on who you ask, I guess," I nudged him playfully and got to my feet. "Come on, we should probably get ready, or Mum will throw a fit."

I didn't wait for him to reply, still slightly embarrassed, just walked past him and headed inside.

After a quick stop in at the office to pick up Ryan and Peter's class schedules, I walked Ryan to his roll call room.

"This is you." I nodded to the room we'd stopped at, then motioned farther down the corridor. "I'm two doors down. If all works out, I'll see you in Math?"

"That's what this piece of paper says," he said, flicking his timetable.

The bell sounded.

I smiled reassuringly. "Good luck."

When I arrived in my classroom, Nicole was already settled, a knowing smile springing on her face as I sat down next to her.

"Okay, who was that you were walking with just now?"

I hadn't realised she'd seen us. "A friend. It's his first day today."

"Since when did you have a hot *friend* starting here and not tell me about it?" she asked, as if I had committed the worst crime. "Oh wait, maybe it was because you disappeared, ignoring all my messages and calls last week. Apparently, our friendship means nothing to you."

My shoulders dropped at her scrutiny. She wouldn't let this go easily.

Mum and Dad had been thorough in spreading the word about my absence, thanks to Havasek's memory modifications. Unfortunately, Nicole still hadn't forgiven me for not telling her myself.

"Ryan's arrival slipped my mind," I said.

She rolled her eyes, not believing a word.

In truth, it had slipped my mind. After being locked up at Havasek for a week, and the need for secrecy in my Eleun life, I'd just applied it to everything else. Plus, I wasn't like her and felt the need to share everything that was going on around me. Especially since it was Ryan's first day, and he deserved to figure the place out on his own, not be bombarded with people he didn't know.

"So, where's he from? How do you know him, and why aren't you dating him already?" Nicole peppered me with her questions as if I should have already answered them.

I sighed, not at all surprised she was trying to set me up without even meeting the guy. We had been friends since our first year at high school and she had a knack for knowing everyone and everything, the social butterfly of our grade.

She would make it her goal to know everything she could about him by the end of the day.

"At least tell me you have his number on speed dial and have been texting non-stop!"

Finding her excitement amusing, I said, "Come to think of it, I don't think I even have his number…"

"Oh, hell no, we are going to rectify that immediately," she said, earning a few looks from our classmates. "How are you not flirting with him? Have you seen him?"

Heads turned in our direction, and I shrank a little lower in my seat, heat flaring in my cheeks.

Laughing, I said, "How can I not? He's sleeping in my spare bedroom."

Nicole just about fainted right there.

"That's it, you are officially the weirdest girl I've ever met," she said.

"I told you, we're just friends. Besides, it's been seven years since we saw each other. I hardly know him anymore," I said, my voice hushed, willing the eyes to divert.

"Well, this I can guarantee. You have until tomorrow to make up your mind about him, because after that he won't be on the market for much longer." She sat back in her seat. "And I take no responsibility for any of my actions when I'm around him, so let it be known that I warned you."

I laughed as Mr Jackson called us to attention.

Being cooped up at Havasek all week, I had wanted nothing more than to get back to my normal life, including school. But now that I was here, I found it hard to concentrate.

It was like a switch had been flicked, unleashing all this energy that I was supposed to use up somehow. I was agitated all the time, making it difficult to sit through hour long classes.

More than once, someone had to verbally tell me to stop bouncing my knees under the table, Nicole physically restraining me when it became too much during Math class.

During the day was the worst when I'd barely done anything after waking up. Running in the morning had helped, but it wasn't until after both Reku and Eleun training that I finally felt less pent up.

I didn't understand the added spark in my step until I questioned Katalya about it on Wednesday afternoon.

"As an Eleun, your instinct is to move, to be active. Sitting still is not in our nature. Now that you've completed the Myundun and you're able to manipulate your ability better, your Eleun needs to be used, and often. Not only this, but your body is also capable of so much more than you're used to, and it's telling you to utilise it."

"Is that why everyone in this place trains so hard, all the time?" I asked.

"I thought they were preparing for a war."

"Yes, our bodies were not designed to lay dormant, just like the elements that surround us. They are always working, even if you can't see them do so," she said.

I hadn't expected the answer, but it made sense. I decided to try to work harder in the mornings on my early run, so I wasn't so jumpy at school.

For the next two weeks, I focused more on my secret life than the one that everyone saw.

Eleun training was far better than Reku.

Katalya continued to produce new Elementals to face me daily. Each time, I was instructed to defend only, with the encouragement to try different ways in which to do so.

I fast became sick of the defence routine. Sometimes, I attacked back.

At this, Katalya would stop us, reprimand me for not following orders, then instruct us to proceed.

I complained quite a bit on those occasions, but she seemed not to hear.

My physical training continued to be brutal. Every second day focused on a martial art, where I would learn upper and lower body strikes. Naomi explained what parts of the body each one was best to hit. The other days I trained on the gym floor for strength and conditioning.

Naomi encouraged me to keep up my cardio as well, explaining that endurance was an important role in bringing my fitness up to speed, and when I told her of my early morning runs, she said that was acceptable.

My mind raced with all the things I'd learnt in the most recent lessons and when I thought I was alone, I would run through them physically, hoping it would help them stick.

But as much as I was trying, Reku didn't come as naturally as using my element. I continued to finish a lot of sessions with bruises, bumps and even a dislocated shoulder when I'd landed wrong in a progression of moves, to which I'd been taken to the infirmary and had it mended by one of the Entina Eleun before returning home that night.

Many times, I wondered if what I was doing was the right thing. But each time I doubted the course I was on, all it would take was a look at that small blue book and I would get this overwhelming feeling that it was for a good purpose.

During our drive home on Thursday, Jayden came up with an idea that would explain all my afternoons away from home.

"Babysitting!" Mum exclaimed, when I proposed the new 'job' to her. "Well, I must admit I never expected that to be your first job. Are you sure it's what you want to do?"

"Yeah, why not?" I said. "The family I've been talking to said it'll only be for a few hours after school some days and maybe one day of the weekend."

She deliberated, turning back to stare at her computer screen. "I don't know… I don't want this to affect your schooling. When will you complete your homework?"

"They promised it wouldn't go late and I'd be home before dinner. I can do it then." I'd rehearsed the answers with Jayden on the drive home, making sure we covered every angle. "Honestly, Mum, it's better than getting a part time job at a fast-food place. Those shifts are always longer and then there's paperwork to fill out and it just seems too messy for me right now. I want something simple and low key. It's perfect."

She sighed, placing both her elbows on the table, and lacing her fingers through her hair.

Finally, she said, "Well, if you've made up your mind, I'll discuss it with your father. But I'd like to meet with this family just so we're on the same page."

I thanked her with a hug and kiss on the cheek before disappearing into my room.

Mum and Dad met with the family I was 'babysitting' for the next day.

Jayden had made all the arrangements by recruiting Bradley, who was part of my Remana team, and Celia, a Breezen or Wind Eleun, to play the parents. Max and Emily, two children from Havasek, role-played the kids.

We all sat in the small living room of a cottage not far from my place. The entire house gave me the feeling of returning home, and I relaxed as I settled into a chair.

Emily, with her royal purple eyes, focused on my parents as Bradley and Celia spun a story Mum and Dad would believe.

Mum and Dad agreed to everything that was said to them, expressing how much they liked the idea of me finally taking on some responsibility. That was a bit much on their part considering what Mum had said the night before.

However, I knew it wasn't entirely their own words, given the constant smiling and nodding.

Emily's gifts gave her the ability to influence other's decisions.

I held back a grin as the young girl smiled sweetly back at me.

I stayed behind once Mum and Dad had left, under the guise of getting to know the kids a little better.

"I can't believe that worked," I said, falling back into the armchair.

"I guess with only two weeks among your own kind, I can understand why you'd say that," Bradley said, scratching his chin. "But this is pretty much our day-to-day life."

I stared at him. How often did they need to mislead people like this?

But Bradley didn't catch my concerned look as he said, "Let's head out."

I hadn't talked much with Bradley since meeting him. But from the little I'd seen he was quiet, and observant, silently learning bits and pieces about everyone around him without having to say much. I got the sense he preferred it that way. I felt a kinship with him. Maybe it was because he was also an Aquenel Eleun, or maybe we had similar traits, by liking our solitude.

Max was the first out the door, Emily, and Celia, not far behind. I stayed with Bradley as he pulled out a key and began to lock up.

"Whose house is this? We didn't just break into a random one, did we?" I asked as he pulled the front door shut.

He laughed. "No, it's Katalya's. She often lends it out for things like this, since it looks friendly."

"I thought she lived at Havasek?"

"Only when she has to," he said, skipping down the front steps. "It's encouraged to live in the world. It helps us adapt to everything and connect with others."

"But isn't that dangerous with all these kidnappings? I mean, wouldn't that make them prime targets?"

Bradley was quiet for a moment as we moved down the path.

"Maybe, but we're pretty sure they're after undeveloped talent, which is why your job is so important."

I followed him into the black van we'd borrowed from Havasek and he slid the door shut as I mulled that over in my head.

No wonder there was a lot of stress that I was prepared when Salyunda divulged a name. If it was untrained Eleun that were being sought out, then my being trained to defend them was crucial.

By the next Friday, I was ready for a hot bath and a long nap that would somehow magically take away the pain in all my muscles.

I'd organised to have the evening off from training, which meant Naomi and Katalya had only worked me harder the night before and insisted I double the length of my run the next morning. I'd groaned but done as they'd asked. I had planned an evening with Nicole, one that involved manicures and pedicures, a facial and, if her Mum was up for it, a relaxing massage, since that was her profession.

It wasn't my usual go-to for a fun night, but after my week, I was looking forward to unwinding.

Walking out of my last class for the day I started for the exit. Something in my bag rumbled. I stopped by the stairs leading to the top courtyard, and as I crouched down to rummage through the books and paper, my hand fell on something that warmed under my touch.

I felt a need to pull the object out and found myself looking at Salyunda, but this time there were intricate silver lines weaving along the cover.

I blinked a few times to make sure my eyes weren't playing tricks on me.

The silver lines *were* moving.

Reality hit me, and I almost dropped Salyunda.

"You'll know when it happens," Katalya had said.

Was this it?

With shaky fingers, I flipped the pages, one after the other.

The crisp white sheets were filled with symbols I'd seen through the Havasek library. Like the cover, they shifted and moved as if trying to form words.

Ten or so pages in, I stopped turning and followed the symbols until they assembled and stopped in their movement. Something in my conscious mind took over and the first few lines on the right-hand page began to make sense.

CHAPTER

SEVENTEEN

Drew Hadwin – Furno.

The words stuck out like a light in the dark.

All I could do was stare at them, numb.

What was I supposed to do?

"Paige. Paige."

I blinked, the words disappearing before my eyes as the symbols returned to their unreadable state.

"Hello, Earth to Paige!"

Looking up, I found Nicole standing less than two feet away, a concerned look on her face.

"Um, hi," I replied, the shock still seeping away. "What's up?"

"Why didn't you pick up your phone? Mum's waiting in the pick-up bay."

My mind raced to catch up with what she was telling me.

I was still at school, and it was Friday… the day I was going to Nicole's for a girl's night.

Uh-oh!

"Um… the thing is, Nic, I um, don't think I can come anymore." My words were slow, as I searched for an excuse she would accept. "I have to babysit Liam and Eva tonight. Mum and Dad want a date night."

Nicole surveyed me, clearly not believing me.

"So, ditch. Liam's old enough to watch your sister." She shrugged "Or

173

ask Ryan. He does live with you, right?"

Damn it!

"Well, the thing is, Sharon's taking the family out, and… Liam is actually going to a friend's house for the night so really it's just Eva…"

Nicole's shoulders dropped as she sighed. "If you don't want to come, just say so. Seriously, it's no biggy."

I knew she was hurt, and honestly, I didn't blame her, I hadn't spent any time with her since school started back. What sort of a best friend was I to ignore the only person at school who hung out with me?

"No, no, that's not it at all," I insisted. "Honestly, I was really looking forward to tonight, but you know… things happen. Look, why don't we do it next week? Invite other girls along. It could be a real blast."

Nicole loved our one-on-one girl time but thrived off the gossip of many.

"Fine," she said, thrusting her finger in my direction, "but you owe me big time."

"Got it, chocolate roses and Tim Tams will be present next week, all for your consumption." I saluted.

After a quick hug she waved goodbye, and I watched her disappear around the corner.

I dug through my bag and pulled out my phone. Ignoring the two missed calls from Nicole. I dialed Katalya's number.

"I wasn't expecting to hear from you today," she said. "What can I help you with?"

"The book… Salyunda," I started, trying to search for the right words, while keeping my voice hushed as students walked by. "It did something weird and I think an Eleun needs my help."

There was a moment of silence before she said, "Are you sure? Did you find the name?"

"Yes, positive. I…I think it's a boy. His name is Drew Hadwin with the fire element." I was caught off guard when someone's bag almost knocked me over. "What am I supposed to do now? Do we know where to find him? Salyunda didn't say."

"Never mind that. I'll take care of it," Katalya said. "For now, just get to Havasek."

"Um, okay, is anyone near my area? I'm still at school, so I might be a while."

My only option was catching the bus, which would take time.

Katalya didn't answer right away. Chatter issued in the background.

"Jayden's on his way," she said. "He'll meet you out the front of the school. Be ready."

I nodded, then realising she couldn't see me and, said, "Okay, thanks."

Swinging my bag over my shoulder I started up the stairs. At the top, Ryan stood with a group of girls.

He was listening politely to a tall girl from our year level named Catherine, her red hair draping across her shoulder, as she explained something. He laughed, nodding, before Sophie grabbed his arm and whispered something to him.

Eyes narrowing at the exchange, I forced myself to continue walking.

Now was not the time to be ogling a guy.

I kept my head down, making a bee line for the gate.

"Hey, Paige!"

I spun quickly to the voice I had both been wanting to hear and not at the same time.

Ryan gave a wave. "Have fun tonight!"

I grimaced, covering with a nod, before hurrying away.

I waited in the pickup bay, looking for Jayden's silver car.

It was another fifteen minutes before it arrived, leaving me one of the only people left waiting. Ryan had driven past ten minutes earlier, and I'd turned to avoid him noticing me.

The Likonan and Bradley were going over a map on a table in the Rekulanna as we entered, quietly planning a route. Katalya had Nicolas and Naomi on either side of her and the two listened carefully as she read from some papers she held in front of her.

Libby stood aside from the rest looking bored. My appearance caused her to scoff before she turned away.

Jayden bent down to the floor by the table leg and passed up a set of clothes.

"You'll have to change," he said, eyeing my school uniform. "We don't want anyone identifying where you're from."

Taking the pile, I noted that everything was black. The rest of the team were all wearing similar outfits that conformed to their bodies, much like the Jalin.

I hesitated. Likonan Harmsworth had said I wouldn't be going out into the field to start with, so why was I being asked to change?

Before I could ask, Jayden joined the Likonan, listening in to the plan. Not wanting to disturb them, I headed to the bathroom.

After changing, I rejoined the group, where they'd formed a circle.

"The route we've chosen shouldn't attract any unwanted attention," the Likonan said to the group, "but just in case, stay on your guard."

"Once in range, I want regular updates about what's happening. Let's keep it tight and secure. I don't need to remind you of what could happen."

I'd only heard a little about previous attempts at finding Eleun, but her tone was enough to set my nerves on edge.

"Right, off you go. We can't afford to be the last ones there this time," she said.

All around me, the group gathered bags. Despite our capabilities with our various elements, there were a lot of weapons among the group.

Around Jayden's waist sat a brown leather belt with four knives sheathed within their frame. Nicolas had two straps across his chest with some silver disc objects attached to them. Naomi had secured a coiled whip to the belt of her right hip, a large dagger on the left. Both Bradley and Libby had guns strapped to their belts, though Bradley also had knives secured to his left leg.

I swallowed loudly. Were all these items necessary?

"Paige, a word please?" The Likonan's deep voice broke through my reverie, and I nodded before joining her and Katalya, off to the side.

"Miss Munro," the Likonan began, surveying me as if my being here was a bad idea.

I didn't altogether disagree.

"Despite my insistence you remain here, I have been reminded that it is your mandate to take to the field." Her eyes shifted toward the ceiling as if there were someone else listening, but the moment passed, and she continued. "You'll need to wear these."

She passed me two objects. One was an earpiece, a black hook curving to attach to my ear. The other was a circular band large enough to fit on my wrist, a glass screen inlaid to one side.

"The earpiece is so you can communicate with us and the team," she said. "Should you be separated. The wrist band, is Alu-Lamek… your mode of transport."

I hadn't even thought about how we would be getting to wherever this boy was, and looking at the device on my wrist, I became even more confused.

"Normally, it takes months of training in order to operate Alu-Lamek," Likonan Harmsworth said, "and given the proximity of the boy, being in our area already, we'd generally use other methods of transportation. However, with the situation being so dire and with our need to arrive as quickly as possible, I've allowed the use of these devices."

"What is it?" I asked, still not following.

"In simple terms, instant transportation. It allows you to move from one location to another, instantly."

Words failed me as I took in her meaning.

"Like teleportation?" I finally said doubtfully, waiting for everyone to burst out laughing at my expense.

"Very much like that, yes," she said.

"It's one of the few technological devices we managed to bring along with us from Marcious," Katalya added. "Marcians were not only gifted with extraordinary abilities, but our civilisation had been around far longer than Earths', giving us plenty of time to hone our talents and use them to enhance technology."

She smiled as if this should have been enough for me.

I was still coming to terms with the idea of teleportation.

"How does it work?" I asked, turning my wrist over to get a better look at it.

"There's no time to explain the details, but the Alu has been reconfigured to Earth's geography. This one is pre-set and linked to the rest of the team, with co-ordinates close to the boy's location, where you'll arrive and vacate from." Likonan Harmsworth said. "Once Bradley activates his, you will travel as one and land in a cleared location."

She hadn't answered my question, but I could see she was eager for us to be off, so I nodded, hoping to ask Jayden before we were whisked away.

"During tonight's mission, your role is strictly observatory," the Likonan said glaring at me to let the message sink in. "You will follow orders from the rest of the team and do so without hesitation. Do I make myself clear?"

When I glanced at Katalya, she nodded, and I followed suit. I guess this was trial by fire. No chance to back out now.

"Good. Let the others take care of the boy," the Likonan said. "They know how to handle the untrained."

The Likonan nodded curtly, before leaving us alone.

Katalya smiled at me. "Don't be too intimidated by her words. Missions are rarely performed according to plan. Go with your instincts but be on your guard and remember whatever happens out there, trust in your team. They know what they're doing."

I smiled weakly, as a sick feeling gnawed through my stomach.

"This is safe, right?" I held up my hand to indicate the Alu-Lamek, "I'm not going to be sliced in half by accident, right?"

She chuckled. "It's very safe. The training is for those who wish to use it based on their thoughts. This option is fail proof, I promise."

She motioned for me to join the rest of the team and I inched over to them.

This was it. I was being sent out to find someone, who, like me, was discovering their abilities for the first time. What would I find? Was I really ready for this?

I glanced toward the bathroom where I had left Salyunda in my school bag, stuffed inside a locker. I didn't want to accidentally misplace it while we were gone. I missed the reassuring warmth the book gave off whenever I doubted my role. Somewhere during the week, I'd grown to rely on it to keep me going, to remain strong. Now I was alone. Now I had to find my own motivation to see this through.

I considered my first experience with my Eleun taking over. I'd been scared, unaware of what was happening when the lightning had almost struck me. Then Dominic and his group had chased me, and I hadn't known what to do, my power my power taking dominance in an unconscious attempt to protect me, feeding off my emotions. The situation could have turned out so much worse.

I remembered Jayden and Katalya's whispered conversation outside my room and knew that they'd been talking about another Eleun that had been taken.

I didn't want anyone else to feel that way or be thrown into a scenario like that.

I couldn't let Dominic get his hands on any more innocent people.

"Hold on, Drew, I'll save you," I muttered to myself.

With my new resolve, I joined the others.

Everyone gathered around Bradley's burly form, creating a circle.

Heart pounding, still disbelieving that I was about to teleport, I turned to look at Jayden, needing to know what was about to happen, but words failed me.

"Relax, it's painless. Just take a deep breath and we'll be there before you can release it," he said.

"Counting down in three…" Bradley began, and my heart jumped into my throat as panic took hold.

I searched for something to grasp onto, anything solid, familiar, not this completely foreign and barely explained mode of transportation I was about to undertake.

"Two…"

My hands shook as I sought some sort of support.

Something warm and strong wrapped around my fingers, squeezing tight.

Jayden stared down at me. As Bradley finished the countdown, Jayden stepped in front of me, wrapping his arms around my waist and saying, "Deep breath."

As I inhaled deeply, a clear thin substance expelled from our wrists, expanding to surround us, the two merging to create one large bubble encompassing the both of us. Before I could wonder at it, the bubble shrunk, conforming to our bodies, a strange elastic feeling against my skin. Then we were no longer inside Havasek but stood in a school field.

The elastic substance disappeared, revealing a chill in the fast-darkening sky.

I stared up at Jayden, who was watching me carefully.

"You okay?" he murmured.

I nodded, not trusting my voice, especially with him so close.

He gently released me, taking a step back.

"Wait here," he said.

He headed toward Bradley and Nicolas on the other side of our circle.

I still had so many questions, but now didn't seem like the right time to ask them.

You'd think suddenly appearing in the middle of a primary school field would have attracted some attention. But all was quiet, nothing but grass and trees to greet us.

The field was enclosed on two sides by a line of trees, the main road just beyond. The remaining side held classrooms, which were dark and quiet.

Reaching the others, Jayden crouched, pressing a hand to the grass, obviously feeling for movement in the surrounding areas through his element.

Nicolas and Bradley kept a look out.

The three nodded to one another, confirming all was clear.

Jayden, standing once more, beckoned the rest of us closer.

Bradley handed something over to him. Jayden pocketed it swiftly, my eyes too slow to notice what it was.

"I'll stay behind and secure our exit," Bradley said. "Make sure it's not hindered. Keep in touch."

Jayden waved for everyone else to follow his lead.

We crossed the field at a run, reaching the main road quickly. Without a word, Libby kicked off the footpath, springing into the air.

On the ground, Jayden took the lead, followed by Nicolas, then me, and Naomi at the rear.

Keeping to pathways and roads as much as possible, we moved at a steady pace. Regularly, the Likonan's voice would sound through the earpieces. First Jayden would respond followed by Libby, and Bradley, before all was quiet once more.

Houses slowly brightened up as lights were turned on and shadows moved behind curtains, bringing to the forefront how shady our movements would look if anyone were to peer outside right at his moment.

Not that we were doing anything wrong. If anything, we were trying to do the right thing.

I was surprised by the lack of cars on the road and concluded that we must have been in a remote area for it to be so quiet at this hour, since it was peak hour travelling time.

We turned down a street that wasn't lit up by streetlamps and my eyes adjusted to the darkness that engulfed us.

Jayden whispered for us to stop. I almost ran into the back of Nicolas. Following the direction everyone was staring, I made out a house, completely blacked out and silent as a grave.

The house looked like a typical Australian outback home: rectangular shape, with a veranda running the entire perimter, and a roof which looked like an over-sized bush hat. Trees in the front yard concealed parts of a small flower garden, which looked well-tended.

"Arrived at destination, approaching now." Jayden's hushed voice entered my ear.

"Affirmative. Proceed," the Likonan responded.

Jayden crept toward the rusted gate, Naomi close behind. Nicolas's hand came down on mine, his look telling me to wait.

Jayden and Naomi were swallowed up in the night before we started for the house. By the time we reached the front door, they were nowhere to be seen.

Sensor lights flickered on as we approached. Nicolas stepped forward to rap on the door, then moved back to a respectful distance to wait.

When no one answered, Nicolas tried again.

He put a hand to his ear. "We've got no response on our end. What's yours like?"

Naomi's voice cut through. "Clear, but you better come round, looks like we got here too late."

My heart sank, defeated.

Around the back, we were greeted by a blinding flashlight as Jayden approached.

"It looks empty, but we haven't searched it thoroughly," he said.

"How do you know we're too late?" I asked, still holding out hope.

He shone the light in my direction. "The back door was smashed, and the whole place looks ransacked. We've seen it before. They enter, take the

Eleun, make it look like a robbery, and leave."

"It could've been a robbery and the family are just away on vacation?" I suggested, though I felt slightly silly.

The corner of his mouth curved up.

"A robbery involves expensive things been taken, but their T.V is broken, there were two laptops on the kitchen bench, and I found a bunch of jewellery in the main bedroom." He shook his head. "This wasn't a robbery."

I sighed dismally.

He motioned for us to follow him. "Let's do a sweep. Make sure there's nothing that will lead back to Eleun existence."

He led us through the back door, our shoes crunching over broken glass and other tidbits lying on the floor. Nicolas and I took the bedrooms, while the other took the living areas.

"We're looking for any sign of Elemental work, anything that stands out and would cause suspicion to the human eye," Nicolas said, veering toward the main bedroom. I took a smaller one.

A single bed lay in the back corner, its cover ruffled from someone sitting on it. Directly across from it sat an old TV, an X-box next to it, the controller smashed on the ground. Clothes were flung around the room, the cupboard doors open and emptied of everything.

They'd left nothing to chance. Even if Drew had hidden, they would have found him.

My heart sank even lower at our failure, remembering my own brush with capture. I'd let this boy down and now he'd been taken by those crazy lunatics.

We should have been faster.

If only I'd not been so new at this…

I did a quick sweep of the room before I could handle it no longer, exiting to lean my back against the hallway wall, trying to hold back tears that threatened. Had he been as scared as I was?

Was I really the best person for this job?

"You, okay?"

Startled, I looked up to see Nicolas crouched on the floor in front of a linen cupboard.

Sniffling, I ran a hand over my eyes to wipe away the tears.

"Yeah, just… disappointed, that's all."

He looked at me, a shadow cast over his face from the torch he held. "It's not your fault. You know that, right? This isn't the first time and probably won't be the last. We'll catch them, and they'll pay for everything they've done."

Turning back to the cupboard, he placed a hand on a shelf, sighing.

"I don't think they left anything behind." Using the shelf to heave himself up, he stood. "Let's find the others and go home."

I pushed off the wall to head back to the kitchen, Nicolas in front of me.

Only when I tried to lift my foot, it refused to budge. That was weird.

Grunting I put more force into the movement. Still, I remained stuck to the floor.

Then I heard a voice in my head, the sound so fleeting I thought I had imagined the whisper as it drifted through my mind.

"He's still here."

I blinked. A feeling of truth swelled inside me that I couldn't dismiss.

Was this another avenue of my Eleun gift? Or part of my connection with Salyunda as Remana? Either way, I wasn't going to ignore it.

"Wait," I said to Nicolas, who stopped at my voice. He'd travelled almost the entire hallway. "I think he's still here."

I felt more than heard it as the voice whispered once more. *"In the cupboard."* My gaze fell on the open doors and empty shelves, bed sheets and towels scattering the floor at the base.

"In there," I said, pointing, even though I didn't know how he could be in the cupboard, since it was clearly empty.

"How do you know that?" Nicolas said.

Feet no longer stuck to the floor, I stepped toward the indented wall running my hands along a shelf. I didn't know what I was looking for, but when I reached the right inside wall, I felt the sliver of a crack beneath my fingers. I leaned forward to get a better look.

The crack ran perfectly straight down one side, two adjoining crevasses at the top and bottom.

I began pulling out the shelves, handing them to Nicolas, who had stepped up behind me, not pushing his question.

Once all the shelves were on the floor, we looked at a square outline laying flush with the rest of the wall. There was no handle, so I pressed my hand against the square.

The wall clicked, revealing a door.

Nicolas and I shared a look, eyes wide, before I pulled the door open.

It was dark inside the hollowed-out manhole, but in the silence, I could make out the slightest breathing.

Slowly, I let my torchlight shine inside, and gasped.

Curled up in the back, tight as a ball, sat a boy with dark skin, black hair, and shocking red eyes.

"Looks like it wasn't a failed mission after all," Nicolas said over my shoulder.

Jayden's voice entered my ear, and I jumped, startled.

"Nick, Paige, anything down your end?"

Nicolas chuckled. "In fact, yes. Come see for yourself."

Nicolas crept closer to the hole, and I stepped back, remembering the Likonan's instructions for the others to look after the boy.

"What's your name?" Nicolas asked kindly, though I was pretty sure he'd already figured it out from the eyes. "Are you hurt?"

The boy's eyes darted from him to me, then back again before he answered with a shake of his head. He looked no older than fourteen, and he gripped his legs, his face stricken with fear.

"Can you tell us what happened here?" Nicolas prodded, but the boy only shrugged back against the wall as if trying to sink deeper into it.

"It's okay, we aren't here to hurt you," Nicolas said. "I promise we're here to help."

Bending down next to Nicolas, I gave it a try.

"He's right. We won't hurt you. In fact, I can barely put one foot in front of the other without tripping." I grinned.

The boy cracked a brief smile. I turned my torch around and rolled it into the hole toward him.

"Here, now you'll be able to see us properly. I'm not too fond of being in the dark either."

Hesitantly, he picked it up, shining the beam on our faces, Nicolas first, then mine where he held it.

"Whoa there, don't blind me on my first day." I threw up a hand to deflect the light, but he didn't move it away. He stared at me, trying to get a better look.

"What, is there something on my face? I haven't had dinner so it can't be food in my teeth…"

"No, it's… it's your voice," the boy said.

I stilled abruptly.

"You… like the sound of my voice?" I asked sceptically. "Thanks, I think."

"No, I mean, yes but… I've heard it before."

"Oh, well I can't say anyone's ever told me that before," I said, trying to keep him talking. "Have we met?"

"No, but I remember you, from… from my dreams."

Nicolas and I shared a stunned look.

"What exactly did I say in your dreams?" I asked.

His words put me on edge, but he looked comfortable talking to me, so I ran with it.

"You told me to wait for you, that… you'd save me," he whispered, eyes flitting to Nicolas and back to me.

I didn't know how to reply.

Nicolas shrugged, just as confused as I was.

I had said something like that before we left. No one had heard me. How did it end up in Drew's dream?

Jayden and Naomi chose that moment to arrive, and we both looked up.

"What did you find?" Jayden asked, his gaze shifting down the hall then back to us.

"Take a look for yourself." Nicolas motioned to the hole, standing up as both Jayden and Naomi bent to get a closer look.

Naomi sighed in relief.

"Thank goodness," she said, facing Nicolas. "Does he know what happened?"

Nicolas shook his head. "Not sure."

Tuning out Jayden reporting back to Havasek, and Nicolas explaining what the boy had said, I turned back to the hole.

"Won't you tell me your name?" I asked the boy. "I'd hate to have to make one up that you don't like."

He cracked a smile. "Drew."

I smiled warmly. "It's nice to meet you, Drew. I'm Paige."

"I know," he said softly. "You already told me."

"Uh…" I said, before catching on. "In your dream?"

Drew nodded.

He didn't seem comfortable talking about his dreams, so I changed the subject.

"You look awfully crammed in here," I said. "Do you want to come out?"

His eyes darted around the small space, the movement of the flashlight in his hands casting a shadow that made the shadows look more ominous. Then he nodded.

I stood back as he shuffled out of the hole. When he stood up, he was half a head shorter than me. He kept his distance even though he appeared more comfortable with me than the others.

Naomi, picking up on his shy stance, suggested she and Jayden head back to do a sweep of the outside.

"They didn't get what they came for, so they mustn't be too far away," she pointed out.

Turning to face Drew, I asked, "Do you remember what happened?"

He looked down, his features darkening at the memory.

"It happened really fast," he said. "Dad came home early… He said we had to leave, that we weren't safe. Then Mum and Dad had a fight, and the back door broke. Dad grabbed me and told me to get in the cupboard hidey-hole. After that I just heard noises, a lot of yelling and crashing and then… nothing, until you arrived."

He looked up, pleading for me to understand. "I have no idea why they came or who they were, honest."

"I believe you," I said.

"It's all clear out here," Naomi said. "Let's get moving."

I turned to Drew. "It's still not safe for you here. We can take you somewhere… where these people won't find you. Will you come with us?"

He looked around the dark house, unsure of what to do.

I didn't blame him. His whole life was here. He would be leaving everything he knew and loved.

"What about my parents?" He sounded lost, utterly defeated.

Bending down, I looked him in the eye. "I'm not going to lie to you, we don't know where your parents are, and I don't know if we'll be able to find them, but we'll try."

I grasped his shoulder for comfort. "In the meantime, its best if you aren't in danger yourself. We can help."

Slowly, he nodded, and I smiled in return.

We followed Nicolas through the house and out the back door where Jayden and Naomi waited for us.

"Let's keep it tight," Jayden said, all business. "Nicolas, you've got the rear, then Paige with Drew. Naomi and I will take point. Libby," he looked upward briefly, "be on the lookout. I don't know if they're still around but keep your eyes open."

Jayden kept a steady pace and although I was more than up for the task, I felt for Drew who might not have been. The Likonan's voice sounded twice as we jogged along the road and Naomi gave a brief check in before all was quiet again.

We turned onto the street that would lead us back to the school field.

Libby yelled. "Look out!"

A large oak tree along the roadside snapped and slammed into the ground directly across our path, blocking our route.

There was dead silence after the crash, and I put my senses on high alert.

"Libby, can you see anything?" Jayden kept his voice low as he searched our surroundings.

"There…" was all we heard before the earpiece crackled and went quiet.

CHAPTER
EIGHTEEN

"Libby!" Jayden yelled. "Libby!"

There was no answer, and I shuddered at the silence. I hoped she was all right.

Jayden took the earpiece out, tucking it into his pocket before motioning for the rest of us to form a circle around Drew, each with our backs to him.

Jayden didn't have to tell us to keep our eyes open. We already knew something was wrong.

A scream echoed from above. To our horror Libby's body came hurtling down toward us. Her arms and legs flailed about as she tried to gain control of her flight ability.

I sucked in a breath, sure she was falling to her death. At the last moment, half a metre from the asphalt, she stopped. Her body flattened out as if she'd hit the ground, but she hadn't. She floated just above the ground.

"You couldn't catch me sooner?" She glared at Nicolas.

I looked between the two, confused.

Nicolas shrugged and with a wave of his hand, Libby was positioned upright before landing softly on her feet.

Jayden grasped Libby's arm. "What happened? What did you see?"

"Not much, a bit of movement up ahead, maybe three, but it's too dark to be sure."

Jayden cursed before searching our surroundings, then he bent to the cement at our feet, using his gift to sense movement.

"We can't go back," he said, standing. "We're surrounded."

Fear ran down my back.

Jayden organised us into formation. Libby took my place in the circle, as I joined Drew in the centre.

The idea was for me not to have to fight at all, with the others surrounding us, but if whoever was out there did get through, I was to keep Drew safe at all costs.

As Jayden relayed instructions, I merged with my Eleun, feeling my power flow through my body.

It was as easy as breathing.

Turning to Drew, I asked, "How you doing?"

He stared a little warily at Libby, who he'd just seen fall out of the sky and land without a scratch.

"I guess that was a bit strange for you, huh? There's a lot we have to talk about, but not here. What you're probably going to see is a little crazy… Just remember that we want to keep you safe, okay?"

Drew nodded, hesitantly.

"You said in your dreams I'd save you. Well, that's exactly what I'm going to do."

He seemed to gain a little more confidence from those words.

Squeezing his shoulder, I gave him a smile.

"Three this side," Naomi called out. "Two male, one female."

I turned to look but couldn't make out much of them in the darkness. All I could tell was that they were in no hurry and approached as if they'd taken a casual nighttime stroll.

The female came along the grass by the footpath. Nicolas turned to face her, being closest. The two males approached along the road, toward Naomi.

I pushed Drew behind me.

"Same here," Jayden said.

I turned to the fallen tree as another female jumped over the trunk. A male stepped from around the branches of the tree on the other side. As he breathed out, red flames escaped his mouth, illuminating his red eyes and dark smile.

Libby crouched slightly in preparation.

I already didn't like our odds. Then the final member of their group rose from behind the middle of the trunk as if he floated there, and I felt as if we should just surrender.

Six against five didn't bring me much hope.

Drew grabbed hold of my arm.

"Well, if it isn't our favourite league of do-gooders," the man who stood on the trunk called out, in a patronising tone.

Recognition flooded me. I could've picked out that voice anywhere. This was the man who'd led the chase after me outside the school not so long ago.

I clenched my hands together but refrained from saying anything.

"You might as well hand over the boy," Dominic said lazily. "We'd have him already if it wasn't for his father's incompetence in following orders – that, and we clearly out-number you."

"He doesn't belong to you," I said, unable to hold back. "Where are his parents?"

Jayden shot a warning look my way.

Dominic laughed. "That is where you're wrong. You see, his father worked for me, and he made a vow to further my experiments, which included handing any Eleun first discovering their abilities to me. But he broke that vow, and now he will pay, just like his wife."

Drew shuddered against me. I wanted to strike out at Dominic with my abilities, but I refrained.

"Now that the air's been cleared," Dominic said in a tone that suggested we were discussing a minor disruption, "we'll just be on our way. Come, come, boy."

I placed an arm around Drew's shoulders, emphasising that he wasn't going anywhere.

"Well, I had been hoping to do this the easy way, but if you insist." Dominic raised both his arms, placing them palm up as if to say, 'they're all yours.'

His companions took a step closer, one laughing with excitement.

When they didn't attack right away, I worried there was something we were missing.

Jayden slammed his foot against the ground. It trembled, and a mass of rocks sprung into the air before shooting off in the direction of the red eyed man, Dominic, and the two girls along the grass.

Dominic shielded himself with the aid of the branches from the fallen tree as they flung around, whip-like, in front of him. The girl near Nicolas screamed from the impact, but the second woman managed to duck out of the way. The red-eyed man managed to swat the rocks away, then glared at Jayden in anger.

Behind me, someone sucked in a sharp breath. I turned, a chilling wind slamming into Naomi, Drew and me. We were bowled over, the gale loud in my ears, pinning us down.

Digging my fingers into the ground, I tried to get my knees under me to rise but was flattened.

When the wind stopped, Naomi leapt to her feet, unwinding a long wiry coil from her hip and ignited it with flames. She lifted it above her head and lashed out toward the breeze blower. He darted to one side. She snapped it again, continuing this dance to keep him occupied so he didn't bowl her over again.

With Naomi's whip alight, it was easier to make out what was happening. Nicolas scratched his face as he worked to dislodge something. The girl nearest him was lying on the ground unmoving. Jayden was playing defence with the other girl who was hurling sharp ice darts at him. He attempted to throw rocks at her in between the ice missiles, but the girl was too quick.

To my right, Libby was goading her opponent with patronising words.

The man's eyes narrowed and teeth showing, he growled.

He'd been with Dominic the first time we'd met.

The man opened his mouth and a long column of flames erupted out, heading straight for Libby. Eyes widening, I sat on the ground helpless to stop the stream of fire as it encircled her completely.

"Libby," I whispered, my heart stopping at the dread of having witnessed someone being burnt alive. "No."

As the flames died down, I began to turn away, unable to handle seeing her chargrilled body. She stood, her arms spread wide, completely intact.

I did a double take.

"That all you got, pyro?" she yelled. "Come on, I thought you were a challenge!"

The red head grinned, like he was glad for the challenge she posed. Then he scrunched his fists together and charged toward her. She swung at him.

Turning to see where the sixth member was, I found an empty space. Where had he gone?

I twisted around, hoping he hadn't gotten the jump on me, but there was only the fight and Drew.

Drew stared wide-eyed, more than a little scared by all that was happening.

Crawling to him, I took his hand.

"It's okay. Remember what I said, we'll get you out of here," I said, though I wasn't sure if the words were for me as well.

Together we stood, but before I could devise a plan to get him out of here, his eyes widened, and he pointed behind me.

I spun around. Long snake-like branches slithered through the air toward us.

I barely thought about my response, just felt for the closest source of water and flung it at the flying branches.

The ice darts that lay abandoned from the girl Jayden was facing, hurtled through the air. They imbedded into the bark of the oncoming branches, throwing them off course.

Dominic brought the branches back on track.

With the ice still connected to the bark, I had access to it. With all my willpower, I battled Dominic for control of the branches. I melted the ice and moulded it around as many of the branches as I could, spreading the water thin.

The branches swayed from side to side as if the wind was bristling them. I fought with all my strength to keep them away from Drew and me.

I honed into defending. Katalya would have been proud.

To be the victor, I needed the advantage… which was more water. I seemed to have the only element that didn't have a great excess, not yet anyway.

I used a burst of energy and thrust the iced-over branches into the ground where they stuck looking like an above-ground entanglement of roots at the wrong end of the tree.

Pulling my focus back, I turned it to the sky.

This was my first deliberate conjuring of a storm, but just like every other time, I barely had to think, and it came willingly.

I felt the clouds roll and tumble in upon themselves, the density and friction it caused making thunder rumble through the sky as it built up to unleash its waters upon us.

It was nothing like the storm I'd created outside the school, its size far smaller and precise now that I had control over my Eleun, and I knew it wouldn't last very long. But all I required was for water to fall, then it was free to move back to Nature's grasp.

The clouds, heavy with rain, were ready to unleash. As I prepared to discharge the water, the ice around the branches broke, releasing the lethal weapons. They surged toward us.

Desperate and caught off guard, I grasped onto something that felt strangely familiar and swiped it through the space in front of me. A sharp blast of air sliced through the branches, and the ends fell to the ground.

I stared at the danger-free zone in front of me, completely baffled at how I'd managed such a feat.

The sky gave a rumble. Now wasn't the time to ponder the situation.

The storm raged of its own volition. I released its waters. Rain pattered against my cheeks and arms.

Dominic had begun to manipulate what looked like thousands of tiny fluttering creatures as they clambered together to form a humanoid figure that stood not ten feet in front of me.

"What is that?" Drew asked behind me.

I shook my head, taking in the monstrosity. "That… is a good question."

Fully formed, the creature bent down and grasped the end of a discarded piece of branch. It started toward me.

Fear crept up my back and I took a step away, wary of what the creature might do.

Drew yelled out behind me. I spun to his aid, forgetting my own demise.

He was on the ground, a hand to his head as if someone had hit him. But everyone was locked in battle. Chocking it up to a loose missile, I moved forward to help him up.

Before I could reach him, something hard slammed against my head. I tumbled to the ground.

Another blow rammed into my back as I tried to rise, and I cried out in pain.

Gritting my teeth, I swung my legs around and tried to kick the creature down, but my leg merely passed straight through the form. Its legs reconnected as if nothing had happened.

Was this creature made of… Leaves?

The more I thought about it, the more I realised what an ingenious weapon it was. It was solid enough to attack, but any attempt to harm it would pass straight through.

A third and fourth battering to my back followed my kick. I got the 'stay down or pain follows' message clearly.

Thank goodness for stronger skin and all, or else I'd be out cold by now.

Drew gave another cry and I turned to see him sliding away from me, only he seemed to be struggling against thin air.

I wasn't stupid enough to encourage more beatings so instead, I reconnected with the storm. I encouraged it to add a little more juice to its ferocity, building up enough energy and friction to give me a weapon I could use against this creature.

Aside from my two encounters with lightning, I'd never actually practiced with it, but after my knowledgeable experience at the harbour, I knew how it worked. I could only hope my aim was just as precise.

Blocking out all the noise and distraction of the fight, I felt the air crackle around me, electricity tingling through my body. Concentrating on the leafy creature, I sent a bolt of lightning hurtling at it.

With all the rain falling, the leaves had been soaked through. The lightning spread throughout the entire creature's form. Its leaves shriveled and burnt out. Dominic watched in amazement, letting his creation go easily as he had formed it.

Breathing a sigh of relief, I started to rise.

I could already feel bruises forming.

Dominic jumped from the fallen tree and made his way toward me. I spared a look at Drew who lay on the ground unmoving. Nicolas seemed to be doing a strange kind of dance as he twisted and turned, fighting a foe he couldn't see.

I faced Dominic again and almost jumped out of my shoes. The remaining branches had sprung to life and were splitting down the centre, loose bark and small twigs flying everywhere. They rose in the air and shot in my direction, veering around their master as he approached.

A fluke attack wasn't going to save me this time. I needed an actual plan.

Pulling as much water together as I could, I built up a wall in front of me. It thickened as each drop was added, pulled from the sky midfall or up from the ground where it lay.

I felt when the branches entered the water and used a current to knock them off course. Two branches managed to exit. They sprung at my legs, winding around my calves like tentacles. I tried shifting the wall of water to the side to dislodge them.

The branches flipped me up and I landed on my back, letting out a loud huff.

The branches split down the middle again, creating two more. They wrapped around my arms, restraining me tight. I wriggled and squirmed, fighting to be released, but there wasn't much I could do.

Dominic rounded the wall and came to stand next to me.

"It would seem you've learned a trick or two," he said, intrigue filling his tone. "I must say, I'm impressed with your progress, considering the small amount of time you've had. I almost wish you'd been on my side tonight."

"Let me go," I spat, struggling against the bonds.

Dominic laughed. "Oh, I can't do that. You seem to possess something that fascinates me." He squatted beside me. "I've never seen anyone with your capabilities before, creating a storm like this. That can't come from just water. No, you'll make a very interesting test subject."

"You won't be doing any testing on her!" an angry voice said from my left.

Jayden hurled rock after rock at Dominic, who ducked and rolled out of the way.

I continued to struggle but it wasn't doing me any good.

As I searched my surroundings for a way out, my eyes rested on the wall of water.

A crazy idea formed.

Taking a deep breath, I let the water fall and encase me, my body floating amidst a bubble of water. The branches still held me tight, but the feeling of revitalising energy ran through me. I churned the water against the branches with growing speed until my arms and legs were free. Standing up out of the water, I inhaled deeply, my encasement coming to my thighs in a perfect dome.

Nicolas had revealed Drew's attacker, a tall girl with half her dark hair shaved off one side of her head.

Naomi darted in and out of wind blasts, her hands aglow as she hurled balls of fire between the gales directed at her from the man she fought.

Libby was in the air, taunting the red head as he attempted in vain to light her on fire, before she grabbed the front of his shirt and took off into the night sky.

Jayden was still aiming rocks at Dominic, but he was only trying to keep his attention on him as the roots of the fallen tree slithered along the ground behind Jayden.

Wanting to get the hell out of here, I split my watery base up, sending half of it tumbling and turning toward the roots that threatened Jayden. The force snapped them at the point of impact, halting their progression. The remainder of water I sent to Dominic.

He barely had time to inhale a gulp of air before he was at the centre of his very own water balloon. He tumbled and turned as I kept him moving so he wouldn't break free.

The anger I felt toward him grew exponentially as I recalled his words.

You'll make a very interesting test subject...

To hell I would!

He struggled within the water, a panicked look spreading along his face as he desperately searched for air.

"Stop, Paige!" Jayden shouted. "We need him!"

I didn't listen.

Something within me had risen to the surface, and it liked what was happening.

He deserved to die. If he had taken all those people and had been doing experiments on them, then I had no doubt he hadn't been kind to them. People like him didn't get second chances.

The stirring inside me grew until I felt a blaze of life overcome me, until it *was* me. My outstretched hand rotated as if on its own as I looked at the tumbling man in the globe.

I barely heard the yells of my teammates as their battles finished, the sight of their boss caged in a watery prison scaring the remainder of Dominic's goons.

The water compressed around him. Glowering, I waited for the final act to happen.

Then everything went dark.

CHAPTER
NINETEEN

"Paige, Paige, wake up!" someone said. "We have to go!"

Stirring, I became aware of pain coursing through my body.

Why did my head hurt so much?

The voice called my name again and I recognised it as Jayden's.

"Come on, please, wake up," his said, his voice a little desperate.

Opening my eyes, I focused on him. He gave me the full force of his smile.

"Hey, there you are." He brushed some hair away from my face. "How are you feeling?"

"Sore…" I moaned, trying to sit up. "What happened?"

"You don't remember?"

"I remember leaf man, roots and rocks, then water…" I sucked in a breath at the memory that I'd wanted to kill a man. "Did I…"

I couldn't say it, because saying it would make it true.

Jayden hushed me. "It's okay. No, you didn't. Libby hit you over the head before you could."

I relaxed, grateful I didn't have blood on my hands, even if it would have been a psychopath.

"Where is everyone?" I asked. We were alone and I hoped nothing had happened to the others.

"On their way to the school, the Alu-Lamek will only let us leave from there as the co-ordinates were pre-set for that location," he said. "Where we should be going. Do you think you can walk?"

"Let's find out."

Jayden helped me to my feet, and I kept an arm around his shoulders. My legs buckled, so Jayden scooped me up. He started off down the road.

"What happened after I blacked out?" I asked, feeling awkward in my current predicament.

I looked over Jayden's shoulder. Dominic and the rest of his group were gone, though the damage from our battle remained.

The tree that had blocked our path lay over the road, its branches broken and scattered everywhere. Upturned Earth and concrete dotted the footpath and grass from where Jayden had pulled rocks to use as ammunition. Parts of the grass was scorched and smouldering, and everything was soaking wet from the storm I'd unleashed, the evidence of that squelching under Jayden's feet.

Jayden snorted a laugh. "Most of them took off when you got their leader. The girl who had been near Nick, she had been out for most of the attack, but she woke up as Libby knocked you out, the ground started shaking… the Earthquake was so big none of us could move. Fortunately, she had some sense when she saw it was only Dominic left. While we were all stranded, she walked over, just fine while we were stuck, and dragged him off with her."

"What about Drew?" I asked, remembering the boy and how scared he must be at this moment, not to mention confused.

"He's fine," Jayden said. "A little shaken up. That was a hell of a scene to watch."

I was relieved to hear that he was still with us and not them.

We were silent until Jayden said, "We should really talk about what happened at the end there."

I downcast my eyes, not proud of the moment I'd chosen to be judge, jury, and executioner.

Honestly, I didn't know what came over me.

Yes, I hated the man who had tried to kidnap me, but that didn't mean I wanted to kill him. I didn't want to kill anyone for that matter.

But while he'd been encased by all that water, the desire to watch him die was all that consumed me. And yet, I knew it hadn't been my thoughts. It was like someone else had been making the decisions and had control over my body to do it.

"Paige, you almost killed a man. What were you thinking?" Jayden said, oblivious to my mental interlude.

I shook my head dismally. "I don't even know if I was thinking."

"What's that supposed to mean?" he said, as if I had intended to be absolved of my guilt.

"I don't know. It was weird. One second, I was me. The next…" I shook my head. "It felt like someone else was calling the shots and I was just there to witness."

"Is that supposed to be some kind of excuse?"

"No! I just don't understand what happened," I said, and when he continued to look like he didn't believe me I added, "I would never kill anyone. I don't even know if I could!"

Just thinking about it made my stomach roll.

He took in my expression and sighed. "Fine, but you should probably know that your eyes turned weird as well."

"Weird? How?"

"Like, your whole eye turned blue. It was freaky."

I tried to think why that had happened, but nothing came to me. It seemed there were a few freaky things about me that no one could explain.

First, my unusual power which, despite Jayden and Katalya's attempts to convey that nothing was out of the ordinary, it had been clear that everything I was able to do should not have been possible at either this stage of my training, or at all, given the scoop of what I could manipulate within the element of water. Then there was the voice in my head from earlier.

Now my eyes were turning crazy blue and something strange was trying to control me.

My life was turning into a freak show.

"Was there anything else?" I asked.

Jayden shook his head. "The Likonan's going to have a field day with this though."

I groaned. "Do we have to tell her?"

I was already not her favourite person, and tonight would not go in my favour.

"The others saw it too," he said with a shrug. "No way she's not going to hear about it."

Something about the Likonan learning about my crazy blue-eyed performance turned my stomach. It felt wrong, as if that piece of information shouldn't be shared with many people.

At least for now.

"Can we just say I… I lost control?" I sounded desperate, but I felt that option was better than the alternative, though I was still unclear why. "I don't exactly want to be known as the girl who tried to kill someone on her first outing. It doesn't look good!"

He looked at me, concern flooding his features.

"Honestly, I had no idea what was happening. I didn't even feel in control," I said. He still did not look convinced, so I kept going. "I would never deliberately try to kill someone."

I shuddered just thinking about it.

"I can't lie to the Likonan," he said. "But I'll tell her your part of the story as well."

Unsure if he was doing me a favour or not, I fell silent for the rest of the walk.

Everyone was already gathered when we arrived at the school. Jayden placed me on my feet to join the circle.

Drew stood opposite me, already sporting a black wrist band that someone had brought along. He was jumpy, eyes darting from side to side, his arms folded protectively around himself.

I tried to summon a reassuring smile when he looked at me. It obviously didn't do much to ease his state of mind.

Everyone appeared ready to collapse. Nicolas's face was covered in dirt, leaves clinging to his hair and clothes. Jayden was wet from the waist down. Naomi and Libby didn't look too bad, a little ruffled maybe but in better spirits than the rest of us.

I noticed that everyone's clothes were still intact, not a single burn or rip to be seen in the material. What were these uniforms made of? I decided now wasn't the time to ask that question.

Each of them looked my way, and I knew they wanted answers about what they'd witnessed. Not willing to divulge anything, I kept my eyes down.

Thankfully, Bradley started the countdown. I worked to keep my breath steady, keeping my arm securely around Jayden's shoulders. Bradley reached three and the elastic bubble expanded, then contracted, shifting our surrounds to a more familiar one.

"What the hell happened out there?"

Barely had the clear substance vanished into the Alu-Lamek did Likonan Harmsworth's voice enter our ears.

Jayden looked down at me to silently ask if I could walk, before leaving the group in the Likonan's direction to answer her questions.

The rest of us followed at a slower pace.

Nicolas motioned for Drew to follow him. Drew turned in all directions, shock from the Alu-Lamek travel still plastered on his face. I knew how he felt.

Naomi, Libby, and Bradley moved ahead of us, the latter collecting the black wrist bands from us all as he went.

Not really knowing what I was supposed to do, and feeling awkward watching everyone go about their jobs so promptly, I caught up to Nicolas and Drew. I wanted to make sure Drew was okay.

I listened to Nicolas's explanation to Drew of Havasek.

Arriving outside the hospital corridor, we escorted Drew down the long white walls and into the same room I'd awoken in on my first day here.

Karen, the doctor who I'd also met on my first day, entered the room as if knowing we were here.

She smiled, giving off a warm vibe as she instructed Drew to sit on the bed so she could make sure he wasn't harmed.

She gave him a once over, before declaring that he didn't have any internal injuries, before looking at where the invisible girl had knocked him out.

I turned to Nicolas and whispered, "How can she tell he's fine?"

"X-ray vision," he said just as quietly. "It's the reason she became a doctor in the first place, as her gift gives her the perfect means to see damage in the body."

Amazed, and possibly a little intimidated by someone being able to see right through me, I nodded.

"Unfortunately, it's no good out in the real world," Nicolas said, "others would ask too many questions if she told them of an injury without first doing an x-ray with a machine, so after finishing her studies and training, she came to work here, where her talents would be better utilized – and believe me, we keep her busy."

With that sort of gift, she would be one of the best doctors around, spotting injuries others couldn't. I could understand why she couldn't work in the normal world, though, and I wondered if she liked that or not.

I didn't voice my question, leaving her to complete her work.

Karen declared that Drew was as fit as a horse physically, then in a smaller voice said she wanted to keep him here overnight as she planned on giving him something to sleep peacefully so he wouldn't have any nightmares.

After she checked Nicolas and me for injuries, we bade Drew a good night. The two of us promised to see him in the morning, before we exited the room as Karen handed over a vial of clear liquid for him to drink.

I wished there was more I could do for Drew. After everything he had been through today, he had to be out of his mind on the inside, not to mention worried for his missing parents.

As we traversed the corridor, I turned to Nicolas. "What happens now? With Drew, I mean."

Nicolas gave me a curious look. "Forgotten already your first days here, Paige? I was on guard a few of those days you were trying to find your way out of here."

He'd deciphered my question incorrectly. I ignored the heat in my cheeks and the laughter in his eyes. How could I forget my arrival here? Had that only been three weeks ago?

"I mean, as Remana, am I supposed to organise his training and tell him about Eleun history, like Jayden and Katalya did for me?"

"Your role as Remana lies in the finding of our kind," Nicolas said, as we entered the main atrium. "From what I understand, once you read the name from Salyunda, there is a connection formed between you and the Eleun whose name you read. That connection remains intact until either you find them, or they manage to complete the Myundun successfully."

We headed for the kitchen.

"Is that how I knew where to look for Drew tonight?" I asked. The voice I'd heard was still a mystery. Perhaps it had been this connection?

"How did you know he was still there? You didn't say a word once you'd pointed to the cupboard," Nicolas said, watching me intently.

"I heard a voice in my head telling me he was there and where to find him. Is that normal as Remana?"

He considered my words.

"I'll confess I don't know a lot about your role, for the most part knowledge of the finer details is limited, even for those on the teams in each Havasek," he said, a look of apology on his face. "But I have heard that each Remana has their own experience with Salyunda, like, it speaks to them in a different way."

So, it was a high possibility the voice had been from Salyunda.

Great, now a book was speaking to me.

In the dining room, we walked toward the glass windows usually steaming with food. The room was empty at this late hour, the dinner rush long since passed, the trays and windows empty of food.

Stopping at the far end of the room, Nicolas grabbed a mug from a silver tray. He filled it with hot water from the kettle along the left wall, then added in a packet of chocolate and milk before giving it a stir.

A thought occurred to me.

"If there is this connection between Remana and a developing Eleun, why didn't the last Remana come to find me?" I asked.

Nicolas paused in his selection of some biscuits on the tray next to the mugs.

"He didn't come, because you were the next Remana," he said, and it sounded like he wasn't sure if he should be telling me this. "That connection wasn't there anymore."

"So he decided I wasn't worth the trip?" I asked.

So much for finding Eleun as fast as possible.

Nicolas shook his head. "I'm not the right person to be answering this. All I was told was that a new Remana had been chosen and Jayden had been assigned to find and tail you. When the Likonan gives an order, we follow."

I didn't need him to elaborate. Jayden had already told me I'd been bait, something I still wasn't overly pleased about.

"But to answer your earlier question about assigning Drew a Myundun Pina," Nicolas said, taking a step back, holding a small plate filled with biscuits. "Sometimes you might need to relay information to them, but usually the Likonan will assign someone to help the person out. So, no, you won't have to do those things, especially given you're only new to our ways as it is. We'll take care of it until you're fully trained."

I nodded, grateful for the reprieve, the anxiety that I didn't realise was there dissipating.

"Feel free to help yourself," he said, waving the hand holding the biscuits toward the trays.

Not wanting to assume I could just take anything, I'd been looking at the evening snack longingly.

My stomach started to grumble.

"If it's not enough, you can fix yourself something in the kitchens." He thumbed toward the back wall, where a door stood open off to the right. "Missions can really take it out of you."

"Thanks" I said reaching for a blue mug. "And what about Drew's parents? Will anyone try to find them?"

Nicolas sighed sadly, watching my snack being prepared. "We'll do our best to locate them, but if what Dominic said was true, then there might not be any hope in us finding them."

My shoulders dropped. I'd hoped his answer would have been different but with everything we knew about Dominic, there wasn't a lot to go by.

"What happens now?" I asked as I filled it up from the kettle. "Do we need to tell the Likonan about tonight?"

"Jayden will take care of that. You're free to go home if you want."

Sighing, I ripped the chocolate packet open. "Jayden's my ride, so I guess I'll have to wait."

"He shouldn't be long. Hopefully…" He moved to the door but paused, turning back to me. "I don't know if anyone has told you yet, but you did good tonight. For your first time out in the field. You held your own. It's more than a lot of us expected. Though, if you don't mind me asking, what happened at the end there? It was like you couldn't hear any of us."

Forcing myself to continue pouring the milk, I swallowed, thinking about what I should say, a feeling inside me warning me to be careful. Why was that?

"I think I lost control at the end," I finally said. "Everything was moving really fast. I don't remember a lot of it."

Accepting my explanation, albeit cautiously, he wished me goodnight and exited the dining room.

Finding a seat along one of the benches, I settled in to drink my hot chocolate, dunking my biscuits in the warm liquid.

Time rolled by and midnight struck when Jayden finally strolled through the door, a bag hanging off his shoulder.

I'd long since finished my late snack and was resting my head on the table, trying not to fall asleep, exhausted from the day's events. I didn't want to miss Jayden when he arrived and had decided to wait here.

He walked over to me as I lifted my head.

"What took you so long?" I said, suppressing a yawn.

"There was a lot to talk about. Harmsworth wanted thorough details. It's the second time we've come out unharmed or even at all with our target." I noticed his features were grim. "Now that we've gotten a look at the kidnappers it might give us a lead."

I bit my lip, wondering what was wrong. Had he held up his promise?

"Then what's with the expression?' I asked.

Jayden lowered his voice as sat down beside me.

"I couldn't tell her," he said, eyes dark.

"Tell her what?' I asked.

"About your crazy-blue-eyed murderous rampage," he said, a little angrier.

I swallowed, not understanding why he was mad, but relieved he had decided not to divulge that information.

"I feel like I'm missing something. Why are you angry at me?"

He exhaled hotly.

"Because I *tried* to tell her, but the words wouldn't come out of my mouth. It was like someone was holding my tongue. Likonan thought I was choking," he said, shaking his head. "Care to explain why I couldn't talk about it when everything else came out smoothly?"

Taken aback by his allegation, I blanched. Did he think I had something to do with this? How would I have stopped him from talking?

"I...I don't understand," I said. "How is that possible? I mean, I wasn't in the room. Do you think an Entina Eleun was controlling you or something? Because I don't see how this is my fault."

My words didn't help his mood. He opened his mouth to speak a few times. Finally, he deflated.

"I'm sorry. You're right, but you're the only one I've talked to about this, and seeing as you asked me to keep it a secret, I could only assume you knew something."

"So, what *did* you tell Likonan Harmsworth?"

He rubbed his eyes, exhaustion from the night's events showing in his features.

"I told her you lost control," he said. "It was the only thing that would come out, though if I'm being honest, I don't think she bought it."

I remained quiet. Why hadn't he been able to say anything except what I had asked him to say? Was this somehow my fault?

Jayden watched me. I got the sense he was searching for deceit.

And just like that, he didn't trust me anymore. A lump formed in my gut at the feeling. I thought we'd been starting to become friends. But apparently, weeks of travelling to and from Havasek getting to know each other, was ruined by one event that neither of us could explain.

When he didn't find anything, he said, "It's late. You should go to bed."

He was changing the topic to avoid whatever it was that now lingered between us.

"Oh, you aren't going home?" I asked, noticing he'd missed the part where we got in the car to leave.

He shook his head. "I'm far too tired to drive right now. Will your parents mind if you stay the night at 'the babysitting house'?"

I cracked a smile, briefly.

"No need. My parents think I'm at a girls' night," I said, grimacing when his smile didn't lift.

"Good."

Motioning for me to follow, he led me out of the dining room and up the curved stairway. I followed him to the girls' quarters, and he stopped outside the room I'd occupied during my first week.

"You remember where everything is?" he asked, tersely.

"Yes." It hasn't been that long, I thought dryly.

He waved me in and I entered, looking at the symmetry of the room. Still the same bland room I remembered.

Shrugging off the bag from his shoulders, he handed it to me as I realised it was mine.

I sighed with relief that I'd packed extra clothes for my night with Nicole, which also included my pajamas.

Jayden started to move to the door but stopped as he reached it. Gripping the handle he paused, eyes closing tightly. Abruptly, he checked each corridor before closing the door and turning to face me.

I swallowed. What was he doing?

"I have to be frank," he said, staring me down, his earlier anger fading. "When I was in talking to the Likonan, I couldn't stop thinking about you…"

My nerves spiked a little at the possibilities.

"I couldn't get the picture of you out of my head with bright blue eyes and that murderous look on your face."

Strangely, I relaxed. It wasn't as though I didn't like the guy, but I'd barely had time to figure out who he was let alone my own feelings for him, and then there was…

I shook my head, trying to focus on what he'd said.

"I told you, I don't know what happened," I said. "This is all still so new to me."

"And I get that, I do," he said, "and I'm sorry for accusing you of doing something to me earlier, but I can't help but feel like this is the beginning of something… big, something we've never seen before."

What was he saying?

Thinking back to when I wanted to eliminate Dominic, I recalled the power that had coursed through me and the feeling that nothing was going to stop me. It had made me feel powerful, like there was nothing that *could* stop me, and it scared me. Not because of the intent of my actions, but because I'd liked it.

That was a worrying thought.

"I don't know what else to say," I murmured, trying to hide the shiver that ran down my spine.

Jayden came to stand in front of me, resting his hands on my shoulders. "Explain everything that happened, everything you felt. Maybe there's something you're missing, something… you didn't understand."

I didn't understand any of it.

I was taken aback by his sudden closeness, my mind going a little fuzzy at his touch.

"I…" I started but didn't know how to continue.

"Please, Paige," he said, mis-interpreting my hesitancy. "I don't like nasty surprises, and since you've been here, I've seen you progress far quicker than anyone in history, not to mention your abilities surpass even the original Eleun. What happened tonight just adds to the crazy you've brought with you. I only want to help, even if I can't talk about it with others. You understand, right?"

I bit my lip, unsure of what I should do. I had kept something from him. But he was going to think it was crazy.

"Okay," I said softly, still not entirely convinced I should bring the information up.

We both sat down on one of the beds and, crossing my legs, I turned to face him.

"But honestly, there's not much to tell," I said. "Like I said earlier, when I went all scary eyes, I felt as if I wasn't in control, like something was taking over… not like when I lose control of my element and it goes crazy."

I shook my head as he started to say something, "It was like there was someone inside me who knew how to use my power perfectly and had complete control of everything."

He scratched his nose. But he remained attentive.

"Then there are the strange dreams I've been having ever since my element first made an appearance. At first, I thought they were just weird dreams, but some have repeated and I'm starting to think they're warning me," I said, trying to make light of it, even if they scared me.

"Dreams? Why do you think they're warnings?" he asked.

"Well, the day before Dominic found me at the field, I had a dream of him, or at least someone with green eyes, chasing me. He's popped up in a few other dreams as well, but nothing that's come to pass yet, not like the first one."

Jayden remained quiet, mulling over what I'd said, and I was grateful he was taking this seriously.

"What were your other dreams of?" he asked at last.

"Bright lights, strange symbols, and a mountain in some forest..." I shook my head, unsure of what it all meant. "That's where I saw Dominic too."

Jayden stared blankly over my shoulder.

"Does that mean anything to you?" I enquired, but he shook his head.

"No, the symbols might be Marcian, though."

"I had thought that, but I haven't found them anywhere to learn what they mean," I said, resigned.

"Is there anything else?"

I shook my head again. "Not unless you count me showing up in Drew's dreams. That was weird. Or the voice in my head telling me where to find him, but Nicolas thinks that might relate to Salyunda and my role as Remana, so maybe it doesn't count."

"Nick told me about that." Jayden ran a hand through his hair. "Something like that would be connected to the Entina Eleun, which isn't possible, so he's probably right. The same with Drew's dreams."

"For the record, I don't actually recall visiting Drew's dreams, so I don't think that counts," I said.

"Yes, well, it's still all a bit confusing nevertheless," he said. "You've become a grade-A mystery, Paige Munro."

"Yippee," I said dryly, waving an invisible flag over my head, glad he seemed to have forgotten his anger.

Jayden stood. "I should probably let you get some rest. Heaven knows you've given me a lot to think about. Let me know if you figure anything out or have any more strange dreams."

"I guess I don't have to worry about you telling anyone," I said. It was meant to be a joke, but his frown told me it hadn't landed.

"Too soon?"

The frown lifted, the barest hint of a smile forming.

He turned to leave.

"For the record, I feel like I can trust you," I said, meaning every word. "I'm sorry you had to lie to Likonan Harmsworth, truly."

He met my gaze. Understanding passed between us and I knew he had let the accusation go. At least for now.

"I'll see you in the morning," he said, breaking the moment as he opened the door to leave.

"Goodnight," I called as the door slid shut behind him.

Sighing, I lay back on the not-so-comfy bed, feeling the relief of having talked to someone about my strange life. Though I was still left with plenty of questions, somehow the weight of it felt a little lighter.

The knowledge that I was only part human had been a lot to take in, and now there was what had happened tonight… which was a whole other level of crazy.

What it all meant remained a mystery, but I couldn't agree more with what Jayden had said: this felt like the beginning of something.

I planted my face into the pillow and let out a muffled scream.

Why couldn't I just be normal?

I was flying through the sky, soaring high above the mountain tops, and the same mountain I'd seen on numerous occasions came into view.

My flight sped up as I zeroed in, heading straight for the domed peak. Everything went dark.

I blinked my eyes open, my blurry vision vanishing, revealing that I was looking at a domed cavern.

I was lying on my back. I didn't know where I was, but an Earthy smell filled the place. When I tried to get up, something prevented me, and I lifted my head enough to see my arms restrained by my side. I pulled against the restraints, but they remained firm, the same true with my legs.

What was going on?

To my left stood two people, their backs to me, looking over an array of tools and strange equipment. They were speaking but I was too far away to hear their words.

I tried to release myself again. A groan escaped me.

A man standing on the other side walked to the table where I lay. He stared down at me.

If I hadn't been strapped to a table, I would have fled.

It was Dominic.

"What's going on?" I heard myself ask, in a foreign woman's voice. "Where's Casa and Micky? They need me. They don't have anyone else to look after them!"

I had no idea who Casa and Micky were, and I realised then that it wasn't me on the table. I was looking through the eyes of another. Not just looking, feeling; everything she felt as well.

Dominic smirked at me. "Oh, I wouldn't worry about the kids, Mumma Cortez. They're making good use of our accommodation here. I may have use of them yet."

I struggled to get up, but it was pointless.

"You, on the other hand..." He circled the table, my eyes following his movement. "Your use is valuable, now."

"And why is that?" I said through clenched teeth.

"If you're successful, then I'll enlighten you," he said simply. He beckoned to one of the two people by the table. "Doctor, it's time."

The male doctor stood by my head. His wide-rimmed glasses reflected the woman's large yellow eyes, her mouth open in protest. He held a large needle filled with an amber liquid.

He looked at me sympathetically. "I'm sorry, but this is going to hurt, quite a lot."

His expression showed that he didn't want to be doing this but had no choice.

Taking a shuddering breath, I felt the needle enter my arm. I clenched my teeth to stay strong.

It was just a needle…

A scream filled the cavern as I felt the liquid ooze through the woman's body. The sensation was horrible and… wrong. Whatever Dominic was doing, he'd defied some law of nature. It was going to kill this woman.

CHAPTER
TWENTY

"Wake up," a voice said. "Wake up, it's just a dream."

A loud scream filled my ears.

"Please, stop. You'll wake everyone up," the voice said.

My eyes fluttered open, It was me doing the screaming.

I zoned in on the face of a girl with dark hair hanging loose around her shoulders, still in her night clothes.

Surprised, I pushed backwards, scuttling into the corner, heart pounding in my chest.

Amelia stepped back, hands raised. "I'm sorry, it's just… you were screaming, and no one could wake you."

Whispers caught my attention. The doorway to the room was crowded by girls still in their nightwear, all staring at me with surprise and shock.

Someone pushed to the front, and a relieved sigh escaped me.

Jayden.

"What happened?" he asked, taking in my panicked state.

"I saw him," I said. "Dominic. And he's…"

I couldn't finish, unwilling to voice what he'd done to that woman and began to cry at the pain she'd felt.

Jayden crawled over the bed and halted in front of me, his arms outstretched.

Hesitantly, I shifted into his embrace, and he wrapped his arms around me, pulling me close.

"It's okay," he said, rubbing my back. "It was just a dream."

"It wasn't just a dream," I whispered for his ears only.

I was shaking, the memory still fresh, the sensation strong. That poor woman, her family…

"Go get some water," Jayden instructed Amelia, and she slipped away. "The rest of you, go back to your rooms. She'll be all right."

More whispers ensued as our audience shuffled down the hallway.

"Tell me what you saw," he said gently.

I did, down to the last detail. It was scary how much I could remember.

I wanted answers, but who was going to give them to me?

Jayden continued to rub my back as I finished, and I closed my eyes with my head against his chest.

"I wish I could've helped," I muttered. "No… I need to help her!"

I felt Jayden nod.

"If they're still alive…" he said it as if the thought was hopeless.

I shuddered.

Dominic was a monster!

"There's nothing you can do right now," Jayden said. "But I can get people looking into their disappearance. If they haven't been taken, then there's nothing to worry about, and we can rule out your dreams being real."

I didn't need anyone to clarify if they were real or not. I knew with every fibre of my being that they were. However, I didn't contradict him. Perhaps something would arise from the search for the Cortez family, that would lead us closer to Dominic.

Shifting back, I wiped my eyes, needing to pull myself together.

I didn't make a habit of crying.

Then I realised how close I was to Jayden and not wanting him to get the wrong impression, I said the first thing I could think of.

"I need to have a shower."

A worried expression clouded his face at my abrupt change.

Again, trying to cover, I said. "Mum will be expecting me home soon."

Jayden narrowed his eyes at me in concern. "Do you know what time it is?"

Searching the room for a clock, I came up short.

"No, why, did I over-sleep?"

"It's five o'clock in the morning… on a Saturday," he said. "I doubt your parents are even awake yet."

Well, that explained why I was still tired. I'd probably only had four hours of sleep.

I suppressed a yawn. "I don't want to go back to sleep."

There was no way I would close my eyes again to be pulled back to Dominic's testing lab. It was just too horrid a place to visit again.

Jayden's brow furrowed. "Paige, it's what your body needs, especially after last night's events."

I began to respond, but stopped as something else occurred to me. "Wait, how did you know it was me screaming?"

"After everything you told me last night, I couldn't sleep, so I was in the hallway thinking it over. The screaming wasn't easy to miss. I only figured out it was you when I saw the horde of girls around your door."

I felt a pang of guilt for burdening him with my problems and regretted telling him.

As if reading my mind, he placed his hand under my chin to make me look at him. "I'm glad you told me! It's just a lot to take in, that's all."

His hand was warm against my skin, a rush of nerves and confused feelings coming to life with him being so close.

I'd never thought about him in a romantic way before. The idea did flash across my mind as he looked at me. Right before another face took his place, green eyes instead of silver, and everything inside me became twisted and confusing.

I needed to figure things out before I did something stupid. I climbed off the bed, pushing the urge to curl back up in his warm arms again from my mind.

"I'm glad it was you who came," I said. "I'm not sure what I would have told anyone else, but I should still think about getting home."

His hand dropped. "Okay, but promise me you'll rest when you get there."

I shook my head defiantly. "It's nothing a splash of water can't fix. It'll give me the energy I need to stay awake."

I walked past him to the wardrobe, picking up a towel folded there.

"I don't think you should rely on that form of energising," he said, wearily. "Rest is the best thing for your Eleun and your body. If you become too run down, then you…"

An inner voice was telling me to listen to him, but I had no desire to close my eyes and feel whatever it was Dominic was doing to those people again.

"I know," was all I said before grabbing my bag and stepping out into the hall.

After my shower, I felt energised and refreshed enough to face the day. Unfortunately, it didn't remove the memory of the woman's fear and pain from my mind, which left a sour taste in my mouth every time it crossed my thoughts.

By the time I entered the dining room, it was six o'clock and a few people were already there eating breakfast.

A television mounted along the left-hand wall displayed the morning news, its volume turned down low enough for only the closest table to hear what was being said.

I filled my plate with eggs, bacon, toast, and tomato sauce, piling it all up into a sandwich, and then sat down in a relatively empty section at the middle table.

I was almost done when a voice from across the room caught my attention.

"Jay, you should probably see this!" Someone shouted as Jayden entered the dining hall.

The voice belonged to a blond-haired short man who sat closest to the television. Another man strode up to the TV and hit the volume button so everyone could hear.

"…they were found by a couple driving out of town in the early hours of the morning," the male reporter, said as images of flashing lights belonging to police and ambulance cars filled the screen. "The couple reported that it was dark, and they came out of nowhere, causing them to swerve to avoid hitting them. Upon exiting the vehicle to make sure they hadn't hit anyone, the couple were bombarded with questions by the three, who were confused by their identity and where they were. After the couple called triple zero, an ambulance and the police arrived."

The screen changed to show a middle-aged man with brown hair combed neatly to the side, a microphone clipped to his suit jacket.

"Now this is all we've been told about the situation, but we were able to speak with a paramedic who confirmed that the three had suffered severe memory loss and couldn't identify themselves, saying they woke up in the forest and blindly made their way to the road."

Another voice sounded through the television, asking, "Were you able to find out where they've been taken, Tony?"

The man in the suit nodded. "Yes, they've been relocated to the Cornal hospital, where it was said the military have set up a secure section to undergo a special investigation about the disappearances."

"Do we know for certain that they were among the missing?" the news presenter asked.

"No," Tony replied. "As of yet nothing has been confirmed, but from what I was able to glimpse, it didn't look like they were any of the people we'd previously listed as missing."

"Thank-you, Tony."

The screen changed to picture a woman sitting at a desk in a studio. "We'll check back with you later as more information comes through, but in the meantime, police are asking that if anyone recognises these three people, to please come forward to identify them to help with the investigation."

Action shots from this morning's finding were shown on the screen: a woman with dirty blonde hair in jeans and a T-shirt, and two men. One was tall with dark hair and in a suit. The other was a head shorter with shaggy sand-blond hair and in pyjamas. All three of them had dirt splotches covering their clothes and faces and looked as if they hadn't slept in days.

I stood up at the sight of the woman and got closer to make sure my eyes weren't seeing things.

"That's her," I muttered, more to myself, but Jayden came to my side.

"Who?" he asked. "Do you know them?"

"No, but that's the woman in my dream. I saw a reflection of her in the doctor's glasses. It's her."

Jayden looked from me to the television.

Drew and Nicolas walked through the door, then halted. "Dad!"

His crimson eyes were glued to the screen.

Jayden and I exchanged a look.

"Is that your father?" Jayden asked, pointing to the screen.

Drew nodded. "The one in the suit. He was wearing it last night. Why is he on TV?"

He turned to look at me as if I knew the answers.

I had a theory, but I wasn't going to get his hopes up. "I'm not sure."

"We have to get on top of this," Jayden said. "Nicolas, the woman, she has two kids, Casa and Micky Cortez. Could be nicknames, I'm not sure. Find them and you'll find the woman. We need a way to get into that hospital, someone to pose as family, maybe. They won't let just anyone in."

"But how do you know all this?" Nicolas said. "This only happened this morning. The police don't even know who they are."

Jayden shook his head. "It doesn't matter right now, just get on it. We'll talk details later. We have to beat the military, or else they'll suspect something."

Nicolas gave a quick nod and disappeared back out the door.

Jayden headed out of the room.

"Where are you going?" I asked, completely lost.

"To see the Likonan," he called over his shoulder. "You two coming?"

Drew looked more lost than I did, but at the prospect of seeing his father again, he hurried out the door and I followed.

Likonan Harmsworth was pacing behind her desk, a phone to her ear and a frustrated look spread across her face.

She ushered us in, continuing to listen to the other end.

"Yes, I'm aware of the risk, but this could be the lead we've been looking for…" Her voice grew angrier. "I don't care what you do, so long as the Welka receives the message in the next half hour. Time is of the essence, so make it happen!"

Before they could reply, she hung up. "Bloody idiot, who ever put him in charge needs to rethink a few things."

"I take it you've seen the news?" Jayden said.

"I've been trying for half an hour to get a doctor in there, but no one can get a hold of…" The Likonan looked at Drew and me as if only just seeing us and changed her sentence. "Never mind. What can I do for you?"

"We may have a way in to the hospital." Jayden said. "Though I don't think you're going to like it."

She eyed us warily, motioning for him to continue.

"Likonan Harmsworth, this is Drew." Jayden turned to Drew as an introduction. "He's the Furno Eleun we rescued last night. Drew recognised one of the men from this morning's find… as his father I believe we could use that as a way to get in and see the patients."

Likonan Harmsworth stared down at the boy.

"Not only that, but someone also recognised the woman in the trio." He didn't even hesitate in his explanation as he skipped over the exact details. "Enough to remember a name… Cortez. Apparently, she has two children."

The Likonan lifted an eyebrow, but didn't question him further, to my relief.

"With this head start, we should be able to create false identities and send someone in to get information out of them," he said.

I stared at him dumbly, my mind wrapping around his rash plan.

False identities? Were we secret agents now?

So many questions ran through my mind. Was this normal for Havasek, pretending to be someone they weren't?

How did they even make that happen? Surely with today's online presence, it was impossible to pretend to be anyone with so many facial scans and IDs required to prove they were who they said they were?

Undoubtedly the government had already run the victims' faces against databases to locate family members, friends, or associates to notify them. Wouldn't it be too late to create fake IDs to use?

I wanted to pepper Jayden and the Likonan with my questions, but seeing as I wasn't the latter's favourite person right now, especially after my 'loss of control' last night, I held them in and let the two talk it out, hoping some of my queries would be answered.

"It's not a bad plan," the Likonan said, "risky, but it might work. Drew won't be able to go in, however."

Drew's head shot up as shock spread over his face. "Why not? He's my father. They have to let me see him!"

The Likonan's expression turned sympathetic as she looked down at him. "I'm sorry, but if you turn up alone, they'll question you about your mother and since she is still unaccounted for, I just can't risk any type of exposure."

"Why not get someone to pretend to be her? Use fake IDs," he argued.

He was a quick thinker. He would need that in his new life here.

The Likonan shook her head. "Your eyes will be too much of a giveaway. They're too unnatural and security will become suspicious."

"So, give him contacts to shade them darker," I piped up in his defence, unable to remain silent anymore. I would have fought to the end if it was my father we were talking about.

I couldn't bear that he would miss the chance to see his family, even if he had been working for Dominic.

The Likonan glared at me, as if to say, 'who asked you', then said, "We can't wear contacts. Our Eleun are too powerful that they dissolve them within sixty minutes." She turned back to Drew and placed a hand on his shoulder. "I'm sorry but you'll have to sit this one out."

I shrank back, chastised. Drew looked defeated.

After everything that he'd witnessed last night and all the things he'd been told about our way of life, seeing his father alive would have been the perfect antidote to get his spirits up again.

The Likonan turned back to Jayden. "However, Mrs. Cortez's children could be a solid lead, as long as we get on top of it soon."

Jayden was already nodding as if having expected her response. "It's in progress as we speak. Nicolas is on it."

"Hold on," I interrupted, annoyed that none of my questions had been answered and not willing to wait any longer. "How is anyone going to stand in for Mrs. Cortez's kids? What if we find out they're three and six? The government will know. We can't send adults instead."

Everyone looked at me. Jayden opened his mouth to respond but the Likonan cut him off.

"I don't understand why you're even here, Miss Munro." She looked at me with a frown.

I tried not to take a step back, even as my insides screamed to run for the hills to hide.

"You may be our Remana," she said, "but that doesn't give you jurisdiction over any other business that might happen around here."

My fists balled at my side.

What was her problem? I had just tried to add another perspective to the situation.

"It was partly her idea," Jayden cut in before Harmsworth could continue her lecture, and I stared at him dumbfounded.

Luckily, the Likonan had also turned to face him and missed my surprised look.

Jayden held his poker face. "She suggested we use Mrs. Cortez as a way in."

It wasn't all a lie.

I was the one who had recognised her, though the Likonan couldn't know that without explaining how I'd identified her.

Boy, did I owe him.

The Likonan didn't respond right away.

"Still," she said, "there was no need to involve her further. I've put you at the head of this investigation, which is no place for an untrained seventeen-year-old girl. I expected more, Jayden."

She looked down at me from over her nose, disapproval emanating from her very skin as we locked eyes.

The news that Jayden was at the head of figuring out where the missing people were barely registered as my fists tightened.

I wanted to show her where something didn't belong.

I felt a stirring in some close pockets of water and reined in my anger so as not to give her a reason to throw me out.

"I beg to differ," Jayden said, voice calm. "She may only be seventeen, but she has surpassed every test we've thrown at her, well ahead of some of the more advanced Eleun. She has control like I've never seen before. She can handle herself just fine. I think she may even be ready to prepare for the Velta, and I think we could use her insight in the investigation."

Even as my cheeks heated at his praise, my temper cooling, I wondered what the Velta was.

The Likonan shook her head. "As eager as I am to see her through that trial and deemed worthy of her title, I'm not willing to risk it on a whim, not with the stakes so high. We need to be sure she's absolutely ready before we open that can of worms, and after last night's events, that time is not now."

She spoke as if I wasn't in the room in front of her.

"Because you know as well as I do what the ramifications will be if she fails," the Likonan added. "We finally have the honour of housing the Remana. Let's not mess it up on maybes."

Jayden pressed his lips together in a tight line.

Feeling the tension in the room, I kept the rest of my questions at bay. I could ask Jayden about the Velta later.

"I don't want her anywhere near this investigation," the Likonan told Jayden, eyeing me. "Keep her focused on Reku and Salyunda."

Her phone started buzzing then.

"We'll revisit this later. Do what you can to set your plan in motion, and I want a full update and briefing." She looked at her watch, gritting her teeth. "Let me know as soon as you're ready."

With a dismissive wave, she shooed us toward the door.

"Alone this time," she clarified, the phone halfway to her ear as she pointed at Jayden.

His jaw tight, Jayden nodded then led the way out of the room.

Drew and I followed in silence as he made his way to the lift.

There was so much I wanted to ask him, but given Drew's presence, I kept quiet.

After ascending to the top floor, Jayden tracked down Nicolas as he came out of a doorway along the same wall that ran away from the medical wing.

They exchanged a few quiet words, which I didn't catch, before Nicolas beckoned Drew to follow him so he could introduce him to Danny, who'd be training him to control his ability.

Jayden waited until they reached the staircase before turning to me, looking like he was somewhere else, and said, "I'm sorry, but I have to take care of some things. Can you find your own way home?"

Since he was about to leave, I said, "What's the Velta and why can't I take it?"

"It's not important right now," he said, clearly caught off guard. He took a step toward the door Nicolas had ventured through. "Can we talk about it later?"

"No!" I said, annoyed he wasn't cooperating, considering how serious Likonan Harmsworth had made the Velta feel back in her office. "Tell me now. If I'm going to do it anyway, I want to know what it is and why."

He sighed, giving in.

"It's essentially a trial," he said, his voice lowered. "To test your Eleun control, along with your physical capabilities under pressure."

I didn't like the sound of that.

I'd known there would be some kind of test to assess my competency, though the details had been scant. Hearing that it was a trial didn't make me feel any better about it. The word trial made it sound like I would be judged and under constant surveillance.

"What exactly does it involve?" I pressed, trying to find a bright side.

"It's a rite of passage in Marcian tradition," he said, looking as though he wanted to be elsewhere. "Every Eleun wanting to show they have control and are ready to seek out further endeavours in the community would undertake an obstacle course meant to challenge you physically and Elementally."

"Like an exam?"

It made sense. Sending untrained supernatural people into a world that didn't know about us didn't sound like a great plan. On the flip side, having to sit any type of exam also didn't sound fantastic.

"What did the Likonan mean by there being ramifications if I failed?" I asked, remembering her sombre note at the end.

When she'd mentioned housing the Remana, it had sounded like it was an honour, like it came with benefits others wouldn't receive because of it. Was she trying to prolong those benefits to make sure I passed this Velta?

Jayden surveyed me before responding, as if he didn't want to elaborate.

He noted the few Eleun in the atrium.

Reaching down he gripped my wrist, pulling me into step behind him, our footsteps echoing around the high-ceilinged room as he walked toward the long bare wall at the back. And then straight through it.

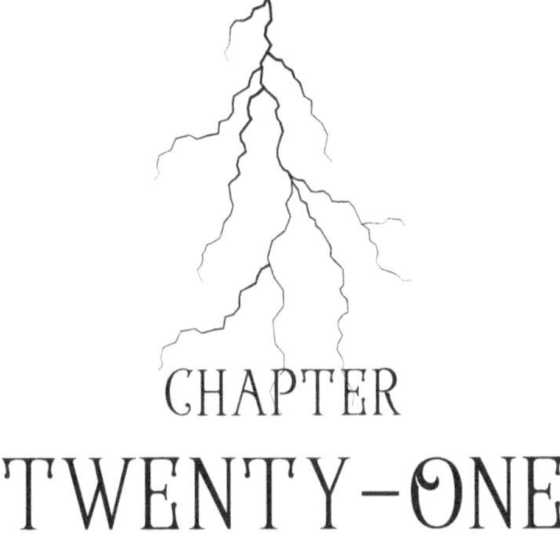

CHAPTER
TWENTY-ONE

Jayden didn't allow me time to process what had happened. He just continued our trajectory along the grassy landscape leading me around the back of the mountain that backed onto bushlands.

Reaching the edge of the trees, he let go of my wrist, turning to face me.

"On Marcious, the Velta was a coming-of-age test," he said, his words hurried, "and if you failed, you'd have to wait another year before you could take it again, halting any progression forward until you passed."

A year? Wait… was that it? That didn't sound so bad. Likonan Harmsworth had made it out to be something deadly.

"Oh, is that all?" I shrugged. What was another year in the grand scheme of things? "I can handle a small failure, so long as I can take it again later."

Failure was the key to success and all that.

"No, Paige, that's not all." Jayden's face turned hard. "Look, there's a few things we haven't told you regarding you taking on the role of Remana."

His words reeled me back in.

"There have been some issues raised about your competency to fulfill the title…" he said carefully.

I swallowed, unsure how to respond.

"In the past, Salyunda usually produces the name of an existing, trained Eleun, before it vanishes to the nearest Havasek, allowing them to immediately get to work on locating and helping new Eleun when their names are read," he said, making sure I was following. "With you, however, there have been a few comments about whether you're suitable for the role, seeing as you knew nothing about this life before we found you."

I didn't know where this was going, but from his grave look, it didn't sound positive.

"What do you mean by comments?"

He exhaled sharply. "There are some who are asking to have you removed as Remana."

"Is that even possible? I thought Salyunda chose the Remana?"

He grimaced. "There are ways of doing it, none of them… optimal."

I lifted an eyebrow, waiting for him to elaborate.

"Death is the easiest option," he said, holding up a finger. At my appalled look, he hurriedly added. "Which has been outlawed for thousands of years, so that won't happen."

He held up another finger. "Declaring you unfit for the role, which will more likely be what happens, but not until after a lengthy trial which will involve a lot of important people having their say, which could lead to either imprisonment – not likely given your age – or the binding of your powers, because without your powers you won't be considered Eleun anymore and Salyunda will recognise that and move on."

I took a step backwards, fear and uncertainty flooding through my body.

"They can do that?" I spat out, feeling faint.

Jayden dropped his hand, his eyes conveying that he wished he had better news to share.

I didn't want any of those options to happen. After last night's events and remembering how good it had felt in rescuing Drew, I knew I couldn't turn my back on it.

My powers and Salyunda were a part of me now and would be for a long time.

I wasn't about to let anyone take that away from me.

I contemplated the only option that seemed likely – binding my powers.

I had no idea what that would involve, but just the thought of it caused my skin to prickle with fear.

I may not have chosen these powers, or this lifestyle, with all its secrets and training and rules, but my abilities were mine.

Sure, maybe I'd briefly wondered if it was possible to be rid of them, and what it would take to do so, but now, I couldn't fathom it.

There was no question about it. I was not giving up my powers for anything.

In a weak voice, I forced myself to ask, "Do they bind people's powers often?"

His sorrowful expression didn't ease. "No, it's not something that's practiced, except in the most extreme circumstances where it comes down to the life of the individual and those around them."

I nodded slowly, taking that in.

"But because you're Remana, and the youngest one we've ever had," he said, "and still untrained, they could very well decide to choose that option, considering how important the role is and what it means for our people and our future."

"If they're so worried about me being so young and untrained, why am I only just hearing about this and the Velta now? It would have been nice to know someone wants my head on a platter."

Taken aback by my words, Jayden said, "Your head on a platter is a bit extreme. I didn't say anything because you were so new here and still learning the ropes. I didn't want to scare you off, plus, we'd managed to put a pin in it promising we'd give you the best training in order to get you up to speed, which was agreed to so long as everything went smoothly. The fact that last night was a win in your favour really helped, so those who were pushing for your release have backed off… for now, but that doesn't mean we can ease off. They won't stop until you've passed your Velta, and even then, there might be problems."

I had been feeling a little better as he talked, but once he got to the end, I deflated again.

"So, when will I have to take the Velta?" I asked, not sure I wanted to know the answer but seeing as it was on the radar, I did.

He sighed. "Hopefully not for a long time if I can help it. We've managed to come to an agreement with the Welka, our leaders, so that each Havasek will take care of anyone in their area when a name is read while you're training, but that only means we'll need to continue pushing your boundaries in training."

"So why can't I start practicing for it now?" I asked curious as to why the Likonan had turned it down.

"Because as soon as we announce that the Remana is preparing for the Velta, the pressure will be on. I don't know about you, but I'd rather hold off on that. Pressure over anything is never good for success, especially if we only have one shot at this."

Knowing that I wouldn't be required to take the test any time soon helped to calm my nerves over the situation, though only slightly.

"Relax," Jayden said, placing a hand on my shoulder. "I'll look after you. No one is going to pressure you into anything until Katalya, Naomi, or I say so, okay?"

Steeling myself, I nodded.

Wanting to move away from the subject of trials and bindings, I returned to some of my earlier questions.

"If you're the head of this whole Dominic situation," I began, unsure whether I should ask the question, "why did you stand up for me back there in Harmsworth's office when you weren't supposed to bring anyone else in on what you knew?"

Sticking his hands in his pockets, he sat back on his heels. "Simple. We need you."

I looked at him, confused. "How? The Likonan doesn't trust me, and according to her, I don't have enough control to be of any use."

He tapped the side of my head. "Because of what's in here."

"I don't follow."

"When you told me about your dreams last night, and then this morning, I didn't think much of them. I'll be honest, I was sceptical, even after you claimed your first one came true," he said. "But when you told me the woman on the news briefing had been the one in your dream, it got me thinking. If you really are seeing Dominic and snippets of what he is doing, then why couldn't we use that to our advantage? That was why I took you with me to Harmsworth's office. I had planned on getting Harmsworth to allow you to work with us on the investigation."

Technically, he'd asked if I was coming with him to the captain's office, but I didn't correct the detail. I was just grateful he believed me that my dreams were real.

"Only I didn't expect talk of the Velta would overshadow it," he added, "so that could have gone better."

"Stuff what the captain says. Put me on the team." I was determined more than ever to see Dominic brought in. "I want to help bring that psycho down!"

"I wish I could, but I'm not the only one on the team. If she finds out, then there will be hell to pay, and not just for me, but you as well. Seeing as your relationship with her is already… rocky," he said, with a knowing grin, "I don't want to push those buttons."

"So don't tell her," I shrugged. "Don't tell anyone. Just fill me in from the sidelines and I'll give you whatever information I can from my dreams."

His grimace didn't dissipate, though I could see he was considering my suggestion.

"Okay," he said, still not looking overly happy with the decision, but willing to compromise. "Deal."

The offer wasn't ideal. I wanted to be in the loop. No, I needed to be in the loop, but given his determined expression he wasn't going to cave any farther, and there wasn't a chance in hell that Harmsworth would agree to clue me in.

"I do have a few more questions, though," I piped up before he could change the topic.

He held up his hand. "As much as I would love to stand here and answer them, we're on a time crunch. I need to be getting back to see where we're at with this plan."

Although I wanted to fight him on it, I knew what he was doing was important.

"Okay, then just answer one," I said, holding his gaze before thumbing over my shoulder. "Please explain how we walked through a wall on our way out here."

He chuckled. "So much for the serious moment we just had, but sure, I can explain that."

Walking back to the wall, Jayden said, "There's a Terralin Eleun from another Havasek who can turn solid objects transparent, while they still look solid."

Jayden waved a hand through the wall, no barrier to stop him.

"During the day it's left open," he said, "but at night there's an actual wall that slides underneath it for security."

"Handy for moving in furniture I'm sure," I said, also waving my hand through the space with a smile.

I remembered Bree telling me on my first day here that I'd have more luck walking through this wall to find an exit. I'd thought he'd been telling me it was pointless. Apparently, he had actually been helping me.

I enjoyed a few trips from one side to the other, marvelling at how real it looked and yet, I felt nothing as I passed through it.

Jayden just stood back and laughed as I disappeared and re-appeared multiple times before I noticed a few onlookers staring at me from the balcony and decided it was time to stop.

I needed to get home before Mum reported me missing. Since Jayden was caught up with his side project, I didn't want to take him away from the important role, so opted to catch the bus home.

Jayden pulled me aside before he disappeared.

"Try not to worry too much about the Velta, okay?" he'd urged. "I know it's a big thing and we need to prepare you for it," he said, then squeezed my wrist gently, "but please, go home and get some rest. Trust me when I say I've got this under control."

Dread rose in my chest, and I tried to cover it with a front of humour.

"Why can't I use one of those Alu-Lamek things to come and go from Havasek?" I asked, trying not to let the fear of the unknown get to me. "It would save me a whole lot of time, and you petrol, every time you pick me up."

"You're not licensed for it and even if you were, very few people are actually allowed to operate them for everyday usage."

"Let me guess, I won't ever be one of those people?" I asked, then crossed my arms.

The corner of his mouth lifted. "Not yet anyway."

"Jayden, we need you," someone called from across the atrium floor.

"I'm sorry, but I have to go," he said.

He jogged away.

Jayden and the Likonan had given me a lot to ponder, enough that my thoughts were well occupied on the bus ride home.

With Jayden's promise to keep me informed of anything important in the missing persons' case, so long as I gave him anything I might see in my dreams, I didn't plan on missing any sleep.

Still, I was nervous about closing my eyes and seeing the horrors of what Dominic was doing play before my eyes like a movie.

I was still shaken up from last night's visions and everything I'd felt. A shiver ran down my spine.

But I knew deep down that if Dominic was going to be stopped, then Jayden needed every lead he could get. If it meant a little more pain for more of a glimpse of what he was up to, then I would put up with it. The fear that Dominic could show up on my doorstep and threaten my family was far too real, especially after what had befallen Drew's home, and what had become of his parents.

"You're home later than we expected." Dad's voice pulled me away from my thoughts, as I walked up the driveway. He held a bag of rubbish away from his body on his way to the outdoor bin, wind sweeping his unkempt dark hair to the side. His pale blue eyes peered down over his glasses at me.

I spun around to walk backwards as I smiled. "We slept in. It was a late one."

"Remember, you promised to stay on top of your schoolwork," he called over his shoulder. "That was part of the agreement that went with your new job and any extra activities."

Giving him a salute in response, I turned to walk normally again. "I remember, Dad!"

Thankfully, he didn't push the topic and I entered the house to do just as he'd suggested.

"Hey Paige!" Ryan launched himself over the back of the couch to sit beside me, as I laced my joggers up for a run five hours later. "Mind if I come?"

My mood lifting at the sight of him, I nodded.

I hadn't seen the Drakes for most of the day. Sharon had taken the kids to the storage unit holding all their belongings. They'd arrived back about an hour before I called it quits on my homework, apologising as they made a lot of noise passing me through the kitchen.

Ryan had offered his help with the Math and PE homework, since we shared those classes together, but I'd refused.

Truthfully, I just didn't think having him around would help me get things done faster, even though I had struggled through a few of the Math questions.

Now, however, I welcomed any form of distraction.

Turning to him with a teasing grin, I said, "Tell me, do people run often where you're from? Because it seems like you struggle to keep up every time we go out."

Ryan had joined me on my morning runs almost every day since I'd started back up. I'd gotten comfortable with him tagging along.

Smiling wickedly, he jumped to his feet.

He was dressed in running shorts and a T-shirt that conformed far too well to his chest.

Apparently, he'd already decided to come regardless of my answer.

He extended his hand toward me and pulled me to my feet.

"Oh, is that how it is?" he said, laughing as we headed for the door. "Sorry to be such a burden on what I thought was a great bonding experience."

"You should be sorry. You're bringing my PBs down."

"I could run our normal route in half the time if you weren't with me. I've just being going easy on you."

"Prove it," I said.

Smirking, he took off without another word, his laughter trailing behind him.

This should be fun.

We ran to the town centre. Then we ran a few kilometres past it before turning around and heading back home.

Collapsing on the grass, I rolled onto my back, spreading my arms wide, my heart pounding against my chest.

Ryan, falling to his hands and knees beside me, said between heavy breaths, "You just… don't stop…"

He sounded impressed.

"Well, you managed to keep up, so maybe I underestimated you… just a little bit," I said, holding up two fingers with a sliver of air between them.

Laughing, he rolled to his back. He began stretching.

"How was last night?" he asked. "You haven't said anything about it."

Standing up, I kept my gaze low so he wouldn't see my dishonesty and started to stretch as well. "You know, girly stuff."

I bent to lunge forward, feeling the burn in my legs from all the exertion, and the sour taste in my mouth at the lie.

It felt wrong deceiving him, especially since I was so comfortable around him.

But I couldn't tell him the truth; I'd been specifically told that I couldn't. Would he even accept me if he knew the truth?

The thought made my heart drop, but I pushed the feeling aside.

He didn't need to know. We could still be friends regardless of who I was.

As the sun sank a little further, we headed back to the house.

When we reached the driveway, Ryan captured my hand, pulling me to a stop.

My heart jumped as his warm hand encased mine.

"Can I ask you something?" he asked, sounding nervous.

I stuttered, "Yes, of…of course."

Our eyes locked, and I was instantly reminded of how beautiful his were: deep, dark, and green. I could've gotten lost in them, never wanting to emerge.

He took a breath. "Are you busy next Saturday?"

It took me a moment to register his question and my heart sped up at where he was going.

"Um, not that I know of," I replied, slightly giddy, but more nervous than I cared to admit.

"Can I take you out somewhere? We can do whatever you like, mini golf, beach, a movie, anything," he said, sounding a little like he was rambling.

I smiled. As it turned out, he was cute when he was nervous.

Then the realisation of what he was asking hit me.

A date. He was asking me out on a date!

Excitement rippled through me.

I hadn't thought he was interested in me like that, especially after the last week. He'd been bombarded with every girl in our grade.

The knowledge that he was singling me out to spend time with me-was surprising.

My insides did a funny sort of dance at the prospect of us spending more time together, alone...

I was glad he couldn't see my heating cheeks in the darkening sky.

"Yes, I'd love that," I replied in a hushed tone.

A tingle of emotions, mixed with a tug that felt oddly connected to my power source, spread through me as it sounded like he sighed. A breeze simultaneously blew between us, muffling any further noise.

Puzzled by the feeling, I stepped back, my hand slipping out of Ryan's. I felt light-headed.

What was that?

The tug had almost been akin to what it felt like when I merged with my Eleun, only I hadn't been doing that this time.

"Are you all right?" Ryan asked, concern lacing through his voice as he moved to my side.

"Yeah," I said, not so sure. I worried that perhaps I didn't have as much control over my abilities as I'd thought. "Probably just tired. It's been a long day."

He nodded, his expression worried. "We should get inside. A meal and then sleep ought to help."

We resumed our path to the house. Despite my moment of dizziness, it hadn't taken away the tingling feeling inside me at the prospect of spending more alone time with Ryan.

I tossed and turned in bed all night. My dreams chopped and changed from one thing to the next, none of it making any sense, nor of any use in locating Dominic.

I was exhausted the next morning, and I wished there were some way to get a good night's sleep without dreaming.

After seeing the early hour of five o'clock, I lazed about in bed, flicking through Salyunda, the symbols on each page changing every time I turned a page.

I'd done this multiple times since first acquiring the book, amazed at how the ink on the pages shifted and rearranged as if by magic.

Despite being the Remana, I was unable to read a single word in the first half of the book. These pages, solely dedicated to the names of all the Eleun it had found over the generations it had been active, were only legible when a new Eleun emerged.

The second half of the book, however, I was able to read.

This half included a brief history of the Eleun people, how they'd arrived on Earth, a day they called Nelayunda, and the importance of keeping our way of life a secret from humans for our survival. It also held information on each of the elements.

I'd learned that although I could read this half whenever I wanted, no one else could.

These pages had been put in for the use of the Remana, so they could explain all these details to the new Eleun that were found, since it was their role to find and protect them until they were safely able to control their abilities.

Most of what was written I'd already been told, but the information about the five elements drew me in. I should become familiar with that section if I ever came across an out-of-control Eleun that needed to be calmed down.

According to Salyunda, if someone lost control of their abilities, they had the potential to wipe out a sixteen kilometre radius as their Eleun took over.

It was a scary thought, but it drove home how important my role was, and why there were people who doubted my ability to perform the job.

Not wanting to go down that train of thought, I snapped the book shut as noise began to sound beyond my bedroom door. I got up and headed out to see what everyone's plans were.

I joined Ryan, Liam, and Peter on the front lawn in a game of soccer, which pegged Liam and I against the Drake brothers. It was an intense match, which resulted in our loss of the game, but it worked wonders in occupying my mind from everything Eleun-related.

We all headed inside, our stomachs complaining of food deprivation, to which Sharon and Mum happily pulled together a mini feast for our enjoyment.

It was a pleasant lunch, spent re-hashing the game we'd just played for the rest of the family to hear, though most of the laughter and loud noise came from those who'd played.

Eventually, the conversation died down. I was about to excuse myself to get ready for my training session, when the discussion turned to another topic.

"Angela, was there any news on identifying the victims they found yesterday?" Sharon asked as she stacked plates to clean up. "I didn't catch the news this morning."

I froze mid sip of my smoothie, listening for her response.

The mention of the found victims sounded strange amidst the walls of my own home now that I knew it was an Eleun problem.

Mum shook her head. "Not that they're saying, though I'm sure it won't take them much longer."

Placing my cup back on the table, I tried to look interested in the conversation, but my mind went to other places.

If they hadn't figured out who the missing people were, it really had been a stroke of luck that I'd recognised the blonde-haired Mrs. Cortez from my dream, and Drew had identified his father for us.

What were the odds that the authorities would identify these people before Jayden could put his plan into motion?

Jayden had said he wanted to get on top of the situation quickly, so they didn't miss the opportunity to get in and speak with them, to find anything they could of Dominic and his location.

Was that still the plan? Or had the strategy changed?

Would we even get anything new out of them?

I felt helpless, sitting here contemplating different scenarios that might or might not happen, what we may or may not learn from these people.

Frustration getting the better of me, I stood up.

"I'm going for a walk," I said, startling everyone with my abruptness.

Mum looked at me, having been halfway through a sentence when I'd stood. "Okay… don't go far. It's still not safe out there."

I nodded vaguely, making my way to the door.

I hit the road at a run. When I made it to the corner, someone called my name.

Ryan chased after me, and I cursed.

Not stopping, I shouted over my shoulder. "Ryan, no offence, but I really don't want company right now."

"Are you sure?" he yelled to me, not stopping. "You can talk to me."

Gritting my teeth, I said, "Positive."

Picking up speed, I took off down the street before he could change my mind.

CHAPTER
TWENTY-TWO

As much as I enjoyed Ryan's company, right now I just wanted to be alone. To let loose some of the pent-up anger inside me. I hadn't had an Eleun session yesterday and I felt as if the only way to release some of the anger was to use my element.

Having Ryan along for the ride would only complicate the situation.

Pulling out my phone. I texted Jayden where I would be when he came to collect me for training later, then continued on my previous path.

The field where I liked to run had a small bushy section that backed onto it. A path wound through it, along with a small creek that was often popular with young families on hot days.

Most of that was flat and well looked after by gardeners. Further off to the side, however, the ground sloped down, leading to un-tended wild shrubbery, before rising again on the other side backing onto fenced off properties.

Most of those places had high fences, preventing people from jumping, or seeing over them.

I headed there now.

I'd discovered the place a few years back when Mum had brought us here one Saturday so we could burn off some energy. Liam and I had been kicking a ball around when I'd sent it down the back slope.

Liam had called 'not it,' so I'd had to climb my way down to retrieve the ball. I'd stopped to marvel at the small little pocket of untouched quiet that no one seemed to be utilising.

It would be perfect for what I wanted now.

The conversation about the missing people had brought to the forefront everything Dominic was doing, and how little I could do because of my 'untrained' status.

Standing at the bottom of the gorge, I connected with my element, feeling the welcoming embrace it sent through me like a long-lost friend opening its arms with joy.

I lifted some of the water from the trickling creek as it moved down the slope. Spiraling it through the air in front of me, I made it rise well over my head, then twirled it around in a circle so it looked like a giant twisted lollypop.

I condensed the water into a ball, and it floated mid-air a metre from me. Extracting a small section, I shaped it into an arrow tip.

Focusing on a tree farther downstream, I lined it up and sent the water arrow toward it with a mental burst of speed. The arrow under shot by a metre or so, landing on overgrown grass and rocks with a splash.

Not allowing myself to get downhearted, I withdrew some water from the ball of floating water, fashioning the same object, and then gave it more of a mental push toward the same tree. It overshot by three metres, the water splashing to the ground out of my sight.

I huffed out hot air in annoyance.

I focused and tried again… and again, and again, one after the other, aiming to hit the same tree each time, until finally I got it.

Not pausing in my victory, I continued pulling out more water from the floating ball. The splashing sound the water made each time an arrow hit the bark sent a spike of achievement through me.

My training with Katalya hadn't involved any offensive attacks. Her instruction focused solely on the defensive manoeuvres, which were supposed to give me enough time for the more experienced Eleun to come to my aid.

After Friday night, however, I knew I couldn't play the victim again. My shift from defence to killer mode had made that clear. Since I hadn't had any exposure to attack options, perhaps that was why something inside me snapped and took over.

I wondered if I had just lost control of my element. That my Eleun decided that it wanted to take over, like it had in the beginning.

If that were the case, then I needed to expand my knowledge on how to attack so it didn't happen again. No matter how much I hated Dominic, I was not a killer and had no desire to become one.

Taking it up a notch, I attempted harder ways to strike the tree, curving the water to the left and right, from down below and up above, spinning on the spot before aiming once more.

The concentration involved took its toll more than the physicality of the moves. Each time I sent an arrow of water through the air, I had to release it at the precise moment, so the water held its shape and remained on its trajectory in order to hit the target.

I spun and dropped, swerved, and dived to the side in a succession of movements, all water arrows hitting the intended target. The water ball depleted, leaving the space empty. I jumped up from my crouched position and punched the air.

"Woo!" I called, before cringing and eyeing my surrounds in case anyone was nearby.

I played around with water shaping, creating various animals and inanimate objects, hurling, or moving them around the space to see if I could, like the kids at Havasek had in the common room.

I'd never really taken the time to play around with my gift and found it soothing and comforting. I should do it more often.

I realised I'd probably lingered longer than I should have and made my way up the gorge.

Reaching the top, I pulled out my phone. Jayden had replied to my message, to say that training had been cancelled as all hands-on deck were needed for the upcoming hospital mission.

Groaning, but also slightly relieved, I pocketed the phone and headed home.

When I entered the house, Ryan was sitting in the lounge room reading a book, the same one I was yet to finish for English.

Looking up, he nodded with a small smile as I entered, then focused back on the pages in front of him.

Sighing, I remembered how I'd dealt with him earlier, and stood in front of him, pulling up all the courage I could muster to admit my fault.

"Hey…" I began, unsure of what I should say.

He took in my partially wet clothes with splotches of mud. "Hi, did you clear your head?"

Not elaborating on my makeshift training session amongst the trees, I nodded, dropping down next to him like a heavy sack of rocks.

"I'm sorry about earlier," I blurted out. "I didn't mean to blow you off like that. Honestly, I just needed time to think."

Ryan turned the book open on his knee, shifting his upper body to face me. "It's okay. We all need to be alone sometimes."

He smiled reassuringly.

Smiling back, I said, "I feel like I need to make it up to you."

"No, you don't have to do that."

I placed a hand on his knee. "Seriously, you were just trying to be nice, and I was rude, so I believe I owe you a favour. Whatever you want. Lay it on me."

He stared at me, trying to decide if I was being serious or not, then said, "Okay, but be warned you may not like it."

The corners of his mouth lifted in a cheeky grin.

Laughing at his attempt to cheer me up, I said, "I doubt there is anything I wouldn't like. I hope. Just name it and it's yours."

I nodded to confirm the offer.

Part of me was curious as to what he might suggest…

His lopsided grin lifted further, and I wondered what he was so amused about. Before I could question him, he closed the distance between us and gently pressed his lips to mine.

A horde of butterflies took flight in my stomach at the touch of his soft lips, and my heart skipped a beat.

My eyes closed, against my better judgement, and I couldn't help but revel in the feel of him being so close. His lips were warm and comfortable, and he smelled of freshly mowed grass. I breathed in his scent.

"Paige, is that you?" Mum's voice sounded from the kitchen. "Can you come help with dinner?"

Ryan pulled back, his face lingering inches from mine, his eyes blazing green.

He whispered, "Consider the debt paid in full."

I woke to buzzing and in my half-sleep state, I reached over and attempted to whack whatever it was stirring the silence. The noise persisted as I failed to locate the source.

Groaning in annoyance, I finally registering the sound. I blindly patted my bedside table until my hand fell on the phone that rested there.

"This better be good," I answered sleepily, thinking the call was Nicole requesting something impossible. I'd not bothered to check the caller ID.

"Hey, shouldn't you be getting ready for school?" Jayden's voice sounded far too happy for this hour of the morning.

My eyes shot open, and suddenly I was awake.

"Jayden, hey, what's up?" I stuttered, sitting upright in bed. "And no, it's bloody six o'clock in the morning. I still have at least a half hour of solid sleep time left, so thanks for robbing me of that."

He laughed. "Well, consider this your early wake up call, 'cause it's happening today."

"What's happening?" I rubbed my eyes. "You all of people should know that not everyone can read minds."

"The mission…" he prompted, as if that should be enough and when I didn't respond, he continued. "You know, the one I said I'd try to keep you in the loop about?"

I inhaled, realising that he was talking about getting into the hospital to see the victims.

"Oh, that mission. How's it playing out?" I asked.

"I don't want to go into it over the phone… But I wanted to let you know that I haven't forgotten about your training. It's just been crazy busy here. Even though Naomi and I won't be there this afternoon, I've organised for something else, so don't be late."

I sighed dismally. "What sort of something?"

He laughed. "Don't sound so excited. I think you'll like it. Keep an eye out for Bree; he'll explain."

Before I could question him further, he said, "Oh hey, I have to go, sorry. See you after, yeah?"

"Okay, good luck," I mumbled, and the phone went dead.

My nerves spiked over what was about to go down. Who had they recruited to play Mrs. Cortez's children? What would they learn from her? Would it be enough to locate Dominic and stop him?

Today was going to be a long day.

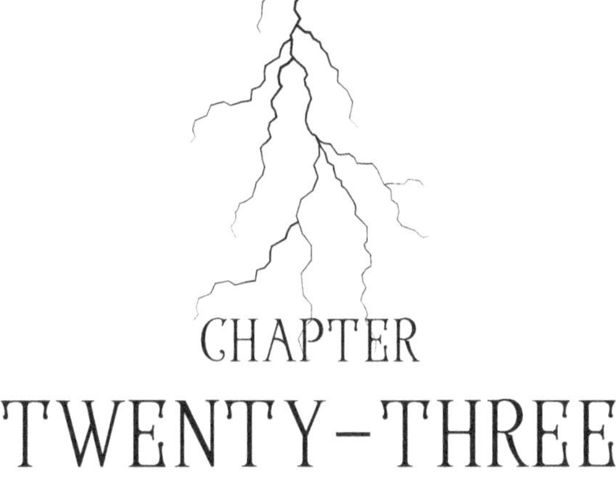

CHAPTER
TWENTY-THREE

By the time I returned home from my early morning run, I had convinced myself that it was better to not think about Jayden and the hospital mission. I would learn what I could after school.

Jayden would fill me in on anything important. He'd promised me that.

I headed inside to ready myself for school and found everyone in the front loungeroom waiting for me.

"Finally! What took you so long?" Liam said with a dramatic wave of his arms, getting to his feet.

I could tell he didn't care as he moved past me for the door.

"Yeah, isn't it normally you waiting for us?" Eva asked, pulling her bag over her shoulder.

Ryan stiffened, his expression slightly guilty.

Did he think my being late was his fault? That I was avoiding him because of his kiss last night?

Heat flushed through my cheeks at the memory of his lips against mine, and I shook my head, hoping he wouldn't notice.

We hadn't had the chance to talk after our intimate moment. I'd been dragged into the kitchen to help Mum, and Sharon had taken the family to walk through their new house, leaving a lot of things unsaid between us.

"Just ran a little longer than usual this morning. Can't I have a little leeway?" I said. Ryan hadn't joined me as I'd left earlier than normal.

Ryan relaxed. "Right. Shall we go? I'm driving."

With his words, we all headed out to the car, grateful to not get wet from the rain. Which had nothing to do with me.

The younger three took the back seats, leaving me with the passenger one.

Beating me to the door, Ryan opened it for me with a lopsided grin, and I felt my cheeks heat further as I ducked in front of him to take my seat.

We were going to have to talk about that kiss at some point. I just hoped I was prepared when the moment came.

My leg bounced madly as we travelled to school, my mind ablaze.

"You okay?" Ryan glanced at me. "You seem on edge."

I forced a smile. "Yeah fine, just another day at school. What's there to be edgy about?"

I'd said that way too fast. I gave myself a mental kick.

Were these nerves about the mission, or about his kiss?

Probably both.

After dropping Lucy and Eva at the primary school, Ryan pulled the car into the senior school parking lot, and we all got out. Peter and Liam took off, leaving Ryan and me alone.

My stomach twisted into knots as we fell into step, heading for roll call.

"I'm going to be honest," he said as we passed the gates, sounding like he needed to get something of his chest, "because I can't hold it in anymore."

"About what?" I asked.

"About yesterday… When I kissed you."

My breath hitched at his openness, my stomach fluttering.

"I haven't stopped thinking about it all night," he said, "and honestly… I want to kiss you again."

The pleasant fluttering turned into a full-on torrent, and I dipped my head slightly to hide my smile.

I hadn't been able to stop thinking about his kiss all night as well. It had been my first ever kiss, after all.

Well, first ever *real* kiss, I corrected myself.

"Oh," I said, unable to find anything coherent.

I envied his confidence to speak so openly, like this wasn't something completely new and foreign, as I struggled to gather my thoughts.

When I didn't do so fast enough, he said. "Is that… not something you want? Because it doesn't have to be. I just needed you to know how I felt. It's totally okay if I over-stepped and you want me to back off."

"No." I blurted out. "I mean, yes. It was nice, and I enjoyed it too. It's just…"

I swallowed, telling myself to get a grip. "This is… new to me, and I don't have a lot of experience with all…that." I waved my hand through the air to indicate our intimate moment the day before.

"I came on too fast," he said with a sigh. "I'm sorry. I shouldn't have assumed…"

"No, it was perfect, really. It's just I don't know what to expect when it comes to dating, and in my head, it was moving a little slower…"

He reached down to brush his fingers against mine and pulled us to a stop outside his roll call room.

"Hey, it's okay." He smiled reassuringly. "I'll slow down. No more unexpected moves until you're ready."

Warmth in the form of gratitude flowed through me, and I squeezed his fingers.

"See you later?" I asked.

He nodded, then reluctantly he let my hand go and walked through the door behind him.

Was I ready for a relationship? Could I even sustain one?

With everything in my life a little crazy, with all the secrets surrounding me, I didn't know if pursuing a relationship was the right move to make.

I hadn't considered any of that when he asked me out.

Groaning inwardly, I cursed my secretive life.

Why did it have to be so difficult?

Or did it?

If I just never mentioned that part of my life to him, then maybe it wouldn't be a big deal. Perhaps he wouldn't question all the time I spent away from home…

It was a wild thought and one I knew wouldn't be viable for a relationship. But just for the moment, I allowed myself to think that it would be; that I could have this.

An image of Ryan being so close to me entered my mind and the feelings he'd erupted inside me returned.

I couldn't deny the truth: I was falling for him, hard.

In my own roll call room, I sat down in the chair next to Nicole, who barely looked at me.

"Hey, how was your weekend?" I asked.

Nicole sighed. "Oh, you know, my best friend ditched me, and I had to resort to lame-as TV as my mum went on about her new boyfriend."

I grimaced, realizing that I was the source of her pain. "I'm sorry, but I did promise a bigger, better one this Friday night, so…"

Her droopy face slowly turned to a winning smile before she grabbed my arm. "I know, and it's going to be the bomb. I've already called Catherine and Isabella. I'll talk to Sophie and Tanya today. That'll make six, including us." She squealed with delight. "I can't wait!"

Inwardly, I groaned. Sophie and Catherine were invited? This was going to be a disaster.

I would never say that in front of Nicole. She was friends with everyone, and they all loved her, so it would be hard to convince her to cull a few people.

She gushed a long spiel detailing everything she had planned, and I tried not to drown her voice out as names were called to mark the roll. I owed her at least that much after I'd let her down.

I tried hard not to think about Jayden and the plans to infiltrate the hospital throughout the day. My mind wandered off, considering what might be going on, or if they were being caught right this minute.

It still felt weird that this was my life now.

"Who are *you* texting?" Nicole cooed from over my shoulder, at lunch, as I sent Jayden a message asking for an update.

I knew he wouldn't respond if he was busy, but I couldn't help myself. There was so much at stake, so much we could potentially learn about where to find Dominic.

"No one," I answered quickly, flipping my phone over, hoping she hadn't glimpsed what I'd been writing, then sheepishly said, "It's not important."

"Uh-huh," she said, before crunching down on a carrot stick, eyeing me.

One would have thought I learnt my lesson after that close call, but during Math, I found myself staring at Jayden's text chain, trying to come up with the words to say, 'give me information or I'm going to combust,' without sounding desperate, or helpless.

Today's Math quiz landed on my table. Ryan was looking over my shoulder, having been asked to hand out the papers. My phone was under the table, Jayden's name on full display.

I tucked my phone into my pocket, but it was too late. Ryan had seen it all, his expression confused as he stood back.

I smiled, trying to brush it off.

Had he seen how edgy I was?

Just another thing to add to my worry list.

When the bell finally rang for the last period, I sighed with relief. I headed straight for the gates, eager to learn anything I could about what was going on with the mission.

I entered Havasek via the holographic wall, which I still found amazing, and stopped short.

The Jalin in the guard house nodded to me in welcome before resuming their conversation with each other.

A group of kids headed for the stairwell, their excited chatter trailing behind them as an older Eleun with red eyes attempted to get them to keep their voices down.

Most of them looked my age.

A Jalin exited the surveillance room on the left-hand wall and hurried toward the lift, looking like he was on an important mission.

If I had to hazard a guess as to where I would find information, aside from asking Likonan Harmsworth herself and I wasn't about to do that, that doorway would be it, since that's where Jayden had disappeared the other day when the mission was first devised.

As I began to move for it, a voice called out to me.

"Paige, over here."

Bree stood by the stairs, beaconing me over to him. Remembering that I was meant to meet him for my surprise, I stopped, and he ran toward me.

Peering over my shoulder, in the direction I'd been headed, he said, "Why are you here so early? I thought you'd still be at school."

"Study period." I shrugged. "We're supposed to study, but no one ever does."

"Sounds nice. Wish we had those here." He thumbed over his shoulder toward the stairs, which led to the rooms they used for schooling. "You still trying to get into the surveillance room?"

He pointed at my destination door. I recalled he'd stopped me from entering the room on my second day here.

"Yeah," I said. "Jayden told me they were trying to find information from the victims the police picked up over the weekend. I wanted to see how it was going."

He laughed, though it sounded like a snort. "Yeah, good luck with that. They're being tight-lipped about the whole situation. My brother, Justin, is on the team as well and he wouldn't give me a sliver of info. There's no way you'll get inside there. You're better off waiting till they get back. They'll be more open once it's finished."

I let my shoulders slump. I had no doubt he was telling the truth. Likonan Harmsworth had been clear that she didn't want me anywhere near the investigation, and I didn't think she would have changed her mind since Saturday morning.

What was I going to do now? Jayden might not be back for hours.

"I wouldn't worry," he said, reading my expression wrong. "They're professionals. They know what they're doing."

"Any idea when they'll be back?"

He grimaced. "Sorry, no."

"Great, guess I'll go read a book or something."

He chuckled. "Sure, if that's your thing, or you could come join us now. We're headed down to the field to play an early game of Elemucka."

I recalled him mentioning the game that second day here as well. Who came up with these names?

"Come on, at least watch a few games so you get the hang of it."

With nothing else to do but wait, and my competitive side piquing with interest over this element-based sports game, I followed him to the lift, where everyone had already disappeared downstairs.

By the time we reached the field, it was already buzzing with activity and Bree stood with me to explain the rules.

This particular version of Elemucka was played with ten players, five for each of the two teams. The aim of the game was to shoot the black soccer-sized ball, made of Maela, an element-resistant material, through any of the five rings around the field to score different points.

The rings themselves were each a different colour to match the five elements, their positioning either low or high off the ground and scattered around the field. All members were allowed to score goals, and the element the Eleun wielded and the colour of the ring they shot the ball through determined the number of points received.

"If you score a goal in any ring with your hands or feet, it's one point." Bree said as we watched a dark-haired boy scoop up the ball in his hands. Running with it under his arm, he jumped up and threw it through the blue ring in the middle.

"If you score a goal in your element's ring with your element, you get five points." Bree clapped as the field reset to find all players gathered in the centre around the red-eyed adult I'd seen upstairs. "And if you score a goal using your element but the ring is not yours, then you get ten points.

"The game is designed to improve your accuracy and precision, along with your control over your element. The rings are set for each element and changed around for each new game."

The game looked chaotic, with elements flying everywhere seemingly of themselves. But I was intrigued by the looks on the players' faces and the cheers from spectators.

We watched the current game play out till Adam, the red-eyed adult, called time so the players could be switched out.

"I want to play," I said.

Bree blinked at me.

"It's more for experienced players. Maybe you should give it a try without the interference before jumping in?" he said, and I could tell he didn't want to hurt my feelings.

"You think I can't handle it?"

"Um, it's not that," he said carefully. "I just think you might want to watch for a little longer, get the lay of the game a bit more. It's a dangerous sport, not like human sports matches. Maybe wait till you've mastered your Eleun a bit more."

I stared at him as if he'd just insulted me. His words weren't enough to deter me. But then again, he hadn't seen my progress since the night in the common room.

"I'll live. Plus, fast healing." I flicked my shoulder. "Isn't that supposed to prevent me from any lasting damage?"

"Um... well, that's not..." He stammered, his eyes roving as he searched for the right thing to say.

"Jayden asked you to bring me here," I said, folding my arms. "Surely that says enough about my abilities."

He nodded, though looked unconvinced.

"Fine, you can play, but don't say I didn't warn you," he said, then headed toward the other onlookers.

Smiling, I followed, eager to get my hands on that ball.

After falling over while trying to jump over a stream of fire, tripping over rocks that appeared out of nowhere, slipping on a wet patch, and getting twisted in my own attempt at shooting a goal, I was ready to call time out.

The game was so much faster than soccer, with so many more elements to it than I'd anticipated.

Even the fight I'd been in with Dominic hadn't been this fast, and for a moment I wondered why he'd held back so much, instead of using speed to claim what he thought was his.

Bree approached me as I lay on my back.

"I told you it wasn't easy," he said, "but I'll give you props for staying in it when most would have given up by now."

I didn't deserve his praise, but smiled anyway, feeling lost.

"Come on, only five minutes left." He hauled me up and we found our position around Adam as he tossed the ball into the air.

I sprung forward, pulling at water beneath my feet from the pipes that gave us access along the ground, shooting it toward the ball. I overshot by a few centimetres, and I whipped it back around.

Bree, whose ability allowed him to jump extremely high with great gusts of wind emitting from his feet, appeared out of nowhere, grasping the ball in his hands. He jetted higher in staggered bursts toward the yellow ring.

Following at a run beneath him, I saw a line of fire shoot upwards toward him.

Giving my arsenal of water a sharp thrust, I sent it skyward, dousing the flames before they reached him.

A growl issued behind me, and I knew that the owner of it had been the fire wielder.

Not looking back, I pulled more water to my aid from the side of the field. The flames had evaporated a lot of my attack.

Bree continued his progress for the ring. Then he tumbled in the air, his momentum faltering as he lost his grip on the ball and began falling to the ground.

I lashed out for the ball, but so did everyone else. Two columns of fire shot through the sky. A blast of air that messed around my hair sped past. A line of soil spiralled upwards, followed by a tree branch, and then pellets of water from the other water Elemental.

I didn't know or understand how the Entina Eleun were attempting to reach out, but they stood close by with concentrated looks on their faces.

Everything clashed together in the middle. At the last second, I pulled back. It would be pointless to join the fray and just be caught in an endless battle.

Bree came to my side, looking up at the mass of water, air, soil, fire and no doubt mind control as well.

"We'll be here all day if we don't break that up," he said. "Think you can get the ball through the ring if I get it out?"

Shocked, he was asking this of me, I shrugged. "I guess we'll find out."

"Be ready to catch it, 'cause you'll only have a few seconds," he said, crouching low.

I had no idea what he planned to do. He sprung up directly into the mass, arms outstretched in hope he could grip the ball.

I started to yell that he was crazy, but I barely got the first word out when he pierced the muddy expanse. Then he dropped back into view, ball in hand.

He was barely out when he tossed the ball toward the yellow ring. With no chance of it going through, I sent my flow of water at the ball and guided it through the ring.

Shocked I managed to score a goal, I let my hold over the water falter, and the ball dropped to the ground below.

Cheers from our team went up, and ten points were added to our score.

Bree landed heavily beside me, slapping me on the back. "Good job!"

Four other players came over to congratulate me, and I smiled back at my teammates. We didn't win, but I was pleased I'd managed to do something right.

I played the third game, then opted to sit the last game out, but I had every intention of participating in another game the next chance I could.

When Adam called the end of the fourth game, I joined the group back inside, enjoying hearing everyone's chatter and excitement over the various plays they'd seen or managed to pull off.

They gave me recognition for my one goal, out of politeness, but I brushed it off saying it had been a fluke shot and that I was keen to play again to improve.

Up until now, I'd viewed Havasek as the place that locked me up, despite my acceptance of my abilities and role as Remana. But in this moment, I felt at ease for the first time, like I could belong if I gave it more of a chance.

After encouraging me to join them next time, a few players waved before they headed upstairs in search of food.

Bree turned to me with a smile. "You weren't half bad. A little more practice and you'll be scoring more goals in no time."

I smiled, accepting his praise as voices sounded behind us.

"Hey, they're back." Bree waved to a male in the front who could have been his double, aside from his older appearance. Remembering that he'd said his brother had been on the hospital mission, I felt my heart rate pick up as Jayden exited the meditation room, a few people behind him.

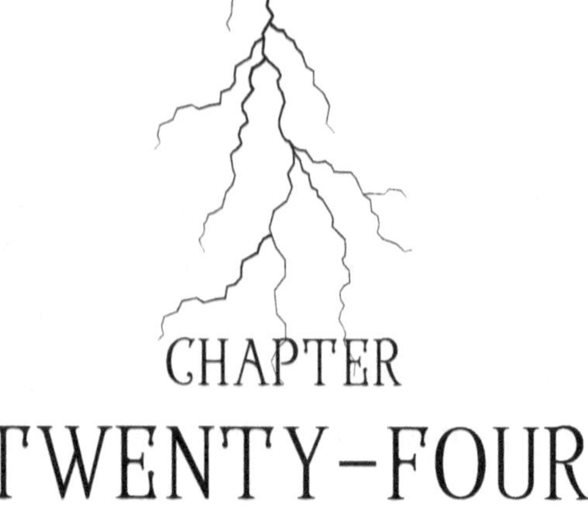

CHAPTER
TWENTY-FOUR

I hurried toward Jayden, eager to find out how the mission had gone. Jayden looked tired, but otherwise unhurt. That had to be a good sign.

He gave me a small smile as I approached.

"Looks like you had fun," he said, taking in my muddied and wet appearance.

"How did it go?" I asked, wanting to for go the chit-chat. "Did you learn anything?"

"Straight to it, okay," he said. "It wasn't what we'd hoped for, but we got a little bit of information. Just not enough to act on."

"What do you mean?"

"They didn't have any memory from their time with Dominic, nor it seems did they have any memory from the past few years." He looked like he was still trying to figure out why. "On top of that, none of them had any Eleun powers, nor any sign that they did."

Scrunching up my face, I said, "I saw Mrs. Cortez's eyes in my dream. She had an ability."

Jayden held up his hands. "I believe you. We have evidence that she did. But she doesn't anymore."

"Evidence, how?" I asked. "If she has no memory, how do you know?"

He waved me into the meditation room. "I'll show you."

Inside a few people talked in the corner in hushed tones, and when I was sure that Likonan Harmsworth wasn't one of them, I sighed with relief.

He motioned to a wall of the room, and the sheets of paper with paintings on them scattered around it.

"One of the Entina Eleun we sent in undercover as Mrs. Cortez's son, can see what someone else has seen with their eyes. Even with their memory gone, the imprint of the image remains." Jayden led me over to the start of the line up to view the pictures. "You've already met Josh, who can pull images from others minds and turn them into art pieces, which is how we got these."

I nodded, amazed by the different abilities that kept appearing.

The paintings showed the story of Mrs Cortez, the woman from my dream. She and her children had been taken at night by a group of three people. I recognised the red-headed bulky guy from both occasions I'd faced Dominic.

They'd used Cassandra and Michael, her children, as bargaining chips to get her to co-operate, then taken the three of them in a dark van to a bushy location. It was hard to make out what she saw because it was so dark, but there was an outline of something in the distance when she'd first emerged from the van, the slight tinge of the rising sun lighting part of the image.

It vaguely registered something in me, but I couldn't place it, so moved onto the next images.

Mrs. Cortez and her children were placed in what looked like a dirt-lined room with bars along the only exit. The three of them didn't look well. Their clothes became dirtier and shabbier as the images went on, and they went from standing at the bars seemingly yelling, to just laying down and accepting their fate.

There were a few images of other people walking past their cell, and I was sure if we compared some of their faces to the ones from the news, we'd find a match.

The proof of Mrs. Cortez's power came in the form of her trying to attack those who escorted her out of the cell, to no avail, her wind element untrained and no contest for those who had been doing this for far longer.

Finally, the scene I'd witnessed play out in my dream appeared. I skimmed over them, having felt each and every emotion Mrs. Cortez had experienced at the time.

The last image was of a silver-haired man, in an army grey and green uniform.

"Who is that?" I asked, not placing him anywhere else in the images.

Jayden looked up from his inspection of a painting not far away.

"That's Commander Larsen," he said.

"Commander? Of what?"

Jayden pressed his lips together, as if reluctant to share this bit of information with me, before he said, "Of a government task force dedicated to hunting Eleun down. He hates us."

"There's someone else hunting us? I thought you said no one knew about us?"

So much for not letting the knowledge of us get out to the public eye…

"For the most part, they don't, but Commander Larsen happened across us years ago and we haven't been able to get close enough to him to wipe his memory of us. Now it's too far gone, and it wouldn't matter if we took those memories away, too many people know. They've kept it quiet for now, so we try to stay off his radar."

"So why is his face up here?" I pointed to him, taking in the older features and stern look.

"Because… we ran into him today," Jayden said.

"I take it that's bad," I said, not needing his response.

"With him involved with the missing persons' case, it means he knows the missing people are mostly Eleun. We're just going to have to be extra careful."

I swallowed hard, not liking the sound of that. I wanted to ask more about him, but Jayden changed the subject.

"Do the pictures line up with what you saw?"

I nodded, pointing to the few that mimicked my dream.

"These do, but the rest are new to me," I said, gravitating back toward the faint outline against the dawn.

Why did this image feel so familiar?

"What is it?" he asked. "Do you recognise something?"

"I'm not sure. It feels familiar… but I don't know why…" I trailed off as I moved to get a closer look.

Then something clicked into place, and I gasped.

Scanning the room, I found Josh sitting in the corner, fingers pressed against his temples as if he had a headache.

Walking toward him I called out.

"Josh, can you pull something from my memory?" I asked.

He looked to Jayden, a little confused by my request, then at Jayden's nod said, "As long as you've seen or visualised the image, then I can access it to bring it out."

My heart rate quickened at the prospect of a possible lead. "Got any paper?"

Jayden left us to retrieve a few sheets.

Josh locked eyes with me and said, "Focus on the image, and I'll find it. Close your eyes."

He placed a hand over my face.

It wasn't hard for me to bring up the image. I'd seen it so clearly many times now, though I had no idea why. However, it seemed there was a reason and I hoped beyond hope that it would lead us to where Dominic was hiding.

Josh lifted his hand from my face, and when I opened my eyes, the piece of paper was no longer blank.

Jayden saw the picture the same time I did and gasped.

His eyes shot to mine, then the painting behind me. He pulled it off the wall and compared the two.

I thanked Josh for his help, and he drifted off, not interested enough to stick around.

Before I could take the two paintings in, Jayden beckoned me to leave the room.

I followed him to a door to the left of the garage entrance, which turned out to be a storage room with rows upon rows of shelving running its length. The shelves were filled with camping equipment, food supplies, and weapons.

Jayden closed the door behind us, and made sure no one else was around, before pulling out both pages.

The page from my memory showed an image of the mountain I'd seen over and over in my dreams. It was tall and ominous, rising high above the treetops, one side leading to the sky in an unbroken incline, a slight divot in the middle showing off two rounded peaks. The first peak was broken by a dent as if an axe had cut it out, the side of the mountain declining to the ground. The bottom of the mountain was shielded from view by the numerous trees that surrounded it, their full green tops appearing as if they were moving.

"It's the same. This one's harder to see," he said, motioning to the darker picture. "But they clearly have the same outline."

I hadn't been crazy to think the same thing. And Jayden, knowing how I didn't want my dreams as public knowledge, had taken measures to keep it private.

"Which means, if we find this mountain, we'll be close to finding Dominic," Jayden said, flicking my dream picture.

I hadn't thought it out, but it seemed the logical explanation, seeing as I had no idea why I was dreaming this mountain, or how…

"You said Mrs. Cortez didn't show any sign of holding an element anymore. How so?" I asked.

"Her eyes were brown," he said.

A thought occurred to me.

"You don't think Dominic is trying to take people's abilities, do you?" I asked hesitantly.

Jayden looked up from the pages in front of him. "It's one of the theories, but nothing we've proven."

The thought was chilling. That it was even possible to take such an incredible power was scary. Binding someone's powers was bad enough, but taking them away entirely… I couldn't even imagine the process involved.

Jayden transferred the pages to one hand and reached out with his other to grip mine.

"It'll be all right. We'll figure this out," he said.

I nodded, though remained quiet. Jayden broke the silence by changing the subject.

"We should organise a proper session for tomorrow. I'm glad you enjoyed Elemucka. It's a good game to get you thinking on your feet and will come in handy for the Velta as well."

"Does this mean I don't have to do any more training tonight?" I asked hopefully.

He laughed. "Yes, you're off the hook, but only because I'm needed for a meeting with the Likonan. Give me an hour and I'll take you home."

He let me lead the way out of the room.

Libby and Naomi happened to be passing by on their way to the lift. Libby's eyes darted to the pages in Jayden's hand. He quickly folded them up and slipped them into his pocket.

Smiling politely to the ladies, he nodded to me once and headed for the Likonan's office.

Libby smirked at Naomi in a way that told me what they thought we'd been doing in the storage room, and I blushed.

I followed them to the lift, noting how hungry I was after my sporting ventures from earlier.

The silence was deafening as the doors closed in front of us.

"So…" Libby piped up behind me as she leaned against the opposite wall, her arms folded, eyes surveying me, "you and Jayden? Isn't he a bit old for you?"

I shot her a glare.

"There's nothing going on," I said, maybe a little too fast. "We were just talking."

"So that's what the kids are calling it these days, 'talking'" she said with air quotations. "I must remember that one."

Libby nudged Naomi and the two of them chuckled.

I remained quiet. They could think what they wanted. I didn't care.

My stomach satisfied and body ready to collapse in bed, I found myself in the passenger's seat of Jayden's car rounding the bend to my house.

As he pulled into the driveway, the headlights illuminated a figure pacing in front of Dad's white car.

Ryan's eyes snapped toward us.

Uh-oh.

I prayed the bright lights prevented him from seeing inside the car. Although he hadn't met my fake babysitting parents, it would be obvious that Jayden was not one of them. He was far too young and drove a car like this. Not exactly the car of a young family's father.

"Everything all right?" Jayden asked as I unclicked my belt.

"I hope so," I replied.

Giving me a roguish grin, he said, "Let me know if you need me to rough him up a bit."

I shot him a shocked look, and he chuckled.

"Kidding."

Frowning at him, I pushed the door open and stepped out.

The light faded as Jayden pulled out of the driveway, throwing Ryan and me into darkness.

"Hey, what are you doing out here?" I asked, though I could only just see him from the light on the veranda, the low tree that stood between us and the light blocking a lot of its brightness.

"Just thinking," he said, sounding at ease.

That was a good sign.

"Who was that?" He pointed at the now-vacant spot where Jayden had parked.

"A friend," I answered simply.

He inhaled deeply.

"Do you know him well? I've not seen him before," he said conversationally.

"We've known each other for a little while," I said, taking care not to disclose how little time that was, or why he might not have met him before now.

"You guys seem friendly. Is that the guy you were texting today in Math?"

He had assumed there was something going on between us. Apparently, it was in the water.

"Yes, but it's not what you think," I said. "He isn't *that* type of friend…"

I left it there, feeling slightly awkward over the subject, especially after our chat this morning. Talking about feelings and relationships wasn't my strong suit.

I liked Jayden, but did I see him as anything more than a friend? I hadn't given it a lot of thought.

But there was also Ryan and whatever was happening between us. I was surprised he had so quickly jumped to these conclusions, though seeing me in a strange man's car would have anyone wondering.

"So, what type of friend would he be then?" Ryan asked, guarded.

"The type that gives me a ride home when I need it, since we don't get to see each other a lot," I said, then bit my tongue at the lie.

He mulled that over before saying, "So there's nothing else going on between you?"

I felt as if he wanted to ask a heck of a lot more questions, but was refraining from doing so out of respect, giving me the benefit of the doubt.

I smiled, relieved we were getting somewhere. "I promise, we are just friends and I have no plans to change that."

"That's good to know," he said casually, though I was sure I could hear the relief in his voice. "How was babysitting?"

Glad for the subject change, I said, "It went well, but I'm exhausted."

That much was true.

A yawn escaped, and I covered my mouth, embarrassed it had snuck up on me.

Stepping closer, he snaked an arm around my waist and placed a hand on the small of my back, guiding me to the front door. "Let's get you inside before you fall asleep out here."

My insides doing somersaults over his proximity, I let him direct me, trying and failing to hide my stupid smile.

However, the reality of my situation came crashing down on me. If there was a chance at something more between us, starting it with half-truths wasn't exactly a good thing.

Ryan didn't deserve that treatment, and I began to re-think my decision to allow something to happen between us.

"I'm thinking sexy but cute," Nicole said, pulling my attention to her as she re-styled her hair to sit messily on top of her head.

It was Friday afternoon, and we were preparing for Nicole's long-awaited girls' night. Though my current position on her bed may not have shown my excitement, I was glad this was the plan for the evening and not the rigorous training regime Naomi and Katalya had drilled me on all week.

Between the early morning running sessions with Ryan, the full days at school, Reku and Eleun training in the evenings, and my lack of sleep thanks to the dreams that continued to plague my nights, I was physically and mentally spent. I'd resorted to dousing myself with water most days for the extra kick it gave me.

No matter how often Naomi told me my Eleun blood and lineage was helping my body to adapt to my new schedule, I needed this break.

"What are you wearing?" Nicole asked, as she shimmied out of her skirt.

I diverted my gaze, taking in the array of drawings that lined her bedroom walls. Nicole was the biggest fashion lover I knew, and that spurred on her love for designing clothes.

Most of the art pieces I'd seen before, but there were a few new additions that would look incredible once she got to working on them.

"T-shirt and pants," I said.

"Really?"

When I looked back, she wore grey shorts and a yellow singlet.

She looked at me, appalled at my choice, though I could see she wasn't surprised.

"You know Sophie and Catherine will bring their A-game. You should at least try a little bit. Besides, you never show off what you've got."

I chuckled. "It's not a fashion parade, and I'd rather be comfortable when I'm sleeping."

She placed her hand on her hip, one eyebrow raised as if wearing the right thing was the whole point of the night.

I tried not to let her comment about Sophie affect me.

I didn't hate Sophie, not really. She was just one of those people who got under my skin. That, and she had taken to latching herself onto Ryan's arm almost every day, as if the two of them were attached at the hip.

I'd almost convinced myself that Ryan was just appeasing her. After all, I was the one he had asked out, not her.

The doorbell rang and Nicole squealed.

"They're here." At the chest of drawers that stood along the same wall as the door, she rummaged around. "Get out of those clothes and into these ASAP!"

She threw two items of clothing at me, then skipped out the door to greet the others.

Sighing, I closed my eyes. I would get through this night without wanting to knock someone out. I'd already ditched Nicole once. I would tolerate Sophie for her.

I held up the clothes she'd given me, and my jaw dropped at the lack of material.

Knowing I would cop it later, I shoved the clothes back into her drawer and changed into my own blue tank top and long star-spotted pajama pants. I pulled my hair tie out so that my long brown strands hung loosely around my shoulders.

It didn't come close to what Nicole would expect, but it was as far as I was willing to go.

The night went as well as I expected, from chick-flicks while doing mani's and pedi's to eating junk food, to playing two truths and a lie and finally truth or dare.

I found myself yawning quite a bit as the last game started and doubted I would last much longer.

By the time my turn came, my head had already hit the pillow. I waved them off as I fell asleep.

I felt someone trying to wake me, but the dream I'd been pulled into was too deep, and it begged me to see what it had to show, promising me I wouldn't be disappointed.

CHAPTER
TWENTY-FIVE

Heeled shoes clicked through the foyer and, in my mind, my vision cleared from a haze. I found myself in the Havasek atrium.

It was getting late, curfew about to be enforced, but a group of five teenagers stood by the library chatting and laughing away. As I neared, I noticed they were all boys.

"Hey, boys" I said, and they all turned to stare at me. A few ogled me up and down as if they weren't sure if I was talking to them.

"What's happening? Trying to be rebels, I see… Staying up right to curfew. I like it."

It sounded like I was trying to fit in with them, make them feel comfortable or at the very least, that I liked them.

But it felt forced, as if I wished I was anywhere else.

A few of the boys nodded.

I lowered my voice. "I'll let you in on a secret. It's not that great. The Pina will just yell at you to hurry up. They're lame like that."

The boys groaned, and a few started for the staircase, taking my warning to heart.

"Drew," I called out, and the dark-skinned boy with jet black hair and crimson eyes turned around. "Mind if we talk?"

He looked around at the other boys, shrugging to say he didn't know why he was being singled out, then moved to stand in front of me. "What's up?"

"Walk with me," I said heading toward the lift.

He fell into step with me.

"How are you settling in?" I asked. "I see you've made some friends."

"Yeah, they're cool. I've seen some amazing stuff since coming here, but it's still… a little weird." He kept his gaze averted.

He scowled, like I was the last person he expected to care about his well-being.

"Yeah, it can be that way to begin with," I said. "You'll get used to it. Once you master your element, it'll feel amazing."

He slumped, face falling to a frown. "Yeah, whenever that's supposed to happen. So far, I can't even light a candle, let alone do half the tricks the other boys are doing."

A sliver of intrigue rippled through me. "You haven't been able to do anything yet?"

A note of sympathy entered my tone, however unwilling it sounded.

Drew shook his head. "Not a thing. Not even this Myundun thing. Sometimes I wonder if I even have powers."

Placing a hand on his shoulder, I said, "You know what you need? Fresh air."

He looked up at me. "But I'm not supposed to leave the building until I've mastered control, plus curfew?"

I bent down to his level.

"All work and no play are a bad combination." I winked, watching for his reaction. "What say I take you out for a drive? Surely there's something you've been dying to do."

He bit his lip, then caved.

"Well, I have been dying to eat a cheeseburger from McDonald's. I mean, that used to be our weekly eat out place and I do miss my parents, but… No, I'm not allowed. What if something happens and I hurt someone, or that Dominic guy finds me again?"

I smiled wryly.

"Come on, Drew. I was there when we rescued you, remember? I know how to fight off unfriendlies, and if you do lose control, I'm skilled in that area too." I nudged him in encouragement. "You deserve a break."

Drew looked back toward the stairs, still unsure.

"I promise we'll be back before eleven," I said.

"I guess if it's only an hour, sure, all right," he said, his eyes lighting up with the prospect of getting out of here.

"That's the spirit."

Leading him to the car park, I unlocked a red Honda Civic and motioned for him to get in. Rounding the car to the driver's side, I saw my reflection in the window.

Straight blonde hair that hung just past the shoulders, yellow eyes, and small waist.

I was Libby.

Trying to process what the revelation meant, I opened the car door and slipped into the front seat. Starting the car, I said, "You ready for some fun?"

Drew smiled with a quick nod, then the car was moving out of the garage and onto the road.

Libby turned on the radio, telling Drew to pick whatever station he wanted. He didn't have a preference, just turned to the local station with the latest music.

Libby sung along, trying to get Drew to join in, but he seemed to become a little edgy the longer the car moved.

Finally, he spoke up.

"Um, where exactly are we going? We should've hit a McDonald's by now." His sounded worried.

"Relax, we're almost there," Libby said, her tone far too chill.

Drew nodded slowly.

Libby nudged him with a smile.

"I've just got to get petrol first," she added, looking down at the dashboard.

She pulled into a petrol station and reached into the backseat, shuffling things around. "Where did I put that damn wallet? Oh, there it is."

She brought her hand to the front, but instead of holding a wallet, she had a needle the size of a table knife.

Drew leaned away. "What's that…"

Libby rammed the needle into Drew's neck, emptying the syringe.

Drew's head rolled then dropped to one side, his eyes closed, his breathing slow.

Libby removed the needle and threw it in the back.

"Ugh, longest drive ever," she said to no one, then added with little emotion, "Sorry, kid, but the boss needs you."

Pushing the door open, she rounded the car and filled it up with fuel.

Then she was back on the road, speeding down the highway toward a mountain range.

The road seemed to continue into nowhere as houses were left behind, and streetlights eventually stopped appearing. All that was left to see were black roads surrounded by trees and dark shapes.

I paid close attention to every single sign, trying to figure out where she was headed with the boy I had rescued.

Finally, after what seemed like hours, the car turned off the main road and down a dirt one, dust spraying everywhere as Libby sped along it. She slowed when she came to a small car park, which was empty except for a large white van.

Pulling up next to the van, she rubbed her eyes then pushed her door open.

"Man, I hate driving!" she complained to the night air, slamming the door behind her as she started around the car.

"There's no rule against you flying," a voice said through the dark, and I felt Libby smile as she stopped in her path. "You would get here quicker, leaving more time for… extra activities."

Libby turned around slowly, her head rolling to the side lazily as a form drew closer. "You know it would have taken everything for me to carry him here and I prefer to have plenty of energy when I see you."

Her voice was playful as he scooped her up in his arms, pressing her back against the boot of the car.

The light in the car was still on, illuminating the man's features enough for me to recognise him: red hair, red eyes, pale skin, and big broad shoulders. It was the fire-breathing Eleun I'd encountered outside the school and when rescuing Drew.

Despite my connection with Libby at this moment, I felt my heart speed up. Libby was working for Dominic. She'd been feeding him information about us and any new Eleun this whole time. She was no doubt the reason Dominic got to them before we did.

Before I could think too much about her role, the red-haired man brought his mouth down over Libby's, hard, and she responded in kind.

I was stuck in the mind of Libby, feeling everything she felt, both physically and emotionally, just like I'd been with Mrs. Cortez.

The man grasped and groped her, pressing his body hard against hers, running his hands all over her body.

I pushed and screamed, trying to get out of her mind, not wanting to see this.

A loud thud from the car sounded, followed by a yell. That paused the two in their frantic movements.

Libby groaned, and she kicked the car with her heel. "That was supposed to knock him out for another three hours. Way to ruin the moment."

The man laughed, reluctantly letting her go with a playful bite to her ear. He whispered, "We'll continue this later."

"Damn right we will," she said. She opened the car door and motioned to Drew. "He's all yours."

The red head bent down and picked up Drew, slinging his small body over his shoulder with ease.

Drew kicked and punched at the man, but it was to no avail.

Libby shook her head. "It's pointless, buddy. No one can hear you out here. Just accept your fate."

Even though Drew looked horrified, he still called for help.

I tried to tune out his voice and concentrate on the path the two were taking. They had torches out to light their way and were using them to guide a path through the forest.

To start, they stuck to the path, but part way down they turned off, following an unmarked trail through the trees.

It seemed they were just walking past tree after tree and not going anywhere at all until a flat surface rose in front of them. They stopped before it, torches searching in the darkness.

The man nodded to something a few metres away, then led the way to a large rock. Libby moved forward and knocked twice, not that anyone would have heard it. Not even Libby's ears seemed to pick up the noise, and her knuckles hurt from the hard rock.

The rock shifted to the left, grinding loud in the night air, revealing a gaping bright hole in the side of the incline.

Without hesitation, the two walked inside and the rock slid shut once more.

Drew had stopped trying to fight, staring in awe at the vast cavern he'd just been carried into.

It was another sight from previous visions. Crates and containers filled the bottom half of the cavern, walkways and doors littering the surrounding walls. They were inside a mountain. They'd cut their hide-out from the inside of the mountain… just like Havasek. Only this still had the rough interior that came with digging through dirt. Havasek had at least decorated.

Libby and the man manoeuvred their way through the cluttered ground until they came upon two men.

One turned to them: Dominic.

He smiled at the sight of Drew.

"One untrained Eleun, as ordered." The man holding Drew dumped him to the ground in a heap.

"Very good, Marco," Dominic said, then when Libby coughed, he added. "Yes, you too, Libby."

Dominic squatted to Drew's level. Drew looked up at him, his eyes widening in fear.

"Oh, don't be scared, boy. You're here for a great purpose, one that will change the tides in this war." Dominic grinned widely. "For now, you might as well get comfortable."

He looked to the man he'd been talking to before Drew's arrival. "Take him to a room."

The man hauled Drew to his feet. "Come on, boy."

Dominic nodded to Marco and Libby, then headed further into the maze.

Marco turned back to Libby, a wicked grin caressing his face. "Now, where were we?"

I had a view of Libby moving toward him as the vision ended, and I heard other voices.

"Wake up, Paige, please. You're making a racket," a voice said.

My eyes slid open, my breath coming out in gasps, my forehead covered in sweat.

I moved to wipe it away but found my arms restrained by my sides.

Nicole gripped my wrists, a worried look across her face.

"Oh, thank goodness." She released my arms. "You are one strong girl."

Blinking, I took in the rest of the room. It was dark except for a light in the far corner, not enough to brighten everything but plenty to make out the five worried faces.

Everyone looked bleary-eyed and fearful at what they'd just witnessed, unsure whether to call someone or ride it out.

"What happened?" My voice was hoarse, and I cleared my throat.

"Um, screaming and thrashing about like a crazy person is what happened," Catherine said from across the room. She was half out of bed, closest to the lamp by the window. "Seriously, some of us need our beauty sleep!"

Ignoring her, I turned to Nicole who gave me an apologetic grimace.

Shutting my eyes again, I sucked in a few deep breaths, trying to calm my racing heart as I processed what I'd just witnessed.

I understood now why I'd been privy to the strange dreams and visions. For whatever reason I was seeing them, it wasn't by accident.

I was being led to the source of our problems and now I knew exactly how to get there.

Sitting up right, I scooped up my phone from the ground and hurried away from my crowded bed.

Entering the bathroom, I locked the door behind me.

Fumbling, I tried to find the right buttons. It began to ring.

Sitting on the toilet lid, I waited, tapping my foot against the tiles. The line continued to ring.

Come on, come on, pick up!

Jayden answered on the fifth ring, and I could have kissed him.

"Jayden, you need to come get me, now!" I said into the phone. "We have to go get him. He's in trouble, and I know where to find him."

"Whoa, whoa, slow down," he said, his voice groggy as if he'd just woken up. "Get who, from where?"

"Drew, they took him, well, Libby took him, and now Dominic's got him, and I know where the hide-out is and we have to go now, or we might never see him again!" I stood, gesturing, as if that was going to help.

"What do you mean? Drew's here. Libby should be too. It's the middle of the night. Are you sure you're okay?"

I grunted. "No, they're not!" Something occurred to me. "Wait, are you at Havasek? You can check to make sure they're still there. Please, you must check, because I just had the craziest dream and I'm pretty sure I'm one hundred percent right."

He groaned on the other end. "Fine, I'll check, but if you're wrong, you owe me big time. I've barely had any sleep this week and you woke me up from the first solid five hours I've had." There was sound as he got out of bed. "I'll call you back."

The line went dead, and I collapsed on the toilet seat.

I felt bad for waking him like this. He'd been M.I.A. all week, working to find a lead to Dominic, which left me to find my own way to and from training and home. The times I had seen him, he'd seemed distracted.

There was a knock on the door.

"You okay, Paige?" Nicole asked.

"Yeah, coming out now," I said, reaching back to flush the toilet. I ran the tap as well and splashed water onto my face, using my element to soak it in to regenerate me.

I would need as much energy as possible for what was to come.

Opening the door, I emerged slowly.

Everyone was still up, though Sophie, Catherine, and Tanya were lying on their beds. Isabella and Nicole stood by the door waiting.

"Everything all right?" Nicole asked again, her expression wary.

I smiled, putting everything I had into it. "Yeah, fine. Sorry I woke you all."

I didn't need to look at Sophie to feel her rolling her eyes as she let out a low, "Oh, she's sorry… way to freak us out."

She slid under the covers and turned over.

Nicole smiled. "Don't mind her. We've barely been asleep for two hours. We're all tired."

I smiled apologetically. "I really am sorry."

"Don't worry about it," Isabella said. "It's all in the fun of sleep overs, right?"

"I guess, but I might get some air for a bit," I said, motioning to the front door.

Nicole said, "Need me to come?"

I shook my head, already starting toward the door. "I'll be fine. Thanks though."

They watched me the whole way out. Sighing, grateful to be out of surveillance, I dropped to the first step, leaning back against the wood, running everything I'd seen in the dream through my mind.

There was no way my subconscious made it all up. The dream felt too real and there were parts that made total sense now that I looked back on it.

Libby had fought the red headed Marco when we'd rescued Drew, but we'd only seen the two of them for the first part before Libby flew him out of sight.

What had they really been doing?

I shook my head, not wanting to know.

Then there was the look Libby had given Jayden and me the night we'd come out of the storage room. Her eyes had gone straight to the pictures as if she needed to know what was on them.

My phone buzzed in my lap.

"Tell me I'm wrong?" I said when I answered, willing to give Jayden his chance to prove it.

There was a pause, then he said, "Neither of them are here, but that doesn't mean they've gone to Dominic. I mean, it is a pretty big theory, Paige. How sure are you?"

I growled. "I'm so sure I will do an extra hour of training for the next month if I'm wrong."

"Okay, that's not necessary. What did you see?"

"We don't have time for this. I know where they are. Can you please just come get me and I'll take you there?"

"It's four o'clock in the morning, Paige; we need a plan. I need to tell the Likonan. We can't just run in there and hope they'll hand over everyone peacefully." He sounded far calmer than I felt.

"But you want proof, right?" I pressed back desperately. "If I take you there, then you'll have it, and in the meantime, you can tell the Likonan you've got a solid lead, so she can make plans."

Jayden was silent.

"Okay, fine," he said at length. "I'll come by your place in an hour. Let me just set things in motion. Can you at least give me a location to leave with Monica, just in case things go bad?"

Thankful the signs had been so clear I said, "Dual Top Mountain in the Charleston National Park. It's about two hours away, and I'm not at home. I'll text you the address."

"Got it, see you soon."

Putting the phone on the ground next to me, I ran my hands through my hair, relieved, then thought about my next problem. Glancing back over my shoulder, I saw that the lamp had been turned off, but I could still hear voices.

How was I to get away from them?

Figuring it might be best to just pretend I was okay, I re-entered the house.

Quietly, I moved to my bed and slid back under the covers.

Nicole whispered a hushed goodnight, then everything was quiet once more.

My heart was racing way too fast to fall asleep, which served my purpose, but it also meant I had to wait for everyone else to drift off. It felt like hours before I could clearly make out five slow and easy breathing sleepers, but when I checked the time, it had only been twenty-five minutes.

As quietly as I could, I crept to Nicole's room and changed into more appropriate clothing, thankful I'd had PE yesterday and had packed my runners. With leggings and T-shirt on, I scribbled a note for Nicole on a piece of paper, leaving it on her dresser for later. It was far from what she deserved but it would have to do.

Grabbing my bags, I tip toed back out of the room and over to the front door. Carefully, I turned the handle and slipped out, then eased the door shut behind me.

Jayden hadn't arrived yet, so I dropped the bags in the gutter and sat next to them, my mind wandering to Drew.

Why take him now and not earlier? Libby would have had plenty of time to lure him out since we'd rescued him, so why now?

What were they planning on doing to him?

CHAPTER
TWENTY-SIX

Headlights lit up the street and I squinted as Jayden's silver car pulled up in front of me.

Throwing my bags in the back, I ducked in the front. Jayden took off before my belt was even on.

"Nice morning for a stroll," he said, his features stern, all business. "So, are you going to tell me what you saw?"

I explained everything I'd seen from the beginning.

Hours later we turned off the main road and onto a familiar dirt one, and I leant forward looking for a place to park the car.

We'd agreed to leave the car a little distance from the car park, hopefully, to avoid Dominic and his followers finding it, then walk the rest of the way in.

"Over there," I pointed to the right, toward a bunch of trees that would help conceal the car.

Jayden veered off the dirt road, and a pained look clouded his features as the car bounced up and down. He pulled in behind the line of trees.

The sun was only just starting its ascent into the sky, giving us a little light to walk by.

"We're only going to scope the area out," Jayden said, as he killed the engine. "Once we have proof, we call the Likonan and wait for back up, got it?"

He'd accepted everything I'd told him about my dream, though I felt that perhaps some part of him still didn't believe me.

"Yes, sir." I saluted. "Orders heard and received."

"I'm serious, Paige."

"I heard you," I replied in a more understanding tone, just glad to be headed to Drew.

"Just wanted to make sure we were on the same page," Jayden said. "Think you can guide us from here?"

I smiled. "Maybe. It wasn't exactly easy to see after the drive, but if all else fails, just head to the bottom of the mountain and walk till you find the big rock…"

He didn't look encouraged but followed my lead anyway. After sending our current location to the Likonan. Just in case.

Up until this point, every turn, road, and sign had been etched into my mind. Whoever, or whatever, had shown me the dream had made sure I remembered how to get here.

Keeping the dirt path in sight, we trekked through the bush a few metres away, staying out of sight, which was eventful given it wasn't a smooth path, with trees and shrubbery we had to navigate around.

By the time we reached the car park, the sun was high enough to light everything around us, and I was grateful it wasn't summer.

The white van from my vision was still in its place, along with another car I didn't recognize at the other end of the parking lot. When we rounded the van, Libby's car came into sight.

Jayden gritted his teeth, his fists clenching. This was the first bit of solid proof he'd seen that Libby had in fact betrayed us. Clearly, he'd been hoping for a different outcome.

If I was being honest, I had too.

I placed a reassuring hand on his shoulder.

Jayden shook his head, not wanting to discuss it, and motioned for me to keep moving.

From the car park, my memory got a bit hazy. It had been dark as Libby, Marco, and Drew had made their way to the entrance with only torches to guide them. It would be anyone's guess where they had turned off the path and headed for the large rock that was the door.

I prayed my instincts, or some other intuition would kick in as we started along the walking track. By the time I'd registered the path had begun to incline too much, we'd gone too far, so we had to double back about twenty minutes before deciding to go off-track in search of the rock.

It wasn't easy, considering the stakes we were up against. We were constantly on the lookout for any sign or sound of approaching feet or voices. At every twig or rustle we dropped out of sight, our Eleun on high alert ready to attack if we were caught.

We trampled through the bush for two hours before we were ready to give up.

I plonked onto a fallen tree trunk, my legs aching from all the walking.

"I need a drink," I said, wishing I'd brought a water bottle along. It wasn't the first time I'd said it this morning, but now I really meant it.

Jayden leaned up against a tree. "Ditto. Are you sure we're in the right place? It could've been the other direction."

That had also been asked a few times today.

I sighed. "I'm not sure of anything right now. I'm exhausted."

We'd basically walked the entire base of the mountain, continually staring up at the cliff face hoping to catch sight of something that would lead us in the right direction. But each time we got closer, I concluded that we'd gone too steep and had to trek back down to start again.

"Maybe it's time to call it," Jayden said. Although it wasn't a particularly hot day, he had red cheeks and looked tired. I doubted I looked any better.

I scanned the area again, willing something to appear. All around us were trees, grass, and blue sky, along with the sound of birds twittering high in their nests. I groaned in dismay.

The fatigue was catching up and being on constant alert wasn't making things any easier.

I was about to agree that we needed to give up for now. A sound caught my attention. I slipped off the tree trunk to hide.

The sound came again: laughter, in a man's deep voice.

"Oh, I like that one," the man said from out of sight. "Be sure to pass it on to the boss next time you see him. He could use a good laugh."

Jayden had hidden behind the tree he'd been leaning against and was peering through the branches trying to get a look at the owner of the voice.

The next words became muffled, the voices heading away from us.

Jayden motioned for me to follow, and we hurried through the undergrowth in the direction the sounds had come from. We made a lot of noise, but no one heard us.

The owners of the voices stopped just out of sight, but their words were clear enough once more.

Hidden behind a tree stump and a large rock, we peered around to see our guides.

It was two men, one taller than the other by a head, and with a dark mustache and beard. The other had sandy hair a little on the shaggy side.

The bearded guy ran his hands over what looked to be moss and grass that had sprouted over something.

"Where is that damn stone?" he muttered, continuing to search.

The shorter one shrugged. "I dunno, I can never find it either. Beats me why they have to camouflage it. No one is going to come out here."

"Ah ha!" the taller one said, and he stood back.

The moss and grass vanished, leaving a large stone the size of a truck in plain view.

I sucked in a breath.

How had he done that?

Seeing as there seemed to be a lot of things I was yet to learn about this life, I didn't ponder on it.

The man tapped the rock twice with his knuckles, like Libby had done, and waited. The rock began to move to one side. It was as loud as it had been in my dream as it shifted.

The two men entered the cave before the rock slid back into place as if nothing had happened, the moss and grass reappearing once more.

I tipped my head, trying to figure it out but coming up blank.

"An illusion…" Jayden said. "They must have an Entina Eleun who can create illusions, clever…"

Well, that made sense.

Moving safely behind the tree stump, I turned to him. "So, do you think you can move that thing? I mean rock is your specialty."

He crouched down. "It would draw too much attention. Whoever is moving that rock on the inside would feel it shifting. They'd know we were here, and the element of surprise would be gone. I think we've gone as far as we can. We need to re-group."

As I peered around the stump, my heart sank a little. Drew was in that cave, along with who knew how many other captives, and I was about to walk away, when we were so close.

"Come on," Jayden whispered, scuttling back the way we'd come.

Reluctantly, I followed until we were a safe distance away and could see the mountain path once more.

Stopping, Jayden took out his phone and began to type.

I still felt very exposed and wondered why he didn't just wait till we were back at the car. Anyone could come across us here.

"That's one long text message," I said. "Sure it can't wait?"

He shook his head. "I don't want to risk it. The Likonan needs to know what we found. She'll want to get a team out here as fast as possible."

His fingers moved madly across the screen until he finally stopped.

"Damn it! No signal. We'll have to go farther down the track."

We started down the path, Jayden raising and lowering his phone to try and catch a few bars of signal, his frustrated noises telling me he wasn't having any luck.

We kept going until a distinctive click sounded behind Jayden, something that was not a nature sound. We both stopped.

"Now, that's a funny dance. I'm not sure I was ever taught that one," a female voice said from behind us.

Another click issued, and my heart rate spiked.

The clicking had sounded an awful lot like a gun safety being released, and although I'd not had a lot to do with any real guns, somehow, I knew that was what it was.

Swallowing deeply, I peered from the corner of my eye at Jayden, whose jaw was tight.

We slowly turned around, coming face to face with the end of two gun-barrels, each pointed at our heads.

Involuntarily, I took a step back, but the woman in front of me followed.

"I wouldn't do that if I were you," she said, pressing the tip to my forehead, grinning. "I would love to use this."

Freezing, I looked past the gun to the slim, dark-skinned girl with purple-coloured eyes. I'd not seen her before, but she looked older than me, and in control of the weapon in her hands.

The man in front of Jayden wasn't tall by any sense, but he was well built. He had yellow eyes and brown hair, and I recognised him from when Dominic had chased and cornered me outside the school. He'd been there along with Dominic and Marco.

Then a third person stepped out from behind a tree, his eyes down cast as he flicked a bug off his wrist. I didn't need to see his face to know who it was.

"I guess you were bound to find us eventually," Dominic said. "My only question is... how?"

He looked up, and his gaze rested on me. "Why bring a rookie?"

He walked around my captor, green eyes fixed on me, and stopped at my side, surveying me. I squirmed despite myself.

"Though I did wonder the same thing the last time we met. Someone so young and new to our way of life, being sent out on such a dangerous assignment… What were those crazy fools thinking? Even if you are Remana." He was smiling as if he knew something. "Then I saw what you could do and realised you weren't just some untrained girl after all. There is something special about you, isn't there?"

He walked around, his smile widening, though I didn't follow for fear of trigger-happy Jane in front of me.

I didn't like the way he was looking at me. It made me feel like a prize to be won, as if all his dreams had come true at once.

What was he so intrigued about?

Dominic turned to Jayden with a scowl. "You, however, are just a pain to deal with. Always showing up at the wrong time. I should shoot right here."

My heart plummeted. I felt around for any source of water in case I needed to act.

I found…nothing.

That couldn't be right. Panic rose inside me as I tried to figure out what was wrong.

Why couldn't I feel anything?

I'd been consciously aware of my powers all morning, had felt the constant pulsing all around me and now… nothing?

What was going on?

"But," Dominic said to Jayden, his wicked grin broadening. "You could still be of use."

Jayden clenched his fists.

"Oh, I see you're angry," Dominic said. "I bet you just want to hurl something at me, cause the rocks to crumble at my feet and bury me in the ground, am I right?"

Jayden didn't say anything, and Dominic laughed, the girl in front of me joining in with a chuckle.

"But you can't, can you?" He shifted his face right into Jayden's personal space. "You can't feel a thing. It's almost as if there are no elements around, but wait…"

He stepped back, arms spread wide. "You can see there are. Rocks at our feet, wind blowing through the trees. There's even a stream not far from here, but why can't I feel the elements?" he asked dramatically.

He took another step back, enjoying his solo conversation on our behalf.

Neither of us spoke. I didn't understand what Dominic was getting at. Why couldn't we feel our elements?

Dominic smiled and placed a hand on the woman's shoulder.

"I've spent a lot of time picking my followers, and it's not easy to find the ones who will follow me without hesitation, but this beauty is one of my favourites." He squeezed her shoulder then dropped his hand. "Jasmine here has the ability to block Eleun gifts. Of course, it also blocks my own power, but as long we're prepared…"

He motioned to the guns to finish his sentence.

He spoke about his followers as if they were prized puppies and not people.

The look in his eyes when he'd seen me earlier made more sense.

Jasmine merely smiled, and her companion showed no emotion at all.

The perfect guard dog.

My mind reeled over the advantage Dominic had with such an ally, especially since most of his biggest enemies would be counting on their elements instead of other weapons.

This didn't bode well for any sort of reinforcement that might come looking for us. That was, if Jayden's message had even gone through.

"So now that we've cleared the air and decided that escape is futile," Dominic said, his carefree manner changing to get back to business. "Shall we skip to the unpleasantries? Chris, Jaz…"

I barely had time to register what he said before both Jasmine and the man swung their guns at our heads, hard.

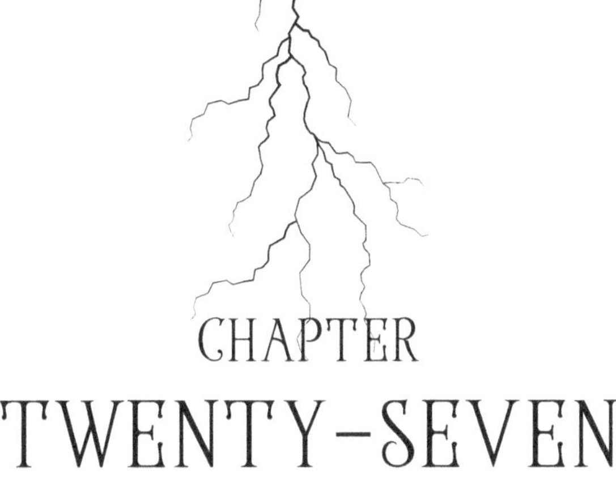

CHAPTER
TWENTY-SEVEN

An aching pain pounded inside my head.

I groaned.

Pain flared in my right side as I tried rolling over and found more hard ground. I opened my eyes to stare up at an uneven brown ceiling.

It took me a moment to realize I was looking at dirt… on the ceiling?

Brown roots curled and disappeared all over the interior, sinking and re-appearing like a sea snake moving amidst water, a few patches of green appearing as new life began to sprout.

Blinking to make sure I wasn't dreaming, I turned to look at the walls and found the same texture surrounding me. We were underground. Or more accurately, in the cave I'd dreamt about so many times.

Alarmed, I sat up.

The room was probably only three metres wide each side and it was completely bare, except for another body. Jayden.

Scrambling to all fours, I crawled toward him. Hesitating slightly, fearful that he was dead, I rolled him over and sighed with relief that he was still breathing.

"Jayden!" I whispered, shaking his shoulder.

He didn't respond.

It took a few more attempts before he finally started to come around. Groaning, he lifted a hand to rub the top of his head. He had a purplish bruise on his face, and I winced, knowing I held a matching one, if the pain was anything to go by.

"Where are we?" he asked, blinking rapidly, not attempting to rise.

"I'm not sure, maybe underground?"

Finally, he got up, albeit slowly, and his gaze landed on the wall behind me.

I turned around, and my stomach knotted.

"A cell might be more appropriate," he said.

Metal bars blocked our only exit.

Together we approached them, my muscles protesting.

Cautiously, I looked out from our lodgings, wondering if anyone was keeping watch. The dirt flooring extended a little beyond the bars, creating a walkway around the walls. Beyond that there was open air leading to a large chasm falling away from the edge.

Floodlights had been set up around the cavern, allowing us to see other rooms lining the walls next to ours, high up off the ground, though we couldn't make out if anyone resided in them.

Across the open space, on the opposite side, wound more walkways, layered like a tiered cake, doorways and rooms set in between the spaces. People moved in and out of them freely.

In the vast space between the walled sides was a maze of large containers, crates, and boxes stacked everywhere, with a walkway weaving from one end to the other. The enormous, exposed underside of the mountain loomed over everything.

The area toward the back held expensive-looking equipment, along with tables and monitors to observe whatever went on down there.

A scuff against the dirt flooring caught our attention. We backed away as Chris, the man who'd held Jayden at gun-point, walked past. Hands behind his back, Chris glanced inside our cell before continuing along the walkway.

Not underground. We were inside the mountain.

"Well, at least we can confirm we found the right place," Jayden said optimistically, if dryly.

I rolled my eyes. "Yeah, but will the others get the message?"

"Not that I saw, but I dropped the phone before they knocked me out, so it could've sent before they found it."

I let out a hopeless breath. The cavalry wouldn't be showing up to save us.

"What I wouldn't give to find out what Dominic is doing down there," Jayden said.

"Don't wish too hard. You might just find out." I snorted.

"I don't like the way he looked at you earlier," he said a little softer. His head was bowed but he was still looking at me. "It was… possessive, like you might be the answer to something he needs."

"You sound a little protective there. Should I be worried about you too?" I smiled and he chuckled half-heartedly.

"I just mean I'm not looking forward to seeing what he has planned. If it's anything like you've explained from your dreams, then it can't be good."

I looked away, my mind going back over everything I'd experienced in those visions: the screams, the calls for help, the looks on the faces of people Dominic had chosen.

No, it wasn't going to be pleasant.

A shiver ran down my spine, along with a feeling of fear and dread at what I'd brought us into.

I pushed off the wall. "We need to get out of here. I'm not sticking around for torture hour."

I tried to shake the bars loose, but they held firm. Giving them a frustrated push, I turned back to Jayden. "This place is probably surrounded by rock. Can you shift some of it to make a way out?"

I could sense water nearby but refrained from using my gifts in case it alerted someone.

"Maybe," he said. "But it's going to make a lot of noise. We'll have to be quick."

Crouching down, he dug his hands into the soil and closed his eyes. He tensed as if trying to shift something heavy… but nothing happened.

He opened his eyes. "That's weird. Why didn't it move?"

Closing his eyes again, he tried once more, but again nothing happened. Standing up, he looked around the room, as if it would explain things.

"You don't think that girl, Jasmine, is still blocking us, do you?" I asked, turning back to the bars to try to find her.

"That's a pretty big range if she is," Jayden said absently, his mind elsewhere as he inspected the bars. "For some reason, I don't think Dominic would want to be left totally defenceless in case of an attack, or have his best weapon completely drained when he needed it most."

I wondered what was so interesting about the bars. It was just metal.

"But they have guns, so they're not defenceless," I pointed out as he rapped his knuckles against a bar. A ringing sound vibrated down its length, and he placed his ear to the bars.

"True, but like any Eleun, their first response would be to use their gifts," he said. "It's in our nature. I think he'd still want full access to it even if he wasn't under attack."

I shook my head, annoyed he was still knocking on the bars.

"Okay, but that doesn't explain why our gifts aren't working… can you please stop that and concentrate?" I threw up my hands. "The ringing is really annoying."

He stood back, eyes still on the bars. "How did he get his hands on that?"

I stared at him, completely lost. "Excuse me?"

Jayden pointed to the bars. "Those have Valiquim in them. That's why our elements don't work."

I blinked twice. "Val… what?"

"I forget you haven't been around long. Valiquim. It's a metal from Marcious. It blocks us from using our elements. Mostly it was used for cells like this." He motioned to our prison. "Havasek has cells just like it underneath the Rekulanna."

I scowled at the bars. "How come I've never heard of it till now? I mean, couldn't you have used it to stop my crazy outbursts?"

"I guess it never came up." He shrugged. "And no… well, I guess we could have, but it would have only delayed the process and the energy would have built up quite a lot, causing even more damage. It's better if you're trained and taught to use the element first before resorting to something like this."

I nodded glad I hadn't caused anything worse than a few storms.

"They couldn't have picked a nicer name, or easier?"

Jayden snorted. "I heard once that they gave it such a harsh name because it suppressed what was in our deepest nature, wielding the elements, and they didn't want to reward its presence by naming it something nice."

"Right…"

"I'd like to know how he got so much of it, though," Jayden said. "It's not like it's a common metal on Earth. In fact, it's rare."

"What do you mean?" I asked.

"There was only so much brought along in the ships that landed from Marcious and as far as I'm aware, it was all used for cells at Havasek. It's usually kept under lock and key… literally." He gripped a bar to emphasise his point.

"Well, clearly, he's gotten some, which ruins our plans for escape," I said. "So, what's plan B?"

He sighed. "I don't know… wait till they let us out and make a run for it?"

I banged my head against the bar, then regretted it. "Fantastic. Looks like torture hour is coming after all."

Moving to the dirt and weed wall, I fell against it with a sigh. Sliding down to the ground, I pulled my knees up to my chest, hugging them close.

"Guess we might as well get comfortable." Jayden stood beside me.

The morning's events caught up to me, and I inhaled sharply.

"Are you okay?" Jayden asked, looking down at me.

"Yeah. Although I may not be when my parents arrive at Nicole's house to see I'm missing."

"You didn't leave a message to ask to stay another night at your friends? Where does your friend think you are, for that matter?"

"I left a note saying I went home early. She would have been okay with it after my crazy nightmare that scared everyone, but now…"

I left it hanging.

"Ouch, that is a problem, but…" He paused until I looked up at him. Caution filled his eyes. "You know we have a fix for that. Memory modification…"

I cringed.

I hadn't liked it the first time they modified my parents' minds and was intent on not resorting to it again. But maybe I wouldn't have a choice. I didn't want to commit to anything, and seeing as we weren't leaving anytime soon, I diverted his question.

"What about you? Do you have anyone who will miss you?"

Letting his head fall back against the wall, he said. "Not really. My mum died when I was young. Cancer…"

"Oh, I'm sorry. I shouldn't have asked," I said, but he shook his head.

"No, its fine. It was a long time ago and I've come to terms with it."

"What about your dad? Any siblings?" I asked, hesitant, though curious all the same. He had never talked about his family before.

"No siblings, and my dad wouldn't miss me if I disappeared for a month, so all good on that front," he said in a rush.

Curiosity spiking, I couldn't help but ask. "Why not? Doesn't he call to check up on you?"

He huffed out a laugh.

"No, he doesn't call to check up on me." He slid down the wall to sit next to me. "Not unless I've got important documents that he needs, but even then, he has other people to do that for him."

I scrunched my face up, not following.

"It's a long story, but I work for my dad's company. It's his first and only love, well, after my mother died, that is." His tone turned sour at the mention of his father. "After I discovered my abilities, and Havasek found me, they became my family. The only reason he keeps any type of contact is because he wants me to run the company one day when he's not around, keep it in the family name and all."

"Do you want to run the company?" I asked slowly.

Dropping his head between his knees, he shrugged. "I don't know. It's not exactly my thing. But he's the only family I have left, and I don't want to lose him, no matter how cold-hearted he is. Plus, he can be very persuasive when he wants to be."

I wanted to ask him what that meant, but I knew he wouldn't answer me, so instead asked. "What do you want to do with your life then?"

"Havasek," he said simply, with a smile that told me he held a great deal of affection for the place, though I already knew that. "They've been more of a family to me than my father ever was. On top of that, it's a worthy cause, helping people who can't help themselves, building a place where we can be safe. What's not to like about it?"

I had my reservations about the place with all its rules and secrets, but ultimately, he was right. It was a good place, a haven for those who needed it. The rules, however annoying, were put in place so we could exist alongside humans.

I took his hand and squeezed gently. "It is a good cause. I don't know about anyone else, but I appreciate the work you do for Havasek."

He smiled, squeezing my hand back. "Thanks."

I sit in a chair. People surround me, eyes watching my every move. They expected something from me, something I'm unwilling to give them.

One of the people points to a figure curled up on the ground just a few metres away. If I don't give them what they want this person is going to get hurt.

I care for this person. They are important to me.

He is important.

I can't make out his face, but as I stare at him, two of the group beat him, grunts and groans forced from him.

I scream for them to stop, tears flowing from my eyes.

How could I have let this happen? He doesn't deserve it.

The figure rolls over and I recognise his face…

My eyes snapped open, and lurched forward, dust rising into the air from my movement.

Sweat beaded my face, my breath coming out in gasps.

"Paige, what's wrong?" Jayden stood from his seated position against the wall.

I wiped a dirty and sweaty hand across my forehead, trying to get a hold of myself.

"You're, okay?" I managed shakily, speaking out loud what my mind was having a hard time grasping. I closed my eyes, relieved. "You're okay."

Jayden looked at me curiously. "Of course, I'm okay. We haven't moved since we got here."

My hands were still shaking, my breathing erratic, as I took him in, willing my mind to believe what was before me.

Jayden, concern, and fear on his features, crawled to my side. I fell into his arms, resting my head against his shoulder, his warm embrace finally convincing my mind that this was real and not the dream I'd just seen.

"It's all right." He rubbed a hand across my back and as, if having read my mind, said, "It was a dream. You're awake now. Just breathe."

The presence of his warm body helped, the continuous movement of his hand a soothing remedy. Soon I was breathing normally, my shaking hands easing.

"Sorry," I mumbled, not wanting to move away. In this dank, dirty place, it was nice to be near something real and alive.

"It's all right," he repeated. "Do you want to talk about it?"

I didn't want to tell him what I'd seen, so shook my head.

"Paige, you don't have to hide anything from me. We're in this together now. You can tell me anything."

Remaining quiet, I prayed for him to let it go, but he nudged me back to look me in the eyes.

"Even if it's bad, I want to know," he said, holding my gaze.

My resolve caved.

"I think we were down there." I pointed beyond the bars, the memory still vivid. "I was in a chair, and they wanted me to do something… I'm not sure what, but when I didn't, they started beating you."

I said the last bit slowly, waiting for his reaction.

He barely moved, continuing to stare into my eyes, displaying no anger or even fear of what I'd said, even though he knew full well that my dreams often came true.

He was no longer seeing me, his mind drifting elsewhere.

"So, is this supposed to come true?" he asked. "Or is it just a 'could happen' dream?"

I shook my head, uncertain.

"Well, whatever happens, whether it comes true or not, you need to do what you think is right. If it means I get beaten then so be it, understood?"

His whole face was dead serious. Anger flashed through me.

"No!" I pulled back from him. "I won't let them hurt you!"

His mouth turned to a hard line but before he could say anything, another voice interrupted.

"Well, that will make my job very easy."

CHAPTER
TWENTY-EIGHT

ominic came to a stop outside the bars. He was dressed in long dark pants designed for the outdoors and a light loose-fitted grey T-shirt.

"I was expecting more of a fight," Dominic said, replying to my comment meant for Jayden. "But as long as I get what I want, I'll take it."

Jasmine, Marco, and Chris stood to Dominic's left. Jasmine smirked at our accommodation, clearly enjoying seeing us behind bars. Chris looked bored, like he was fifteen minutes out from clocking off his shift to go home.

Jayden pushed to his feet. I followed a little slower.

"What do you want?" Jayden snarled, leaning slightly in front of me.

Dominic smiled. "A bit protective, I see. Why do you assume the worst? I only want to talk."

Jayden spat an unamused laugh.

Dominic leaned back, observing us like we were two priceless pieces of art on display. "I'm not going to lie. Your presence here worries me. Unless of course you're here alone…"

He pulled something out of his pocket.

Jayden's phone.

"Your distress message didn't go through." He smiled knowingly.

My heart sank. We really were on our own.

No one was coming to save us.

I stepped up beside Jayden, taking one of his hands in mine.

Whether it was for me or him, I didn't know.

"Now that's settled, let's move on to more important things." Dominic's eyes lit up and, taking a step back, he motioned to the bars.

Chris stepped forward with a set of keys and unlocked the door. It creaked open. He, Marco, and Jasmine headed straight for us.

We backed up, my heart pounding in my chest.

Jasmine's hips swayed from side to side, her features neutral. Marco grinned, eager to get his hands on us.

When our backs hit the wall there was nothing else we could do.

"Tie them up," Dominic said.

"Turn around," Marco said to Jayden and me, pulling zip-ties out of his pocket.

When neither of us obeyed, Marco's smile broadened. "I'd be happy to knock you out and drag you along the ground..."

Jayden's mouth pressed into a hard line and slowly, he turned around. I followed suit.

My arms were pulled roughly behind my back. I winced as the zip ties were yanked tight. We were spun back around and instructed to walk.

Jasmine walked in step with me while Marco stayed behind with Jayden. As we exited the cell Dominic took the lead and we followed him to the end of the walkway.

I peered into the adjoining cells as we were guided by them, and my heart sank.

Children huddled in the corner of one cell, five or six of them at a quick count, ages ranging from five to late teens. They didn't look hurt from this distance, but they cowered as we passed.

Most of the other cells only held one or two people, some asleep on the floor, others propped up against the walls or pacing the small space, all eyeing us warily. A lot of them sported bruises and nasty wounds, and they were all dirty and looked like they needed a decent meal.

I glared at Dominic, wanting to break out of my restraints and make him pay for harming these people.

Reaching a gap between the ledge we stood on and the one that started back up along the other side, we stopped.

How were we going to get down to the ground?

I stumbled back when the ground trembled beneath us. A large section of dirt, weeds, rock, and grass appeared, filling in the gap perfectly.

Dominic stepped onto it, and we all followed.

The dirt shifted again, and I had to balance myself against falling over as we descended. The section of Earth hit the ground. A green-eyed man standing at the base stepped out of our way with a nod.

Dominic led the way in silence through the maze of boxes, crates, and containers.

Finally, we reached the open section of the cavern where all the equipment was set up.

To the left stood four rectangular tables, one next to the other, upon which stood four computers, an occupant behind each one typing or monitoring the screens.

Directly in front of us sat a single chair. Further behind was a single table lined with various equipment I couldn't identify but reminded me of sharp knives.

Dominic strolled ahead to speak with the woman behind the first computer.

Standing beside Jayden, I became frightfully aware that this reminded me of the dream I'd had. My heartbeat increased at the prospect of what might be coming.

I glanced at him with a grimace; he gave me a similar look.

Dominic returned to us.

"Now, before we begin, I would very much like to know how you found us." He looked between us. "I have taken a lot of precautions to hide this place, including making sure all my people are loyal, so I'd like to know who the weak link is."

I swallowed. Even if I told them the truth about my dreams, would they believe me?

Jayden shook his head ever so slightly, and I pressed my lips together in solidarity.

Dominic sighed. "Marco."

In one quick movement, Marco punched Jayden in the gut.

A cry escaped my mouth. Jayden doubled over with a grunt but remained standing.

"How did you find us?" Dominic said, his patience thinning.

Jayden took in a breath and bravely tried to stand up straight. I was torn between telling the truth to save Jayden more pain and following Jayden's instruction not to give in.

Dominic motioned to Marco. This time, it was a right hook to the jaw. Jayden staggered back a step.

I whimpered, scurrying to his side, not sure what I was going to do. Jasmine grabbed my arm, pulling me back.

"Shall we continue?" Dominic tipped his head.

My lip quivered, but I held my tongue.

Marco swung again. Jayden tried to block the blow, but Marco was too fast.

I closed my eyes against the tears forming as Jayden groaned in pain.

The pain of watching Jayden beaten became too much. Why was I just standing here? After everything he had done for me, in rescuing me from Dominic and taking me to Havasek where I would be safe. This was how I repaid him.

I ran at Marco.

His frame was three times bigger than me, but I crashed into him anyway.

He only took one step back.

Marco swung at my face, sending me to the ground with a cry of pain.

Through all my training with Naomi, I'd never actually experienced a punch, let alone one to the face. The closest I'd ever come to feeling this kind of pain was during a track run when I'd tripped and fallen, landing on hard cement, my face taking the first impact, only this had more force and precision behind it.

As I struggled to get up, a boot landed against my stomach. I curled up, coughing.

I regretted my decision to run at Marco, even if I'd diverted the attention from Jayden.

Marco grabbed my shirt, hauling me to my knees, only to knock me back down again with his fist.

Pain registered where his blow landed, and all I felt was agony.

Letting all other feelings go, I focused on one: the hate I had for these people. I hated them for what I was going through right now, but mostly I hated them for the damage they'd caused to so many innocent people's lives.

Everything they were doing was wrong. They deserved to be punished, but fighting back was pointless. All I could do was accept my fate.

Things were going to get a lot worse.

Something clicked into place, like a key catching in a lock saying I could enter, and my connection to my Eleun was there again.

Was this some sort of trick?

Marco reared his foot again to strike.

A scream ripped from my lungs as I felt the dead air split apart. I hurled it into Marco's stomach, and he staggered back.

"What the….?" He looked for the source of the attack.

The pain only slightly eased as I registered what I'd just done.

Somehow, I'd attacked with an element, except instead of water… I'd used air.

The memory of wielding the wind still fresh, I pulled at it again, sending it across his side. He stumbled and fell to the ground.

Painfully I got to my knees. Jasmine looked shocked someone was using their element while she was still blocking. I hurled the next gust at her. Her knees gave way and she fell to all fours in the dirt with a disgruntled groan.

Dominic's eyes followed the line of destruction. As I turned to him, comprehension dawned on his face. He raced at me. Using wind as a barrier, I sent a torrent at him, pushing him back.

He yelled something, which I couldn't make out over the sound of the wind. Then I was on my back, the heavy weight of Marco pushing against me, his forearm secured over my windpipe.

The lack of oxygen caused me to lose control over the air attack and it died out.

"Hold her down!" Dominic yelled, as movement darted around us.

I struggled under the pressure on my throat, my air supply quickly running out. Frantically, I searched for anything to help and found water nearby. I pulled it toward me, and it slammed into Marco's side.

He rolled off me, water soaking the both of us.

Coughing, I twisted in the other direction. I climbed to my knees and drew the water from my clothes, I readied it for my next attacker.

"Who do you think is faster?" Dominic called.

My heart sank. He had Jayden on his knees, with a knife pressed against his throat.

Jayden's eyes were barely open, and I saw his unspoken apology, as if it were his fault he was utterly defenceless right now. But there was also amazement on his face at having seen me wield two elements.

I didn't know what to feel about this development.

Gritting my teeth, I let the water drop to the ground with a splash.

"There's a good girl," Dominic said with a smug smile.

Motioning for Marco to take his place, he turned to me, eyes narrowed.

"Interesting…" he said. "You were able to get past Jasmine, and it seems we saw two elements at work. Care to explain yourself?"

I kept my mouth shut, even though I was just as curious. I wasn't going to discuss it with him.

"You know, I knew there was something different about you." He sauntered toward me, and I took a defensive step backwards. He didn't slow, just circling me as he eyed me up and down.

"When we came to claim the boy, I wasn't sure what I was seeing. There were a lot of elements at work after all… But now I see things far more clearly and it intrigues me."

I gritted my teeth. We'd come to rescue Drew, and I hadn't even seen him so far, let alone had any way to escape with him.

A sharp sting erupted in my neck, and I cried out.

One of the women from the computer desk slunk away from me, an empty syringe in her hand.

She'd snuck up on me as I'd followed Dominic's progress.

"What was that for?" I snapped.

"Something to help you lose focus," Dominic said, his smile calculated. "I can't have you breaking out again."

I blinked as he moved away, my vision unfocused, balance disappearing as I staggered to stay upright. Hands grasped me from behind, dragging me backwards. Everything was spinning wildly as they dumped me in a chair. My arms were released only to be re-tied to the armrests at my side.

I tried fighting the man and women who'd grabbed me, but concentration was difficult.

"What do you want… from me?" I slurred around the dizziness.

Why was I fighting it? I wanted to close my eyes and sleep. Yes, sleep would be nice.

"To see how you tick…"

I gave a small jump to find Dominic standing next to me with another woman in jeans and purple top.

The woman moved in front of me, my vision producing two of her.

"Whenever you're ready." Dominic's voice floated around me.

"What are you going to do?" I asked drowsily.

"Oh, nothing you will remember."

The woman placed her hands on either side of my head, which only slightly stopped the spinning.

I felt her presence in my mind. She had entered just like Katalya had those first few lessons.

I wanted her out.

The woman sifted through my memories, flashes, and scenes from my past flitting through my mind.

Then her probing stopped.

"I've found it." Her voice echoed around the cavern.

"Good, show me." Dominic slid closer.

The woman lifted one hand off my head and placed it on his, her eyes closed.

I cried out at the stab of pain as she returned to my memories. This time, more recent images ran through my mind, and I felt her replaying them to Dominic.

No! They couldn't see those. They were private.

The memories continued. My training sessions with Katalya. Our rescue of Drew...

More private memories came forward and I yelled, "Get out of my head!"

A force pushed out toward the woman.

She stepped back with a look of shock on her face.

Had I managed to knock her out of my head?

I'd been desperate for her to get out of my mind, but I hadn't thought it would work.

The woman stepped behind me, resting both hands on my head again.

"What happened?" Dominic looked from me to the woman. "There was still more. I need to see more!"

"She's fighting back!" The woman grunted in annoyance. "I don't know how. The drug should have knocked her out."

The probing intensified and I fought with everything I had, my eyes screwed up tight, my head pounding in my ears.

She was far better at this than I was, but I had to try, even if I didn't know what I was doing.

Dominic wanted something from me, and I was not inclined to give it to him. After everything he'd done, it almost certainly had no good ending.

She changed tactics and instead of trying to see my memories, she searched for something else. My eyes snapped open as I followed her movements. She was looking for the source of my Eleun.

It'll be less painful if you don't struggle. Her voice resonated through my mind. *Attempting to fight will only make things worse.*

Growling, I pushed back harder.

"What's taking so long!" Dominic's voice boomed.

"She's putting up a strong fight." The woman sounded flustered, giving me hope that I might be able to win this.

When she dove in again, my barrier was stronger, and she couldn't get past the surface.

I will get through and if I don't someone else will. Her voice sounded strained in my head.

You'll have to kill me first! I mentally replied.

Another jab pierced my neck, and I knew it was another dose of the drug they'd given me earlier.

Panic rose in my stomach, my focus wavering.

My defences fell as the drug entered my system, and she delved deeper for my Eleun. I was powerless as she hovered on the fringe of my mind, just observing. Then, ever so slowly, she moved forward, somehow, clasping onto me, the two of us entering together.

The rush of power soared through me like it always did, energy and excitement filling my body. The only difference was, I had no control.

"I'm in," she said, her voice struck with awe at what she was feeling, what we were both feeling.

"Show me what she can do!" Dominic said. He was all but salivating at the prospect of unlocking my secret.

I opened my eyes to see him staring at the space in front of me. A column of water materialised from the puddle I'd dropped earlier. The column spiralled upwards, rising ten feet in the air, then split halfway, the separate columns curved sideways creating two archways.

It was a strange sensation. I could feel everything the water was doing, and yet I was not in control.

Not unlike another time…

"That can't be it," Dominic said. "Show me more!"

The water dropped, spluttering to the ground.

"Oh… there's more," the woman said in awe, "but I'm not sure a storm inside a mountain is the smartest choice."

Dominic turned to look at her. "Anything else?"

A breeze picked up, blowing along the ground, stirring up the dirt. It swirled between the feet of those watching before turning into a light whirlwind. Dust and loose items flew in the air, joining the spectacle as everyone watched.

"Amazing!" Dominic called over the noise the wind was making, his gaze alight with excitement. "What about together?"

The water on the ground swirled as it had before, recreating the spiral, and the two spun simultaneously.

"Mytheleun," Dominic muttered.

It hadn't fully sunk in, as I'd fought Marco, that this was possible. But staring at the two spiralling elements before me, feeling their movement, somehow it felt… right.

Even though I'd been practicing and wielding water for weeks now and was familiar with it, the feel of the wind was so natural, like I'd always known it was there but just hadn't asked it to do anything.

But even as I thought this, I realised I had used it.

The memories crawled forward as if waiting to be acknowledged. Once, when Dominic had attempted to come closer during Drew's rescue,

I'd used wind to throw off the branches. Again, when Ryan had asked me out, my emotions sparked in a new way.

This was what Dominic had been searching for the whole time. The looks he'd given me, his interest.

Nearby, still kneeling on the ground, Jayden watched enthralled by the sight, like everyone else. His whole life he'd been led to believe that no one could wield two elements, and yet here I sat...

Dominic looked overjoyed, as if fate were about to change in his favour.

It scared me to think of what was going through his mind.

"Penny." He turned to the woman behind me. "Find everything she knows, even her memories. Maybe there's a key to why she can hold two Eleun. Kyle, I want to know what makes her different. Get her..."

I didn't hear the rest as Penny began to dig through my memories once more. Images flashed through my mind as she searched for anything that would give her information.

I tossed my head back and forth, the sensation making me feel sick.

"Stop it," I yelled. "Please, it hurts!"

"Then don't fight it," Penny responded calmly.

How could I not fight? This was my life she was rifling through like the pages of a book, my mind she was controlling, my body they were talking about examining.

I would fight with everything I had.

Then something stirred. Something Penny didn't notice at first. It awakened as if from a deep sleep, becoming aware of what was happening.

And it was angry.

I recognised it, not sure if its reappearance was a welcome one or not. The last time it had almost killed a rman. The same man, that wanted to turn me into a lab experiment.

That one simple thought was all it needed to rage forward and take control of my body. My limbs went limp as the presence swirled through my bones, coursing through my veins. The power was exhilarating, and I couldn't help but want more.

I let it take over.

Penny screamed both out loud and inside my head, her probing stopping abruptly. Then there was a thud as something hit the ground behind me.

Gasps and shouts rang out as people rushed to her side.

What had happened?

I couldn't turn to find out. I couldn't even open my eyes, the other subconscious part of me completely in control.

"I'm not getting a pulse," someone yelled from behind. "I need an Entina!"

Footsteps pounded on the ground, heading away.

I felt hands on my cheeks, as someone lifted my motionless face up, then side to side. The person placed two fingers against my neck, then let my head slump back down.

"She's fine," Dominic drawled, and I noted his relief. He didn't want his prized pony being damaged. Penny was replaceable, but the girl with two elements… not so much.

Anger stirred inside me.

How could he care so little about what happened around him?

I snapped my eyes open. Dominic startled, then took a step back.

I knew my eye were solid blue, the way Jayden had witnessed before when I'd attempted to kill Dominic.

The whirlwind, which had been twirling this whole time, changed course. It collided into Dominic, throwing him to one side. The water spiral stopped, splintering, and hardened into sharp ice daggers.

I didn't know I could do that!

The daggers rubbed against the ropes on my wrists, and the restraints fell away.

My body stood, stepping away from the chair and the commotion behind it.

This new part of me wasn't concerned with what happened to the woman who had forcefully invaded my mind. In fact, it didn't care for a single person in the mountain. It wanted to show them what real power could do.

"What do you think you're doing?" Dominic asked, though he sounded annoyed.

I spun to face him.

"Your boyfriend's life still resides in my hands." He motioned to where Marco still had Jayden at knife point. "Take one more step and his life ends."

I pushed against the barriers of my mind, wanting to enforce that Jayden was important to me. But the other part of me wasn't inclined to defer from its mission to destroy.

My head cocked to one side, as we both took in Marco's face. My subconscious wasn't sure whether it should take pity on the helpless man on his knees or just leave him to the fate it had reserved for everyone else in the cave.

I pounded against the inside of my mind, pleading with the presence to have mercy and save him.

It didn't respond to anything I tried.

Instead, it turned my back to Dominic and said in my voice. "Do what you like with him."

No! I shouted, but nobody heard.

The winds picked up and everything was thrown into chaos.

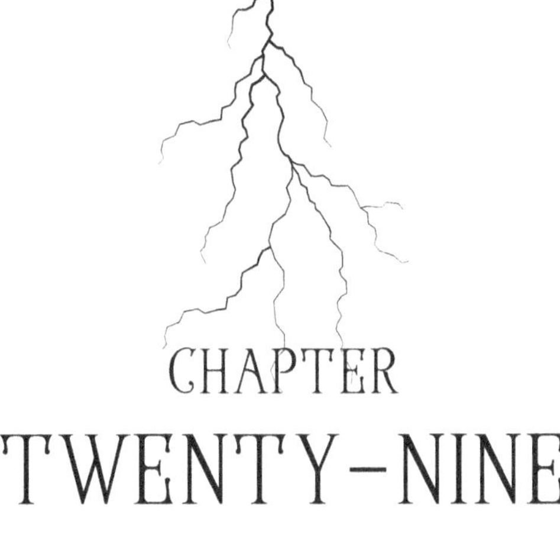

CHAPTER
TWENTY-NINE

Wind blew through the cavern, billowing dust, and dirt everywhere. It whipped through the towering boxes and crates, whistling among the cracks and crevasses as people ran for cover.

The wind tossed my hair back and forth, obscuring my vision, but from the calls and yells, I knew the wind was wreaking havoc.

I was no longer merely the controller of the elements with a partial influence over them. I was now the creator, or at least… this other part of me was.

An explosion erupted at the opposite end of the cave. A large and heavy object sent flying through the air crashed down on the wooden boxes. I couldn't make out the object, but a torrent of wind rushed in through the now open entrance confirming it had been the stone door.

The rush of wind joined the already rampaging rage that cascaded through the cave.

Screams sounded with this new intrusion. People ran in all directions to avoid flying debris.

I desperately hoped Jayden wouldn't be hit by anything, if he was still alive, given my declaration of not caring for him had been announced.

I'd lost sight of him, Marco, and Dominic in the ensuing windstorm.

As the winds churned inside the cavern, I felt something building outside and I was made privy to what this other part of me was planning. It wasn't just the winds it was stirring up: it was the skies as well.

A loud *boom* echoed outside, reverberating through the ground.

Dominic was going to see that storm after all.

White fog swirled in through the entrance, rising fast to the ceiling, the whiteness turning dark to form thick grey clouds, which rubbed together in anticipation of causing disaster.

When the top half of the cave was filled with clouds, rain began to fall in thick, hard drops. Everyone left out in the open raced for cover. I remained motionless and calm, my body drinking in the feel of the moisture hitting my skin.

The free roaming winds were pulled in to surround me. Before I realised what was happening, they picked up speed, spinning hard and fast in a low whirlwind, lifting my feet off the ground.

My head tilted to the roof, as a blast of thunder echoed. Lightning flashed amidst the clouds.

With my arms outstretched, I could feel the two elements working together to cause as much carnage as possible.

Even though this subconscious was saving me from experimentation, I wanted it all to stop.

This was not me and I wouldn't consciously cause harm to people in this way, no matter how much I hated them.

Lightning struck a crate below, blowing it apart, sending wooden splinters in all directions. Another followed, hitting the electronic equipment. It burst into flames.

The striking continued. Flames blazed everywhere as I destroyed anything they could use against me.

The rain turned to hail, making the sound in the cave deafening, Thunder boomed both inside and out, the storm leaving little place for anyone to escape.

Something collided with my gut, and I doubled over in pain. Control snapped back to me, and my airborne state faltered slightly.

The presence took back control, but not before I managed to keep a part of me on the outside of the barrier.

This was my chance to right things.

I focused on me, who I was, how I lived my life, the person I wanted to be, hoping it would work. This had to be the key to taking back what was mine.

It wasn't easy. The elated feeling of so much power emanating from my body was enticing, but I had to do it, or else many lives were going to be lost, lives who had merely been pulled into this situation because of what they were.

I pushed against my other half, widening the space I'd already consumed, the battle for my body raging.

Another blow to my stomach sent us both reeling back. I leapt forward to gain as much ground in my mind as I could.

The presence pushed against my barriers, its desire for destruction and violence radiating through me. But this was my body. Whatever this was did not belong in control.

Breathing hard against the exertion, I took hold of the storm that raged around me. Ice turned back into water, then ceased entirely at my command. Swirling and twisting the winds, I used them to push the clouds back through the entrance, out into open ground where they dissolved into Mother Nature's grasp. As I lowered the pressure of the wind, my body slowly fell back to the ground, which was now mush.

Silence filled the cave as I took in the destruction, everyone cowering under cover, not that there was much left to call cover.

Most of the boxes and crates lay battered and broken, the maze we'd walked through earlier completely gone, just a pile of broken wood and debris. Lab equipment was strewn along the ground, glass bits sticking out at odd angles.

I looked around helplessly.

What had I done?

A groan sounded to my right, and I turned to the noise. A shape rose slightly from the ground, before falling back down in a splutter.

"Jayden!" I created a path by pushing the thick mud to the side as I ran to his side.

He was completely soaking. Skidding to stop beside him, I bent down, helping him into a seated position. His face was red, his bruises starting to colour from the beating he'd received. When he saw me, he staggered back, uncertainty covering his features.

"Paige… is it really you?" His voice was hoarse, and I cringed at his condition.

"Was I that scary?" I asked, not wanting to hear his answer.

He tried to sit up but winced. "A little, yeah."

Moving to his side once more, I said, "I didn't hurt you, did I?"

He grunted. "All these injuries are courtesy of Marco."

"I'm sorry you had to see all that," I said. "It's not exactly a party trick to show off."

"I guess a few things have come out from our little field trip." He shook his head. "Did you know you could do that?"

"Not consciously, but it felt like I've always known, deep, deep down." Not wanting to talk about it here, I said, "Come on, let's get out of here. We need help."

He slung an arm over my shoulders and, together, we stood.

We hobbled, Jayden trying not to force too much weight on me, in the direction where the entrance of the maze had once stood.

Dominic strolled toward us. The corner of his mouth lifted to a grin.

"That was quite a show," he said.

"Leave us alone, Dominic," I snarled.

He laughed. "You don't scare me. That was merely a puppet's play compared to what you can really do."

What did he mean by that?

"You can't control me," I said. "I'm not some pawn you can discard when I don't follow orders."

"Oh, I don't want to control you," he said. "Once you know the truth, the full story, you'll take matters into your own hands and do it for me. You'll be giving the orders."

"You're crazy if you think I will believe anything you say, after all you did to those people up there." I pointed to the cages, my temper growing hot. "If you had any decent humanity left in you, you'd have done things differently."

He stared at me, then finally said, "You may not see it now, but you will eventually."

As if on cue, four people surrounded us. Marco and Jasmine were the first two. The other two were a girl with olive skin, and blue eyes, and a tall man with purple eyes. They all moved to box us in.

We were outnumbered, and with my compassion back in tow, and energy levels hovering dangerously close to empty, there was no way I was risking Jayden's life again, especially since he could barely walk, let alone fight.

Easing Jayden's arm from around my shoulders, I helped lower him to the ground. He grunted in relief from the strain of standing.

"Wise choice," Dominic smiled. "You might as well get comfortable too, my dear."

I lowered to the ground, sitting cross-legged next to Jayden.

Now that the storm had dissolved, people were starting to move around again. Debris was being removed and assessed to see if it was in working order. Electrical equipment sparked, and I couldn't help but smile.

Turning back to Dominic, I decided that this was the perfect opportunity to understand what he really sought. He clearly wanted me to join him. Perhaps I could appeal to that desire to get answers.

"Why do you want me on your side?" I asked, hoping he wouldn't answer with the obvious.

He grinned, looking away from a group of people rummaging through the computer pile. "All my life, I've searched for someone like you, someone who could hold more than one Eleun. I always thought that goal would be achieved through science; finding the right person capable of being able to hold them. Never did I expect someone to be gifted that way through birth. It was an impossible notion."

"Wait, you're telling me that's what you've been doing this whole time? You've been trying to give another Eleun to someone?" I paused, thinking. "But where would you get another one from?"

Even as I spoke, I realised the answer was right in front of me.

"From here…" I looked to the cells higher up, or more precisely, at the figures inside them. "That's why you've been taking Eleun. You've been experimenting by taking their Eleun from them, but then… you've been doing this for ages. Where's your dual Eleun?"

"There lies the problem…" He looked annoyed. "You see, an Eleun cannot survive outsides its host. It feeds off our life force, beating in time with our heartbeat. Once removed, both the host and the Eleun die."

I sucked in a breath, horrified at what he was telling me, then stopped, a thought springing to mind.

"But Mrs. Cortez… She's still alive, but her eyes have changed colour. How did she survive?"

He still looked angry, like that experience had annoyed him more than the others.

"It's all about control. You see, if someone hasn't learnt to fully control their ability, their link to the source is frigid, unstable, whereas when one has complete control and mastery over their gifts, the line between soul and Eleun is solid and the two are linked indefinitely. What happens to one, will happen to the other."

I was starting to understand where he was going, but remained quiet as he continued, hoping all the talking would give us time to figure out what to do next.

"The reason Mrs. Cortez is still alive is because she hadn't gained control over her powers. She hadn't made that connection to become one with it, so although it was part of her, it didn't result in her fatality. Once her power had been removed, it caused her to be nothing more than a mere *human* with memory loss." He spat the word out as if humans were worthless to him.

A spark filled his eyes as he looked at me.

"How did you know her eyes changed colour, or even that she was an Eleun?" he asked, finally realising that I should not have known those pieces of information.

I bit my lip. He may know that I could control two elements now, but he didn't need to know about the rest.

"We looked her up when she was found," Jayden interjected. "Her profile showed yellow eyes and I assume you know we paid her a visit. It wasn't hard to notice the difference to brown."

He coughed at the end.

I breathed out, thankful for his quick thinking.

After making sure Jayden was okay, I turned back to Dominic.

"So, did you succeed?" I pushed. "Did you make someone like me?"

"Do you think I would still be here if I had?" He sneered. "Powerful though our Eleun might be, they don't survive outside our bodies for very long without a host, so no, I have not succeeded… yet."

I swallowed at his deathly look. Inside, however, I was torn between an array of emotions. Relief that we were finally beginning to understand what was happening, which might give us the opportunity to stop it. And sadness for the fate of all those who'd been subjected to his experiments, those who had perished, and those whose lives had changed completely due to memory loss.

The Eleun inside needed us. They survived because of us. I'd not considered that before, nor had anyone mentioned it. Perhaps they hadn't known?

I pulled myself together, needing more answers. "But why are you trying to make someone like me? What's the point of all this?"

I waved my hand to indicate the inside of the mountain.

"Now you're asking the right questions." His features lost some of their dark air, though only slightly. "I was told long ago that I was destined to find the Dual Eleun. So, I knew it was possible, but never in my dreams did I think it would be this easy. *You* are the answer to everything I've built. *You* will be the one to bring about peace in this war. There is no doubt about it. All you must do is open your eyes and see the truth."

He pointed in my direction every time he said the word 'you' to emphasise his point.

"War?" I shook my head in disbelief, lost again. This was the first time I'd heard of any war. "What war? Look around. There is no war going on and if there is, you're the one who started it. If you're destined to be the one to finish it, why start it in the first place?"

All this talk about destiny was starting to make me feel uncomfortable.

"You are so naïve. There is so much you still don't know, so much that place you call *Havasek* hasn't told you." He drew closer, and I leaned back. "Like I said, open your eyes. You'll soon see the truth."

He held my gaze as if trying to convey something without speaking, then grinning, he turned away.

"Who told you about the Dual Eleun?" I asked, but my confidence was wavering, and the question came out softer than I'd intended. "Who said I'd be the one to end the war?"

"That is something I will only share if you co-operate." As he walked away, he called over his shoulder. "Theresa, Ricky, with me."

The two new faces moved to follow him, Marco and Jasmine repositioning to stand either side of Jayden and me.

I still had more questions, but it didn't seem I was going to get anything new out of him. Which meant it was time to find an escape route.

"What are you going to do to me?" I yelled after him. "Cut me open?

Pull me apart? Inject me with more drugs? What's the plan?"

Dominic glanced back at me before he discarded me and continued away.

"You know you can't get me angry, or maybe next time the mountain really will come down," I yelled. "So, what are you going to do?"

"Jasmine, Marco," he said. "Take them to a corner somewhere."

Hands grabbed under my armpits and dragged me upright as I struggled in their hold.

"You'll never get away with this," I said. "You will pay for everything you've done!"

I stumbled backwards as Jasmine dragged me away. I let her.

Three goons down, two more to go.

They dropped us by a half-standing crate in a small, secluded area by the right-hand wall. I could just make out the cavern's entrance around the next bend and it was wide open.

My storm had at least given us a way out.

Marco and Jasmine stood a few feet away to keep an eye on us, blocking our only escape route.

Jayden crawled to my side and whispered. "That was clever. Well done."

He smiled at me knowingly, as if he could read my intentions to decrease our opposition.

"We still have to deal with these two though," he said, nodding to our constant surveillance. "But at least we know what they've been up to all this time. Nice thinking getting him to talk, even if half his story doesn't make any sense. The Likonan is going to get an earful when we get out of here."

At the mention of the Likonan, a strong, urgent feeling came over me.

"You can't tell anyone about my wind ability," I said, the feeling confirming my words, telling me it was vital we keep this under wraps.

"Why? This is big. Everyone will want to hear of it."

Biting my lip, I waited for the feeling to return; it did.

"Think about it. If Dominic wants to tie me down and conduct experiments on me, then who's to say others won't? I mean, I trust Havasek and am grateful for everything they've done for me, but I'd rather not go through that scrutiny."

"We don't know what will happen," he said slowly.

"I'd rather not risk it," I said. "Can't I decide who knows and who doesn't? It's my power."

He narrowed his eyes. "That's the second time you've asked me to lie about something. Why don't you want people knowing? Am I even going to be able to say anything if I try, like before?"

I grimaced at his accusing words. Like it was my fault he couldn't relay my secrets.

"Not everyone can be trusted," I said. "Libby already betrayed you. Who else might be a spy? Besides, it's not lying, it's just omitting. It's a feeling, please. At least let me try to figure out why I'm different before we go spreading the word…"

His jaw tightened. "Fine, but if it compromises us in anyway, I'm telling someone."

Considering he couldn't say anything the first time, maybe I had nothing to worry about.

"Okay, deal." Dragging the conversation back on task, I said, "This is pretty much where my plan ends. Any ideas?"

He looked around, my request for secrecy filed away for later. "Let me think about it."

As much as I knew now wasn't the time to talk, the silence between us was all it took for my mind to go crazy with questions. I couldn't help but vomit a bunch of them right then and there, interrupting his thought process.

"What did Dominic mean when he said I didn't know the whole truth? And what's this war he mentioned? Or is he just crazy and making things up to get us on his side?"

Jayden's expression was uneasy as he said, "There are plenty of things you don't know. Heck, there are plenty I don't know, but I haven't a clue what he was talking about. And this war? You were right when you said the only thing we are fighting is him. It's the first I've heard about it on any bigger scale."

He turned away, but not before I caught a hint of relief.

He was hiding something; something he didn't want me knowing. Or perhaps couldn't tell me. I wasn't sure how, but I would find out.

Deciding that now wasn't the time, and that he was my best chance of getting out of here, I left him to it.

Instead, I watched Jasmine and Marco talking. Their voices were low, and I couldn't make out what they were saying. Marco kept turning his body toward us as if wanting to approach, but Jasmine would grab his arm and pull him back before saying something in a rough whisper.

From what I had seen of Marco, he was the muscle around here, so the only explanation for his eagerness to join us would be to batter us up a bit.

Perhaps he was still angry about earlier. Dread filled me.

I nudged Jayden. "I think we might have a problem."

Following my gaze, he said, "Are they debating whether we get a hot meal?"

"If they are, it'll come at the price of Marco's hot fists." I groaned as Marco moved closer.

Jasmine followed, trying to pull him back, and her words finally hit my ears. "You can't. Dominic wants her unharmed. She could bring this whole place down around us. Believe me, I want revenge, too!"

She might as well have been mute for all the attention Marco paid her.

He strode up to us, his face determined, his gaze fixed on me.

"Now might be a good time for that plan," I said to Jayden, getting to my feet and starting to back up.

Jayden followed a little more slowly, his injured leg hindering him.

Marco was close now.

"No one surprises me and gets away with it." He growled, balling his fists at his side. "You're gonna pay for making me look like a fool!"

This was not good.

Jayden grabbed my arm and tried to push me behind him, but I pulled away from his grip and took a stand.

"You want another ride, do you?" I goaded Marco, my heart racing madly at the size of him. "Out of the two of us, who has the upper hand here, me or you?"

I lifted my hand and sent a small volley of wind at him, my powers still at my disposal while his weren't. It circled his middle, spiraling up to his head before disappearing into nothing.

A wave of fatigue drifted over me at the effort.

Marco tightened his fists even more and growled.

"Jaz, give me my fire?" He barely moved his lips, his eyes fierce and determined.

Jasmine looked between the two of us. "You know I can't do that. Dominic would know."

"I don't care."

Jayden tried to pull me back, saying under his breath, "Paige, you don't want to mess with him."

I pulled my hand away from his and stood my ground. He was right, but there was also no way to stop Marco, so this was going to happen whether I goaded him or not. Since Jayden was already hurt, there was no way I could bring him into it again.

On the downside, I was about tapped out. The being, or consciousness, whatever… that had taken over had used a lot of my energy and I was feeling the effects more than I cared to admit.

I needed to end this before it turned ugly.

When Jasmine didn't unblock his element, he said, "Fine, I'll do it without."

He covered the remaining steps between us and grabbed the front of my shirt.

Jayden cut in from the side, knocking Marco's arm down, and threw a punch at his face. Marco's head flew to the side before he turned back to Jayden with murder in his eyes.

"You, I can hurt," he said with a grin.

Jayden limped back, his fists raised. "Paige, get out of here!"

There was no way in hell I was leaving him.

Before Marco could grab Jayden, I wrapped my arms around his neck from behind and used my weight to pull him back. He was far heavier than I'd anticipated, and I only managed to cause his head to shift slightly. He reached round, trying to pry me off. I clung on tight, preventing him from attacking Jayden.

Something grabbed the back of my shirt, yanking me off him; I fell hard against the ground, mud splattering on and around me.

I found Jasmine standing over me.

"Just because I won't lift the block doesn't mean I'm on your side," she hissed, then dove toward me.

I rolled to the side, and she stumbled. I got to my feet, barely finding my balance. She ran at me. Before she could reach me, I sent a blast of wind into her side, knocking her off course. She landed in the mud.

Marco had Jayden backed up against the wall and was throwing punches at him. Jayden was doing all he could to block him, but Marco wasn't letting up. Jayden winced as fresh blood dripped from his lip and cheek.

I ran at Marco's side as if playing rugby, only when I impacted, he barely shifted an inch.

Getting a grip around my waist, he threw me off. I landed on my back with a thud, coughing as the wind was knocked from me.

Starting to rise, I was pushed back down as a heavy weight pressed against my middle.

Marco sat on top of me, his legs on either side of my waist. He restrained my arms with one of his hands, a menacing smile creeping up on his face as he lowered it closer to mine.

I turned away. Mud coated my cheek, but it was better than smelling his disgusting breath.

"A little eager for a beating, aren't we?" He exhaled through gritted teeth. "Since you can't seem to keep away, I'm happy to oblige."

He smiled wryly, wrapping a hand around my jaw, and squeezing.

I felt the urge to spit in his face, but his hold was tight.

I pulled at the water in the mud. Just as I was about to throttle Marco with it, a loud cracking sound echoed through the cave.

My heart leapt, fearful something had exploded and we were about to be buried.

Marco turned his head from side to side, looking for the source of the noise. I would have done the same, but he still held my jaw, his body obscuring everything.

The enormous cracking sounded again. Marco cried out as something wrapped around his throat, his grip releasing to claw at whatever held him. His head jerked backwards, then his weight was gone.

Rolling to my stomach, I coughed and spluttered, before turning to see who had rescued me.

Jayden limped toward me, a relieved grin on his face. Following his gaze, I smiled as well.

Marco knelt in the mud, hands still clawing at his neck. Behind him stood Naomi, whip in hand, pulled tight as she held it like a leash, staring down at my would-be assassin.

Further up the path, people I knew spread out through the wreckage and engaged in battle with those they encountered.

Bree crouched low, then sprung into the air. He landed on the first level where he ducked and weaved to avoid fists and flying weapons headed in his direction.

Nicolas raised his hands, and four broken pieces of wood took to the air, soaring at a man and woman charging him.

Justin, Bree's brother, seemed to be neither here nor there as he zipped from one place to the next. Every time I blinked, he was somewhere else, knocking down this person or tying up that one. It took me a minute to realiee he was running faster than my eyes could see.

Adam stood in one spot, turning his head from side to side, fiery red beams shooting from his eyes in short spurts, landing at the feet of his targets, deterring them from going anywhere he didn't want them to.

There were others as well, all dressed in the black uniform of the Jalin, heading in different directions as the need was required.

When the once-crowded entryway was left bare, only three people remained: two Jalin and Likonan Harmsworth.

CHAPTER
THIRTY

Likonan Harmsworth marched over to us, her gaze fierce and determined. She was like a lion on the prowl, head high and shoulders back, as if she'd been in control the entire time, her entrance planned down to this very moment.

Naomi remained behind Marco, her leash tight.

Searching the area, I found Jasmine unconscious in the mud not ten metres away.

I sighed in relief.

With her knocked out, we had a better chance of winning.

"I assumed that because you didn't call, you needed help," the Likonan said, looking to Jayden, but then she turned her gaze to me. "We followed the unexpected storm to get here, though I'm still not sure why Miss Munro is here. But now isn't the time to discuss it."

I didn't shy away from her scrutiny. If it hadn't been for me, they would still be searching for this place.

She glanced toward Marco, who was turning purple. "Let him go, Naomi. We need him alive."

Naomi loosened the whip, slightly.

Marco gasped for air.

His hands began to flare red. Likonan Harmsworth lifted her hands at him, two long vines shooting from her palms. They wrapped around Marco's body, securing his arms by his side. He fell back in the mud with a splatter.

I did a double take, wondering at the mechanics of how her power worked, considering that the vines seemed to come from inside her body and were not just something that she manipulated like most Eleun.

Given how intimidating she was, it was highly unlikely I would ever ask her outright about it. Though the thought that she could shoot vines from her hands did make me like her a little bit more. But only a little.

She bent over Marco as he writhed on the ground. "I'm allowing you to live because you have valuable information, that is all. Remember it!" She turned to address the two Jalin. "Get him out of my sight. Tie the girl up as well and keep an eye on them."

The Likonan turned to Jayden with an air of authority. "What do I *need* to know?"

"They're trying to create a weapon, someone who can wield two elements." His eyes darted to me, and I could see that he was fighting the urge to tell her about me. "That's why they've been taking new Eleun that haven't connected with their source yet, because the less trained they are the –"

"The more pliable the Eleun is to remove before it dies in transition," Likonan Harmsworth finished for him.

She didn't seem surprised to hear this news.

"Anything else?"

He shrugged. "Plenty… but it can wait."

She turned back to Naomi. "Go help the others; see if you can find Dominic. He and I need to chat."

Naomi, having released her whip from Marco when he'd been dragged away, expertly coiled it up and attached it to her hip, before taking off through the wreckage.

Likonan Harmsworth looked Jayden and me over. "Are you hurt?"

"I'm okay, but Jayden can barely walk. Marco beat him badly."

Jayden fought to stay upright. His left leg was bent in the middle as he rested on his good leg, his face covered in bruises.

Likonan Harmsworth grimaced. "You don't look too good, Jayden."

"I'm fine," he said between clenched teeth. "I can hit where it counts."

"Always the martyr… Fine, why don't you find us a way up to the levels?" She motioned to the gap between the two ledges overhead. "Your gifts should be perfect for that."

Jayden hobbled toward the entrance where the rock lift we'd travelled on earlier had appeared. I moved to follow him.

"Where do you think you're going?" The Likonan's tone held a slight hint of disapproval, and I cringed at what she was about to say.

I faced her, finding the gaze I met terrifying.

"I don't know what he sees in you," she said, nodding after Jayden. "But he should never have brought you along. In fact, I'm not sure what's gotten into him lately. I get the feeling he's not telling me something…" She paused, her stare unwavering as if she could see something about me she hadn't before. "Now isn't the time to discuss it, though, so we'll continue this later. For now, stay here and help guard those two."

She pointed to Marco and Jasmine, the latter slumped against the wall. "Do you understand me?"

Before I could reply, someone yelled, "Marco!"

A current of air blew above our heads. Libby landed between the two Jalin standing over Marco and Jasmine.

She punched the first Jalin in the face, then kicked the other in the stomach. She leapt through the air, to push the first against the second. They barrelled into one another. She ran to Marco's side and began to work at the vines.

I stepped forward, ready to stop her, when the Likonan's voice boomed over me.

"Libby, what do you think you're doing?"

Libby glared at us.

"What I have to!" she spat. "You think I was ever a part of your *society*, where I just had to lie down and follow orders? Ha, not a chance. This is where I belong and you're all fools for following those *pretenders*."

She bent low and lifted Marco up to his feet. Wrapping her arms around his middle, she took off through the air and disappeared.

Likonan Harmsworth looked surprised by this turn of events. Clearly, she hadn't anticipated a mole. Or maybe she had but had guessed wrong.

She strode forward, pointing to the two Jalin. "You two, go after her. I want them both alive."

The Jalin took off, trying to locate where she'd flown.

The Likonan turned back to me. "You stay here. I'm needed elsewhere."

She raced farther into the mountain, out of sight.

The mountain was filled with loud bangs, crashes, screams, and explosions. I couldn't see the chaos, the partially standing maze obscuring my view.

I hated sitting here playing babysitter to Jasmine while everyone else tried to help those who'd been captured. I desperately wanted to find Drew, to see him with my own eyes and make sure he was safe.

Jasmine groaned, stirring on the ground.

I stopped, torn. If I left, Jasmine might block everyone again making everyone powerless.

Only Dominic was prepared for that scenario.

Balling my fists, I turned back to her just as her eyes opened. She took me in, then the empty space around me. There was no Marco to help her.

She hauled herself at me. We tumbled to the ground, fresh mud coating our clothes and skin. Rolling, I landed on top of her. I swung my fist at her face.

I groaned, pulling my hand back and giving it a shake. I'd never actually punched anyone before and found it none too comfortable.

Jasmine laughed beneath me. "You've got no power behind it. Here, let me show you how it's done."

Grabbing my shoulders, she pushed me off her. I landed a few metres away. Her form came into view as I rose, her face contorted in a snarl. Lifting a foot, she thrust it into my ribs.

I yelled out, coughing as I cradled my arms around my middle, mind unfocused.

This wasn't going well.

Another blow came before I could gather my thoughts and I rolled to the side, catching the end of it. She pounced on me, and I fought to keep her off. Her fist connected with my right cheek, and I collapsed to all fours, spitting out blood.

Fear swelled inside me.

She stood just shy of me. "You're hopeless. What good is having two elements if you can't even protect yourself? I'm surprised you've lasted this long."

She started toward me again.

She was right. I did need to protect myself… just not with my fists.

When she was two steps away, I shifted the mud under her foot. Skidding backward, she fell flat on her back with a splatter.

I smiled and, groaning, got to my feet.

"You're right. What good is it if I don't use my abilities?" I mocked, my voice weak and hoarse.

Growling, she started to rise.

I shifted the mud under her again, and she fell back down. I needed to get her out of here, away from everyone else in case she decided to initiate her blocking power.

Wrapping the mud around her ankles, I weaved it up her legs and secured her waist. I stalked toward the exit, Jasmine trailing along the ground, her body leaving a slushy muddy mess behind her, as I used the water in the mud like a rope to drag her over piles of broken wood and other material.

Cries echoed through the cavern, and I paused when a loud *boom* sounded, the stairs Jayden had been constructing crumbled heavily to the ground. Then gunshots rang out. I shot a look at Jasmine, my watery rope still intact.

Unfazed by the commotion she'd caused by using her ability, she yelled. "How are you doing this? Why can you still use your ability?"

Panic filling me, I strode straight through the arched exit, heading for the tree line. I needed to get her as far away from the fighting as I could.

It had grown dark outside, giving the bush an eerie feel.

A few metres in, I stopped, forcing the girl upright as I manipulated the water in the mud to place her against a tree trunk. Separating the water from the dirt, I wound the liquid around her whole body, securing her to the tree.

"I'm going to make you pay for this!" she said through gritted teeth, struggling to free herself.

I ignored her.

I wasn't sure about this next part. If I just left, then the water would fall to the ground, leaving her free to return and aid Dominic. I had to make this more permanent.

An idea struck me.

I placed my hand against a section of the water encasing Jasmine's body. Closing my eyes, I concentrated, thinking of cold things, imagining the water turning to ice, as it had when I'd been under the influence of the other being. The act came naturally, as if all I had to do was think about it and the liquid hardened under my hand, spreading out along the watery restraints until frosty steam floated off the top.

Jasmine tried to move, but the ice held firm, too thick to break.

"Don't move," I said, though my words were pointless, seeing as she couldn't.

Babysitting complete, I headed back inside.

Loud crashing and banging from all over continued to rage. Balls of fire, cascades of water, and bits of Earth moved through the air. A strange whistle emanated between gaps and crevasses of the debris, and I assumed that meant there was plenty of wind being used as well.

The rock staircase led to the first and second levels. Jayden, at the top looking drained and exhausted, worked his way to the third floor as he manipulated the stone that lay beneath our feet.

More of our people hurried around on the bottom levels now, securing rooms, fighting off Dominic's followers, or getting people out of cells.

I smiled at the progress we'd made and searched for Drew, hoping he was all right.

I found him on the opposite side of the cavern to where we'd been kept. He was keeping pace with Nicolas as he fought off Theresa, the dark-skinned girl I'd seen earlier. She hurled ice darts in their direction.

I started up the stairs. Shouts rang out behind me, and I turned to see the Likonan, Naomi and two Jalin charging my way.

Fire spewed out behind them, hot and roasting. I covered my face with my hand, feeling the heat from here. When the fire died down, a blast of wind bowled forward, and Naomi and one of the Jalin took a tumble through the mud. Likonan Harmsworth and the other Jalin tried to fight back, but there was only so much that vines and an Entina Eleun could do against this lot, as the wind bellowed down on them.

Naomi and the Jalin stood their ground. Fire erupted from Naomi's hands as she launched two balls into the air. The balls of fire landed on some broken wood, the surface flaring up. The Jalin drew water from the mud and lassoed two long whips at the pair that followed.

Dominic's followers dipped and dived, and I got a better look at them. One was Marco, his red hair hard to miss anywhere. Libby must have freed him. The other was Ricky, another one from earlier.

The ground began to shake.

I tried to steady myself, willing myself to stay upright, ready for anything. But the shaking intensified, and I fell to the ground, struggling to stay on all fours.

Everyone had fallen as well.

No… not everyone.

Dominic strode up behind Ricky and Marco, followed by a girl with shoulder length sandy blonde hair and green eyes. None of them seemed to be affected by the trembling ground.

Dominic gave orders. Ricky and Marco ran back into the mountain, as Dominic started forward, the ground he moved on remaining firm.

The sandy-haired girl kept pace with him, one foot always connected to the ground, as she slid in an almost dance-like motion, and I noticed that she was barefoot.

Did she need to be physically touching the ground to use her ability?

Dominic walked past Naomi and the Jalin, giving them a little berth to keep them out of the safe zone. He reached Likonan Harmsworth, stopping a few feet away from her.

"I feel honoured that you came to collect me in person." He held a hand to his chest as if he really meant it. "Unfortunately, today is not the day you detain me. My plans have only just started to come to fruition."

The Likonan scowled at him as he sauntered past the Entina Jalin, heading toward me.

"What do we have here?" he said with a smile. "A package all ready to go."

Reaching into his pocket, he pulled out a large, capped needle.

I tried to scoot back, get as far away as I could, but the vibrating ground made it impossible. I was frozen as it continued to shake violently.

Uncapping the needle, he leaned over and stuck it into my neck.

Gasping, I felt the drug enter my system, my strength beginning to falter. My elbows bent, and then I was on the ground, suddenly incredibly tired.

There was no escape. Whatever he'd injected me with seemed worse than before. Dominic knew how much to give me this time. He'd seen what I was capable of and wasn't taking any risks.

It was useless. All I could do was lie there and accept my fate. I didn't have any fight left in me and all I wanted to do was sleep.

The ground around me stopped shaking as Dominic stepped closer to me, preparing to lift me up.

A cry issued from overhead. Someone fell, landing heavily on the blonde-haired girl. She screamed, her connection to her power severed under the pain.

Dominic glanced from the girl, to the Jalin that were preparing to fight, to Likonan Harmsworth who yelled to detain everyone, then to me.

Rage filled his gaze. He wouldn't be able to take me with him and escape.

"This isn't over," he growled.

Before I could even try to respond, he bolted for the exit.

Flashes of elements erupted across my vision as he was pursued, but I was too tired to pay attention.

Darkness surrounded me as the drug took full effect.

CHAPTER
THIRTY-ONE

Waking, I found myself in the hospital wing of Havasek. The fact that I was back at Havasek and not locked in a cell, caused relief to swell within me. We had made it home safe. I only had to hope everyone else had as well.

I tried to sit up, wanting to be anywhere but in the hospital, and grimaced when pain burned through my stomach. Collapsing back against the pillow, I took slow deep breaths.

Finding my phone on the nightstand, I slowly reached over to grab it, wincing at the pain.

There were thirty missed phone calls from Mum, another twenty from Dad, and five from Nicole, with just as many messages.

I groaned again. Things were going to be interesting when I got home.

Noting the early hour, I dropped the phone, my mind scrambling for a way to explain my disappearance for a day and a half.

Staring up at the ceiling, I wondered how I'd gotten back here without waking. The drug Dominic had given me must have been a big dose to knock me out for so long.

A soft tap on the door drew my attention.

"Mind if I come in?" Katalya's voice called out from the open doorway.

I shook my head.

"How are you feeling?" She surveyed me with a piercing gaze.

"Sore. I tried to get up, but… my stomach really hurts."

She smiled apologetically. "Yes, Karen said you had some bad bruising. We'd hoped it would have healed already. But seeing as it's taking longer than normal, I'm here to speed things along."

Having experienced an Entina heal me once before when I'd dislocated my shoulder, I nodded.

I winced at her cold fingers as she touched my bruised skin and closed her eyes.

A cool tingle spread through my middle and, when Katalya opened her eyes, I sat up and looked at my stomach. The bruised colouring had disappeared, only a small ache remaining.

I ran my hands over my skin. "You must never get injured with an ability like that."

Katalya laughed. "Yes well, avoiding such circumstances also helps."

"Did everyone get back all right?" I asked. "Is Drew okay? What about the other captives? What's happened to them?"

I had only meant to ask the first question, but as it came out, more had followed.

She smiled. "Looks like I healed more than your bruises, with those questions. Yes, everyone got back. Drew is fine, and the other captives have been taken care of medically, with their memories wiped, aside from those with Eleun who will undergo training."

"And Dominic? Did he escape?"

Katalya's face softened to a frown.

"Unfortunately, yes, he did. But we were able to detain a few of his followers. They have been secured in the cells below Havasek awaiting interrogation."

I frowned at the news that Dominic had gotten away. I would have slept better if he was also behind bars.

"So, no one was hurt or killed?" I asked uncertainly, not wanting to ponder Dominic.

Katalya tipped her head to the side. "There were plenty of injuries. That's why we didn't heal you right away. It's taken all our Entina Eleun to stay on top of the situation. We've almost run dry."

"Thank you, for this." I waved my hand over my shirted stomach. "It feels much better."

"It was my pleasure." She tipped her head. "Jayden brought some of your things up if you want to shower and change clothes. I can't imagine being covered in mud is very comfortable."

I grimaced, having already noted the mud caked all over my clothes.

Before she could leave, I said, "Katalya, I have one other question."

She lifted an eyebrow for me to continue.

"What does Mytheleun mean?"

"Where did you hear that?" she asked with a scowl.

"One of the men in the mountain said it. I was curious." I shook my head, not wanting to make a big deal about it. "It's silly. Forget I asked."

She reached for the door handle, then turned to say. "It means Dual Elemental."

Keeping my features blank, I nodded in thanks, and she left me alone to clean up.

Looking at myself in the bathroom mirror, I cringed at the sight. Mud had dried through my hair, bunching it into clumps. It splotched over my face and had made my clothes stiff, and the stench needed to be rectified immediately.

I undressed, trying to avoid touching the bruises on my face and arms. I considered calling Katayla back, but decided it was best if she saved her gifts for those who needed the healing more. I would just cover the bruises with make-up until they healed completely.

Once showered and in the fresh clothes I'd packed for the sleepover, I heaved my bags out to the foyer. A group of teenagers stood chatting by the library.

"Drew, you're okay?" I called, catching the attention of everyone in the room as I ran toward him.

Drew turned as I came to a stop in front of him. He gave a broad grin and wrapped a hug around my middle.

"Jayden told me you helped rescue me, but they wouldn't let me see you. They said you were pretty hurt," he rambled on, still holding tight. "How did you know where to find me? They wouldn't tell me anything. They're just treating me like a kid who doesn't need to know anything. Its sucks."

I laughed. "I feel ya, dude."

"Hey Drew, aren't you gonna introduce us?" one of the boys behind him asked.

He pulled back, his cheeks red after having hugged a girl in front of all his friends.

"Sorry," he mumbled, running a hand through his hair. "I didn't mean to…"

I brushed it off. "It's fine. Who are your friends?"

He introduced me to the four other boys, who all seemed eager to talk. Jayden entered the room, and I excused myself politely.

I called to him across the room as he headed for the dining room.

He turned and searched the crowd for me, and his face lit up when he saw me. I met him halfway at the foot of the staircase.

"Hey, I thought you were still out, sorry," he said. "I would have come to see you."

"I only just woke up a short while ago. How are you?" I took him in and cringed. "You look like you could do with some healing, too."

His face was still covered in purple and blue marks, but he was walking fine again.

"I told them not to worry. Of course, they insisted I get my leg done, so I wasn't going to fight that." He laughed. "What about you? Feeling better?"

Nodding, I started fidgeting with the bottom of my T-shirt, feeling nervous.

"What did you tell the Likonan about… last night, with the storm and all?" I bit my lip, hoping he caught my meaning.

He glanced around, making sure no one could hear him, then lowered his voice. "The truth… well, most of it anyway. We took prisoners who followed Dominic willingly, plus there were captives in the cells who saw what you did, so I couldn't outright lie and say someone else caused all that damage. I just left out all the parts that might suggest you controlled another element and the… crazy stuff."

He pointed to his eyes to indicate how mine had changed. "By the way, we still need to talk about that. You spoke this time and somehow, I don't think it was you…"

"Not here, later."

Truthfully, I didn't know what to say about what had happened. All I knew was that it had freaked me out and although it had saved me from enduring whatever Dominic had planned, I had no intention of letting it happen again. As for the revelation that I was even more of an anomaly and could control two elements, I didn't know where to start.

He gave me a disapproving look. "Anyway, I doubt it's going to be long before someone mentions you controlled two elements. They haven't started interrogations yet, but it's bound to come up. It might be better if you just come out with it."

"No," I said, my voice rising slightly. "It's hard to explain, but I've a feeling in my gut. I need time to figure it out and I'm really grateful you didn't mention it."

His eyes narrowed, but he didn't argue.

"I was just headed to breakfast," he said straightening back up and speaking at a normal volume. "You want to join?"

At his mention of food, my stomach rumbled. I hadn't eaten since Friday night.

After breakfast, Jayden told me to go see the Likonan. She'd instructed Jayden not to take me home until I'd given a report to her. So, I went over everything I needed to say to line up with Jayden's story on my way down.

The downside of not telling the truth was that I openly had to claim that I'd lost control again, to which I received a serious scolding for being so irresponsible, the Likonan reiterating that I should not have been there in the first place, untrained as I was.

"In light of all this and seeing as you so desperately want to put yourself in harm's way and be treated like an adult," she continued. "I've decided it's time for you to prepare for the Velta."

I swallowed hard, nerves riddling me at what this would mean.

"Beginning next week, you'll start the Veltanish training under close supervision, preparing for the end of year intake. I suggest you take it seriously as most trainees are given years to train for it and not a few months."

Her anger filled the room, and I nodded to placate her, eager to leave.

I left feeling disgruntled that I'd not been able to ask any questions.

I wanted to know about this war Dominic had mentioned, and although I'd taken his words with a grain of salt, something inside me still wanted answers.

On the way home Jayden and I talked about my incident with the storm inside the mountain. He had plenty of questions, none of which I could answer. I told him how it had felt, that someone else had been calling the shots while I had just watched on like a spectator.

"It wasn't until I was hit in the stomach by something that I was able to get control back. It was strange… like it was aimed at me," I said, thinking back to that moment.

"Yeah…" Jayden said sheepishly, "that was me. I figured since Libby knocking you out the first time had worked, I had to try… though I was kind of aiming blindly. You were so far up and covered in cloud."

Jayden had saved me more than once yesterday.

"Don't be sorry," I said, even though the pain was still fresh. How could I be angry at him for helping? "I was able to take back control from 'other me' so it worked."

He looked a little confused. "I think I understood what you just said, but it's still weird."

I laughed, not entirely sure I understood it either.

Jayden pulled up a few houses away from mine, but I didn't get out right away, fidgeting with my shirt again, nervous about what I was about to face.

"You okay?" Jayden asked, turning to face me slightly in his seat.

"Not really. Mum and Dad tried to call all yesterday. They're worried."

"Well, there's always memory wiping," he said.

I grimaced at the idea.

"No, it's okay. I should face it, teach me to make better decisions in the future," I said grimly.

"Okay, but just so you know, the offers on the table," he said. "Hope you've got a good excuse?"

I groaned, throwing my head back against the headrest. "No."

I'd listened to a few of the messages left on my phone. Mum had tried Nicole and learned that I'd left to come home, courtesy of my note, but of course I wasn't there, which sent everyone into disarray. Nicole seemed just as anxious, and said that I needed to call Mum because she sounded frantic. I'd only been able to listen to a few of Mum's messages as they all sent my stomach into knots of anxiety at making everyone worry so much about me.

"Sure you don't want to wait a few days and show up with the rest of the captives, pretend you were kidnapped?" Jayden offered lightly.

"You should've offered that back at Havasek." I eyed my front yard. "But I'm here now, might as well get it over with."

"Good luck," he said as I pushed the door open to get out.

With a wave, he drove off and I watched him go before starting toward the house.

Standing at the end of the driveway, I stared at the house, willing myself to move.

Where did they think I'd been?

One step after the other, I slowly made it to the door. It was unlocked and pulling it open, I stepped inside.

Mum poked her head around the corner of the kitchen. Her face turned from worried to relieved as she ran to me.

"Where have you been?" Her voice was halfway between yelling and soothing. "We've been worried sick!"

She pulled me against her, squeezing. I tried not to cry out as she pressed against the unhealed bruises.

"I'm sorry," I said, when the pain had dulled. "I didn't mean to worry you, honestly."

She let go, holding me at arm's length, her expression turning serious. "Well, you did, and you owe us an explanation, young lady!"

There was no getting out of this one.

"We thought you'd been taken. We called the police, filed a missing person's report and everything!"

I cringed.

Great, now I was going to have to tell the police where I'd been.

"Your father has a few things to say to you as well." She took my arm, leading me into the kitchen.

Dad, Sharon, and Ryan were all seated around the dining table, and I felt a lump in my throat at the sight of the latter.

Sharon stood as we entered.

"We'll let you talk," she said, nudging Ryan in the shoulder, and he followed her out of the room, suggesting to the younger kids that they take a walk to the park.

Mum motioned me toward a chair, and I sat as we waited for the house to clear.

When all was silent, Mum and Dad looked at me expectantly but all I could hear was my heart thrumming in my chest.

I took a breath and began to lie.

Afterwards, I sat on the front lawn, trying not to think about the way my parents had looked when I'd told them I needed some time to myself, to get away from everything that'd been going on lately. I didn't go into detail about what 'everything' included, hoping they would assume it had something to do with my workload from school, but they'd taken it as me running away.

I completely deserved the lecture I'd gotten, but I still felt like I was getting the bad end of a horrible deal.

Not for the first time, I cursed the situation I was in, having to keep a secret from them to preserve their minds.

I hated that rule.

Not being able to share this side of me with the people I cared about most was downright mean, and lonely. If there was one thing I would change about everything I'd discovered over the last few weeks, it would be that. Opening up to them would make a world of difference.

Burying my head in my hands, I shook off the thought. It was pointless. They didn't know the truth, and if they did…

How would they react if they knew?

Either way, it didn't matter, because I wasn't about to risk their minds just to learn what their reaction would be, like a science experiment.

I would take their punishment in silence, and act the repentant daughter. They deserved that much.

Lifting my head to the sky, I wanted to scream all my frustration out at it.

A scraping sound came from behind me.

Ryan leant against the brick wall, one leg bent, arms folded against his chest, watching me.

I sprang to my feet. "Hi…"

How long had he been standing there?

His expression was blank as he replied, "Hey."

The hurt in his tone clenched at my heartstrings.

After everything I'd gone through in the last day and a half, I couldn't help but feel afraid. Facing him was harder than going up against Elemental forces or feeling defenceless when Dominic filled me with that drug. And yet here Ryan was not a few metres away, just watching me, probably judging me, as he should.

Butterflies flew through my stomach. Once I would have loved the feeling. Now I resented it.

"Will I be receiving a half-thought-out apology as well?"

His question caught me off guard, but he looked expectant, like I should know what he was talking about.

My mind raced, trying to find meaning to it.

Why did he think he deserved an apology from me?

Then it hit me, and I held my fist over my mouth.

Saturday was supposed to be our date. The one I'd been debating canceling but hadn't had the guts to bring up with him for fear of making him feel bad.

Instead, I'd done something far worse: I'd stood him up.

My stomach knotted tightly as I moved closer to give him my best apology.

"You know what, don't worry about it." He held up a hand to stop me in my tracks. "If you didn't want to go out with me, you could have just said so. I would have understood."

He pushed off the brick wall. "I'm a big boy. I can handle rejection just fine."

"No, that's not it, I promise. I…" He wouldn't let me finish.

"Then what, Paige?" he snapped. "What was so important that you couldn't pick up the phone and tell me you couldn't make it last night, that you were okay and just needed some time to yourself? Or better yet, tell your parents who, by the way, haven't slept because they were so worried about you?"

I didn't know what to say.

"I don't suppose you'll tell me where you were? Seeing as you clearly didn't tell them the truth." He pointed at the house then looked at me expectantly.

I couldn't answer. I couldn't bring myself to lie to him.

Instead, all I could do was shake my head, dropping my gaze to avoid looking at him.

It was cowardice, and he deserved far better, but I couldn't look at him, not with his eyes pleading with me to open up and trust him.

He snorted. "I don't know why I bothered asking."

He started for the house.

"Ryan, wait!" I called, the words exploding from me before I could register what I was saying. I still had no idea what to say to ease his mind.

He spun around as I reached the brick wall, and I took a step back, startled by his sudden movement.

"This is crazy," he said with a sigh.

Maybe he hadn't given up on me entirely.

"Why are you being so secretive? What is so important that you can't share it with me, or anyone?" he asked.

His eyes were earnest, filled with hurt and the need for me to trust him.

I couldn't look away, my heart reaching out to him, wanting to comfort him, to give him solace that what I was doing was important and that he had to trust me.

My lips, which had parted at the start of an explanation, faltered and I closed them again. I needed to get out of here. To be anywhere but facing him right now.

Without saying anything, I turned and started down the driveway.

He cursed, following me. His footsteps picked up before his hand wrapped around my arm, spinning me around.

I let out a sharp breath, reaching to remove his hand. I'd forgotten about the bruise on my arm and cradled it gently to my side.

"What's wrong?" he asked, anger replaced with concern. "Are you hurt?"

His tone added in a sharp note of speculation, his eyes blazing with fire.

"It's nothing." I shook my head. "I just…"

Before I could stop him, he pulled me closer and rolled up the sleeve of my loose jumper, revealing the bruising along my wrist and forearm.

I yanked my arm back and shoved down the sleeve, but the damage was already done.

"Who did this to you?" His eyes lit with fury. "Was it that man, the one you claim is your friend? Tell me!"

I hardened up, dropping my arm. "No, Jayden would never do this to me. I'm fine."

"Paige, you are not fine! You're…" He leaned in closer to get a better look at my face. "Is that another one on your cheek? What the hell is going on? If he's hurting you, I'm going to –"

"It's not him, all right!" I yelled over the top of him, then before I could think about it too much I said, "The person who did this will get what they deserve, so leave it!"

"How can I leave it when you come back looking like this?" He motioned to my cheek and arm. "You need to tell someone."

"The right people know and will deal with it," I said, though I couldn't help but think I was fighting a losing battle. "So can we please drop it?"

He gritted his teeth. "Let me help you!"

Why did I feel so attached to him?

Ever since he'd come back into my life, I'd felt this connection, something drawing us together. It was easy being with him. The way we talked and interacted felt… right.

Even now, I wanted to reach out and touch him. I felt a constant pull, always drawing me to him. It was like we had an affinity with each other. I wanted to hate the feeling because he could never know my secret and that made it hurt more when I realised what I needed to do next.

Looking to the ground, I inhaled deeply. "You can't, so just let me go."

I didn't return my gaze, too afraid at what I might see.

He said in a soft voice, "Okay, I won't bring it up again. I'm sorry I couldn't help more."

Then he was gone.

The first tear trailed down my face and dropped to the ground.

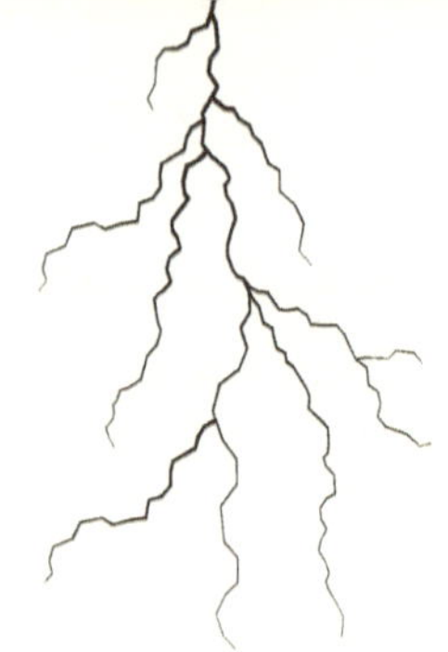

EPILOGUE

My phone buzzed on the outside table, and I diverted my gaze toward it.

Shutting off the water in the hose I held, I closed the distance to pick up the phone.

It was Nicole, checking in to see how I was holding up under my grounding.

Smiling, I leant against the table, fingers dashing across the screen in reply.

I'm alive, barely. Any chance you want to send sugary sustenance to get me through, or better yet, come and help me? Car washing will go faster with you here.

I'll get on that, she replied, followed by a wink emoji.

Which told me she would do no such thing and I was on my own.

Letting out a groan at my hopes being dashed, I returned the phone to the table and continued the task Dad had assigned to me before he and the rest of the family headed out to watch Liam's basketball game.

I'd had no interest in joining them at the game. I was so far behind in my studies that I needed the day to catch up, so had opted to stay home and get started.

It had been two weeks since I'd returned home after spending the night unaccounted for, and since then I'd done everything my parents had asked of me. School and home became the only places I was allowed to go, and my babysitting job, which of course they didn't know was Havasek. But even then, I'd had to make some drastic changes as Mum and Dad insisted they drive me to and from the house every evening I was required.

Havasek had been accommodating and had organised the house to be available, as well as having someone present at the door to continue the façade.

The Likonan, who seemed to approve of my grounding, had organised pre-set Alu-Lamek devices, which I was slowly getting used to, for my travel to and from the house to avoid time lost in my training for the Velta.

The Likonan hadn't been kidding when she said I would need to work hard to get up to scratch. The Veltanish training was twice as intense as what I'd been doing with Naomi.

Every second day I had to pretend I was headed to look after two kids, when in reality, I pushed myself to my absolute limits on the field and an old obstacle course set in the bush-land behind Havasek.

Unfortunately, with my disappearing act still fresh in their minds, Mum and Dad had decided I needed some extra enticement to remain at home today in case I got any ideas about sneaking off without their permission. And seeing as I was grounded till the end of term, they listed a few jobs I could complete once my schoolwork was finished.

Washing the car was first on the list, which I'd thought absurd seeing as Dad usually took it through the drive-through car wash weekly.

Not willing to push my luck, I'd grumbled my acceptance of the tasks and waved them goodbye.

So here I was two hours later, having completed my homework, hosing down the car.

I made sure the vehicle was good and wet on this side before turning to grab the bucket, only to realise I'd left the bucket and detergent inside, along with the cloths.

Slumping, I moved to turn off the hose, then thought better of it.

There wasn't anyone home, and the car was around the back of the house at present. The neighbour's fence was tall enough that they wouldn't see anything.

Despite this, I looked over at the fence, biting my bottom lip.

I shouldn't use my ability here… should I?

But it would be so much quicker if I did. Besides, once I got to scrubbing, it would be easier to have a steady stream of water at the ready, and with only one person, that wasn't possible.

Dropping the hose to the ground, I diverted the steady water flow from spreading over the pavement and instead arched it up and over the car, circling it to rain down on the side I hadn't reached yet.

Holding it steady, I entered the house in search of the equipment I needed.

I dumped the bucket and chemicals on the pavement, then pulled at the stream of water to fill the bucket while I added the detergent. I plunged the cloth into its depths to soak it up.

I scrubbed and wiped and worked my fingernails at the tougher marks that refused to come off. All the while, the water from the hose floated up from the ground, where the head lay, through the air, and onto the section of the car where I worked. Every now and then, I directed the water to spray lightly over me.

It was hot out here and the sweat was real.

Shifting around to the back of the car, I motioned for the water to arch vertically around the car and spray from behind me to rinse off the section I'd just completed.

Grimacing at the mud caked on the underside of the boot, I took a step back and quickened the flow of the water so that it loosened the dirt, focusing on pulling more water from the source to keep the pressure on.

"What the hell!"

I spun around, shocked to hear a voice. My hands inadvertently directed the water in the direction of the speaker, spraying her right in the stomach.

Nicole squealed and tried to shield herself, the two bags she'd been carrying dropping to the ground beside her. Cursing, I waved my hands to divert the water from her, allowing my hold over it to loosen, so it began to spray wildly over the ground once more.

"Nic, what are you doing here?" I stammered. My heart was racing.

She shook her hands away from her body, droplets flinging everywhere as she looked down at her now-wet apparel.

"I was coming to give you sustenance! And company. I never thought you'd douse me as a welcome."

I smiled sheepishly at her.

"Sorry," I said weakly.

She narrowed her eyes, clearly annoyed, then her gaze dropped to the hose head, which lay on the ground at the opposite end of the car.

Her eyes widened as if she was just putting together that something had been amiss. Her soaked attire didn't matter anymore as she pointed at me and then the hose.

"What did I just see?" she asked, her expression demanding an explanation.

I bit my tongue for a count of three to stop from saying something stupid.

How long had she been standing there?

What had she seen?

"I was washing the car," I replied finally, "like I said in my text."

But she wasn't having it, and I knew from her look of disbelief that she wouldn't allow me to get away with anything but the truth.

Oh boy, I was in so much trouble!

9 781763 527133